The Contender from Delos

The Contender from Delos

Leo Carrington

ALBION LITERARY HOUSE

Published by Albion Literary House, Salt Lake City, Utah

Library of Congress Cataloging-in-Publication Data

Carrington, Leo. The contender from Delos / Leo Carrington. 348 pages ; 22 cm

ISBN979-8-9912986-0-5 (paperback : alk. paper)

ISBN979-8-9912986-1-2 (ePUB edition)

ISBN979-8-9912986-2-9 (Kindle edition)

1. Wrestlers—Rome—Fiction.

2. Wrestlers—Greece—Fiction.

3. Rome—History—Empire,30 B.C.–284 A.D.—Fiction.

4. Greece—History—146B.C.–323 A.D.—Fiction.

5. Historical fiction.

6. Young adult fiction.

I. Title.

PZ7.1.C377Co2025[Fic]—dc23

Library of Congress Control Number: 2025936322

This is a work of fiction. Names, characters, businesses, places, events, locales, and incidents are either the products of the author's imagination or used in a fictitious manner. Any resemblance to actual persons, living or dead, or actual events is purely coincidental.

Printed in the United States of America

First Edition, 2025

To my children, may you always find strength in virtue, courage in adversity, and wisdom in every trial.

Palaestra

The palaestra—a temple of sweat and ambition, a place where boys become men and men become legends. Its colonnades frame an open courtyard where the air hangs heavy with the scent of olive oil, dust, and sweat-soaked skin. Stone benches, pitted and worn, remember every whispered strategy, every trainer's sharp command, every murmur of those who watch, measure, judge. The sun carves the forms of wrestlers into long shadows across the sand, illuminating muscle and movement in stark relief. Here, discipline is honed like a blade, the lessons of strength, focus, and control seared into flesh and memory alike.

But the heart of the palaestra—the true crucible—is the skamma.

Set apart from the rest, sunken slightly into the earth, the skamma pit is where lessons become trials, where theory dissolves into the unforgiving reality of the fight. Its sand bears the imprint of struggle, churned and darkened with sweat, forever shifting beneath the weight of bodies locked in combat. There is no marble finery here, no smooth stone beneath your feet—only the uncertain, yielding ground that can catch or betray, cushion or consume.

The palaestra trains them—but the skamma tests them. Here, two enter as equals, but only one leaves victorious. Hands find skin, legs tangle, breath comes fast and hard as the pit claims its toll. Dust rises in plumes, marking the moment of impact as one fighter is thrown, his back striking the sand, his defeat imprinted on the earth like a memory. But the skamma is not cruel—only indifferent. It cares nothing for the victor nor the vanquished. It waits, ever hungry, ready to swallow the next battle whole.

And when the fight is done, when the wrestlers stand once more—sweat shining on their skin, lungs still burning—the palaestra embraces them again. Its shaded porticoes offer quiet respite. Here, bruises are tended, lessons repeated, failures studied. Strength rebuilt. Spirit renewed. But soon—inevitably—they return to the pit. Because no man ever truly leaves the skamma. The sand might smooth over, the wind might wipe away the footprints, but the struggle—the test—that stays with them forever.

The Contender from Delos

CHAPTER I

A man isn't measured by his wins in the pit, but by how he handles defeat.
I hear my father's voice in my head.

I don't know though—sounds like something the loser would say. I'd rather win.

I prepare myself for the fight by oiling my body and dusting myself with sand from the pit. The moment calls for me to focus, but the random calls from the crowd are increasing the flow of blood coursing through my veins. I breathe deep to slow the formation of sweat around my forehead and eyes.

The judge approaches the center. He carries a rod in his hand to either prize us apart or urge us forward. His presence stirs the people into a greater uproar—a deafening assault on my ears.

I focus on my opponent. All I offer is a defiant stare. The first attack always takes place in the mind. A battle can be won or lost before you throw the first punch. I weigh him up, looking for a weakness I can exploit.

His balance is off.

He is taller and carries more weight. He'll compensate his slower movement with a frame that is hard to pull down. He'll stand against my efforts to knock him over while delivering blows rained down like hammers—if I stop long enough to let them land. I reassure myself; speed will win this contest. A brief handclasp between us lets me sense arrogance or fear. This man has no fear. He snarls as we lock eyes and offers an insult in a language unfamiliar to me. He's overconfident. He thinks he will have an easy victory.

I am Alexander, and today my name will find fame from the lips of all who witness my conquest. Their memories will weave themselves into the fabric of this moment, ensuring the tale of what unfolds here lingers long after the dust has settled and the victor stands triumphant. A breath of cooler air separates the Palatine Hill from the baking heat of Rome's dense and crowded streets. Gleaming white marble glows under the shining, golden chariot of Apollo. Patricians and their clients, a distinguished audience, gather in the shade encircling the palaestra. Senators, generals, and owners of grand estates mark the occasion with the importance of their presence.

They are witnesses to a contest between the finest wrestlers of Rome's vast empire, building excitement and anticipation with debates on the likely champion. Money changes hands to wager on the strength of their conviction. The combatants themselves have only one aim, to receive the honor of the laurel crown from none other than the Caesar, Marcus Aurelius.

I am daydreaming again.

The crunch of an open hand against my jaw sends my head whipping to the side. A blur of angry faces spin around me as another swiping blow flies through my hair. Close but no contact. My dodge looks like a stumble and gives me a brief second to react and correct. When my opponent resets his stance, reality rushes back in with my instinct to defend.

I'm not in the palatial settings of the Hill. I'm in the back court of a square of towering insulae. A sweltering, makeshift arena, closed in on all sides with the bellowing and drunken anger of a crowd screaming for blood and broken bones. The windows of ever-rising apartments make up the gallery. This jeering audience is enjoying my pain from both around and above.

Is that the best you can do?

A flurry of kicks, advances, and retreats will score no points, but they'll cause the pace of money changing hands to increase. Five denarii, ten denarii, fifty or more... I know I'll win, but those who gamble on my defeat will lose as surely as the man expected to beat me half to death.

Another uppercut sends my gaze back, above me, and the sun fills my sight. I know he's stepping forward. He's too eager for a quick ending. An elbow grazes the side of my face, and I find him straddled over my leading leg. I can take him down in an instant, but instead, I lean in and cling to him. My head buries into his shoulder, my weight tests his resistance. The judge moves in to separate us, while the residents of the Subura cry louder and harder for a ruthless victory.

This judge cuts a striking figure amid the chaotic buzz of Rome's backstreets. A local man, he bears the rough-hewn look of someone shaped by the city's gritty underbelly. His tunic, plain but well kept, suggests a respect for order contrasting sharply with the disorder of our current surroundings. He has seen more than his share of brutality this life offers and has earned the crowd's respect. "Back off!" he barks, his low hoarse voice carrying over the jeers and cheers—a reminder to today's contenders of the ostensible rules of the fight.

Back in our stances, we circle and test. The victim of this play twists and cracks the muscles in his neck. His grin, sinister and malicious, tells me he is already thinking of the large feast the small purse will buy him. He's advancing again but with less discipline. I can choose where he hits me. I take the pain and absorb his blows. To keep the betting high, I have to stay just on the edge of defeat. I'll carry the bruises and the cuts for days. But I will be victorious. Victory is delicious. Its flavor lasts longer than sweet porridge, bread, olive oil, and even the wine the bounty from this fight will bring.

Just a little more.

Then I hear it. A single voice cuts through amongst the noise of a hundred or more. This man has the experience of calling troops through the smoke of war, the clash of steel, and the chaos of the charge. My father, Marcus, makes his presence known.

"Now, Alexander. Now!"

I have the briefest moment of connection with him. I lock on his face. He sits amongst the snarling masses, as if in the amphitheater, bestowing his judgment on the fallen.

I'll take another two strikes for effect and on the third I'll step beyond his reach.

His knuckles smash into my eye, and the sting jolts me awake. His other hand wrenches my neck forward, dragging me into the force of his forearm. When it grinds into my jawbone, I feel the pain pulse through me, but it puts him close enough for me to attack.

A look can give so much away. He knows I'm ready to reply. He can sense he is losing the advantage. Panic grips him as the crowd grows impatient for his last jab to send me to the floor. He lunges forward, and I lower myself. His leg becomes locked in my arms. I pull myself in. My head pushes against his body, and time slows down.

His arms flail, his body lurching as he fights to stay upright. The sound muffles around me, but I can hear the change in the crowd's reaction. A hundred people at once, all realizing that they'll return home much poorer than they left that morning.

Should I let him have one last attack and squeeze a last coin or two from the ever-hopeful? No, it's time.

I stretch my left arm around his waist, while my right still holds his leg firm. I drop even lower, squatting down with his knee pressing against my hip. Then I arch my back and twist. His body is no longer within his control. He glides over and around, carried forward unwillingly by his own momentum. The only thing that will stop him is the unyielding stone below the disguise of a thin layer of sand. His head makes a sickening thud as it bounces on the surface. His back lifts and sinks with the tremor of a shock. His shoulders lie flat and defeated as the power of his own weight forces a yell out from the pit of his stomach. I dive to stretch my body across him. This fight is over. I will not allow him to stand.

The judge grasps my arm and raises me up. I'm declared the victor, but I'm not a popular winner. Arguments break out and outrage spreads like a flame fanned by the hot air of irate words. Fortunately, where there is fire, there are also vigiles ready to put it out. They push their way toward me, imposing their self-declared authority among those who want to cast blame for their loss.

"Stay amongst us, Alexander."

The leader of the vigiles calls me by name. My father will have arranged my safe passage home. I look around for any sign of him, but he's already gone, and all I can see are the lines being drawn between rival groups of armed and dangerous gangs. There's a code that stops them from carving each other up. A win will follow a loss on another day. Their wrath is just a warning that I should play no further part in it. In a city of a million people, it is unlikely any of us will cross paths again. This is where my father comes in.

Arranging a street fight always begins in a similar way. First, he'll visit a taberna at the end of his day's work. He'll pretend to be drunk and start talking about how his son will be the greatest wrestler in the whole Roman Empire. He'll issue a challenge and a wager. There is always someone who will take the bait and offer a bet.

When the opponent steps forward, my father arranges a venue and time. Two weeks will pass to allow the word to spread. A gamble between two people isn't worth the effort. There have to be many others who play a part in raising the stakes.

I once asked him what would happen if I lost. He told me the sewer led to the Tiber, and from there, passage on a boat in amongst the bricks and tufa would cover our escape. I didn't know if he was serious; he always laughed while he described our method to get away from the mob. I'm sure my mother would have something to say about his plan.

The crowd was dispersing. Not all had lost. The gang, who counted me among the other money-making opportunities of their territory, had profited from my win. They wouldn't cause trouble. They kept a watch from a distance. Their presence would be enough to stop others from coming too close.

"Time for you to go back to your father."

"Did you win money today?" I ask the leader of the vigiles.

"Our only gamble is getting you home in one piece. That's how we earn our share."

"Can I go to the baths to clean myself?"

The vigiles laugh and their leader shakes his head. "Marcus doesn't pay enough for that. Let's get going."

***

"Look at the state of him, Marcus."

My mother, like anyone's mother, took pride in her son's appearance. Here I was, surrounded by four vigiles as if they had just apprehended me at the scene of a crime. My skin is covered in oil and the grit they called sand; my hair is matted with sweat and dried blood; an eye half-closed from that last stinging strike and three good-sized bruises are already beginning to darken with what looked like the finest purple dye.

"He'll clean up, Elena, don't worry. You did well today, my boy. I thought for a moment we were on our way to the sewer." My father winks at me, ignoring my mother's annoyance. "The wagers weren't as good as I'd hoped, I'm afraid."

The leader of the vigiles looks unconvinced. "We agreed on a price, Marcus."

One of his men holds tight to my shoulder until they receive the fee. The leader weighs the small leather pouch in his hand. He can tell the payment is correct without counting out the coin.

"Let me know when you require us again," is all he says before disappearing with his three associates into the bustle of the city street.

"Are you alright, Alexander? Come with me."

My mother is small and slim. She doesn't look like she could drag a wrestler about, but there's an unbeatable strength in her determination. She pushes me through a queue of people lining up for food at the taberna run by our neighbor, Caeso. As we arrive at the counter, a broad smile lights up his face.

"Ah, here is the people's champion. Did you give him worse than he gave you?"

"I hope so."

"Caeso, can I ask if Alexander can go through to the back of your shop and take some water to wash?"

"Of course, Elena. One sestertius is all I ask."

"You ask for one sestertius when he won you ten denarii today?" calls Caeso's wife from across the room.

"Are you trying to ruin me? One sestertius for all the fetching and carrying and preparation—"

"Preparation of the water from our roof, dear husband?"

Caeso sniggers along with half the people in the queue. Everyone knows he isn't serious.

"Of course, Elena," Caeso confirms. "Go through Alexander, you know where the water is."

I walk over to the other side of the counter and through a doorway into a small, shady courtyard at the rear of the building. A covered cistern collects the rainwater, and a collection of pots sits beside it to draw out the contents. A wall that comes to just above my head is all that separates me from the busy throng of people walking by on the other side.

I remove my tunic and sandals. As I douse myself in the cold water, I can feel the cuts and bruises react to the sudden change in temperature, but it's a sting I can bear. Another stain on my hip is starting to grow. One of his kicks has made its mark. I gasp quietly, not wanting to cause a fuss.

"Was it a hard fight today?"

Caeso stands in the doorway, offering a strigil to remove the dirt and oil from my skin. I take it from him and begin to scrape the stubborn grime away.

"He had a powerful punch, but he lacked training. I think he was just muscle from one of the gangs."

"Probably," Caeso agrees. "You have to fight smarter, not stronger, to become a great fighter but you know that, don't you?"

"I knew I would win. I trust my father to tell me when."

"Marcus is a good man. I know that he takes great pride in your wrestling. It pains him to put you through these fights."

"It pains me too." We both enjoy a small laugh.

"Your father has dreams of your success. I'm sure they will happen. You are young. Your life is ahead of you." He raises his voice in mock frustration. "Not like mine, stuck with a nagging wife!"

"I'm holding a knife, Caeso," comes the reply from inside, and we laugh again together.

"I have the same dreams as my father, but right now, I'm dreaming about some of the honeyed porridge you serve. I'm starving."

"Coming right up. Just let us know when you're ready."

Caeso turns back to the shop, and I return to cleaning off the soil of combat. I use the strigil to remove the oily, dirt-streaked residue and place it into a small bowl. The most famous wrestlers will sell this gloios to adoring fans. The buyers place it on their own skin, believing it has healing benefits—and maybe even a little magic power to give them strength and courage. I have a long way to go before anyone will seek to obtain what I scrape away. One day, they will.

I'll get to the baths tomorrow. Wet hair will soon dry in the heat, and I feel fresher for the cold shower at least. I'm ready to eat as I head back to my parents, who are sitting at one of the tables placed out on the street.

"You look more like my Alexander now. The boy I sent out with his father this morning."

My mother ruffles my hair until she's happy, adjusting it to what she considers an acceptable look.

"Mother!"

"Elena, he looks fine; leave him alone, don't fuss."

"It's your wish to get him into fights, it's mine to make sure he's handsome enough to find a wife. Do not argue, either of you," she smiles.

Soon the food is being served to us. The porridge I had been waiting for all day, freshly baked bread still hot out of the oven, olive oil, and a jug of posca to wash it down. Caeso had even added a small bowl of dates and figs without us asking for them.

"He doesn't want a sestertius for this?" says my father suspiciously to the server.

"No, it's free. A gift from Caeso," she replies.

We are a happy family, and although we have little, no one is ever alone in the Subura. People look after one another and share the little they have with neighbors and friends. That's why the bowl of dates and figs sets off on its own journey around the taberna after I grab a couple of pieces for myself.

Well-wishers soon gather beside us, asking about how my fight went. My father tells great tales of his days as a marine in the Roman navy, so he's also good at recounting my fights for those interested. He even adds in a few moves that I know never took place. My opponent would always end up taller and larger than he had appeared to me, and then he would ask me to demonstrate my last throw repeatedly, only without an actual victim.

Another jug of posca arrives on the table. I was never sure how much money we won, but there was always a line of others who would congregate to extract their part of the prize. The vigiles earned theirs for security, and then there was the local gang. They earned their share for *not* involving themselves in the fight. Led by a man who was wealthy enough to live on the ground floor of our insula. Flavius would describe himself as a trader, offering services with good fees in return for favors. Mainly the favor of leaving you alone. He was friendly enough, but my father insisted that he would only stay that way as long as it paid him to do so.

He was rich enough to own two slaves for his personal protection. They were Dacians. I never heard them speak, but as they flanked Flavius and helped him clear the seats opposite us, their threatening gaze was enough to reveal their role.

"That was a good match, Alexander. A spectacular finish. You could feel the earth shake the coin from the hands of those stupid enough to bet against you."

"Thank you, Flavius."

"Another jug!" he shouts at one of the servers. "And not the cheap colored water you normally serve as wine."

I watch the server speaking to Caeso at the counter, who looks over, disgruntled. Flavius demands higher quality but is seldom willing to pay a higher price. The amphora soon arrives, and Flavius fills our cups.

"You will have coin for my share, Marcus? You can take Caeso's price from it, before you pass it to me."

"We don't want any trouble," says my father.

"Marcus, you have my respect at all times. You have fought for the glory of Rome. A man we can all thank for your efforts on behalf of the empire. How else would I have ended up with two fine bodyguards? They are always happy to meet with one of the soldiers who helped to bring them to the greatest city in the world. Isn't that right?"

The two men continue sitting in silence. It is hard to feel comfortable in the company of Flavius at the best of times, but his personal protection ensures an added layer of intimidation and fear.

"We're having a family dinner, Flavius," says my mother. "Please tell us what you want and leave us in peace. My son has fought hard today to earn the little we have. He didn't expect to pay for your family as well."

"Elena, my family is extensive, as you well know. These streets aren't safe, and there were many today who grudge a loss. My family looks after yours. I only ask you to acknowledge that when you can. Is that too much? Alexander is not so well known yet, but his fame could easily rise. He earns enough for you and Marcus, but I could take him further.

Fights throughout the city, not just the Subura. Who knows? Other cities, other countries. Then he'll earn enough to allow both our families to dine well at this taberna."

My father can't hide his annoyance. "He will certainly not stay fighting in the Subura. His future is better starred than that. Some of the finest palaestrae in Rome are interested in taking him on. Alexander will soon be a champion among the elite. He'll be fighting for the entertainment of the emperor in no time at all."

Flavius sits back, convinced that an elite palaestra, or any wrestling school for that matter, was just a dream for both my father and me.

"Very well. I won't press the matter—so long as I'm properly compensated for my... restraint. My usual share will do. Just enough to remind me we're still family."

My father brings another worn leather purse onto the table. He spills the coins out, dividing it into two piles until they're even. Flavius nods his acceptance and reaches out for the money. My father snatches one of the coins back at the last minute.

"For Caeso," he says, with his own determined stare.

Flavius smiles. "Of course," he rises from the table, "my offer remains. The business opportunity will always be there, elite palaestra or not."

His departure also steals the cheerful atmosphere. My mother looks tired and frustrated.

"We should take Alexander home, Marcus. His body will ache in the morning, and you're expecting him to help you tomorrow."

"Where are we working?" I ask.

"You can help me carry tools. An old friend has asked me to do some repair work at their domus."

"A domus? That sounds good. Who is the friend?"

"Well, more of a former commanding officer, but we became good friends over the years. We fought beside one another and served in the same places. I haven't seen him since before you were born."

"Before I was born? Was he on Delos with you? Does he know mother?"

"Yes, and yes. He arranged our transport from the island to Ostia."

"It's time to go, Marcus. You both have to be up early."

I never really understood why my mother appeared sad about Delos. She was from the island and met my father when his navy post saw him stationed to help protect the merchant ships from pirates. I can see every day how they love one another, and I understand that my father brought us to Rome in search of a better life. I suppose she just misses her own people, just like I would miss everyone from the Subura.

We pay Caeso his coin for the wine that Flavius ordered. He wouldn't take it until he learned that my father had snatched it back from the gang leader's hand. The evening is turning to a cool twilight. We don't have far to walk, but we stay on the third floor and the staircase is in almost total darkness. Only small patches of light creep through the windows. You have to feel your way along the walls, and avoid those who use the steps to sleep.

Eventually, we reach our apartment. It isn't just ours—a curtain divides our space from others. We have only a narrow strip, with a bit of storage for the few things we own, and a single window that looks out onto more insulae, which in turn stand staring back at ours.

My father is a carpenter by trade, so the residents in our apartment have the luxury of raised wooden platforms to sleep on. He built them from scavenged timber—broken crates from the market, and planks hauled from a collapsed *insula* two streets over. What others would burn, he sanded smooth and fit into place. No one asks where the wood comes from, as long as it holds our weight through the night.

No ropes, no mattress stuffing—just sanded planks, fitted tight and level. They aren't beds like those living on the Hill might enjoy, with cushions stuffed full of feathers and linen dyed in ochre and wine. But they **stand** above the grime of the floor. We lay our mats across them, roll up blankets for pillows, and sleep a little easier knowing what might scurry below won't reach our faces.

Mother is asleep soon after we reach home. Father joins me by the window as the smell of burning taints the air.

"Somewhere is alight. Poor souls," he says.

We stand in silence and listen for a sound that will let us know how close the fire is, but the remaining stragglers in the street drown out any chance. Their voices rise in joy or even song, all fueled by the wine.

"Do you really think I can train at an elite palaestra?" I ask.

"Yes, I do. You have genuine talent and ability. You just need the mentorship of a master to sharpen those skills and help you understand how a champion wrestler thinks, and not just how they fight. You did it today. I watched you. You didn't attack when I signaled. You took your own time, and an extra couple of bruises, I might add. You had him in the lock long before you gripped his leg," my father smiles, "but you were in a dream world again. That first punch could have knocked you over. What were you thinking of?"

"Palatine Hill. Wrestling for the laurel crown, in front of the emperor."

"Well, that's good. That's ambition, but try to keep it away from the actual skamma pit, in the middle of a fight. Anyway, my boy, it's time to sleep. That's the safest place to have a dream."

CHAPTER II

MARCUS

I look at Elena and Alexander as they lie asleep. It's time to waken my son, even though the day has barely started. I feel sorry for him. Rome hasn't lived up to its promise for my family. Like many others, we live a life that earns us just enough to survive a day at a time.

I had learned the trade of a carpenter while I served in the navy as a marine. The business of raiding against pirates often inflicted damage on the ships, so I started by just learning how to make repairs. Then, as we patrolled between the islands of the Aegean, I learned to help build the walls and gates of the forts that housed our small garrison. I always knew it would be my way of making money when my military service was over, but I never considered how many others might have the same idea.

"Alexander," I whisper.

"What?" comes the drowsy reply.

"It's time to get up. We have a walk to reach the house where we're working today."

The only answer is a groan and one open eye. The other remains half-closed under the dark ring of a bruise. He won't be much help beyond helping to carry the tools, but it's better for him to move and take some exercise. A soak later at the baths will help him heal.

"Alexander," I say with more authority. He's unlucky his father has a military background.

"Alright, I'm awake. Where are we going?"

"To the house of my old commander, Aulus Virius. He was our centurion when I was on Delos. When I left the navy, he remained and progressed higher in the ranks. Now he stays in a fine house he's looking to improve. It was luck that caused our paths to cross again. Something that's in short supply, just like coin. So, we can't be late."

Alexander is strong in more ways than he knows. Even from a young age, he accepted that life presented difficulties, and understood he must take his share of responsibilities. I'm grateful for how he has always helped his mother and me without complaint. I feel I owe him his chance for success.

Today, I know there is a faint opportunity to make it happen. Getting him to carry the tools is only an excuse. If I can get Alexander in front of Aulus, then perhaps my old commander's influence might open doors where I could not.

"I'm ready, Father."

"Good. Pick up a tool bag and let's go."

***

We step out onto the street and Alexander asks me once again, "Where are we going?"

"Janiculan Hill," I reply.

A bright sun is trying its best to throw light among the tall buildings crowding around us. The Subura is subdued for just a few hours each night. By dawn, the air is already filling with the scent of freshly baked bread, the tang of blood from a butcher's shop, and the unmistakable aroma of fresh fish.

The hammers of metalworkers beat out a march, as the hooves of oxen and the rolling wheels of their carts spin over uneven cobbles to escape the morning rush.

Greetings, nods, and brief comments on the weather are the first exchanges. It's usually a comment on how hot the day will be, or how warm the morning is already. When it does rain or turn cooler, we'll complain about that instead.

Traders and hawkers begin to set out their stalls. They call out to those who pay the slightest attention, insisting *they* are the cheapest and the best. They'll tell you that you won't find better food, tools, or trinkets than theirs. Well, at least until you walk past another trader selling the same item for less.

This is how my city comes to life each day. The temples, the palaces, the monuments, and the green spaces are still to come into view, but before they do, the streets will fill with an ever-increasing crowd of people. Queues are forming from those who can afford to eat early. Slaves push through the center of the swelling crowd carrying litters bearing the cargo of a senator or a wealthy merchant. The gathering voices merge to create a bustling, vibrant atmosphere of bargaining, bickering, laughing, or cheering. The city of Rome gradually rolls out of its slumber.

"It's busy this morning," Alexander complains.

"There are games set for today. People are arriving early for the sport. Watch out for pickpockets when we get to the Vicus Tuscus."

"They won't come near us." Alexander smiles as he replies.

He's right. I carry a scar or two from battle, and Alexander still looks like he's just returned from the wars. While we're not armed, we're both carrying bags of tools that could easily double as weapons.

As we turn into the main street, we both stop and pause for a moment. Although I've passed it many times before, the sheer size of the Flavian Amphitheater never fails to take my breath away. At this time of day, it casts an enormous shadow over many of the surrounding buildings. Its towering walls house the statues of the gods within decorated arches, and the half-open doors allow a brief glimpse of the arena where many gladiators will face their last day. This is a place of honor, sacrifice, and death. It commands awe and fear in equal measure.

"Will I fight there one day?"

"I hope not, my boy. It would surely mean you had found yourself on the wrong side of the emperor."

"They hold some wrestling matches in the arena."

"Sometimes, but the rules of wrestling rarely allow for a kill. That doesn't suit the patrons of this place."

We push through a dense pack of people who are gathering for the contests. We do our best to hold on to the tool bags and keep sight of one another. Security is tight in this area. There is an obvious presence of cohorts and older gladiators to manage crowd control. It deters all but the most experienced criminal. Being caught for theft here might see you instantly apprehended and given a punishment that forces you to become part of the afternoon's entertainment.

"Head for the Via Sacra," I call out.

Alexander nods back with a slight look of bewilderment, but he does his best to push his way across the crowds, who are mainly heading in the opposite direction.

"Where are we going now?" he asks as he catches up.

"I want to pay a visit to the gods. I think I should ask for a blessing today."

"Which one?"

"The goddess of carpenters, of course. Minerva will help us with our work if we ask her nicely," I smile.

A smaller street leads through to a wide thoroughfare. Warehouses, shops, and buildings dedicated to administration stand opposite an almost unbroken line of temples and shrines. It is no less busy, but there's more room to breathe as we carry on to the foot of Capitoline Hill.

We start to climb a steeper path and leave the chaos further behind. The tool bags drag us with their weight, and we become fully exposed to the heat for the first time that day. We haven't eaten yet, so our energy is low.

"Are you alright, Alexander? I'm sorry, I never asked how you were feeling."

"I'm just regretting taking the extra couple of kicks and punches yesterday. I wasn't thinking about the day after."

"I told you when to end the fight."

"I know. I wanted to make sure of my victory that's all. I had to get him where I wanted him."

"For a spectacular victory, yes. You could have brought him down earlier."

"Maybe, but *how* I brought him down will be the part that's remembered."

A grin appears on my face. I stop in my tracks and turn Alexander by the shoulders so he is facing Palatine Hill. I want him to remember the view.

"Every time you step into the pit, remember that the actual battle isn't against the opponent facing you. It's against those parts of yourself that are hardest to control. Your fears, your desires, your doubts. These are the true opponents. Life, like wrestling, will test not just your physical strength, but more so your inner resolve. You must learn to recognize what's within your control and what isn't. Your efforts, your attitude, and discipline are all yours to command. But outcomes? They're often beyond our reach. Strive to improve, to learn, and to endure, regardless of the circumstances. This is the path to true strength. It's not the accolades or the applause that define your worth; it's the ability to maintain your character in the face of adversity. Hold on to that, no matter what life throws at you, and you'll always be victorious.

"Now you have permission to dream while you're standing here. This is the time to think about the palaestra, the skamma pits surrounded by colonnades, an oiling room, a fountain, and a bath. A place for you to attain perfection. The complete harmony of body and soul."

Alexander doesn't reply, but I can see his imagination fill with what his future can bring. A place among the elite. A name held in the highest regard. A reputation worthy of the greatest wrestlers.

As we stare over the Forum Romano, Palatine Hill rises out of the valley. It's crowned with the white walls and tiled roofs of the Imperial Palace, the adjoining temples, and the surrounding houses of wealthy patricians.

"Do you understand why I want to ask for the intervention of the gods? I don't want to organize another street fight for you. I feel regret for the decisions I've made too often in haste, or out of fear. The truth is, the past is not something within my power to change, but today, well that's a different matter.

"What do you mean?"

"We'll talk more later. After our visit to Minerva."

We walk on again. The steps to the Temple of Jupiter Optimus Maximus are steep and intended to create the feeling that you are entering into the realm of the gods. I hand Alexander a single coin and take one myself from the pouch I carry.

"See the priest sitting before the bronze doors. He has a bowl for offerings. Place the coin in it and then walk forward to the shrine. Stand before the threshold and breathe in her wisdom and power. Feel it draw into your body. Then concentrate on a single thought. Tell her what your heart desires. She will hear it."

"Is that all I need to do?"

"For now, yes, but when she answers, then you must be prepared to follow her guidance. It makes the gods angry if we forget their efforts to help.

I follow him up the last flight of steps, and we place our coins in the bowl. The priest nods slightly and smiles, accepting our offering. We lay down our bags beside him and walk to the door. I can feel Minerva's energy around us. I hope Alexander feels the same. We bow our heads before the goddess and pray.

***

Aulus Virius steps forward with open arms to greet us.

"Marcus, it is truly good to see you after all these years. Delos became too quiet after you left. We did too good a job of removing the rogues."

His welcome makes me happy. His memories of our time spent together in the navy still have meaning to him. His house is beautiful. The atrium bathes us in ethereal light from above, as though the gods themselves have blessed our reunion. It fans out over the tiled floor and the pool below, glinting over a mosaic of blue, green, black, and white. The walls ripple with life—Sirens stretch their arms from the painted waves, their parted lips forever caught in silent song. Nearby, a Hippocampus rears mid-thrash, its coiling tail propelling Poseidon's chariot through a sea of swirling blues and greens. And from the abyss, Ketos surges upward, its serpentine body twisting through the deep, jaws yawning wide to claim a helpless sailor, his outstretched hands swallowed by shadow.

"And this must be your son?"

"Yes, this is Alexander."

"I sense Elena's influence with this name. It's not so common in Rome. I remember when," Aulus pauses, "your parents left Delos... before you were born, but I can see that you have inherited your father's courage. How many punches did you dodge before earning yourself a black eye?"

"A few, but he was taller and heavier," Alexander replies.

"My son is a wrestler. No one has beaten him since he started."

"Really? Now that I have met my old friend after all these years, I would like to see one of your contests. You must let me know when you are competing."

An awkward silence hangs in the air for a few moments. I don't really want Aulus to see him fight in the back courts of the Subura. I have to steer the conversation in the right direction.

"I'm keen to find a trainer for him. His technique is excellent, but he needs more guidance than I can give."

"There are a few I could recommend, but their fees are expensive."

Aulus offers a sympathetic look that speaks so many words in silence. He can see that I would never be able to afford the cost of sending Alexander to a distinguished palaestra. Our lives have traveled different roads since I left Delos with Elena. I have become a humble carpenter while he has risen to the noble rank of tribune.

Alexander's smile also drops from his face. The reality of our circumstances can easily quash the optimism and ambitious dreams that we share for his future.

"Alexander, I take it you've heard the stories and legends of Milo of Croton?" Aulus continues.

"Yes, he's the most famous of all."

"And have you heard of Zeno of Citium, Cleanthes of Assos, or Chrysippus of Soli?"

"No," Alexander replies, "Are they famous for strangling, breaking fingers, or high throws?"

Aulus is teasing. His broad smile is kind. "No. The people I speak of will guide your conduct in life. When you enter the skamma pit armed with their knowledge, then you will really become unbeatable."

Aulus claps his hands and a slave steps forward at his side. "Take Alexander to the culina. Give him some food, and place something on that eye to soothe it."

I nod for my son to accept politely. The slave gestures the way forward, and when they've left the room, Aulus adopts a more serious tone.

"Follow me into the garden."

It is a tranquil place. Far removed from the heat and dust of the streets. Water sparkles from a fountain in the dappled light that breaks through the branches of a fig tree. Pink clematis that had first bloomed in spring is still in flower, and low hedges of rosemary and myrtle line a winding path. Elena would love to spend time here.

"What work would you like me to do?"

"I need, well no, I want some new furniture. A few items, from planters and bird feeders to couches and tables. Something that will impress my more discerning guests. It's important to create the right atmosphere. A tribune has power, but I still need to make an impression on others to maintain my influence."

"I can't lie, Aulus. I'm happy to be a carpenter or a marine under your command."

"Yes, I understand and appreciate that. Do you miss the sea? It's something that the citizens of Rome are too far removed from. I know it still has a hold over me."

Aulus claps his hands once more. The same slave who had escorted Alexander rushes forward into the garden.

"Bring us wine," he commands. "Put down your tools for the moment, Marcus. Sit with me. Your presence here brings so many memories back. More than once, we saved one another from a javelin or a sword. We felt the same anticipation as we prepared to board the enemy ship. The collision, the barked commands—"

"That was you," I laugh.

"Yes, that was me. Though I never had to tell you twice. You leaped into the fight. You feared no one."

"I was young. I didn't fear death."

"There are many outcomes that are worse than death by the sword. At least it's quick."

We fall silent as the slave returns with the wine and cups. He places them between us and fills them with the ruby red liquid. It gives me time to ponder over the words of Aulus. *He's telling me he knows my life has changed for the worse, without embarrassing me. He really is a skilled diplomat, a man of kindness and wisdom.*

"Would you consider returning to the navy? Alexander is here for Elena. I'm sure he would protect her while you were serving."

I shrug and contemplate his question. "I've thought of it in recent years. There is talk of more rebellion amongst the Germanic tribes and the Sarmatians."

"I can tell you the trouble has started already. Even though it might not be a full-scale war just yet. The Danube is an important frontier. It keeps the legions supplied. We are going to need men with your skills and experience. If you could consider it, then I can offer enough influence to see you return as a navarchus."

"To captain my own ship?"

"To begin with. I have complete faith that you would rise even higher in the ranks."

I take a deep drink from my cup and place it empty on the low table between us. The slave instantly steps forward to fill it once again.

"It is tempting, I admit."

"I don't know what you earn working with wood, but I'm sure a ship's captain earns more. It would mean a better life for Elena and Alexander. Two people whom I'm sure you love dearly and only want the best for. I'm offering you the chance to take back control of your destiny. The opportunity you lost when you had to flee from Delos."

"You won't tell Alexander?"

"Marcus, I am your friend and have remained so through the years we have lived our separate lives. It is not my place to tell Alexander about his birth. That is a decision for you and Elena. I *am* suggesting a way to change all of your lives for the better. You can surely see the sense in that? Rome will always face threats around the edges of its empire, but it won't be our end. I would trust you to always make the right choices in the heat of conflict. What's another few years? In that time, you will return and see your son, ready and fit to wrestle the very best. You will have earned the pay and the promotion for your own villa. I guarantee it."

I drink some more wine. It flows down far too easily. It brings back one of my last memories as the ship to Ostia left the dock. Alexander was with us, concealed from prying eyes in soft woolen swaddling. His birth was the secret that sent us back to Rome. I knew after all these years that Aulus wouldn't reveal it now. He joins me in draining his cup only to have them replenished once more.

"How would I arrange for Alexander to train? He needs proper instruction to make improvements. He's good, but not good enough if I'm honest. He takes too many chances. He'll focus on the glory before he's even earned the win."

"Hah!" Aulus laughs. "Then he's just like you, and perhaps me as well if I'm honest. Let's drink to that."

We clash cups and drink again. It refreshes both my thirst and my hunger to return to the navy.

"Do you know the palaestra run by Gaius, on Palatine Hill?"

"Yes, of course. He has a reputation for producing many great, even exceptional wrestlers."

"He does indeed. How would you feel if I could persuade him to accept Alexander for training."

"Gaius?" My mouth drops open, and I can't hide my shock. "You could arrange for this?"

"I *might* be able to arrange something. Gaius, you may know, once had his own distinguished career in the military. He appreciates men who give their best years to serve their Caesar. He trains the wealthy offspring of many of the senators. It pays well, but it doesn't always give him the quality or talent that he wishes to work with. I will warn you, he is a hard taskmaster, but if Alexander can impress him with his effort and natural instincts in the pit, then I'm sure he will see potential."

"That's the best news I've heard in a long while. My son will burst with excitement even to have the chance to show what he can do. But how do I pay for this?"

"Is the wine so strong or your memory too short? I can only feel that our chance meeting is fate. The gods will always put us where they need us to be."

"I made an offering to Minerva on the way here."

"Then there you have it. Her wisdom has inspired our conversation. If I can tell Gaius that Alexander's father is returning to the front line, and if your son can demonstrate this talent you speak of, then I'm sure he can accommodate at least one student who produces results as payment. Gaius is shrewd. He will know that another successful wrestler will encourage the participation of those who will simply provide the money to cover costs."

"Aulus, I don't know how to thank you."

"Drink up. Help me with this plan by first allowing me to find you a ship and a crew. I will speak to Gaius and get his agreement to see you. If he accepts Alexander, I'm sure it will be on condition of him taking charge in your absence. Then all will benefit. He will have a young champion, I will have done something for an old and dear friend, and you will serve with distinction in the service of Marcus Aurelius, for the glory of Rome. Or..."

"Or?" I ask.

"Or you can start to build my bird tables before you have any more wine."

We stand and embrace. The old days have returned, and I feel flushed with optimism and excitement about what lies ahead. We return to our seats and share more wine before Alexander joins us. He's surprised to see that the visit has turned into a social occasion.

"Bring another cup for Alexander," Aulus orders. "Did you eat well, my boy?"

"Yes, thank you. I had olives, cheese, salami, and bread. It was delicious."

Aulus and I laugh. I think it's obvious to Alexander that we've been sitting here drinking and talking all this time. It seems to amuse him as he gulps down his first cup of wine. The day is getting hotter, and it's easy to forget that wine tricks you into thinking that it's quenching your thirst.

"Your father and I have been discussing your wrestling, Alexander. It seems that I may be able to help, but I'll let Marcus tell you."

"Father?" he asks.

"My good friend Aulus has another good friend on Palatine Hill. Someone who runs a palaestra within his private villa. You might have heard of him. Gaius."

"Gaius! *The* Gaius?"

Aulus begins to laugh. "That's exactly what your father said."

"Yes, my son!" I confirm. "Aulus can ask him for a meeting. So he can decide if you have what it takes to train at his palaestra."

"But he has trained some of the greatest wrestlers in Rome. Will he even see me when he knows I come from the Subura?"

"And do you know who else came from the Subura?" I reply. "Julius Caesar was born a short walk from where we live now. Never let that thought go. This is the chance we've been waiting for. What do you say to Aulus?"

"Thank you. A hundred times thank you. I can't believe it."

The late morning progresses with more wine and then food brought out to the garden for lunch. Alexander is full after his visit to the culina, but the chatter and good spirits reawaken his appetite, and he seizes the opportunity to eat morsels of chicken, oysters, and mussels.

Aulus is thoughtful enough to prepare a package for home. Enough food to last today and tomorrow. I know I've drunk more strong wine than I have in a long time, but I remain sober enough to keep the conversation away from my part of the bargain. That talk will be for another day, after I speak with Elena.

Instead, we return to the nostalgia of our navy days. Life was hard back then, but as the past becomes more distant, the worst times are the first to fade from memory. We only talk about the wins and the thrill of life at sea, and Alexander encourages us to relive more for his enjoyment.

The temperature has risen to the full heat of the afternoon as we leave the house of Aulus Virius behind. We make our way back across the Tiber. The roars from the amphitheater dominate other background noises. We seem to reach home faster than I realize, and suddenly, I stand still as Alexander rushes to climb the stairs and find his mother to tell her the good news.

My news will have the opposite effect. Elena will realize that in the end, it will be better for all of us. A brighter future worth sacrificing for in the present. Minerva will not let us down.

CHAPTER III

Weeks have passed since I first visited the house of Aulus with my father. No work was accomplished that day; just two old friends deciding to drink too much wine and tell tales of their days in the navy together. It was funny to watch them talking about life on the Greek islands.

My mother and father rarely talk about Delos. I know enough to realize it must have been a lot different from where we live now. The house where my mother grew up was near the sea. She would tell me how she would love to sit at the shore either early in the morning or later in the evening.

Father speaks about it differently. He concentrates on his life as a member of the garrison. Patrolling in streets that were much smaller than those in Rome, often only wide enough for two people to walk side-by-side, and closed in by terraces of stone walls that climbed the hillside. For my father, Delos was a place to rest between adventures at sea, or at least it was only that until he met my mother.

We returned several times to carry out the work for Aulus after that first day. Father said the money was good. He made a point of not arranging any more fights for me during that time, but he insisted that I train on as many days as possible.

Today, this means a visit to the Baths of Agrippa. They have a public palaestra where I can work out with others who are keen to practice their wrestling skills, play ball games, or lift weights to build strength.

I want to put as many hours in as possible. There's no coaching here, it's just about enjoying the sport. Find a partner to match your size and strength and begin. People aren't in a contest, so it's easy to win submissions without too much effort.

I have a reputation with those who know me here. Regulars to the baths who want to prove themselves in front of their friends offer a challenge, but the easiest victories are often against those who are loudest about their chances.

Now and then, I'll face a stranger who surprise me with their skill. I enjoy these fights the most. I have to think and plan; I have to learn their strengths and weaknesses during the match. These fights don't always end with me on top, but I always take something from the defeat. Either a new idea for a hold or a realization of how to correct a mistake. I'm learning all the time, and that's what I need to do, so I'm ready to demonstrate my skill to Gaius.

I don't want to tire myself. I accept a single match before I make my way through the baths. The laconicum is first to encourage a sweat in the hot and dry conditions, followed by the milder waters of the tepidarium. It's a good idea to take some time to relax and adjust to the heat before I step into the hot water of the caldarium. It feels like I'm boiling alive for the first few minutes, but then I become used to it. It's a calm place, but not quiet. A long procession of people gasping, laughing, and exclaiming about the heat, their voices resounding off the stone walls, echoes throughout the chamber.

As I enjoy the soak, I can only think of what lies ahead. The dream of my test in front of Gaius. I still can't quite believe it. Each day I went with my father to work in Aulus's garden, I would ask him to ask Aulus about the meeting. I knew he would tell me right away, but I wanted to make sure he hadn't forgotten.

On each visit, once he gave me my instructions for the day, he would disappear for a while to speak with Aulus. Sometimes he would return in a strange mood. I couldn't work out if he was happy or sad, or if they had just shared a little more wine.

Eventually, he returned from one of their meetings in excellent spirits. Aulus had told him he'd spoken with Gaius, and he *wasn't opposed* to the idea. That was enough to keep my excitement going for another few days, until one morning when we walked into the atrium of his house. Beyond the open space, Aulus sat further back in his tablinum, a room framed by carved wooden screens, its walls lined with shelves of wax tablets and scrolls. A heavy desk stood at its center, strewn with documents and a half-melted candle, the scent of warm beeswax lingering in the air. This was where Aulus conducted his affairs—settling accounts, reviewing contracts, and meeting those who sought his favor. He beckoned me forward with his finger. I looked around at my father to make sure it was me he wanted. He simply smiled and nodded.

"Don't keep him waiting," was all he said.

I stepped forward to where Aulus sat. He already had some of his clients gathered around him. I think he wanted to impress on them that he was a tribune who could get things done.

"Well, Alexander. It seems that I have good news for you today. Gaius, the foremost wrestling trainer in Rome, trainer of champions and celebrated throughout the empire, has agreed to meet you and allow you to demonstrate your skills at his renowned palaestra on Palatine Hill."

A gasp of appreciation passed around the others in the room. I felt my heart race in the moment. I don't think I had ever felt so happy before in my life. It was a dream coming true for me. I don't know how many times I said thank you, before my father stepped in to congratulate me and take me away to the quiet atmosphere of the garden.

He sat me down on one of the new seats we had built. "This is your time, my son. Work hard and prepare. Be the best person you can be. Gaius won't just be looking at your skill in the fight. He will want to judge your measure as a man. Anything which he interprets as a weakness will count against you. I know you will not fail. I believe in you, Alexander."

"I won't let you down, Father. I will work for this like never before. I will make you proud."

"You have made me proud already, and your mother. Whatever happens next in life, know I will always be proud of you for following the path ahead."

The words draw me back into the surroundings of the baths. I'm unsure what he had meant about *whatever happens next*. There's something about the situation I don't understand. I can't quite puzzle it out, but the thought lingers and then I let it go. I must keep focused.

I step out of the steaming hot water, my skin warm and glowing. Ahead, the cool pool of the frigidarium glistens in the torchlight. For a moment, I pause, knowing the cold will be sharp and shocking. But I take a deep breath and plunge in.

The icy water wraps around me like a sudden winter wind. My whole body tingles as the cold takes hold, every part of me waking up at once. As I let myself sink into the chill, a feeling of calm and joy washes over me. The cold water pulls me fully into the present, clears my mind and makes me feel alive.

Normally I'll finish there. The Baths of Agrippa are free, but today my father provided me with a coin to pay for a massage. He wants me to be as prepared as possible. I gather my belongings before heading to the area used for public massage.

A slave steps forward and takes my coin before leading me to one of the empty slabs. The process begins with the strigil scraping against the skin of my shoulders, back, and legs, then a cloth towel is used to rub hard against my body and loosen my muscles. It's followed by the massage. Hands and elbows apply pressure, followed by stretching and bending of my arms and legs.

Little shocks of pain can cause you to yelp, but the feeling departs as soon as it has arrived. By the time the massage is over, I am more than ready to take on *whatever happens next*.

I rush home. The Subura is in the center of the city. I'm outside our insula in no time at all. I feel good and ready for the challenge, but from the third-floor window above me, I can hear the unmistakable voice of my mother, rising in anger. Then my father shouting back. They never argue. I speed up the staircase to find out what's going on.

Some of my neighbors gather at the doorway to our apartment. They pat me on the back and tell me not to worry.

Worry about what?

I pull the curtain aside. My father has his back to me, and my mother is sobbing, her cries increasing upon my arrival.

"Tell him, tell Alexander," she says, her voice breaking through her tears.

My father turns around and places his hands on my shoulders. "Be strong, my son. Sit with your mother. I have just received news. Sit with her."

He ushers me forward, and I sit on the edge of the bed. She wraps herself around me. Her instinct is to offer protection. I hold her hand as it reaches around my waist. I can tell she is afraid.

"I'm sorry to have chosen this moment, but I have to let you know. I'm returning to serve in the navy."

"The navy. We're returning to Delos?"

"No, Alexander. *I'm* returning to the navy. I have received a post in the north. To help protect supplies to the legion on the Danube. You and your mother will remain here. They are making me a captain. I will earn enough to give us all a better life when I return. Aulus will help where he can in the meantime. He has promised to support you with some work. I'm sure before long, the success you'll achieve under Gaius will pay much better in prize money. I know that this is difficult to understand right now, but it will make all our lives better."

"But I don't want you to go. Mother doesn't want you to go."

"I could have found a better way to prepare you both. I am sorry that it has to be like this, but you are my family. I must do everything within my power to make sure that your lives are the best I can make them. We are only surviving here, and now there's a chance to change all that for good. One day, who knows? We might even live in a house like Aulus, with a beautiful garden and walls decorated with tales of your favorite heroes. I will not be gone forever."

I can feel my mother relax her grip. I feel her letting go of hope as she begins to speak.

"I followed you here, Marcus. Love removed our fear in those days. We could only think of one another, and our baby. It didn't matter that we had nothing. We had each other. The nights we would lay here in hunger. It caused us pain in our stomachs, but we never stopped believing the next morning would bring something better. We had each other, that used to be all that was important."

"Elena, if there was another way, I would have taken it. Nothing will keep me from coming home to you. When we came to Rome, Alexander was with us as our child, but we were years away from having to make decisions on his future. It is different now, and today, he has the chance to go so far, *because* I am returning to military service."

"Gaius is making you rejoin the navy?" I ask.

"No. Gaius has already been told I am rejoining the navy. His role will be to look after you in my absence. His guidance and training will replace anything I could teach you about making furniture."

"Your father is telling you we are the last to know about his plans."

"Is that true? I knew something was happening between you and Aulus. Was this it?"

"It has taken time to organize. Aulus used his contacts and influence to get me the right promotion. I will not be on the front line. I promise. My only job is to make sure that the army supplies reach those who need them. There are no pirates where I am heading. I will be safe. You needn't worry. Either of you."

"Do not tell me not to worry, Marcus. Of course I will worry. Every day until you return. Don't excuse yourself by hoping I won't care."

"Alexander. Please be here for your mother. I have received my orders. There is no going back. You need to impress Gaius, that is how you will find success, but it's also how we find success as a family. Please understand my actions, and please understand what is required from you. Remember what I said at the shrine of Minerva. When the goddess shows us the solution to our problems, we have to listen and act. I have listened. I have acted. What did you pray for?"

"I asked to be given a training place on Palatine Hill."

"Then, my son, you know what you must do."

***

People are going back and forth from the house of Gaius. To one side of the atrium entrance is a shop where small statues are being carved, on the other, a place selling fresh fruit and vegetables.

Groups of men stand and speak among themselves. Plebeians, probably bodyguards, other servants, and slaves, waiting for their masters who are carrying out business inside the house.

They part to allow us through, where Aulus is already waiting. His kind smile makes me feel a little more at ease. I'll admit I was nervous all the way to the top of the hill. Although I don't live that far away, this is a part of the city I have seldom seen.

My mother insisted that both my father and I look our best, but everyone inside the house is wearing much finer clothes. I'm sure they view us as typical working people. None of them will think for a moment that I might join the most elite palaestra in the city.

"Marcus, Alexander, this is an exciting day," Aulus whispers. "Gaius is busy at the moment, but he will see us soon."

He nods toward a stern-looking figure seated among a group of wealthy patricians. The conversation is loud enough for all to hear—a debate on whether a man's fate is already determined or whether he can change it by his own free will. It wasn't the sort of talk that you would hear at Caeso's taberna.

I'm anxious and doubting myself. The people here are so confident. Apart from those involved in the conversation at the far end of the room, there are others walking in and out of the domus. Many are the same age as me. I'm sure they are the wrestlers. They walk through the house unchallenged.

Slaves stand by to await instructions from almost anyone. They look at me as if I should stand beside them.

"What do you think, Alexander?" asks my father.

He is as nervous as I am and as excited. I want him to calm me down, not make me worry even more.

"I just want to get our chance to speak with Gaius. I can't wait to know if he'll accept me."

"Today, you only need to display your virtue," Aulus assures me. "You are a fine young man, and your mother and father have raised you well. Show your respect and gratitude for this opportunity, and I'm sure Gaius will accept you."

I nod back in acknowledgment, my mouth too dry to talk. I'm wringing my hands without thinking about it. Father knows me well enough to realize that I need some distraction.

"Look at the frescos, Alexander. They all depict wrestlers in combat. It's in the Greek style."

"Some of them look like they're street fighting," I reply.

"It's pankration," my father says, "I know there are few rules, but there's still more than street fighting."

I smile and look around the room. As my gaze moves from left to right, I catch Gaius staring back at me. The conversation is still happening around him, but he is concentrating on me. I meet his stare, but I don't feel I have a choice. I think it would be rude if I looked away and I want to give the best impression.

I watch him excuse himself from his discussion. The other men carry on with expressing loud opinions to one another as Gaius stands up. I can feel the hair on the back of my neck stand up. He is heading over to me. I can feel my father's hand on my shoulder, and faintly hear the voice of Aulus.

"Now you get your chance, Alexander."

Gaius is tall and muscular. I don't know if he has led a legion, but he looks like someone who had spent a long time in the army. I can't explain it. There's something about him that just makes you feel as if he would be the best teacher you could ask for. Before I realize it, he's standing in front of me, still staring into my eyes.

He allows the slight slip of a smile at Aulus, before returning to a more serious expression.

"So, this is the man you told me of, Aulus?"

"Yes, this is Alexander, and his father, Marcus, who is returning to service with the legions in the north."

Gaius shakes hands with my father. "You have my admiration. It takes a strong heart to return after years away from the front. We all join up with the energy of youth on our side, but that's often removed by the years of marching and poor rations."

"I served in the Aegean as a marine. There wasn't so much marching."

"Where were you stationed?"

"My last post was on Delos, protecting merchant ships in the area."

"The birthplace of Apollo? I would like to visit there myself. They have great games on the island, I understand."

"Yes, there's a fine tradition of wrestling in all the islands."

"Of course." Gaius rubs his chin with his hand as he turns his attention back to me. I can see his mind working. He's looking at my stance, my shoulders, my arms, my legs, but then he stares directly into my eyes as if he's looking for the person within.

We all stand in silence to allow him to make his considerations. There's so much happening around us, but I feel separated from it all.

"Very well," remarks Gaius, "let me show you the palaestra, Alexander."

When he turns his back, I look at Aulus and my father. They both appear to be happy. As we walk through a garden, Gaius passes comments to some of his students who are sitting amongst the shade of some trees. Just like the others gathered in the tablinum, they're discussing opinions on living a good life.

Gaius pauses for a moment to listen to them, but his attention causes them to hesitate.

"Do not let me stop you," he insists, "I'm interested to know your thoughts. It lets me know if my teaching is bearing fruit."

It's hard to tell, but I think Gaius is being kind to them even if he makes it sound as if they're in trouble. Then he says something that surprises me.

"This is Alexander; he will join us tomorrow. Please welcome him." He turns back to me. "We are all friends in the garden. When you sit here, be mindful of the words you use and the respect you offer to others. That is, if you want to be considered a worthy opponent in the skamma pit."

The other students nod and greet me. I appreciate the welcome, but I also feel intimidated. I don't look like them; I don't think I could talk like them. It worries me, as I realize that I thought it was enough to know the strikes and the holds, but to be the best among these wrestlers there's so much more to learn. I have no doubt, however, that they will be respectful and act according to the careful words of Gaius in the same way he has advised me to do.

We walk on, and within a few more steps we enter on one side of the palaestra. Another rush of blood excites me. There are two skamma pits. One is dry, but the other is wet and lined with mud rather than sand. The smell of olive oil and the baking dust under the heat of the sweltering sun combine to make the air come alive. This is where I am going to learn. This is where I can rise to the top and become a champion. My heart swells. I can feel the others look at the wonder on my face. My father can't stop grinning.

"So, I can start to train here? I'm being allowed to join?" I ask, with my voice trembling in anticipation.

"I am still to know you well, Alexander, but a recommendation from my old friend, Aulus, is something I value. It would be wrong of me to disregard his opinion. I do not know your father either, but I recognize a spirit in him that has helped to build the greatest empire the world has ever known. If you have inherited even half of his standards and devotion to duty, then you will have the discipline that you need to work within our strict codes of practice.

"Your body will mold into shape, like a sculpture appearing from a block of marble. Your technique will grow with practice and training. All I need to know is if you will show gratitude by being the best of men. I have a sense that your potential is good. You will not find me easy to impress. If I sense that you are not what I expect you to be, then I will remove you from this place with the same haste that I welcome you.

"Work hard. Listen well. Be virtuous. At *all* times. Whether inside or outside the skamma." He pauses for what seems an eternity. "Yes, return in the morning and prepare to become a champion." He turns to make his exit, then pauses in his step and turns back to me. "Many have the skills and the discipline, Alexander, but few have the heart of the lion."

***

Later in the evening, it's as if I'm already Rome's most famous wrestler. The word is spreading through the streets surrounding my home, and Caeso is making a point of telling everyone at his counter about how the greatest wrestler in the city is from the Subura and grew up on his food and wine.

I sit at the table outside the taberna again with my mother and father. There's a constant line of well-wishers that queue to offer their congratulations, all asking if I can share some of my good fortune.

My mother has settled down with my father's decision to rejoin the navy. We all knew it was part of the reason that Gaius accepted me as his latest student. There was no point in continuing the argument. She spoke of how proud she was of me. I was a dutiful son who had always listened to his mother. She made sure the neighbors knew that it was her influence that had turned me into a good person, although I suspect they knew that already.

The crowd draws me away from where I was sitting. They all want to hear my story, what the palaestra is like, and the other wrestlers. As I dart between many conversations, I look back at my parents. They're alone, holding hands across the table and looking into each other's eyes. It's easy to see the love they share for one another.

I know they're exchanging hopes for the future. I can sense that this is a moment of pain as well as joy. The air changes around me. People are moving away, the many cheerful voices fading. I turn around to see Flavius, flanked by his Dacian bodyguards.

"You know, I heard your news even though I was in a different part of the city. Word is already traveling about Alexander from the Subura. I knew it had to be you."

"I have to be with my mother and father now."

Flavius's hand pins my wrist to the table. "Do not fear me. We have much to gain from one another. I am in no rush. Just know that I am watching over you." He smiles at his bodyguards and nods in their direction. "We are watching over you. With your father going away, I feel it is my responsibility to look after you and your mother. I do not want others to feel that they can take advantage. I only have your best interests at heart."

"I don't need help. I will look after my mother and the people here all look after one another."

"Is that why they've all walked away?"

He looks around himself, and he's right. People don't linger in the company of Flavius unless they are a member of his gang.

I look at him, about to tell him that people don't stay in his presence because he intimidates and makes subtle threats to their well-being, that he takes advantage by force where he has no right to do so, and that I do not like him, but my father calls to me and saves me from what might have turned out to be something like trouble.

"Alexander! Come over here now, it's time for us to go home."

Flavius lets my wrist go. "Spend time with your father. Soon he will be gone. Maybe you think I am not good enough to sit with you, but

I am more pleasant company than the barbarians of the north. Marcus will know that soon, and like I said, I can wait. I'm sure I can be just as good a father figure to you *and* your mother."

CHAPTER IV

I'm not at my best as I make my way up the hill to the palaestra. I didn't sleep during the night. A mixture of excitement and worry about what lies ahead has been running through my mind since yesterday, looking for something I've missed, analyzing and assessing everything I can think of. At the same time, I'm looking forward to my very first day of training. I want to prove to Gaius that I'll be an excellent pupil. It will take longer to prove I can be a great champion.

The house is quieter than the day before, but some of the other students are waiting outside the entrance of the atrium. I feel as if they're waiting for me. Wanting to be the first to greet me, and maybe judge just how much I know before we face one another in the skamma.

One in particular stands out from the group. The way the others gather themselves around him suggests that he's someone who commands respect. The leader of the small group. An elite amongst the elite. I take a slow deep breath as I draw closer, and a few last rapid thoughts run through my mind. My father telling me to carry myself with strength to earn respect, and my mother telling me to be humble and good-humored to make new friends in the palaestra.

The leader steps forward and extends a hand. "It is Alexander?"

"Yes," I reply.

He clasps my hand. I can detect the strength in his fingers. His arms are strong with wide-set shoulders. His neck is thick and muscular. His confidence is obvious and formidable. Within a few moments of our meeting, I already know he will be a tough competitor.

"I am Lucius. Are you ready for your first day with us?"

"As ready as I can be. When does the wrestling begin?"

"Well, not yet." Lucius smiles as the others laugh lightly. "You are keen. Most of us won't fight until tomorrow. The first day of training is exercise; running, jumping, some weights. Even before that, we will spend some time talking and sharing our thoughts."

"Talking?"

"This school places as much emphasis on training your mind as your body. Gaius expects us to understand *how* to learn, not just what to learn."

"I've only ever used my speed and my strength before now."

I knew my words were wrong even as I uttered them. The laughter from the others wasn't unkind, but it made me feel inferior. I annoyed myself, and, just as if I had left an opening in a fight, I'd created a space for Lucius to impose his authority, a weakness to attack.

"Any animal knows from birth how to attack its own kind. That is nothing more than survival. Gaius demands that we all rise above the base instinct to fight. He teaches wisdom, courage, temperance, and justice, and he expects to see those lessons turn us into better wrestlers."

"I thought it would just be fight training."

"That's what gladiators do. We are above that. Gaius demands more."

"Is he strict?" My question causes everyone else to laugh again.

"He is. You will learn soon enough. I said that most of us won't fight today, but one of us will, against you. He'll want to see what you are capable of. I should warn you, no matter how good you think you are, Gaius will waste no time in pointing out your flaws."

"I'm here to learn," I reply.

The others nod in agreement. It feels like I've passed the first test to be accepted. They return to conversations with one another, and I'm left to stand in silence. It's increasing my tension. I try to settle my breathing, but I want to get inside the palaestra, even for some exercise to settle my nerves. Doubts begin to creep into my mind. *Can I learn all these virtues that Gaius will expect, and how can I apply them to a choke hold or a throw?*

I know I'm tired from the night before. I feel weaker than I should. All the other students look fit and well prepared. My mind begins to wander, telling me that any one of them will beat me and make me look foolish.

Calm down, Alexander. Minerva has placed you here.

A slave appears in the doorway. He doesn't speak and barely makes eye contact with Lucius, bowing and gesturing with his hand toward the inside of the building.

"It looks like Gaius is ready for us," says Lucius. "Welcome to our palaestra, Alexander. Follow instructions well, and remember, you cannot learn what you believe you know already."

The other students smile at him as he leads the way. I take my place at the back of the line and follow on.

***

I thought the garden in the house of Aulus was large, but it doesn't compare with the space within the domus that belongs to Gaius. There are areas for many groups of people to sit and enjoy a feast or entertainment. Water features and sculptures lie within displays of flowers and trailing vines; fruit trees are heavy with young apples, pears, and plums. Pathways wind around the garden, directing visitors to secluded seating where they can enjoy the shade and beautiful views. The surroundings have a calming effect.

We walk into what I can only describe as a small grove. Trees surround a circle of seating, which, in turn encircles a table, laden with plates of fruit to enjoy. There are figs, melon, and grapes, but also more exotic and tempting options such as peaches from Persia and cherries from Anatolia.

I watch as the others take what I assume are their regular seats. Gaius is already sitting at the head. The students spread out on either side of him, helping themselves to their favorite treats. Lucius sits opposite Gaius. I'm sure it's considered a particular honor to sit there. There is no doubt in my mind by now, Lucius is the champion here. The others are content just to be alongside him.

I try to decide where to seat myself, but there's already a place kept clear, beside the left hand of Gaius.

"You will sit here, Alexander," Gaius commands. "Help yourself to some of the fruit. It helps your training."

I take a peach and some cherries. Gaius observes how I head straight for the food that I am not used to eating.

"Cherries will help your muscles when they are tired," Gaius continues. "Peaches are good for your heart strength. What you eat and what you drink can aid your health or destroy it. You should begin to learn about the benefits and the dangers. Use the knowledge gained to make wise decisions."

"Yes, I understand."

"I will arrange for you to have fruit to take home each day. I expect you to eat it, and not to sell it on the streets."

I feel self-conscious. I've already half-hidden a peach away with a plan to take it home to my mother. Gaius has not only spotted the fruit but also the intention. My first lesson learned. An honorable person repays generosity with gratitude.

"Seven students," announces Gaius to the entire group, "seven students. It is a number that carries the auspices of good fortune. The seven hills of Rome, the seven gods with their seven positions in the heavens, and the seven kings who ruled before the republic. Now we are seven, I should see greater improvement in all. Young Alexander joins our ranks. He will bring a fresh challenge for you all to overcome. If you cannot beat him in the skamma, then I will want you to understand why he has won, rather than how he has won.

"Some of you recently traveled to a contest in Palermo, a prestigious event, where Lucius triumphed, and others performed well. Another small group wrestled in Naples, for prizes of coin and titles to add to their glory. Where was your last fight, Alexander?"

I could feel all eyes on me. It was embarrassing to tell the truth, but I felt that Gaius was leaving me no choice. He already knew the answer.

"I had a fight in the Subura."

"The Subura. Where was the palaestra in the Subura?"

"There was no palaestra. A circle of grit laid out in a courtyard enclosed by insulae."

"Grit? Not sand, or mud? That must have torn at your skin."

"We didn't spend too long on the ground. We started in the standing position. My opponent was more used to striking with hands and feet."

"Pankration?"

"Like pankration, maybe with fewer rules."

The others laugh. It's well known that pankration has very few rules.

"And what of your opponent? Was he larger or smaller than you?" Gaius continues.

"Larger, much larger."

"So, there you have it," Gaius addresses the other students. "Alexander can face an opponent without the safeguarding of rules, he can adapt to a distinct style of fighting favored by his opponent. He can beat a man much larger than himself." Gaius pauses. "I assume you won?"

"Yes. I threw him over and pinned him to the ground."

My fellow students nod back with respect, including Lucius. I feel better about why Gaius wants me to tell my story.

"Then none of you should presume a victory against our new student. You must offer the same respect you would accord to those from Palermo or Naples." Gaius turns to look at me. "And for you, Alexander, you have six other students to learn from, not just one. Everyone who sits around this table has something to offer you, whether it's in the heat of combat or the calm reflection of their thoughts. Our palaestra has a reputation for the highest standard of learning. Your aim while you are with us, is to preserve that reputation."

I acknowledge his words in silence. Maybe I should have said something to show him I agreed, but the moment has passed, and the conversation has moved on.

I think Gaius is happy enough for me to just listen to the first morning's lesson, but I get the feeling that he will soon expect me to voice an opinion. If nothing else, I think he'll want to examine my thoughts to make sure I've been paying attention.

The rest of the morning offers plenty of opinions from the others. They discuss examples of good virtue, debate what a person can control in their lives, and what lies beyond our control.

I'm still tired from the celebrations of the night before. Although some of the conversation is beyond my understanding, it's still pleasant to sit in the garden and talk. Almost too pleasant. I'm losing concentration, and the only thing keeping me awake is the thought that I'll soon be called on to fight and show what I can do. I feel nervous. The thought emerges that regardless of who I fight, I'll suffer a loss. I am determined to keep my good humor and not be hampered by worry.

Gaius moves the conversation on. He claps his hands and gestures toward the table for the benefit of one of his slaves. The servant picks up a bronze urn and places it before me.

"And now it is time, Alexander. We must arrange your match for this afternoon. We'll follow the normal contest rules. Within the urn are six pieces of citrus wood. Each one bears the name of one of your fellow students. In a moment, you will draw a piece of wood from the urn and select your opponent for today. Before that, you need to place your own marker on the table. You will need this for future fights so that some can select your name from the urn. For today, place it down and then draw the second marker against it."

Gaius hands over a small cylinder of golden-brown wood, capped at one end with a disk of bronze, and at the other, a smooth surface with a mark. My mark, my name. It feels like I'm being given a piece of gold, made for my arrival today; it means that I'm truly part of the palaestra on Palatine Hill. I thank Minerva as I roll the marker in my hand.

"Welcome, Alexander," Gaius confirms. "Now make your choice."

I place the piece of citrus wood down on the table and reach into the urn. There's an air of anticipation from everyone about who I'll choose. All have their eyes on the prize, the first fight with the new student, as they joke and jostle with one another.

I can feel the markers roll around under the touch of my fingers. It's impossible to read the characters of a name. One particular marker rolls back and forth under my palm, and instinctively, I believe this is the one that the goddess wants me to choose.

I pull it from the urn and look down at the wooden end, which bears the name of my opponent. The result doesn't surprise me.

"Lucius."

***

I was excited to just stand in the palaestra the day before, but now I'm exercising and getting ready to fight. I know how to prepare. A routine

I've run through many times before, even though today is an unfamiliar experience.

The other students are there to help me, guide me, and maybe make me stretch a little further with my preparation and my body. The sun is rising to its highest point in the sky, The skamma pit glows with a golden aura as the sand becomes hotter to touch.

First, some light training with one another. Running through moves in slow motion with softer landings. I notice Lucius is avoiding sparring with me. I know he wants our first contact to be in the bout. An unblemished surprise for us both. We both watch each other from a distance.

I'm finding it difficult to relax, so I lift some small weights just to have some time on my own. I need to focus my mind. I have to believe in myself. Gaius wouldn't have just selected me because my father was returning to war. He has seen something that he recognizes as promising.

Lucius will be my toughest match so far, and even if I don't triumph today, there will come a time when it happens. For now, I can only do my best. *Will that be good enough for Gaius?* I have to have faith that it will. Faith in all that I have been given—my skill and discipline, my intellect in the pit, and my ability to read my opponent.

My teacher doesn't allow me to escape to my own space for too long.

"Alexander, Lucius. It is time. Go to the oil room and get yourselves ready."

An oil room isn't something I'm used to passing through before a fight. Walking into it for the first time is enough to make me feel like a famous wrestler. A powerful scent of fresh and older olive oil mixes with herbs and flowers. Lucius smiles as he looks at me, taking a deep breath.

"Gaius prefers a certain mix of herbs, which he insists is good for us. It also marks out a wrestler from his palaestra. He will expect you to stand out wherever you go now."

Lucius takes me on a quick tour of the room. A bronze brazier sits to one side where they heat the oil on colder days; there's a large mortar and pestle for grinding the herbs, and along one wall, metal strigils hang above a trough to catch the scrapings of the dust and grime from our earlier exercises.

I tread carefully as a lining of oil covers the center of the floor. It's edged with a ring of sand that will attach itself to the soles of our feet when we're ready to leave.

Finally, a center table holds jugs and krater mixing bowls. Lucius offers me first choice of which to use.

While I apply the oil, I can hear the sounds from outside the room. The others are still training. I can hear Gaius barking instructions and corrections. I'll have to do well to avoid his harsher comments. The best I can hope for is to avoid making foolish mistakes and underestimating my opponent.

Then other voices appear. A crowd is assembling. Seats are being pulled into position in the shaded area that folds around the palaestra.

"Gaius has invited an audience for your first fight," says Lucius.

"Is that good?"

Lucius nods and shrugs his shoulders. "It means he's expecting us to have a match worth watching. I know many of the voices. There are dignitaries out there from the palace, a senator or two, tribunes, and other wealthy neighbors who always attend."

Just at that point, Gaius arrives and stands in the doorway.

"Time for our contest. Are you ready, Alexander?"

We follow Gaius back out into the center of the palaestra. A servant hands him a rod as we walk over to the skamma pit. Gaius will judge the fight for the day. We dust ourselves with more sand and experience a brief burning sensation as it fixes itself to our skin. Brushing the excess from our hands, we step into the center of the circle under a cloud-free sky.

Whether for or against me, the calls from the crowd always give me inspiration. Today, most of the voices call out for Lucius, but a few are offering me their support. A one-sided contest will disappoint. I take their encouragement as we both lower our stances.

Then Gaius gives the command. The fight is underway, and the noise echoes around the palaestra. We move around one another for a few brief moments, testing reach and responses. Lucius has an aura of strength that seems to wrap around him like a shield. I can feel the movement of air punching ahead of his hands. There is a powerful sense of his physical size as he places his steps on the hot sand. He is formidable, focused, and fast.

Before I know it, the world is spinning around me as he lifts me from the ground. I'm in a position I can't control, regardless of what happens next. The ground arrives hard against me, with Lucius applying his own force on top. A cheer fills my ears, along with the voice of Gaius issuing a proclamation of the score. First point to his current champion.

There's no time to waste. A pain has shot through me on landing, but it fades as I stand back on my feet; a brief few moments pass before we stare into each other's faces once again. The crowd's support grows ever louder. Sweat and oil run across my skin and serve as protection against an easy trap of my fingers or a firm grip on my elbow. Lucius is aggressive on the attack and forces me into constant defense.

I suddenly see it. That is his mistake. An early point has made him hunger for a quick finish. We clash and grip each other's necks; our heads press against each other. Something awakens within me. I'm close enough to feel a weakness, a lack of grip, or the surprise of my response. The attack that takes place in an instant is only possible from years of dedication and practice. Intent is the beginning of the score, then action follows as I slip my head under from the inside to the outside of his arm. My right hand pulls on his neck, while I drop lower. My left hand locks around his leg. Then a rush of force completes the move. Lucius, the champion of Gaius, has fallen to me.

Now the audience gasps rather than calls. As we stand again, Gaius proclaims that I've earned the point. I feel charged with energy. I've made him fall once, and I can do it again. Lucius smiles before we circle each other once again. I know he won't make the same mistake twice, but neither will I.

The noise level rises. The various calls for each wrestler intensify. This is what I live for. This is where I want to do well. We have the measure of one another. One point each. Gaius won't let us relax. He wants to keep the excitement high. This is a sport I know. Will I take another point against me to keep the tension high? It's a risk that I can't resist. I react to his fake attack. He shifts from one leg to the other, and I collapse to one side. I might tell myself I have given up the point, but Lucius doesn't need a second chance. His arms lock around my neck as he stretches his body out to exert the most force. I have no choice but to offer a submission.

The pain is intense, but the audience is jeering and cheering like never before. Many call for Lucius to take the ultimate point, but a few still call for me. They want to see our match go the full distance.

As Gaius brings us back together, he frowns at me. I shudder as I realize that I've angered him. I feel guilty, but I'm in the heat of the moment and Gaius will not allow me the opportunity to make amends. I can only win from this point on, and now I feel the pressure of my misjudgment.

Within a few moments, we are twisting and stretching around the scorching surface of the skamma pit. Our bodies are dripping with sweat. It's a point where any move can fail to make its mark. Even the best-planned attack can lead to defeat. The force of our muscles pressing on one another, our legs entangling and the unforgiving, blinding sunlight—all combine to imprison us within the struggle. Outside our fight, the noise is ever- increasing; glimpses of reddened faces flash by as the audience draws closer, looking for a champion's winning move.

Time moves between the slow realization of a choke I can aim for and the ferocity of the battle. I summon all my strength to turn Lucius away from me. This is my chance. From behind, my right arm curls under his chin, and I clasp my hands together. I get up enough on my feet to drag him backward, pressing with my shoulder and forearm. He has one last attempt at breaking away, but my strength is holding the advantage. It is his turn to submit to me.

The fight has become more important than any would have imagined. I feel as if this palaestra belongs to me. I'm no longer the shy and nervous student from a few hours earlier. I have the chance to beat one of the most promising wrestlers in Rome. For a moment, I wonder which god he prays to, and hope that Minerva is more powerful.

Gaius signals the score and confirms the next point will declare the winner. We lower our stances once again. Now both of us are eager for the quick win. I can do it. I can beat him. I will prove that I should be the champion. My thoughts distract me just long enough for Lucius to show his experience.

When the last move takes place, all my thoughts of greatness disappear in an instant. I step into a trap as his hand slams down on my head. I feel my arm being dragged across my body. His right hand clamps into place as he steps in and fixes his other hand onto my leg. The point of my defeat follows as he drops his height and rolls backward. The world rotates around me as his body weight stretches my back flat to the ground.

It doesn't need Gaius to award the point. The cheer already erupts for the latest victory of the chosen champion, Lucius.

***

After the match, Gaius disappears to the domus with his guests. Lucius and I clean ourselves in the palaestra bath. We joke about the fight, but there's a sense of dissatisfaction. Lucius also thinks I was careless on the third point. I'm not sure if he suspects my intention, or thinks I made a mistake, but it seems to cause him doubt over whether he has won.

I'm the last to leave. My body is relaxed and has become softer in the past few weeks as I haven't been in any street fight arranged by my father. I think Gaius could overhear my deepest thoughts because I find him waiting for me as I leave the bathhouse.

"Let me make something clear," he begins, "there's no one on Palatine Hill who has trained as many successful wrestlers as possible. My reputation depends on the results I achieve, and my name draws the wealthy parents of less talented children. Do you think that makes me a cheat?"

"No, Gaius." I speak with a hesitancy that gives away my fear. "I know you will benefit everyone that comes to this place."

"But I know some of the others I teach will never make the progress they need. Their heart isn't in it. A distraction will appear, and then they'll leave. Maybe their training will have some benefit in their life, and maybe I will earn more denarii, but neither party will end up satisfied.

"I confess, I don't mind as long as I am sure there could be no other outcome, but," his pause clears the way for the lesson, "if I know that I am being deceived by one who can be great, then that is unforgivable. Lucius, you, and I all know who should have won today. For someone who is such a fine wrestler, I would not rate Alexander as an actor.

"It takes some time for a new student to learn well, to grow in their ability, only then to displease me. It's unusual to experience it all in one day, but today, I have. I only give one warning. You have until tomorrow to decide on returning to be the perfect student every day you spend here. That is your only hope of representing my palaestra. Am I clear?"

"Yes, Gaius."

"The slaves have prepared some fruit for you to take home for you and your family. Everything I do for you from now on will have to be earned with honesty, sincerity, and hard work. Now go."

CHAPTER V

I returned the next day, and the day after. Those days turned into weeks and Gaius forgave the faults of my first fight against Lucius. He is strict. He has a military voice, a tone you feel you *have* to obey. His every instruction is like a command.

My father sometimes spoke in the same way, especially if I had done something wrong. There was a special way he would say my name if I was in trouble—he didn't have to say any more. Like a soldier in the ranks, I would quickly fall into line.

It makes me smile. I didn't think that out of all the things I'd miss about my father, this experience of being issued orders by him would be one.

He left for his ship just a few days after I joined the palaestra. Gaius had invited him to come and watch me train on the day before he left. He was excited and happy, pleased to see that a dream was coming true for his son. I think he was also looking forward to returning to uniform and life in the navy.

There is nothing he won't do for my mother. I know when I was born that he rushed to bring us to Rome. He wanted to create a new life for his family, and he was determined to succeed. He worked hard when wealthy patricians gave him work to do, but the rich know how to hold on to their money and there was always someone willing to work longer for less. At times, there could be boat repairs down at the river, or the reconstruction of insulae that had been destroyed by fire, but all of that work seemed to involve gangs who would claim their share of my father's pay.

As I grew older, I became more aware of his disappointment, but each day he would get up with the sun and try again. He didn't suffer defeat while he was a marine and was determined not to suffer it as a carpenter. I often heard him repeat the saying *amor fati*—the love of fate. It was his way of accepting what he couldn't control while striving to improve life for all of us.

His decision to return to the war was about taking control. He is better at commanding a ship rather than building one. When he made the decision, he was confident his allegiance to the cause of Rome would bring reward to all of us, and he wasn't wrong.

Aulus gives me work on the days I'm not training, and Caeso pays my mother to keep working at the busiest times of day at the taberna. She enjoys a free meal with me when I return in the evening, and the fruit that Gaius provides helps to make us full.

My father's departure is an enormous loss, but I can't deny that life is changing for the better. I'm sure that he's looking to the south each morning just as I look to the north. I know we'll both be speaking the words, *amor fati*.

"What will you be doing today?"

My mother's voice draws me out of my thoughts.

"This the third day of the tetrad. We rest, just some light exercise. Gaius will lead us in our discussions on philosophy."

"Philosophy!" My mother smiles and looks into my eyes as only a mother can. Her tone is quiet and pleased. "I never thought my son would become a philosopher, but it makes me proud to know that you're learning these things."

"I know, and I'm beginning to understand why he insists on it. He says that this is true Greek tradition."

"Of course, Gaius is wise enough to know that many aspects of Roman life crossed the sea from Greece. I expect you to be proud of your heritage."

"I am, but I'm a Roman first."

"You are a Roman, plus a Greek. That is better."

"Maybe—" I pause. "Do you think we will ever return to Delos? I'd like to see it one day."

"You might be bored. It is a beautiful island. The birthplace of the god Apollo, so you wouldn't expect it to be anything else, but it's quiet compared to the city."

"So, there are no sea monsters?"

"No." She laughs. "I never saw a sea monster in all my years there, and the sea is with you everywhere you walk on the island. You cannot escape its power whether it sits placid under the clearest sky or wrathful in the darkness of a storm, but there are no monsters to do battle with. I think you would soon want to come home."

My mother wipes a tear from her eye. "I'm sorry. I suppose there's still a part of Delos within my heart."

"Well, it was your birthplace."

"No," she says sharply, "no one is born or buried on Delos. It is sacred to Apollo, remember. It is a sacrilege for a child to be born there. There is an island nearby, just a short ferry crossing. Rheneia is where I was born."

"Why didn't you live there?"

"That's where the people of Delos bury their dead. But some souls can't move on if they died violently or weren't buried properly. The Unburied, the Untimely Dead, and those killed by violence can't find their way to Hades. It's best not to build a home too close to them."

"That makes me shiver," I say.

"My son the champion? You don't need to be scared. Just pay respect to the ancestors and walk on."

"If you say so. Maybe I will prefer Rome."

My mother's smile covers a sadness as she hugs me. She, more than anyone, has shown the strength and conviction to be the best person she could be. She had coped with everything that her life in Rome had offered, for good and bad.

"Be off with you," she says. "You can't be late for Gaius and your *relaxing* day."

"Training," I insist.

It is true. Not everyone views philosophy as training

***

I sit in the shadier part of the palaestra, near the skamma pit where the mud is kept wet, thick, and ready for training. Wrestling takes place under an open sky, and though the weather is usually warm and dry, we prepare for the worst. Mud slicked over oil turns a firm grip into a fleeting one, a steady stance into a sudden fall. Gaius insists his wrestlers learn to win under any conditions.

The sun blazes overhead, its heat pressing down like an extra weight on my shoulders. Sweat trickles down my back as I shift, adjusting to the uneven ground. Gaius stands before us, arms crossed, his voice measured and steady, each word placed with purpose—like stones in a fortress wall, built to keep weakness out.

"Zeno of Citium," he begins, pacing between us, his sandals kicking up dust. "A man who lost everything and built something greater from the ruins. When he washed up in Athens with nothing, did he wail at his misfortune? No. He listened. He learned. And he founded The Stoa—teaching that true strength comes not from what we *have* but from what we *are*."

A beetle scurries past my knee, its tiny legs navigating the cracks in the dirt with instinctive precision. It adjusts, adapts—without hesitation. How many times have I done the same in the sand of the arena? My stomach tightens. How will I have to adapt in my next bout? Will my opponent test my resolve—my patience?

"Virtue," Gaius continues, his gaze sweeping over us, "is not found in victory alone but in the way you fight for it." His eyes land on me. "Even in the way you *think* about it."

I force myself to meet his stare. Did he already suspect my mind was elsewhere? I swallow and sit up straighter. If I want to prove myself, it won't be with deception—it will be with discipline.

Gaius pairs the philosophy of Stoicism and the virtuous mind with his ideals of devotion to the palaestra. There's an obligation to learn what he wants to teach. Failure to understand or act on his lessons could mean the end of my time as one of his wrestlers. So, this *is* training, and the demands placed on us all to succeed are just the same as winning our contests in the skamma.

Gaius is looking over each one of us in silence. He's considering to whom he should address his words. On this occasion, he chooses me to be the example. He recites the words of the philosopher, Seneca.

"It is not the man who has too little, but the man who craves more, that is poor. What does it matter how much a man has laid up in his safe, or in his warehouse, how large are his flocks and how fat his dividends, if he covets his neighbor's property, and reckons, not his past gains, but his hopes of gains to come? Do you ask what is the proper limit to wealth? It is, first, to have what is necessary, and second, to have what is enough."

Gaius seeks our reaction before offering a response, and the others are waiting for my turn to speak. I know the point he's trying to make, but why does he pick *me*? It's easy to see that I'm the poorest of the students. My clothes aren't the highest quality to begin with, frayed and stitched with repairs. Everyone knows I live in the poorest part of the city.

They have all been kind and never tried to make me feel bad, like I am less than them, but I suffer from a lack of confidence, a sense of not being the same. When we're wrestling, you can't tell us apart. No distinct feature in my physical appearance marks me out as being something less.

It's different during these other lessons. Lucius is from a very wealthy family. The domus where he lives is on Palatine Hill, closer to the Imperial Palace than even the house of Gaius. The others aren't far behind him. All speak about having servants at home. They talk about feasts, and their parents taking part in the forum, or city guilds.

I could only remain quiet at first, but as the time passed, I thought about how my mother had spent time talking about life on Delos. She spoke of how her brother, my Uncle Nikos, was a successful merchant with a large house and servants. She spoke about how the view from his garden gazed over the Aegean Sea.

Being able to talk about that gave me something to offer into our conversations. The others were interested to know how life was different from Rome. Each night, I would go home and learn a little more. My mother and I would sit and share some food while she went over old memories and stories of how my uncle always made her laugh.

I had never heard her talk like this before. Maybe she didn't like to remind my father of how our lives might have been. Although sometimes it made her cry, I think she looked forward to each evening where I would tell her about training, or the work I did for Aulus, and she would tell me more about Delos. It made the time pass for both of us while we waited on my father to return home.

"Well, what do you say, Alexander? Share your thoughts with us." Gaius is waiting.

"I think he means that we should appreciate what we have and value the good in that, rather than comparing ourselves to others and craving what they appear to have."

"Good." He allows himself a small smile. "A man might have more money or a larger house, but is he more content? He may have greater wealth, but he may also have greater problems as a result of having that wealth. It is wrong to assume that you would only share in the good things of his life, should your wish come true. Having less material wealth than him does not make you poorer. In fact, being at peace with yourself, and acknowledging the gifts that are already yours, is the proper way to live your life. A state of gratitude for what you already have, will remove the impulse to envy others. For though one may have less money, they may also have fullness in their heart and a wealth of mind and spirit." He seemed to hold his gaze on me a moment longer than was necessary to make his point.

I can understand the lesson that Gaius is giving, but there's still a part of me that wishes for at least a little more. I just return a nod to signal agreement, but Gaius wants to prove his point.

"Lucius's father is almost as rich as Caesar himself. He faces no challenge to clothe or feed himself, his home is a place of luxury, but even he has to learn this lesson." Gaius turns to face his champion. "Lucius, what does Alexander have in his life that you would like to have?"

I feel terrible, a small giggle of laughter from the others says everything about what they're thinking. Lucius looks at me with pity in his eyes, but he knows he will have to answer Gaius.

"I would like to live on the beautiful island of Delos."

"But you live in one of the finest homes in Rome," Gaius reminds him.

"But I can't rise in the morning and take a few brief steps to the sea. It sounds idyllic, away from the noise of the city. Imagine how good it would be to find a quiet place to contemplate our thoughts, and to exercise the mind."

Gaius signals his acceptance of the answer. "Though you would have trouble attending my classes from there." He smiles.

"A fair trade, I think, to become a contender from Delos," Lucius jests.

"Contender from Delos? Hmmm, I think Alexander might have something to say about that." He looks at me and waits patiently for my response.

"Reputations… and titles, are earned." I say slowly.

"Well said!" Gaius replies with authority. "The contender from Delos, a laurel without a bearer."

The discussion continues for a while longer. Gaius is a busy man with many clients to host and entertain. There is still most of the afternoon left when he tells us to leave for the day. I move closer to Lucius.

"Thank you for helping me out. I was worried that no one would want something from my life."

"I meant it," says Lucius. "Delos sounds like an incredible place. It's true what Gaius is saying; life on Palatine Hill is not as good as you might expect it to be. There are a lot of rules to live by, I think I would be free of much of that if I lived on your island."

"When you put it like that…"

"Will you go there? Would your family move there from Rome?"

"I don't think so. My father loves the city life. In his own way, he lives with gratitude for what he has. If he finds enough work to provide for us, he seems content, but then I see him sharing stories of his days in the navy. I knew he was missing life at sea. It doesn't surprise me he has gone back."

"Have you heard from him?"

"No. It takes time for a message or anything else to return from the front. We might not hear from him at all. He might just turn up one day, and then we'll see. Maybe we will go to Delos then."

"Good, then you can invite me to visit. I'll tell Gaius that I'm going to spend time in reflection, although I'm more interested in seeing if the Greek girls look like Aphrodite."

"I think two young Roman wrestlers will be popular on the island," I laugh.

"Look, the rest of us are going to play dice today. Will you come with us?"

"I'll just need to watch. I don't have coins to gamble."

"That doesn't matter. You can cheer us on." He turns to the others. "Alexander is going to come and learn how to play dice with us."

They're happy I'm joining them. They tell me to watch out for each other cheating and joke with me to ask Gaius for a rod, so I can separate them when the arguing breaks out.

We laugh together, head out of the palaestra, and walk off toward the city.

***

We wander down the hill and into the crowds. The direction we're heading in is taking us to the outer edges of the Subura. I start to become a little nervous about where we're heading as we're getting closer to my home. I'm ashamed to say that even after the lesson from Gaius, I still don't want the others to see where I live.

I needn't worry; we stop at a taberna I've never seen before. It is large and stretches back on the entire ground floor of an insula. Although it's bright outside, with no windows to speak of, it must be lit by oil lamps the further you go inside the building. The dim light cuts it off from the outside world. It doesn't look like a place where wealthy patricians congregate. In fact, not all the people are strangers to me, some faces I recognize from being at one or two of my street fights. If they know me, then they don't give any sign. The various dice games in play are holding everyone's attention.

Cheers and curses break through the rumble of chatter going on between the tables. It's a place where people win and lose money; a place where emotions will naturally run high. I can sense this in the crowd and am mindful of the possibility that fights might break out.

We sit around a circular wooden table. I think Lucius and the others are regulars; they seemed to have a spot they consider as being theirs.

A servant attends to us right away. Lucius orders wine with bowls of olives and nuts. He produces a small pouch of coins, more than I would even win in a fight. He asks for dice and cups to play the game and pays an extra coin over the price of the food.

"Do you need to buy the dice?" I ask.

"No. We rent the table, while we're here. There is a lot of coin that changes hands in this place, it's just the way that the taberna earns its share of the games."

The wine and food arrive first, followed by pieces to play our game; leather cups, knucklebones, and six-sided wooden dice.

"We should start with a game we can all play," Lucius insists. He nods to the others with a knowing look. He's telling them I don't have money to gamble, without saying the words.

I'm glad he does. I'd played the first game before and I'm not bad at it. You scatter five knucklebones on the table, while trying to keep them grouped together. You pick one of them up in your hand and throw it into the air. Then you have to pick up the others in a single swipe, before you catch the one you've thrown.

It's hard to catch all five, but I manage it a few times. I'm competitive and trying my best to win. We spill drinks and food as we scramble to beat each other, but everyone just accepts it as part of the fun. Lucius just orders more to replace anything we've lost from our enthusiasm.

We play the first game for a while. With no money changing hands, some are starting to complain that they want to play for money. I settle down with some more olives and wine to become a spectator for the rest of the day.

They keep playing with the knucklebones but it's a different game where you have to roll four on the same side. One of the sides of a knucklebone is called the *dog*. If you roll that side, you put a coin in the middle of the table. The coins build up as it's far easier to pay money into the game than win it back. At some point, someone will throw the winning combination, and a cheer goes up as they collect their coins.

The games go on for hours. Lucius keeps paying more money for the table, some of the others pay for their share of the wine. I am paying for nothing, but nobody seems to mind. All their attention is being taken up by the game.

The money changing hands is more than I've ever seen in one place, and it's drawing attention. A crowd starts to form around us as the collection of coins grows higher. No one is able to throw the winning combination, and Lucius turns to me.

"I nominate Alexander to take my throw. He is lucky," he announces. "Do you accept this dice roll in my place?"

The others agree. It adds tension for me to take the turn. There's thirty denarii on the table. I can see people around us placing bets with one another on whether I could cast the right combination. When I accept the challenge, feet stamp amongst the audience and then a hush falls on the room.

I go into a state of mind like I'm entering a fight. Concentrating, feeling the weight of the knucklebones in the leather cup, and imagining them rolling out in the right order. All falls silent, except for the rattling of the cup. I cast the knucklebones down on the table and they tumble over, rattling against the wood. Time always slows down for me at these moments, as we watch the last one roll into place.

"I WON!" I shout and raise my arms in the air. The rest of the crowd lets out a great cheer and Lucius holds my wrist up as if I've just won the fight of my life.

"Well done!" Lucius exclaims. "Take your share."

I can't believe it; he's splitting the money between us. I have fifteen denarii. That's enough to pay for a new tunic or sandals, some cheese or meat, about thirty loaves of bread. I should leave now with what I've won, I should appreciate what I've gained, but now I've money to play with and everyone is encouraging me to keep going. Telling me that the gods are making me lucky.

To begin with, I win more. The pile of coins grows beside me. The others are happy I can join in with the game, and for the first time I feel equal to them. I even use some of the money to pay for more food. I become caught up in the moment. Now other men are seating themselves around the table. Some of our group have taken too much to drink and are sitting further back with stomach aches. They watch from a distance as Lucius and I continue playing the strangers.

The atmosphere changes. These are serious gamblers we are sitting with. I can see that the front of the taberna has grown darker outside of the entrance. There is more cursing and more tempers are fraying than earlier. Within a few games, luck is beginning to leave. Lucius is still enjoying the game, even though he is losing money. It doesn't matter to him. He's immersed in the camaraderie and the competition.

I sink into myself again. I see the coins that can make so much difference to my mother, flow away like spilled wine. Before I know it, I watch the last of my money taken from me. The winner is a coarse-looking man, scarred from fighting over losing bets.

"Take this," he says, flipping one denarius back toward me. "You look as if you need it more than your friends. Thank you for the game."

He rises from the table and leaves. It's time to go home. To my friends, it was just a day of playing games, but to me, if I had worked every day for Aulus for a month, I would never have that amount of money. I was angry with myself. I could never tell my mother what I had done or where I had been. It was night, she would worry where I had got to. I wouldn't be able to disguise the wine I had drunk, but the rest would need to stay a secret.

The night isn't over. As we make our way toward the door, we pass another table, which sits piled with coins in the center.

"Get the boy, he will win it for you."

I feel someone pulling me toward the game. Two men are facing one another. This time, it could be a hundred denarii that's weighing the table down. One of the men is a stranger, but the other is Flavius.

"Alexander, what brings you here?"

"You know this man?" says Lucius.

"You might call us family friends," Flavius grins. "What do you say, Alexander?"

"Give him the dice, Flavius," shouts an onlooker, while others agree and push me forward to the edge of the table.

"Does my opponent agree?" Flavius asks the man facing him.

The other man waves his acceptance and once again a cheer quietens into a hush. Flavius passes me the cup and the knucklebones.

"This boy has won money for me before," he announces. "Bring me luck, Alexander."

I can't escape the situation. All eyes are on me. I place the knucklebones in the cup and swirl them around before casting them onto the table. The crowd groans as three land on the same side, but the fourth lies on the opposite face.

Flavius directs a frown in my direction. I want to escape but there are too many people around me. The game continues for another two turns. Each time, I score three rather than four. Then the man facing Flavius takes his last turn. He rolls a perfect set and wins the money.

Again, a cheer rises for the winner. Flavius shakes his hand but turns to me with a colder stare. "You owe me now," is all he says, as he disappears into the crowd with his two bodyguards close behind.

The best day has become the worst day. My friends walk me part of the way home, but I still don't want them to see where I live. They are still full of wine and wish me a good night as they turn back to their own homes.

I race the last few streets. I can see my mother looking out for me from the front of Caeso's taberna. She has a stern look on her face as I draw near.

"Where have you been, Alexander? No, don't answer that. I can smell where you've been. How much wine have you drunk?"

I don't have a moment to answer. She drags me inside, where two loaves of bread sit waiting for us on the counter.

"Caeso says we can take these home. I worked hard today, so he gave me food *and* pay. Let's get you home, you look tired. Who paid for you to drink wine until this time of night?"

"Lucius," I reply.

"Well, Lucius has too much money."

Didn't I know it!

CHAPTER VI

I haven't slept again. I don't know if it's my shame at losing a month's worth of money, or a premonition of bad times ahead. Or if the first will have caused the second. The goddess bestowed good fortune on me and I squandered it away.

The night had been warm and uncomfortable. It didn't feel like there was air to breathe as I rolled from one side to the other. Eventually, exhaustion took over, and before I knew it, my mother was shaking me to awaken.

It's time for more training. Day four of the tetrad. We'll practice certain throws or holds, which Gaius thinks will need more work. We'll train with weights to build our muscles. It requires strength and stamina that I don't feel capable of summoning today.

My stomach is suffering from the wine and the rich food from the day before. I'm not used to eating or drinking so much. My head's beginning to ache and the rays of the sun burn in through the open window.

It's getting warmer, but I feel colder. I just want to go back to sleep, but my mother is determined I'll be ready for the day. As soon as I'm on my feet, she's leading me downstairs to Caeso's, saying that I need to eat something before I go anywhere else.

That's the last thing I need, but when my mother has made her mind up, all I can do is follow.

Caeso's taberna is only a few brief steps from the entrance to our insula. He's standing outside on the street when we emerge into the daylight.

His normal smile is missing. When he catches sight of us, his face is downcast. Two men are talking to him. They have their backs to us, but they're tall, broad-shouldered, and look imposing, looming over Caeso.

Then he points toward my mother.

"Elena, come quickly," he beckons.

The men turn to face us with grim expressions. My mother grabs my hand. She is fearful. I can sense it through her grip.

"Elena, go through to the courtyard with Alexander," says Caeso. "These men must speak with you."

My mother places her other hand to her mouth, stifling a gasp. Caeso ushers us forward through the small queue of customers. I turn my head back. The two men are following us. They look at me with stony expressions.

"Are we in trouble?" I ask.

"Keep going," one of them replies.

We pass behind the counter and head toward the rear door. Caeso's wife is watching the men escort us. She mouths silent words at my mother. I can't make out what she's saying, but my mother begins to sob.

Everything is happening so fast. Caeso places two stools down for my mother and me to sit on. His wife holds my mother by placing an arm behind her shoulders. All of a sudden, the shock spreads to me. I know what we are about to hear.

"This is Elena and Alexander," says Caeso as he takes a step back.

The two men look at one another for a brief moment before one of them starts to speak.

"Elena," he pauses, "and Alexander. I'm afraid I have to bring you bad news."

"No!" My mother starts to weep. I hold on to her, tightening my grip on her hand. I feel a tear start to roll from my own eyes and my fears grow.

"Marcus served Rome well. We were part of his crew. He led our ship when others would have turned from the fight. There wasn't a man among us who wouldn't follow him."

"My father?"

"Sarmatians ambushed us when we were protecting supplies for the legion. Only a small group of men, driven by hunger to take us on. There was a skirmish, nothing more, but Marcus fell victim to the first attack. When we reached him, he was already gone."

A tremor passes through me, my ears fill with the anguished cries from my mother. I can feel every part of my body tighten and tense. The man holds out a small bag for me to take from him.

"We collected small things you might keep in his memory."

"What happened to him?"

"This is not the talk that your mother wants to hear. Take care of her Alexander. Just know that you should be proud of him. His men paid tribute to his passing." He pauses once more. "Your father spoke of you with pride. He told us you were a fine wrestler. He told us you wait for him to act like a Caesar in the amphitheater, waiting for him to give the thumbs down on the opponent you're to defeat. We committed his body to Mars, the god of war. I'm sure he will continue to watch you from above."

I take hold of the small bag as the two men bow and leave us alone.

"It was Minerva," I call out, "it was Minerva that he prayed to."

When they're gone, I allow myself to weep with my mother. She holds onto me as if to keep me safe from any other misfortune that might befall us. My head is swimming with guilt and remorse. All I can think about is my father warning me to always be grateful to the gods for the gifts I receive. I start to hate myself for what happened the day before. What if it *was* Mars or Minerva who had gifted me the money? I had squandered the blessing that was bestowed upon me.

I feel terrible enough with the news, but then there's the knowledge that I could have helped us more, helped my mother more.

Caeso places his hands on my shoulders and looks into my eyes. "You are the man of your house, Alexander. Rid yourself of the tears and ask what your father would do. The same day still sits in front of you. If you are to do him honor, then you must carry on and be strong. Go to your training. We will look after Elena."

"But I can't—"

"Go, Alexander," my mother insists, "we need you to make your father's dreams come true."

"If you're sure."

I rise unsteadily. I don't know what to feel. Caeso's wife takes my place on the stool beside my mother, wrapping her in a tight embrace.

Caeso draws my gaze. "Do what you need to do today. We will keep Elena with us until you return home."

I pass the bag of my father's belongings to Caeso and leave. I decide to pursue my father's crew. Maybe they'll tell me more when I'm on my own. I rush through the taberna. I can feel the eyes of many on me. I'm sure they suspect what is wrong even if they haven't been told. I rush out onto the street. It is already busy with the morning crowds. I look in all directions, but the men are nowhere to be seen. All I can do is turn and walk in the direction of Palatine Hill.

***

I become a little more settled as the house of Gaius comes into sight. I'm late, but sure that even Gaius will forgive me, especially with the news I've just received.

The other students are already inside the house. I make my way to the entrance only to have my way blocked by a large servant. I try to go past, but he presses a hand against my chest.

"It's me, Alexander. I am a student of Gaius. Let me pass."

The servant remains silent, only shaking his head to deny me entry. I can just see Gaius by peering around the servant's body. He's standing in the atrium with some of his clients.

"Gaius, it's Alexander," I shout, and the servant turns his head to look over his shoulder.

"Let him in," says Gaius.

The servant steps aside and Gaius signals for me to follow him. He looks stern and even angry. I can't understand what's happening today. I know he'll sympathize with my reason for missing the first lesson.

We arrive in the garden. It is unusually empty. I can hear the others exercising in the palaestra. Gaius gestures for me to sit in the seat opposite him. The one that's reserved for Lucius.

"How does it feel to sit in the champion's seat?"

I'm not sure how he wants me to reply. "It feels like it should be an honor to sit in this seat."

"It should be." His stare unnerves me. "How do you think you earn the right to sit there?"

"By being the best wrestler," I reply.

"No. You earn the seat by being the most virtuous. By living the best life possible. To refrain from temptation, to demonstrate good moral values, by striving to be the best you can in all things. Success in the skamma doesn't cause this, it follows on from it. Virtue must always be the driving force."

"Yes, Gaius."

"There are many seats around the table, but for some, there's no space. Those who spend their hours coveting the wealth of others, or those who desire the plebeians to know their name. They are just like the gladiators who line up to die for the entertainment of the masses. And then, there are those who struggle to tell right from wrong. There is no such thing as an unjust action that leads to a just cause. If you live a life in the company of wolves, it is only a matter of time before they devour you."

A silence falls. I know he's talking about me.

"I'm sorry I was late, Gaius. I can explain."

"Then do so. I am not a judge. I am only a benefactor. There is no prison where I can send a person who lacks honor. I can only withdraw the benefit I offer as a course of action. Tell me how your day passed after you left the palaestra yesterday."

He knows about the dice game.

"We went into the city. All of us, together." I pause.

"I know where you went. I have neighbors who shouldn't frequent the gambling dens, which doesn't mean that they don't. They are old enough and wealthy enough to acknowledge that they lack the good qualities I demand from my students, but neither will they see me deceived. My neighbors said that you led the group into the taberna. They saw you all drinking so much wine they were sure you must have been stealing it.

"No. No! It didn't happen like that. Lucius took us there. He paid for the wine. Ask him, he'll tell you."

"Oh, I have spoken to Lucius and the others, do not worry. I have doubled their training for today to work the poison out of their blood."

"I swear, Gaius. I had no money to gamble."

"Yet my neighbor saw you throwing dice for a prize of almost one hundred denarii?"

"That wasn't my money. They forced me into taking the throw."

"Who forced you?"

I went to speak and then froze. It would be even worse for me if I explained who Flavius was, and that I knew such a criminal. My silence condemned me.

"You have already had your warning, Alexander. You received it on your very first day. You have shown me you can memorize the holds and techniques of wrestling. At the same time, you demonstrate you have *learned* nothing. Whether throwing a fight or dice from a cup, it is not the behavior I desire in a student of this palaestra."

"My father died," I blurt out.

Gaius sighs and looks intently at me; he's trying to decide if my morals are low enough to lie to him about something so serious.

"When was this?"

"It must have been a few weeks ago. It took until today for two of his crew to find my mother to tell her. He died in an ambush."

"They must have respected your father a lot, to put so much effort into finding your mother."

"They said that all his men would have followed him anywhere."

Gaius allows more silence to fall as he contemplates my fate.

"Life is temporary. It will do you no good to spend your energy on grief. Instead, ask yourself what you can do to honor your father. My suggestion is you fill the gap in the ranks created by his absence. The navy makes fewer demands on living a virtuous life than this palaestra. You can fight, there's no doubt about that."

"No, please, Gaius. All my father wanted was for me to become a wrestler. It made him so proud when you took me into your palaestra."

"Then be thankful he is not here to witness your expulsion from this school. Go, Alexander. Wherever you belong, it is not here. It is not amongst the virtuous."

He claps his hands, and suddenly two large men are standing behind me.

"Can I say one last thing?" I ask.

"Take him away," is all that Gaius says in return.

He rises and turns his back to walk into the palaestra.

The servants pick me up and force me back through the domus hastily. I can hear laughter from some in the atrium as I'm pushed through toward the door. A final shove at the entrance casts me onto the ground. I'm left to pick myself up from the dust as bystanders gossip and snigger. I never belonged on Palatine Hill. Even I know that.

***

I head straight for the Temple of Jupiter. All I can think of is asking for the forgiveness of the gods. I've never known a day like this, with so much misfortune. My mind keeps turning on the thought that I've brought it on myself. I should have taken the gift of the money and walked away. It will be a long time before I forget *that* lesson.

It is almost the middle of the day when I step onto the main square of the temple complex. It is quiet. Most people prefer to carry out their worship in the morning, when it is cooler. The doors to the three shrines are open: Minerva, Jupiter, and Juno. Beside each door sits a priest to offer blessings and accept donations.

My memories come flooding back of the last day I stood here with my father. Before we visited Aulus, before I joined the palaestra, and before he agreed to return to war. I look around myself, hoping to glimpse him among the arches and the colonnades. It's a forlorn hope.

I know that he died on another day, some weeks ago. Maybe I had been working or training hard on the day he fell in battle. I would have been doing my best, and Aulus or Gaius would have appreciated my progress. I'm sure the day didn't influence my father's fate.

His death was also nothing to do with a game of knucklebones, but I could use what remained of my win to bring about a change of luck. I am already holding the single denarius from the night before. The coin that the gambler gave back to me out of pity.

I place it in the bowl of offerings, beside the priest who sits outside the shrine of Minerva. He looks at the coin and looks up at me. Sitting by the goddess of wisdom must have affected the priest, as he seems to know the reason for my visit.

"Minerva will ease the burden of your misfortune. Stand and listen to her counsel."

"My misfortune?"

"A whole denarius says that you feel you have done wrong. If you came here seeking answers from the goddess, then worry no more. You have already set foot on the right path."

"Thank you," I reply. I bow toward him, and he raises a hand as if in blessing before gesturing over to the entrance of the shrine.

I cannot cross the threshold. I offer my silent prayer as I gaze inside the shrine. Other than the priest, there's no one nearby. The goddess looks back at me from her throne. Her owl sits at her feet, with wide eyes to see in the darkness. My father once told me that if you saw an owl, then the owl would have seen you first. If it hadn't flown away, then it was because it was there to help you. Minerva would be nearby.

I finish my prayer. If Minerva is wise, then she will see what lies in my heart. I want my father to know I'll not forget him, and my mother to have a happier life beyond this day.

I turn and bow once more to the priest who smiles in return, then I descend the white steps. The scene before me offers a backdrop of Rome, the greatest city in the world. My father brought us here with hope in his heart. Instead of sharing his dream, a rage starts to build within me as I find myself back in the city streets. I retrace the journey that set events in motion, through the Via Sacra, passing the amphitheater and the bustling crowds, before returning to the Subura. Rome hasn't changed because of my father's death. Those who live well on the surrounding hills will lose nothing in the name of his sacrifice.

I walk to Caeso's. He's surprised to see me back so early in the afternoon.

"Did Gaius let you come home?" he asks.

"Gaius has sent me home for good."

"What? Did you tell him about your father?"

"Yes. He says that I should take his place in the navy."

Caeso spits on the ground. "Then he better not show his face around here." He pauses and looks at me. "You need something to eat. My wife is with your mother at your apartment. She has given her something that will make her sleep for a few hours. Sit down at a table and I'll bring you food, but no wine, I think. I've seen enough of my customers the next morning to recognize the signs."

He's right; I'm tired and I feel drained with the news on top of my own aches and pains. I see some people leave from the table I normally sit at with my family. I take a seat on my own and watch the people on the street go about their day. One of the servers follows me with bread and broth.

"I'm sorry to hear your news, Alexander. We all are."

"Thank you," I reply.

The kindness settles me a little, and I concentrate on the food in front of me. I don't need to look up. I can feel the large bodies take up the remaining seats at the table.

"This is not a good day, Flavius."

"I am sorry, Alexander. I liked your father. His spirit was admirable."

I wait for some sarcasm to follow, but for once, Flavius appears to be sincere. He orders an amphora of wine, some cheese, and more bread, for two.

"Don't the Dacians eat?" I ask.

"Oh yes, but not while they're at work, that's most of the time. How is your mother?"

"Asleep. It's best that she's resting. Do not disturb her."

"Or what? You may be a famous wrestler from Palatine Hill, but don't think you would easily defeat the two men that sit beside me. I am trying to pay my respects. I can help you and your mother. I can see the anger in you. That is the first thing you should seek to remove."

"Yes, I'm angry!" I thump the table as Caeso arrives with part of the order for Flavius.

"Leave him alone, Flavius. Do not make his day any worse. After his father and the palaestra."

"The palaestra?" Flavius asks.

"Gaius expelled me from the school. One of his neighbors witnessed me rolling knucklebones for a hundred denarii. A prize that wasn't even mine."

"Ah, I see. Am I getting my bread, Caeso?"

"Yes, I'll fetch it."

He disappears back inside the taberna. It's obvious that Flavius doesn't want anyone to know his part in my downfall.

"We have both suffered a misfortune from the game. I will recover the money somehow or from someone. Alas, you will not return to the palaestra. So, I find myself in your debt. Let me help you. I want to help."

"What can you do?"

"I can get you the fame you desire. Gaius trains boys that will earn nothing, and he knows it. I've seen his like before. He takes from the rich as much as I do. He dresses his crime up with notions of fine virtue and the study of the noble art, but it is only his house that improves as a result."

"Gaius is a good man. He is sincere. He took no money from me."

"He is a businessperson, and your success would have promoted his business while you remained poor and dining on the crumbs from his table. So much for virtue, I will at least be honest with you. Work with me as you worked with your father. I can arrange more fights for a bigger purse and give you a fair split to show my appreciation."

I know that I am going to regret saying this.

"How much of a share?"

***

The rest of the day passes too fast. First, Flavius and his henchmen lead me into one of the most notorious parts of the Subura. Gangs huddle on every street corner. You can buy anything here, but none of it is legal. It's considered too dangerous for even the Praetorian Guard to enter.

The two Dacians flank me on either side as Flavius moves through crowds of men. He is looking for a fight. Eyes watch over me from afar, weighing me up as a contender, deciding whether to take on the challenge.

Many conversations are taking place when another gang leader emerges out of a neighboring taberna. Flavius negotiates with him over money. They bring another man forward. He is smaller and thinner than me, but he is muscular, scarred, and wears a patch over one eye. He grins in my direction, letting me see that less than half his teeth remain. Then Flavius and the other gang leader shake hands. They have agreed to the terms for the fight.

Flavius beams with delight as he walks back over to us. "You will fight Ahu." He points toward the thin man. "He's won a lot of fights, but he's lost just as many, as you can see. Don't let him get to your eyes. People say that he's searching for one to replace the eye he lost. He doesn't understand that they stop working when you pluck them out."

"It's against the rules to attack the eyes."

"You are here for money, Alexander, not rules. Beat him any way you can, but only when we've collected enough bets against you. Just like your father used to do. I will give you the signal to bring him down, but you will have to break something to stop him from getting back up. Now let's go."

They march me down a series of small streets that lead further into a series of courtyards. Word is traveling alongside us. More and more people are beginning to follow, an excited audience in procession, looking forward to the combat.

I wanted out, but I can't escape now. There's only one way out of here alive, and that's winning the fight. Flavius spits out instructions and warnings to me with every step we take. He tells me that Ahu has a reputation for eye-gouging and strangling. Flavius says he's quick to bring opponents down with a kick. I shouldn't let his size fool me. He assures me that Ahu will kill me for even half the money on offer.

Within a few more brief moments, I am standing alone, facing Ahu in a dimly lit courtyard. There's no sand... and no oil. The crowd forms a ring around us that lays out the area for the fight. Shouts from the windows above taunt me. Ahu is a local hero, that much is obvious. Did Minerva lead me here? No, I reminded myself. This is my doing.

With no rules, there's no need for someone to judge the fight. A communal roar from the crowd starts the action. We adopt a stance while beginning to circle. Punches and kicks are thrown to test distance and reflexes. My mind is racing to look for his weaknesses. I'm giving him too much respect. He will win any way he can.

He aims a kick that connects with the inside of my thigh. Far more powerful than I was expecting, it throws my balance. In that instant he moves in, pulling my head down onto his fist. I must take three or four rapid punches to my face. He's a brawler, not a wrestler. He's pulling me close, but not even trying to restrain me. I absorb the pain of his attack and use both my hands to reach around his neck, bringing his head down with force, I shift myself to the side and push him to the ground. The impact causes him to yell out in anger. I could finish him with speed, but I catch sight of Flavius. He looks annoyed. If it seems that I can win, then no one will place their bets.

The more strikes I take, then the more money I'll make. So now I understand. I might as well be fighting an animal with fangs and claws, just like the gladiators. Ahu tries to wound me in every way possible. He bites, he scratches, delivers more punches, and even more kicks. A cut on my head causes blood to flow into my eyes. All I can do is defend. Push him away when he gets too close. Stop him from getting me on the ground. The crowd doesn't notice the skills I've used to keep him back. They're more excited about him getting the eye that he always seeks.

The noise and anger of the audience surround me. My death would be a bonus to the night's entertainment. I take one last look at Flavius. I don't see him granting permission, but this has to end now. Ahu decides he will pull me forward again. I grab his wrist, clamping his hand between my head and shoulder, and before he can react, I bring my other arm over. I pull his hand free and twist it over on itself. I now hold him with his face pointing down and his arm outstretched within my grip.

I lock my hands on his wrist. He's trapped and complains with another yell. He tries to grab me with his free hand, but I only need to wrench his arm to stop him. A last burst of strength is all I need. I spin myself around as I pass his arm above my head. It twists his body into a violent forward roll, crashing him on his back. A trained opponent would know how to land. Ahu has not had training. As I land on him with my knee and the full force of my weight, the sickening crack on his arm brings the crowd to a sudden silence.

Others rush in around me. For once, I'm pleased to have the Dacians at my side. Flavius steps forward and begins to guide me away from the scene. He has his money, so there is no reason to hang around and no glory for the victor. I have done my job for the evening.

We soon reach his apartment where he shares out the prize. I've earned three hundred denarii. Three times the amount that was lost in the dice game, and twenty times the amount of coin that Lucius had gifted me. Is this how the gods show they are listening? This time I'll hold on to the money, but how will I explain it to my mother? I take a look at myself as I walk home. The cuts and the bruises will be explanation enough.

CHAPTER VII

I sit back and admire my handiwork. It's just a fence, but it's solid and strong and will last a few rainy seasons before needing any more repair. It lines a pathway in a garden, drawing a line between a stone path and colored beds of summer flowers: roses, marigolds, and amaranth sitting among lilies and irises. It's a peaceful place to be. I know the owners will hear that I've stopped hammering and will soon come to judge my work. Sometimes there will be a final haggle on my price. Experience has not only improved my work but also my ability to stand my ground in negotiation.

The last fight for Flavius had changed me. It was the next day that I picked up my father's tool bags and set about finding work. I had thought of trying to go back to the house of Aulus, but I was sure he would reject me with the same haste as Gaius. There was no need for him to offer support with my father gone. So instead, I went from door to door among the domus closer to home, offering to mend tools or make repairs for a bargain price.

I soon adjusted to the regular working days, but my anger was slower to remove. An unexpected part of my training at Palatine Hill had become more important to me. The long hours spent discussing Stoicism shaped my thoughts about life.

Sitting here in the garden, I snatch the small moment of peace to transport me to a place where I can contemplate my thoughts. I know there's a lot for me to be grateful for, and its gratitude that will always defeat my rage. I am taking control of what I can. I'll be ready for whatever comes next in life.

I take a deep breath. The sound of footsteps approaching brings me back out of my thoughts. The master of the house and one of his clients have come out to check over my work. I think the client is maybe a carpenter by trade. He checks the quality of the construction rather than how the finished work complements the garden. I stand, awaiting their approval.

The master seems to be avoiding eye contact; he nods and whispers to his client before leaving us alone.

"You've done a good job. My patron will ask you to call back in a month's time. He will have more work for you."

"Thank you," I reply.

"Now, about the money," he continues.

I tense up for an argument, but he hands me the exact price I've asked for.

"You should ask for more," he confirms. "I'm sure you'll find more than a few will try to work your price down, but very few will argue to put your prices up. Start higher in the future. Your skills are better than you know."

"Thank you for your advice. I've not been working for myself for very long."

"Well, whoever taught you, taught you well."

"I know. He taught me so much I am thankful for."

***

The journey home is short today. I have to walk past other tabernae before I reach Caeso's. The smells are making me hungry; sausages sizzling on a grill, spiced lamb roasting in herbs, and seafood sometimes drizzled with the juice of very expensive lemons.

We can't afford to eat like that, but I know that Caeso will make sure my belly is full and content by the end of dinner. Flatbread and dumplings with some soup or stew. My recent visit to the gambling den has put me off of eating olives for a while, but I still enjoy a small bowl of dates and figs.

The menu doesn't change much but I appreciate it, especially after a long day working in the sun.

As I draw nearer, I look out for my mother. Normally she'd be standing on the street watching for me coming home, but today she's nowhere to be seen. I'm not worried, but it bothers me a little that she's not where I expect to see her.

I push my way through the queue to get to the counter and Caeso spots me approaching.

"Your mother is back at home, Alexander."

"Is she alright?"

"Yes, I would say so. You have a visitor at your apartment. A Greek man, always laughing about something or other."

"Uncle Nikos?"

"Yes, she said he was her brother. I think it's him."

Before the words have left his lips, I'm running at full speed toward our apartment. The tool bag should weigh me down, but I'm too excited. I haven't seen my Uncle Nikos for years. I run up the flights of stairs like a gazelle.

As I reach our floor, I can already recognize his laugh.

"Uncle Nikos!" I shout, as I pull the curtain back.

"Alexander!" he replies and welcomes me with a hug. His laughter booms around the room as he says, "It is good to see you, my boy." He grabs my shoulders and holds me out at arm's length. "You have grown into a man in the years I haven't visited. I've missed so much; I will set that to rights on this trip."

"Are you going to be staying in Rome?"

"Yes. I have a ship berthed at Ostia, some goods and passengers to ferry home for the return journey. Just two days, but if you don't mind, I will stay with you until then."

"I'll make a space for you to sleep, Uncle."

"Don't worry about that now. I can sleep standing up if it's required. Although it tends to upset people if I'm steering the boat at the time."

He holds a serious expression on his face for just long enough before a wide grin transforms it.

"Nikos, behave yourself," my mother says. She looks like all her worries are gone. "Alexander believed you."

"I didn't," I insist, but I think I *could* see Uncle Nikos do something like that.

"So, where can you take me in this fine city to eat? I'd rather avoid fish. I've had my fill of it over the journey here."

"Don't you like it?" I ask.

"Oh, I like it, but it doesn't like me. My stomach could do with something that's roasted into submission rather than still flipping about on the plate. So, where will it be?"

"Caeso makes our meals."

"Is that the taberna just outside of here?"

"Yes," my mother interrupts, "Caeso and his wife have helped us a lot since," she pauses, "over the last few weeks, I mean to say."

"I know, sister. I understand. Then allow me to pay him for the best he can provide, as a thank you for his care. Tomorrow we can go further. When I'd like you to guide me around your city, Alexander. Will you show me the best sights?"

"Yes," I reply with excitement.

"Good. As long as we make it to the races for the afternoon."

"The races?"

"The Circus Maximus, of course. How can I travel all this way and not visit?"

I'm almost bursting by this point. Circus Maximus? Chariot racing? We're going to watch a chariot race? I pinch myself to make sure that it wasn't me who was sleeping while standing up.

We set off down the stairs. Between the three of us, several rapid conversations are taking place at once, and in two different languages as my mother and uncle drop into speaking Greek with one another without thinking about it.

Raised to speak both languages, I can understand most of what's said, but now and then certain words are difficult to understand. I think they know. I get the impression that they're speaking in their own private language at times, referring to events or times that are beyond my knowledge, and they would like to keep it that way.

We take our usual table and Caeso is delighted to serve us his finest menu. Uncle Nikos soon has us all laughing—he always has funny stories to tell. I'm not sure if they are all true, but I think he's told them for so many years and become so good at it that it doesn't matter to people.

Every now and again, my mother and uncle say things that I don't understand. I use these moments in the conversation to enjoy the food that's always been here but never available to us. The stewed pork melts in my mouth, the roasted lamb slips from the bone. having been cooked to perfection. There's Caeso's family recipe of garum sauce, and fruit preserved in honey; even the bread that Uncle Nikos can afford is tastier than the kind I usually get to eat.

Uncle Nikos is keen to find out what I've been doing through the years since we last met. My mother tells him how we've been discussing old family stories from Delos, and she laughs as she tells me about Uncle Nikos leading sixty people along the shoreline in the syrtos dance.

I ask him about the sea monsters. I know he'll tell me a fantastic story. He switches to a hushed, fearful tone and warns me it's bad luck to speak of such things on dry land. He will wait until we sail across the deep black of the ocean, with no moon to light our way—where we drift through the shadows of ships that have sunk with all hands on board, and the first sinuous coils of Ketos rise from the depths, slick with seawater, to claim our fate.

My face must be a picture as even my mother tells me not to worry about setting foot on a ship.

"I don't want you to put him off, Nikos," she smiles.

"Of course not, Elena. I wasn't thinking."

He looks as if he is a small child in trouble as he winks at me. I wish he could stay with us in Rome. It feels like I have a family once again.

***

The next day arrives too soon. I'm already starting to count the time left with my uncle, but it's going to be such an enjoyable day.

I can hear voices from the other side of the curtain. It sounds like my mother is saying goodbye to a neighbor. Maybe they are moving away. I only take a few minutes to get myself ready and draw the thin material back.

My mother is hugging an old friend who has lived beside us for years.

"Is someone leaving?" I ask.

"Good morning, Alexander," says my uncle. "Are you ready to lead us to the sights of the city? You'll need to tell me which chariot team to support. I was thinking of cheering for the blues. That feels a little more Greek to me."

"My favorite color is red," I argue.

"Then we'll need to see which one of us is best at urging our chariot on." Uncle Nikos places his arm around my shoulder and steers me toward the stairwell. "Elena is just following us. She wants to join us for our sightseeing, but she has some things to attend to in the afternoon. So, it will be just us men at the racing, and we'll all meet up again later for a nice dinner. Does that sound like a good plan?"

"Yes, I can't wait," I reply.

We walk downstairs and out of the doorway. We're only waiting for a few moments when my mother appears. She nods to Nikos, and he smiles before pointing me into the streets to begin our walk.

"So where would you like to go, Uncle Nikos? Temples, the Pantheon, or the Forum?"

"I want you to take me to Palatine Hill. I want you to show me the palaestra where you trained with Gaius."

His choice of location startles me a little. "I'm not sure how welcome I'll be there."

"You don't need to go inside the place. They won't allow your mother to enter. I know of Gaius. He often found himself matched against my good friend and business partner, Demetrius. I think Demetrius would be happy to know that I had passed on his regards."

"If you're sure, Uncle?"

"Walk us there and pass through as many beautiful parts of the city that you want to choose, but yes I wish to visit Gaius, just for a brief moment."

I lose my appetite for the day ahead. I'm nervous about returning to Palatine Hill, even in the company of my mother and uncle. I'm worried about confronting Gaius and the others.

Finding the slowest path I can take, I try to delay our arrival, but Rome feels smaller today. I can only twist my way through the streets so much. I ask for street food. I stop to let us watch entertainment on the streets. Uncle Nikos never forces me to rush anywhere, but as time passes, I know I have to carry out his request.

The house of Gaius sits at the end of a quiet road. There are walls and gates at the bottom. You can't just walk past it. It's your only destination on this part of the hill. I can see the normal small crowd of servants who gather outside waiting on their various masters, and among them stands Lucius. He recognizes me in an instant. Even from a distance, I can see him whisper to some of the others, causing them all to turn their heads. I'm sure they're laughing at me.

Why did my uncle want to come here?

I can feel his hand on the small of my back, guiding me forward, and placing me in front of Lucius. I'm experiencing the anticipation of entering a contest. Every nerve ending has come alive. I'm already judging how Lucius places his weight, scanning his face for signs of weakness or fear. I can feel my fingers tighten and then expand. If a fight breaks out, I'm ready.

"Are these your friends?" asks Uncle Nikos. "Please introduce me."

My mouth is dry, but I make an attempt. "Hello, Lucius, it's good to see you again. This is my..."

My words trail off as Lucius and the others turn their backs on me. They walk into the atrium in the full knowledge I can't follow. The same servant who threw me out weeks ago still guards the door.

Uncle Nikos sighs. "As I thought, the elite of this school are not learning the virtues that their parents are paying good money for."

He approaches the servant by the door and asks to be shown in to see Gaius. I hear him mention Demetrius of Delos once again. It works, as within a few moments, he has disappeared inside the atrium. The situation annoys my mother. I can see it in her eyes, but she still smiles at me, kindly.

"I can't wait to get away from here," I spit out.

"Your uncle won't be long," she says reassuringly. "He is a merchant who doesn't like loose ends on an arrangement."

"What do you mean?"

"He's paying Gaius for the training you received."

"Why is he doing that?"

"Because he believes in you and your good nature. Gaius has a lot of influence over those who get to fight in Rome. He doesn't need to be your trainer to affect your chances of success. A few vengeful words spread into the ears of others will stop them from taking you on. Your uncle is merely putting a stop to that."

"Maybe he's wasting his money. Haven't I already failed? I'm only good enough for street fights. Maybe that's all I was ever good for. I never beat Lucius once in all the times I was here."

"Maybe Gaius didn't train you to beat him. You told me each day that you came home from training, about how Lucius was the favorite. It didn't take long for your Uncle Nikos to realize that there might be a reason for that. It is good for Gaius to have a champion from such a wealthy family. If you understand what I'm saying."

"I do, but I still feel as if I failed my father's dream for me. He only wanted people to believe in my abilities. He wanted me to be amongst the best."

"And would he want you to give that up? Losing a match to Lucius should not leave you questioning everything you've strived for. Winning isn't about one result; it's perfecting the fight you have inside of you that counts. Champions aren't always undefeated; you will earn your victories over time, pushing your limits and learning from every misstep or mistake.

"You must be ready to carry on and give it your all. That's what matters, and that's all your father would ever have asked for. Never feel that you ever let him down. I've no doubt you will have victories to savor, but remember, it's the determination to carry on after a defeat that separates you from those who will give up for good. Believe me, that's a quality that your father would always hold in high regard."

"I admit, I thought you would be happier to forget my wrestling after all the trouble it has brought."

"No, Alexander. Nothing could be further from the truth. But I've been talking with your uncle. It's time for you to move on, and not continue to live under the illusion that you have failed. There is so much ahead for you, so much to still dream about, but it's not here, not on Palatine Hill."

My mother is right. The subtle clues begin to join in my mind. The goodbyes with neighbors, the settling of business, the snatched words of conversation over the past few hours.

"You want us to leave Rome?" I ask.

"Your uncle intends to take us back to Delos on the next day's tide. Within a few moments of his arrival, he could see how we were living. He could see how hard life was. Rome offers us nothing. Returning to Greece will provide a future. A chance for us to start again. We will live in his house. It looks over the sea. You'll be able to see the sun as it rises and falls, without living under the shadows of the insulae."

It's a shocking revelation. Just as my uncle emerges back out of the house, our eyes connect. He can read my thoughts.

"You've told him then?" he asks my mother.

***

I say very little on the way back into the city streets. I listen as Uncle Nikos gives his opinion on Gaius. I don't think my former trainer would enjoy hearing my uncle's thoughts.

"Gaius insisted he was only concerned with maintaining the virtue of his other students..." my uncle recounts, "... that was until he discovered how much coin I had."

"And then what did he say?" I ask.

"He started to reason that perhaps he *could* take you back if, of course, I continued to pay for your training. I asked him how much it would cost. He told me how much he wanted. So, then I asked him how much more would I have to pay to have him train you well enough to beat Lucius. Let us just say that the silence that followed was rather deafening." He let out a big belly laugh and I asked him what was funny. "I could not keep myself from reporting the rude behavior of Lucius and the other students toward you. What virtue was that you taught them, I asked him."

"What did he say to that?"

"There are no words to describe his arrogant defeat."

We all pause for a moment before we begin to laugh together.

"You will beat Lucius one day, Alexander, but not through the guidance of Gaius; another will prepare you for that win. You will learn on Delos that the darkest storms pass into the calm stillness of a wonderful blue sky. Today a storm has passed. Now let's enjoy ourselves before the next one comes. It seems we have arrived."

I turn around to look ahead. The Circus Maximus stretches out before us. Long lines of people merge into a crush to be the first to enter the building.

"Look after your Uncle Nikos," says my mother. "We don't want to lose him in all of this." She waves a hand toward the massive structure.

"Don't worry about me, Elena. I'll be easy to spot when I'm in the leading chariot. The blue one, of course."

"I will see both of you later." She smiles and waves as she heads for home. I haven't seen her smile like that for a long while.

"Lead the way," says my uncle.

Even taking our place in the crowd is exciting. There is a lot of talk about who are going to be in the races. Men from Gaul, Africa, and Spain are all racing for the whites, the chosen team of the emperor. They are usually the team to beat. A woman tells me there will be eight and ten horse chariot races today. I can only imagine what that will look and sound like as they race around the track, hooves pounding the dirt in a thunderous display of skill and speed. I grin at my uncle as the crowd pushes us into a narrow channel.

The towering gates creak open. There is no going back now as the surge forward gathers pace. I can feel my uncle's grasp around my arm. He's determined we won't separate as we head into the cavernous arena. It takes my breath away. As I look down just one length of the track, it's longer than most streets in Rome. It stretches out before us, and the surrounding stadium rises around us. My mouth drops open with the sheer size of the place.

We push into the crowds to find a good view. People rush back and forward to grab space on the lower benches. We're met with some vendors selling food and drink; the noise and excitement are incredible, a cacophony of fans all vying for room. I don't know how my uncle managed it, but we find a good place only three rows back.

"You will feel as if you're in the race from here," says Uncle Nikos. "You might be able to jump onto a chariot as it gallops toward us."

"I don't think so, and don't you try either," I reply.

Uncle Nikos laughs and pretends as if he's going to make the jump. It's hard to get him to be serious, but I wouldn't have him be any other way.

The crowds organize themselves while a fanfare of trumpets and the beat of drums announces the arrival of the emperor. It silences all of us as he takes his place, higher in the stand. He's surrounded by his Praetorian Guard and members of his family. He takes a moment to look over his people before lifting a distant hand to signal the beginning of the races.

A grand parade begins with gladiators, wild animals, and the charioteers themselves steering their stallions around the track. The crowd cheers their favorites as they go by. Uncle Nikos and I don't know enough about who is best, so we just cheer with the crowd standing beside us.

"I think this is a good way to finish your time in Rome," says my uncle. "Remember the roar of the crowd when you leave, and it may still be here for you when you return."

"It's still a big thought for me. Moving to a place I don't know, and all of a sudden. I'm a little scared even though I don't want to say so."

"Then imagine yourself on one of the chariots right now. You stand ready to win the good grace of the emperor, or riches from the prize money. There are many things that can happen in the race to work against you, and if you let fears take hold, then you'll never win. The charioteer puts everything to the side in his quest for glory. He only concentrates on what he needs to do to find success. As the horses thunder past, allow yourself to experience the energy, the strength, and the power. Sense their determination to be the best they can be. You should not fear the future, Alexander, and neither should you worry about the days that are far behind you. Trust your Uncle Nikos, I will not let you down."

He ruffles my hair the way that parents often do. I think it pleases Uncle Nikos that we're joining him on Delos. He must have missed his sister over the years, at the very least. As a tense hush descends on the arena, I feel my fears dwindle. Whatever lies ahead, I promise myself I'll be ready to take it on.

The drums and the trumpets strike up once, and the first four charioteers steer their way onto the track. The volume of the crowd pounds against my ears and reaches a level that makes them ring from the noise. A signal starts the race, and a tumbling thunder begins to roll toward us. Four chariots, each pulled by a team of four horses, speed along the track. I can feel the ground shake as they come nearer, the beat of the hooves resounding against my chest. Then they're in front of us. I can see the faces of the charioteers clearly, grim and determined as they fight for the advantage. I've never experienced being so near to anything like this before. It feels like one slip could send a chariot crashing into us, but they pass by, kicking clouds of dust into the air. I choke for air and my uncle pats my back.

"Enjoying it?" he shouts.

"Yes! Come on, reds!"

"No, blue, blue," he laughs back.

The chariots soon appear again as they begin the next lap. It's white that has moved into the lead, but my chariot isn't far behind in second place. Each time they pass us, I get more used to being so near the race, and I get lost in the excitement of shouting for my team. The charioteers drive in the tightest curves around the track; sometimes a chariot rises off of one of its wheels. The entire crowd will gasp or hold their breath to see if it crashes out or carries on and moves nearer the front. I raise my arms as the race enters the last lap. It's clear by now that the whites will win, but my team comes second. They will have another chance in the next race.

"So now, are you ready to fight and win?" asks Uncle Nikos.

"I'm ready to be a charioteer," I reply.

"I think I'll forget to tell your mother that," he laughs.

The rest of the afternoon rushes on. I'm so worked up by the races that I don't even pause talking for a moment on the entire journey home. We're soon at Caeso's, where every one of the regulars at the taberna has turned out to give us their best wishes. My mother smiles when she sees the joy on my face.

"Well?" she asks Uncle Nikos.

"I think Alexander is ready to go now," he grins in reply.

CHAPTER VIII

NIKOS

I gaze toward my nephew, Alexander. He's clutching the rail of the ship and looking ahead over the bow toward the approach of his new home. It's been a difficult few days at sea and the boy hasn't held on to the little food that he's eaten.

I then turn to look back at my sister. She has survived over the rolling swells of the deepest ocean, but her mood has become more subdued as we've neared Delos. I ordered her not to stare at the sea. The water can often consume those who are unhappy with life by tempting them to leave the world they know.

Who should I attend to first?

Elena nods at me. My sister knows my mind better than anyone else. She invites me to ease Alexander's thoughts rather than hers.

I step past crew, sails, and cargo. The ship sits heavy in the water. Each cut through the waves delivers a spray of brine across your face. The wind whips from the northwest. This is the world I love, but I know it's not for everyone. I stand next to Alexander where at least I'll stop some of the Aegean from lashing down on him.

"How are you feeling?" I ask.

"Better," he replies. "I think I'm just starting to get used to being at sea when we're about to make land. I hoped I would enjoy the journey more."

"It's not been the worst. A stiff breeze, but no storms. Apollo wishes us to reach home."

"My mother told me that Apollo was born here. Is that true? A god born on the island?"

"The Greek gods live near their followers. Most of these islands have their own connections with tales of the immortals. Sometimes for good fortune, other times for mischief, which seems to amuse them. Delos is special, of that I'm certain. Even the other islands gather around it in respect. They form a circle of protection. Which is then encircled again by the greatest civilizations of the world. The Egyptians, the Syrians, the Romans, and many others have built temples here, wishing to honor their own gods in such a sacred place, but the temple to Zeus sits alone atop Mount Kynthos. He will not let us forget who rules here."

"I don't know how I feel about having the gods on the island. What if I do something wrong on Delos?"

"I'm yet to know of anyone exploding in a bolt of lightning," I laugh. "Olympus is too busy with making wars to give you any trouble. The island is sacred, and many of the people you will meet don't live here. They visit to make offerings, to ask for problems to be solved, or seek a happier heart. Then there are others that Delos transforms. Even a pirate at sea becomes a merchant when he makes shore. No one pursues their crimes while they are on land. They buy and sell like any other, in wine, dye, oil, and people. If the gods don't take *them*, then I'm sure you'll be safe."

"Does that mean it's dangerous?"

"There are always streets or houses to avoid in any place, but we live in peace thanks to the emperor. It is not good business to ply an illegal trade within sight of Roman patrols. Much better to arrive with cargo ready to sell, and a small tribute for the garrison to encourage their distraction.

"As I said, Delos lies at the very center of the world, and over many years, the rulers of Delos have changed many times. Control of these islands has always been important in increasing the wealth of kings and queens. It's a prize that's often fought over.

"In my lifetime and yours, there's been less trouble. There have been times, many times, that the island has lain for years without a population, but the people will always find a way back. Pilgrims need places to stay and food to eat. They want clothes, sandals, trinkets, and other items to buy; so, the traders follow, and the markets grow. Before you know it, empty buildings and houses begin to fill again.

"Then the island needs people with trades, those that work with stone, clay, and wood. The island replenishes with the resources it needs.

They say that if nature follows its own ways, then a forest will grow, but if it's left to man, then it is a city that emerges instead."

"Then there are other families? People like us?"

"Yes, families live here, but there's one important law on Delos. It is sacrilege for anyone to be born or buried on the island. We transport the dead across the water for burial, while mothers will find places on the surrounding islands to give birth to their children."

"What happens if you break the law?"

"No one breaks that law. So, no one has suffered punishment."

"I am still excited, Uncle Nikos. I'm looking forward to seeing our new home."

"Good," I smile, "I am happy to welcome you to it. It's too big for me on my own, even with servants."

"We'll have servants?"

"Of course, you will live the life of a patrician on Delos. What would Gaius say?"

"Who?" Alexander laughs.

"Yes, who indeed?" I smile. "Get yourself ready to disembark. I just need to speak to your mother for a moment."

I leave him to continue looking at the fast-approaching harbor. It's full of merchant ships, Roman galleys, and fishing boats. The markets are busy with people. The town is a twisting maze of marble and granite which glows under the burning sun, and the slopes climb toward temples and shrines that perch in the cooler air of windswept hillsides. The surrounding sea is clear and reflects the deepest blue. It is good to be home.

Elena is also standing now. I have seen her emotions shift back and forward with the currents over the past few days. I know she is nervous about returning after fifteen years, but I'll look after her and Alexander. I'm sure she knows that.

"Alexander is happy," I assure her. "He'll be happier once he's stepped off onto dry land."

"I know, Nikos. Thank you for bringing us here."

"Rome tries to convince its people that there's no better place to be. I'm sorry, I am Greek. My land is not the same as theirs. In time, Rome will lose its influence over Alexander as well." I pause. "Now what about you?"

"I'll enjoy moving into your house, brother. I think for a while I'll enjoy your garden or maybe walking beside the sea. I will take some time to adjust, to form friendships with neighbors. Delos will grant me the time to reacclimate."

"And whatever you need, just let me know. There are people to fetch and cook for you. Just ask."

"I want to cook, and I want to be able to choose what I buy. I didn't say that I wanted to hide away. I want to embrace this second chance that the gods are giving me. If you don't mind, I'll plant a new bay tree in the garden, in memory of Marcus. I'll make my peace with Apollo, Zeus, and Leto. I'll make offerings and ask that Alexander finds their favor. I will run your household when you are back out at sea. There is plenty to fill my life with now."

"So, then you're happy too?"

"Yes, brother. Thank you."

It fills me with great cheer that my family is ready to join me on Delos. My crew can dock the ship without me, but I choose to give them instructions. The Sacred Harbor is far from serene. It's busy with many faces I recognize. Waves and calls from other merchants welcome me home, while some of the Roman guards acknowledge my arrival. Crowds shift back and forth, some move freely, while others will remain chained until someone pays for their release.

Seabirds fill the air above us, screeching for attention and any crumb of food they can find, some swooping quickly to take a morsel from the hand of an unsuspecting visitor. They prefer the fishing boats, but the crush of people can also provide a dropped meal for the keen-eyed scavengers.

Then come the growing calls of a hundred voices raised in barter. Competing traders negotiate prices loudly, describing weight, quality, and cost in a variety of different words, but the language of trade has a common understanding.

And so, the journey ends. The ship glides its way in, and the ropes are cast and secured to hold us to our berth. On a normal day, I would leap onto dry land from here, but today I provide my family the convenience of docking by a platform to allow them an easy step from the ship.

"Is it how you remember it, Elena?"

"Yes. I can't tell you how much I've missed it. There is something in the air. It's so familiar. I left the island, but it's never left me."

"And what about you, Alexander?"

"It's very busy. I thought we were coming to a quiet island with a few goats on the hillsides."

"There are goats as well. If you prefer their conversation."

"I thought I had peace from that cackling sound for longer," comes a booming voice.

"Ah, Demetrius! I'm sure the silence only made you somber."

My great friend and fellow merchant steps out from the crowd. It's hard to miss him as he towers above most of us. He is older and a long gray beard balances against a shaven head, but he has the strength and physique of a much younger man. We clasp hands. His grip could tear a man's hand from his arm, so I thank the gods we are friends.

"Was your trip successful?" he asks.

"Yes. There was much to bring home from Ostia, but my main cargo was my sister and her son."

"Elena, it is good to see you again." Demetrius offers a bow. "How is Marcus?"

"I'm afraid my husband fell in battle just a few weeks ago."

"I'm sorry, Elena. I didn't mean to upset you."

"The weeks have passed now. I concentrate on the happy memories. It is alright, Demetrius; Marcus always spoke highly of you."

"He was a great friend, and my own family owe him much. Let me know if there's anything I can do for you..." Demetrius pauses and looks at Alexander. "And this young man? Is this your son?"

"And my nephew," I interrupt. "You can see the handsome family resemblance?"

"Yes," Demetrius frowns at me, "he has been fortunate to inherit some qualities of his mother."

"Perhaps you're right," I reply. "Alexander has learned carpentry skills from his father. Do you think we could give him some work here at the harbor?"

Demetrius looks squarely at Alexander. I can see my nephew shrink back under the gaze.

"Yes, we can find something for you to do. Leon!"

The barked call summons forward one of the harbor workers. Not a slave, but a local boy from Delos tasked with organizing people who move the cargo of the various ships that sail in and out of the island on a daily basis.

"Yes, Demetrius," he replies as he appears out of the crowd.

"This is Alexander, he will start work with us in the morning. Can I leave it up to you to show him what to do?"

"I won't turn down any help. What brings you to Delos, Alexander?"

"Alexander is my nephew," I interrupt. "He has come from Rome, but this will be his new home."

"Rome? I've always wanted to go there. You can tell me what it's like to live in the greatest city. Demetrius doesn't work us too hard. There will be time to talk."

Leon offers an impudent smile while Demetrius responds with a grumble.

"If you have so much time on your hands, then organize men to carry the belongings to Nikos's house, and don't get delayed on your way back."

"Yes, Demetrius," Leon replies before he disappears into the crowds of workers who line the harborside.

"Thank you," says Alexander. "I can mend and repair anything with wood. I've brought my tools with me."

"That might be useful. We will find work to suit your skills. The first ships will arrive only a short while after the sun has risen. So, eat well at Nikos's expense and get rested. Knowing how your uncle sails his ship, I'm sure you'll appreciate being back on dry land for the rest of the day."

"You handle the trades," I protest, "I'll bring in the cargo through flat calm or raging storms. Have I ever let you down?"

I spot Alexander casting a look toward Demetrius to confirm that he is indeed happy to be off the ship. Then I see Demetrius almost crack his face into a smile.

"Be careful, Demetrius, you almost displayed a sense of humor," I tease. "We can't have that happening in public."

"It is time I should get back to work," he sighs. "Elena, it is good to see you back home and with your son. I hope that you find your return to this place peaceful and welcoming."

"Thank you, Demetrius. Thank you for helping Alexander."

Demetrius nods and turns his attention to the ship that's already being unloaded. His voice booms across the dock even when he has walked out of sight.

"Now let me lead you to your new home, Elena and Alexander. Your belongings will follow us up to the house."

***

I don't live far from the docks, but the path takes us through markets full of curious traders who want to know everything about the new family that has appeared on the island. Elena is known to some, but not all. Those who remember her are keen to meet her son and talk about old times or discover the new gossip before anyone else.

I can only be polite for so long. When I see Leon with two men carrying the few things that Elena has brought with her, I know we need to make progress. The news always travels fast on these islands. It wouldn't surprise me if the people of Mykonos or Naxos already knew we were here.

I choose a quieter path once we leave the markets far behind us. Small enclosed lanes wind in and out between tightly packed houses, shops, and places that serve food and drink. I can see the maze of twists and turns is different from Rome... from the world Alexander has known.

"You'll get used to it," I assure him.

"How do you know where you are?" he asks. "I'm not sure if I'm walking into someone's house or a shop or just another passageway."

"Most of us like it that way, and those that live here are used to the lost looks on the faces of those that come to visit the shrines. They will help you if you ask. You can't walk off the island, so eventually you will end up in the right place. You can be certain of that. We don't have far to go now."

We climb the hillside amongst more open land. The harbor and the sea have returned into view and Mount Kynthos draws your eye to the highest point.

"Further along this road, the higher paths lead to the homes of the gods. There is plenty of choice."

Alexander is trying to take everything in at once. After living so long in the city, I'm sure it's strange for him to be surrounded by the sea. The wind is blowing a strong breeze full of salted brine, while gulls swoop overhead with their calls piercing above the busy noise from the markets. The sun is becoming hotter, and I know they'll appreciate the shade of the garden.

"Here we are."

Both my sister and her son look shocked at what they see. A small lane leads into a square of tiled ground, dotted with shrubs and trees. Four colonnades support the roof over the entrance hall. My servants appear from the inside and line up to welcome us.

"Is this all yours?" Alexander asks.

"This and some more rooms that you can't see. It stretches back a little."

Elena embraces me. I can feel her fears and worries disappearing in an instant.

"Thank you, Nikos... thank you for bringing us here."

"I'm sure we'll all benefit from having the family together. I've missed you, sister, and I have yet to know my nephew as a young man. I'll enjoy the company. The servants have heard all my jokes too many times before. They just laugh out of loyalty or obedience."

We step into the courtyard. The high walls at the front create a feeling of privacy as the blue sky spreads out above us. Smaller birds jump between shrubs and the branches of trees while a channel of water runs to the side, perpetually filled from an underground spring. The tranquility of this place has kept me here for years. I hope it will capture the hearts of my sister and nephew, especially Alexander. I know a better life awaits him here.

I introduce the servants. "Tigranes is from Armenia, he does all the work of keeping the house from falling apart and lifting anything bulky from the market; Selene and Na'amat look after the cooking and the cleaning. They will serve you with anything you need and will carry out any errands you need. Selene is an excellent seamstress, Na'amat is an excellent cook."

I note that Alexander might be uncomfortable about giving instructions to a servant.

"Don't worry. All three earned their freedom a long time ago, but they have no families to return to in their homelands. The life here is pleasant. All are here because they want to be here. I'm afraid you won't find the same situation at your work on the docks, but up here with the gods we are all happy to exist together."

Tigranes, Selene, and Na'amat all smile and nod to Alexander and Elena. I ask for Selene to escort Elena to her room and help her wash and change before we eat. Tigranes and Na'amat leave to make the other preparations. I point to two stone benches in the courtyard.

"Sit with me for a moment, Alexander. I'm sure your head is spinning by now. Do you think you will enjoy life on Delos?"

"It is different from what I expected. I didn't know that you lived like this, Uncle Nikos."

"Do you think I have too much?"

"No, I just never thought about it before. We stayed in such a small room in Rome, and it wasn't even our own. I think it'll take me time to realize I'm not dreaming."

"I assure you it is not a dream, but I've worked hard to build it. Sometimes so hard that I'm not here to enjoy it. The servants can maybe get peace then and enjoy living here on their own."

"Maybe they have a party when you're gone," he laughs.

"No, no," I tap my nose, "I count all the amphora before I leave."

"But do you remember the strength of the wine in each one?"

"I can see you are going to be useful to have around," I smile. "You will soon fit in, and your Greek will improve over the passage of time. A word of warning about Demetrius. He has a short way of dealing with people. He can appear bad-tempered and unforgiving at times, but he is kind underneath it all. Follow his instructions and he'll think well of you."

"Does Demetrius live near here?"

"He lives down at the shore, next to his palaestra."

"He has a palaestra?"

"Nothing like Palatine Hill. It was already there when he paid for the land. A ruin from many years ago. He has an ambition to restore it. To return it to its former glory."

"You said he wrestled Gaius years ago?"

"Many times. They won *and* lost against one another. That is why they persist in their mutual respect. Their memories of facing each other in the skamma pit returns them both to their youth."

"Do you think Demetrius would allow me to join his palaestra?"

"I hope so. I've already told Gaius that Demetrius will be training you."

"Has Demetrius said so?"

"No, he doesn't know yet. I just wanted to annoy Gaius. I knew that would work."

"I wish I could have seen his face," Alexander grins. "But I could help at the palaestra. I could help to make repairs."

"Yes, you could, and Demetrius is short on talent to train. Leon attends, but he's not the best of students. Demetrius once had a student called Dario; he was good enough to travel for contests. The last I heard he was fighting in games in Sicily."

"That's what I would really like to do, Uncle Nikos. Mending fences earns me money, but wrestling is my passion. I want to be the best wrestler I can be. My father wanted that too."

"And your father is another reason that I'm sure Demetrius will help. They were old friends, and let me just say that Demetrius was in your father's debt due to his actions as a friend. I'll let Demetrius tell the story when he is ready to let you know. In the meantime, work hard and impress him with your skill and I'm sure he'll agree to train you."

I pause and get to my feet. "I'm sure you are going to be happy here. Delos is a special place. It confers its blessings on all that visit its shores. It is men who set out decrees for no births or burials on the island, but it is Delos itself that replenishes the population. Perhaps that is the true will of the gods."

"I feel excited about what the future holds, Uncle Nikos."

"Good. Now go inside, the servants will show you to your room. Yes, you have an entire room to call your own. I will meet you and your mother for dinner later on. Go now, and rest after your journey."

Alexander's smile is wide. It touches my heart to see him relieved of troubled thoughts he may have been harboring. I watch him go, then walk back out into the street.

The sea that is part of my soul opens up the view in front of me. Crisp low waves glide lazily in and out of the shore. The sun gilds them as they roll into ever-changing drifts, and I can smell the salt in the air. Whether I'm on it, in it, or near it, then I'm content. I cannot bear to stray away from its presence. Even one night in Rome was beginning to make me uncomfortable.

I stroll back down through the narrow lanes and steps. It's the hottest part of the day, meaning the streets are quieter. If people aren't buying or selling, then they'll be sleeping to avoid the worst of the sun. For me, it's my favorite part of the day. A peace descends as I follow a well-trodden route toward the shore. The waves and the seabirds are sounds that make me feel at home. The breeze is always present, and of course the warmth from a baking sun.

I turn south when I reach the edge of the water. I stare ahead to where the ruins of long-forgotten buildings still lie untouched—blocks of stone left to bleach and shine among wild, overgrown plants.

No one is buried here; the dying are taken away before their last breath, so there are no spirits left to roam. Yet this part of Delos still makes me feel as though I'm stepping into a more ancient time. Perhaps even back to the birth of Apollo, when the gods themselves walked these shores. It's a custom meant to keep the island pure, but I can't help picturing the grim reality of it—loved ones bundling the sick onto boats, their final journey stripping them of a quiet and dignified end.

I follow the path around some headland, and the colonnades loom into view, still standing out from above the shore. The palaestra is far from its most glorious days, but imposes its presence among the land-scape in spite of its age. Even sitting in silence, I can still imagine the great wrestlers of days gone by, and the legendary contests that must have taken place. I can picture the crowds cheering for their favorite and the triumphant roars of victory. Perhaps a few spirits still languish here after all. I sit and contemplate the challenges we will face, but one thought rises above the rest.

I think you will become a champion here, Alexander.

CHAPTER IX

My eyes open in my new room. It takes a moment to adjust to the new surroundings. Awake from a dream where Flavius is still taunting me to fight again, I find myself in a calm space. The sound of chattering voices and plates being laid out filters through the wall. A faint perfume makes me sit up. Although no one is around now, someone has been here in the room in the last few moments. A brand-new tunic lies across the bottom of the bed. The clothes I arrived in are gone.

"Alexander are you awake?" my mother's voice calls from the other side of some curtains that are draped across the entrance.

"Yes, I'm awake."

"Then hurry. You start work soon."

I haven't forgotten about my promise to report to Demetrius at the harbor, but everything was moving so fast. There has been so much to think about since my arrival.

I jump out of bed onto a tiled floor that feels cool under my feet. I think my room had once been used to entertain guests; it's decorated with paintings on the walls and a mosaic in the center of the floor. I reach for the tunic and pull it on. It's a perfect fit. A pair of brand-new sandals are waiting for me. I rub my fingers through my hair and slap at my face a little to knock the sleep away.

I step through the curtain almost into the path of Na'amat as she carries plates of hot porridge for us to eat.

"I'm sorry, master," she says.

"No, it was my fault," I assure her.

She lowers her head and carries on to serve the food. She's calling me *master*; it feels strange. I want to tell her to use my name, but she is too quick to carry out her duty and remove herself back to the kitchen.

"Come and sit, my son. Eat some food. I'm sure Demetrius will look for you to impress him."

"I wonder what job he'll have for me."

"Your uncle told me Leon's responsibilities include watching over the slaves who move the cargo between the ships and the markets. He takes note of which merchants have agreed a trade and then oversees the goods being delivered to the buyer."

"So, he's a slave master?"

"No, it's Demetrius who owns the slaves. Leon only helps him organize the men."

"I think I'd rather work with wood."

"Take your tools in case you need them. You told him you would bring them along with you."

I finish my meal and stand up. I go to return to my room for the tool bag, only to see that it's already sitting by the entrance to the house.

"I'm going now," I call to my mother. "What's the best way to get to the harbor?"

"Go outside the house. You'll see where the ships are, don't worry," she replies.

I pick up my bag and leave. There's already a heat in the air. The low sun shines across rows of white buildings that step their way down the hillside. Other people are already moving around the paths. Servants sweep courtyards, and visitors from the shrines are already looking for places to eat. Many would have risen to witness the dawn from their chosen temple. So, it's understandable that there are other early risers, up and about to cook and serve the food.

I'm attracting attention. Some people nod a morning greeting, while many look away if I catch their eye. I feel as if they know my story already, or a version that has reached their ears. I wonder what they've heard about me. Is it about a Roman wrestler from the finest palaestra in the city? Or is it the street fighter who earns money from fighting with criminals? I tell myself that none of that is important. My life is now on Delos. If I can gain fame and fortune through the training that Demetrius might offer, then it's this island that will be the setting for my story.

The thought cheers me. As I step through the narrow lanes on my way to the harbor, I'm confident about what lies ahead. I think I'm more excited than when I first met Gaius on Palatine Hill.

As the sloping hillside reaches the level of the shore, the atmosphere changes. I hadn't noticed it when I arrived yesterday because the markets were full, but on the northern side of the town, a large area of flat land stretches out. It's full of people, crammed together and locked in chains. Men and women are forced to sit without shelter, and from what I can see, little food or water.

Men with whips and clubs pace around them, while a Roman patrol walks past to let the captured know that escape is futile. It's common for the wealthy to have slaves. I saw it every day on the streets of my home city, but a scene like this is different. Hundreds sit huddled together. Some show fear in their eyes, while others look defiant. Most bury their heads away from the gaze of the captors.

"If you're not buying, walk on," shouts one of the guards.

I turn my head away. He could be a pirate for all I know. I don't want to get snatched on my first day out of the house. It's a relief when I see Demetrius and Leon standing together in the distance. A large trading ship is docking, and they both have their attention on it as I walk up behind and announce my presence.

"Demetrius."

He turns to face me. As my Uncle Nikos warned me, he looks angry most of the time. I wonder if I'm late or if I've upset him by using his name. Leon offers a grin, and he rolls his eyes to the side as if to make fun.

"I can see you, Leon," says Demetrius, with a scowl. "Put your tool bag down on the ground, Alexander."

I do as he says. He stands in silence, looking me up and down. He takes my wrists in his hands and examines my arms, hands, and fingers. For a moment, I wonder if he plans to sell me.

"Your uncle was down here earlier. He wanted to let me know you were a wrestler in Rome. He said that you trained with Gaius?"

"Just for a short while, but I learned a lot while I was with him."

"Then you best forget everything he told you."

He turns away as the merchant ship begins to tie up at the dock. Without looking at me, he gives out instructions for the day.

"Follow Leon. Watch everything that he does. That's how Romans learn from Greeks. They copy us."

He strides off along the harbor without a second look back. Traders are already gathering to be first to relieve the ship of its contents. Demetrius positions himself at the center to take command of the situation.

"He likes you," smiles Leon.

"Really?" I reply.

"I've seen him pick people up and throw them into the sea if they annoy him, but don't worry, you're almost family because Nikos is your uncle."

"I'm glad about that."

"Come with me for a moment, we should hide that tool bag. You won't need it today, and this place is full of thieves and cutthroats."

I follow him to a place nearby. Oil and wine lie stored next to timber and marble. Leon takes my bag and secures it under some animal skins that are piled together. Another group of slaves watch him tuck my bag out of sight.

"Won't they touch it?" I whisper.

"No, they work for Demetrius too. They will let you place anything you want here. It's their job to make sure that no one removes it. Unless I say so."

He nods over to four heavily built men, and they bow back.

"This is Alexander," he calls over. "He has the authority of Demetrius. Do what he says and all will be well."

I look at Leon as he issues his command. He looks serious and even fierce as he talks to the men. His voice changes as he imposes his authority. It's clear that they won't disobey him, and then they turn and bow to me.

"You can nod in acknowledgment," says Leon, "but never ever bow as low as them. You are the master."

There's that word again. I don't know if I'll ever get used to it. I do as Leon tells me and we return to the side of the ship. It's already being unloaded, and Demetrius waves a hand toward Leon. No words required. We both move with speed.

Leon rushes to the side of the ship. He calls out words in different languages that I don't understand.

"They're Armenian," he says. "There's copper, wool, and grain on board."

"You can speak Armenian?"

"Not really. They know some Greek. We all learn the words for the cargo. Then it's prices and everyone understands about barter and money. Besides that, you just learn the correct welcome and how to wish them a pleasant trip when they leave. You'll pick it up."

I thought Demetrius hired us for our muscles, but that doesn't appear to be part of the job. I stand back, watching as Leon organizes the cargo into specific spaces. He gives instructions to more slaves, keeping an eye on everything as it shifts around him. He calls over to Demetrius every now and again, who immediately picks out the buyers interested in moving supplies onto their own ships while setting some aside for the markets on Delos.

The trades move at an incredible pace; another merchant ship is already making its way to the dock, and further along, fishermen are landing fresh catches to feed the islanders.

Leon tasks me with taking just two men and a hand cart to move grain to the nearest market. It's only a short distance away, but it still feels like a challenge. He places a coin in my hand and points toward a Roman soldier standing at the dockside.

"He is called Valerius. Shake his hand and pass the coin. He'll follow you at a safe distance for your protection."

I nod as Leon gives the instructions to the men who will pull the cart. They've done this many times before. I'm sure that they know what they're doing and don't need me to guide them. All the while I know that Demetrius will keep an eye on us. He'll be watching everything.

"You'll find Krateros with no problem," Leon continues. "He eats as much as he sells, and he'll be expecting you. If he complains about the quality or the weight, *he always does*, then just tell him that Demetrius will come to sort out his problems. That usually settles him down. On you go and get back as soon as you can. There's more to be done when you return."

I set off ahead of the men and the cart. The first job is to bribe the Roman soldier to provide me with some armed support. Valerius watches me approaching and looks either side of himself to check that none of his officers are nearby. When he's happy that there are no witnesses from his unit, he beckons me forward. I shake his hand and place the coin in his palm.

"Where are you heading, friend?" he asks.

"To Krateros?"

Without looking, he rolls the coin around his palm. He knows it's the correct payment for the job.

"That won't take long. Walk on, I'll follow twenty paces behind you. Don't look back. Just know that I'll be there."

I carry on walking over to the market. The men move behind me, straining to pull the cart. The crowds are starting to grow once again. Faces stare at me as I lead the way. This is an island where everyone knows everyone, and I am the stranger. It makes me think of my street fights in Rome where people yelled at me or looked at me with hatred because they were losing on a bet. The locals aren't angry, but it still makes me feel the same. It's not helped when Krateros appears from out of the crowd and calls out at me.

"Who are you? Is this my order? You're late. I should get a discount for my trouble. I've lost business because of you. Did you walk around the entire island to reach me?"

"I'm Alexander," is the only question I answer.

"Alexander? At least you have a Greek name. Where are you from, Alexander?"

"Rome."

Krateros looks over my shoulder. I turn back to check that Valerius is still behind us. I'm relieved to see that he is.

"Did Demetrius buy you from a ship?"

"I live here. I've just arrived on the island and Demetrius has given me work. He asked me to look after the delivery of your grain. He said 'Krateros is one of my best customers. It is important to treat him with great respect.'"

"No?" The trader pauses. "Demetrius said that about me? I am one of his best customers?" He smiles but then his face turns to a frown. "Do you think I'm a fool?! Demetrius only likes my money. He has no time for people. Ask anyone around here. Best customer indeed. I will tell you something for nothing and believe me, my friend, I don't give anything away for free. If you work for Demetrius, you will work every day. He will pay you just enough and no more to make sure you will keep working for him. Take my advice. Find yourself another job as soon as you can."

He pushes me to the side and instructs the men to unload the cart. He examines everything as it's brought to his stall. He takes his time, even stopping to make sales to customers rather than letting them slip by without giving him their business.

"I don't know, Alexander, my friend. The load feels a little light. I'm not sure if it's as good as what I bought before."

"Demetrius says that he will visit you to sort out any problems you have."

"Demetrius says that? How is Leon?"

I think my face is flushing with embarrassment. They all know each other too well.

"Can you fight, Alexander?" Krateros asks.

"I'm a wrestler."

"Now it makes sense. That's why Demetrius has taken you on. Take this package and don't break the seal. I expect my payment to reach Demetrius in one piece."

"Thank you," I reply and nod respectfully. No bow.

"And remember. You buy your grain from here. Don't let the other crooks fool you. They'll sell you the worst. Cheap doesn't always mean good, Alexander."

He slaps me on the back before returning to his customers. As I set off to return to the docks. I hear him laughing with people about how I told him that Demetrius thought he was the best. I think even the two men with the cart are smirking at that. I wonder when I'll fit in here or find acceptance with the local people. Then I think again about what Krateros said.

Has Demetrius hired me to be a wrestler?

***

The rest of my first morning passes quicker than expected. The ships race into the dock early to get their cargo sold before others arrive. I learn that prices can change fast, depending on whether there's too much or too little to buy. Demetrius doesn't control everything, but many of the merchants choose to negotiate with him.

I stand beside the two men and the hand cart. They speak to one another in hushed words, but not to me. They're older, maybe twenty years or more. Maybe they've aged because of the life they've had to lead. I had witnessed that in Rome. Even so, it was obvious how much younger I was, and they had to follow my bidding. I wanted to know who they were. I wanted to ask questions, but every time I caught their eye, they would look away. It was only when I gave a command that they nodded in response.

I wasn't comfortable. Back in Rome, they might have spoken to me. There were those in the Subura who had once been slaves. They had earned their freedom and lived alongside everyone else. Those that sat chained were only at the beginning of their journey. Some might end up with masters who treated them with fairness, but I was sure that wouldn't be the fate for all.

Leon walks over to find me. I think I look unhappy as I stand beside the cart. He orders the men to pull it to the other side of the dock. They react to his command with haste and take the cart to the spot where Demetrius has his own store of goods. They sit on some rocks where they can wait to be summoned again. Now they look at me, but only to be ready if I call them back.

"How are you getting on?" he asks.

"I don't think the men needed me with them. I'm not sure if I've even done anything."

"Don't worry. I gave you a simple job to begin with," he replies. "The slaves could have done it themselves, but then you would have Krateros and the others like him claiming that there was grain missing or wasted. It's not the slaves that you are there to keep an eye on."

"I understand, I think."

"The men you work with will earn their freedom by not breaking the trust of Demetrius. Krateros will never earn that trust in the first place. Men and women captured in war are often better people than those who remain free. Through fate or ill luck, they have lost control of part of their life. To win it back, they must concentrate on what they can control."

"You're talking about Stoicism?"

"Yes, you've heard about it before?"

"I trained in an elite palaestra on Palatine Hill in Rome, near the Imperial Palace. Gaius, who owned the palaestra, would teach us about Stoicism before we began our physical training. He said it was important to understand, to make us better at wrestling."

"Demetrius is the same," smiles Leon. "I do my best to listen and take it in, but I find it hard to concentrate on some of the ideas. I just want to be good enough and strong enough to win contests. I think I frustrate him, to be honest. He says I have talent, but it's still hidden away from view, that something up here is holding me back." He taps a finger to his temple. "He says that it will need a good opponent to reveal it." He pauses and looks at me thoughtfully. "Are you going to join the palaestra? I think it would be good for us to train together. Maybe you can teach me something from the Roman ways."

"Yes, I want to join the palaestra. It's weeks since I've trained. My uncle said that he would speak with Demetrius. Do you think I should ask him now?"

Leon smiles again. "You can't push him. He decides when he's going to take someone on, but he needs a replacement for Dario."

"I've heard Dario's name mentioned."

"Dario was his best student. Good enough to attract the attention of those who wanted to place him in fights all across Greece. He's been away for months. There is no one else good enough to practice with. Although I don't mind the lack of bruises since he left."

"Did he do anything to reveal your talent?"

"No, he just beat me up. If I learned anything, it was how to defend myself."

"Well, that's half the fight, at least."

"I know, but it's the other half I need to work on. I want to beat him one day."

"I know how you feel. I want to beat Lucius."

"Who?"

"He is a great wrestler from Rome. Gaius favors him above all others. He's making a name for himself and helping Gaius keep his reputation strong and the patronage of wealthy families flowing. I suppose that's what the trainers are looking for."

"Not Demetrius," Leon remarks. "He has wealth. He works hard and lives well. What more does *he* need? You will learn he's different. He wants to help people reach their highest level, to be the best they can. He always says that our success is his reward."

Just at that moment, Demetrius appears out of the crowd. He strides toward us with his fearsome look.

"Am I paying the two of you to chatter?"

"We've finished what you asked of us," insists Leon. "Alexander has made a good start. He'll be an excellent help."

"Very well, if Leon is happy with your work, then you can return tomorrow to do more. When I decide to only keep half an eye on you, then I'll hire you as a regular worker. Until then, avoid looking as if you have nothing to do."

"I was talking to Alexander about wrestling," Leon interrupts. "I wondered if he could come and watch me train at the palaestra tomorrow?"

Demetrius sighs. Leon was right; he didn't like to be pushed.

"Maybe Alexander could teach you to be more subtle in your requests, Leon. Your problem is I know your next move before even you know it. Yes, Alexander can come with you, but let's not waste the opportunity. Come prepared to show us what you can do."

I can't help grinning along with Leon. It is going to be good to get back to training. Demetrius maintains his serious look.

"The two of you can go for today. From tomorrow, I don't want to see you standing idle. I want you to either be working or becoming part of this island. Consider this your first lesson from which I will expect to see results. Good day."

Again, he turns and disappears into a conversation with another group of merchants as if to prove his point.

"Are you hungry?" asks Leon.

"Yes, but Demetrius hasn't paid me yet."

"I have enough to feed us. Follow me, I have enough for bread and olives and cheese."

"Maybe I'll leave out the olives. I'm not so keen on them these days."

We set off back into the main part of the town. It's the same place that I walked through this morning, but I feel better as I follow Leon through the crowds. I realize that as the day progressed, Delos hasn't changed, but I've changed.

Leon's offer of friendship seems to echo the lesson from Demetrius. It was how Leon would have started his training; I can see that. He speaks to other friends as we walk through the crowd. He makes a point of always introducing me and letting people know that I am a wrestler like him. Each conversation is brief, but it's a start. These people will become my people. It's not like Rome. You can disappear in the world's biggest city, and few will miss you, but Delos is different. There's something about this place that shapes the people who live here. Maybe it's living beside the gods that does it.

We step back into the narrow pathways that weave like a serpent between packed shops and houses. It's cooler and pleasant out of the direct sunlight; a small space with four tables inside is our destination. Leon receives a greeting from the cook and the server. It reminds me of Caeso's taberna.

"What about a lentil bowl and bread?" he asks me as we take a seat.

"That sounds good," I reply.

A fluent conversation in Greek begins between Leon and the server. I can pick up most of it, but not all. I hear my name being mentioned, and Rome, wrestling, and my Uncle Nikos. The server laughs as she replies.

"She says she will let you stay as long as you don't tell his terrible jokes," Leon confirms.

"I promise," I say in return.

Sitting inside for the hottest part of the day, I learn more about Leon's family. His father owns a fishing boat, and his mother works with clay and makes gifts to sell to the island's visitors. The only thing he tells me about his sister is that she's annoying.

I tell him about my mother and how she's lived on Delos before. I talk about my father, and for the first time I find I can talk about him with a full sense of pride. Remembering stories without feeling sad. I think wherever he is, he will be happy that we've returned to Delos, and I'm sure he'll know that I am returning to the palaestra.

CHAPTER X

My third day on the island of Delos, and it still feels new and different from the city I have left behind. A slower pace of life exists in Greece. No one seems to be in a hurry.

There are things I miss about Rome. Caeso's, of course, and friends and neighbors I once ate and drank with, but Leon is introducing me to new people all the time. He tells everyone about how I am such a great wrestler from a famous palaestra. I ask him to not declare it to everyone so proudly. I haven't trained so much since leaving Palatine Hill and I'm starting to feel as if my skills are maybe not as sharp as they were. Hopefully, I will start to change all that today.

Demetrius has left the harbor before we finish our duties. He's told us he should be at the palaestra waiting for us when our work is over.

"We can go now," Leon says as he takes a last look along the dock. "Time for us to have a fight."

"And I thought we were becoming friends," I smile.

"Yes, but that ends when we step into the skamma," he laughs back.

We set off along the shoreline. There's a path, but the southern end of the island is more overgrown with plants and grasses. It passes through older ruins. Delos must have been a lot bigger before years of invasions and pirate raids. I can make out where lanes and streets might have been. Broken walls lie around archways that still stand. Then I catch sight of what's left of a large amphitheater. It looks like it would have seated thousands. Something that wouldn't have been out of place in Rome.

"Does no one go there now?" I ask Leon.

"Not for entertainment. My sister meets with her friends there."

"Do they put on plays?"

"No, nothing like that. My sister and her friends are Christians. They don't have a shrine or a temple on the island. Are there Christians in Rome?"

"Some. They live in a poorer part of the city. People don't trust them. They refuse to take part in the rituals or worship the emperor. Some people say they are rebels, always plotting to cause trouble."

"Yes, that sounds like my sister."

"Where were you born, Leon? I was told that no one is born here."

"That's true. I was born on Mykonos. My family only moved here a few years ago. My father could fish from any of the islands, but he would often land his catch here, and I suppose he decided it would be easier just to live closer to where he worked."

"Did he want you to fish with him?"

"I did for a while, but I prefer my feet on the land. When Demetrius offered me work, I took it."

"I know what you mean. I hated the journey from Ostia."

"Did you spend most of your time gazing over the side and clutching your stomach?" Leon teases.

"Yes, I'm afraid so."

"That's what I was like, too. People think because we live on the islands that we must love the sea. I like to swim in it, but that's enough."

We keep joking and laughing with one another as we walk onward. Leon doesn't take his life too seriously. He's happy to work and train with Demetrius, so I start to wonder if the training will be less strict and more fun. The idea disappears as we enter the palaestra.

"Head up, tuck your elbows. Circle!" Demetrius steps around the edge of the skamma.

Two younger wrestlers are learning the basics of how to stand and face one another. It must be one of their first lessons. Demetrius catches our eye as we arrive, but he concentrates on the battle being carried out before him.

"Lower yourself, use your head, circle away. Move in again."

Demetrius reacts to every move, calling out attacks and defensive blocks, expecting his students to react immediately to his commands. The afternoon sun is high above us in the sky. It causes their sweat to run, making it harder to grip or hold. All the while, Demetrius drives the intensity of the match-up. His instructions encourage them to keep in the fight and work for the win. Even though they're just starting out, he's already making them hungry for points and victory.

"Grip the heel, elbow flat."

A low attack finds success, but there's no moment to rest. Demetrius stops the fight just long enough to demonstrate a better defense.

"Hold your inner calm, be aware of the power that comes from focus and discipline. These are the things within your control. Now stand and face each other again."

The fight continues. They are just beginners, but they show the same spirit as any seasoned wrestler. Demetrius looks over to Leon.

"You know how to instruct them. Take over the lesson. Alexander, follow me."

Leon steps into the role of teacher. I'm beginning to see why he's important to Demetrius. Trusted to carry out his duties at the harbor and take over training in the palaestra, Leon has virtues that even Gaius would admire.

I follow Demetrius to some higher ground that rises above the palaestra. He sits on a granite slab that has been left lying from another ruined building. He positions himself with a view over the sea and the palaestra. I know he's keeping an eye on the training below us. I think about how he manages many tasks at once. At the dock, he works with buyers and sellers, organizing supplies for the markets, carrying out twenty conversations at once, and still keeping a watchful eye over new recruits like me. He invites me to sit in front of him.

"I do not know you, Alexander. Nikos speaks of you in good terms. I knew your father and mother before you were born. Your father helped my family. I will do my best to repay that debt, but that only creates an opening, an opportunity. How will you use it, I wonder?"

He directs his gaze out to sea and waits in silence. The constant breeze that sweeps around the island whips at my hair as I search my mind for an answer. *This has to be a test.*

"I'll work hard. I can train all day and then train some more. I only want to be a better wrestler."

"I won't twist your words," he replies. "I can hear that you're sincere, but even the two youngsters fighting below are *better* than they were last month. That's not enough ambition for someone who seeks to be a champion. If it's not for you, then I will have to settle for merely making you better and carry on my own search elsewhere."

"I want to be the champion," I panic. "I can be a champion. I won't let you down."

"That's a promise indeed. I'll remember and keep you to it. With every word you speak, you reveal a part of your soul. I already know that you are rash and sometimes too quick to react. There is a harmony created when mind and body are in balance. As yet, you are far from that perfect state. I suspect you have earned injuries in the past by overreaching or believing you had abilities beyond your true capabilities."

All that from one answer? It makes me nervous to say any more. Demetrius allows silence to settle once again.

"It's true I've had injuries, and those have come from mistakes. I can admit that, but my first matches were at the public bathhouses. It's there I learned about the rules, but not always from those that had skills themselves, and not always from within the fight."

I pause again. I want to use words that have value to Demetrius. He misses nothing, and I want to prove I'm worthy of his trust. I allow a few moments before continuing. I want to show him I'm committed.

"I found I could watch others and learn the moves they were *about* to make. I could see how they used their weight and the attacks that they favored. I could see when they weakened themselves with frustration or anger. Then when I faced them in the skamma, I already knew what I needed to do to win. No one taught me that."

"Did Gaius not speak about learning through observation?"

"He did, but I had already been using it. I think he saw that I could read my opponents. It's easier to defend when you know what's coming."

"Indeed, it is," Demetrius replies. "Actions, reactions, and consequences for others make for valuable lessons. What did you see and learn from Krateros? What if you were facing him as an opponent?"

The question surprised me, and Demetrius would know if I was not being genuine with my reply.

"He scared me at first, but then I realized it was more of a part he plays. I had to earn his respect by deflecting his first attack, by letting him know that I could surprise him with my next move."

"And how did you do that?"

"I told him you said he was one of your best customers."

The silence returns, except for Demetrius clearing his throat before he continues. "And how did you win?"

I think hard about the question, but then the answer shows itself to me.

"I followed your training and the guidance from Leon. You set the course of my first attack; Leon instructed me to bribe the guard. The two slaves knew Krateros well. I'm sure they wouldn't have allowed him to steal or cheat. He couldn't win because I had followed all the preparation and instruction. He conceded by offering the correct payment. And from now on, he'll remember how he had to concede. I will have the advantage the next time we face each other."

"Good," is the response. "Krateros was indeed your first challenge, and you passed."

"If I had failed?"

"Then I would know even more about you, but nothing that would have helped convince me I had a champion to train. You must learn to face challenges because adversity is inevitable. They provide the chance to grow and build your character. Embrace them rather than turn away in fear. Use the knowledge you have gained from observing others. And above all, let that learning extend into your body when you wrestle. It is the balance of reason and instinct that will make you a formidable contender."

"I understand."

"Then the talking is over. It's time to start your training."

***

The palaestra on Delos doesn't offer the same comforts as Palatine Hill. There's no oil room to prepare in, only the remains of a place that used to be one. Walls stand on three sides, most of the floor is intact, but there's no roof. The sun burns down around Leon and me while we prepare. Insects buzz around us, but the scent of the olive oil keeps most at bay. The stone floor is becoming hotter below our feet, and we have to step with care across overgrown areas to make our way back within the colonnades.

There is no ceremony, no cheers from a crowd of patrons or gamblers. It's only Demetrius and the younger ones in training who are present to witness the fight. Seabirds call out across the bay, and the distant murmur from the town and harbor are the only sounds I hear as I step into the pit.

I feel the sand beneath my feet for the first time in weeks. Leon smiles all the time, and I don't sense I am in a fight for my life. There is no fear, just a rush of energy that surrounds me. I don't know the age of this palaestra, but I'm sure that many great contests have taken place here over the years, and now I'm going to wrestle before one of the greatest champions it has ever produced.

"Go ahead," is all that Demetrius says.

I begin to circle around Leon, while he holds the center. I remember what he'd said to me, about only learning to defend against Dario. If he can defend that well, then I can't just assume my early attacks will succeed. This match will need patience, and I know we will end up on the ground and exchanging holds for the win. But first I need to bring him down.

There is a glint in his eyes. Leon is confident and smart. Maybe he can't match me in weight or strength, but a simple attack is too easy for him to block. I have to let him get closer. I need to open myself up to encourage him forward. He has speed, but I can use that against him.

"Is this a dance or a fight?" asks Demetrius.

We both can't help grinning, but Leon reacts. I see in his eyes that he's ready to move. He sinks lower and reaches for my leg. I see him dropping, and I step back out of reach. He stands up and presses on my shoulders. My arms are outside of his. I hook under his arm, step in and twist around for the throw. The thud of the landing brings the move to an end as I let myself fall on top.

There's no time to rest. We're not fighting for points. We're competing for the approval of Demetrius. How long we stay in the skamma is his decision to make. If it was a street fight, I would move quick to take advantage of a shaken enemy, but Leon is my friend. I circle again to allow him time to breathe and steady himself.

I catch Demetrius noting my delay. I know that he reads every movement from both of us. As I flick my gaze back to Leon, he rushes in, under my distraction. He almost catches me, but I still block with my forearms. As he breaks away, his speed increases and his grin grows wider. He is observing me and learning from my moves. *Why didn't I expect this?* Leon has always been part of this palaestra. He has been training with Demetrius while I haven't. I have more of a match than I thought.

I see an opening on his leading leg, and I dive for the attack, but the skilled defender knows how to react as he sprawls over me, pressing down on my head and my back. I slide my leg on the sand, which burns against my skin. I pull myself closer and upright. I try to spin around him, but his hands and arms remain clasped around my neck. Before I know it, Leon has hauled me onto my back. I can hear him cheer for himself and laugh, as I collect a mouthful of sand from his triumphant celebration.

"Continue," says Demetrius. He wants to see more.

We battle on; we score more points. I'm ahead, but we move on past the normal time of a contest. Demetrius is testing how long it takes to sap our strength. Choosing the hottest part of the day to wrestle places us under the burning bright light of Apollo. We're both tiring. We take longer gasps of air in the pauses between combat. I can feel my muscles aching from lack of use. I should have stretched and warmed up more. I never thought we would still be fighting.

Leon keeps smiling, but not so wide. The sweat is streaming from him, and I imagine I look the same. The fight moves onto the ground. Neither of us are keen to keep crouching into a stance and we make a silent agreement to end the battle with holds. As we twist around each other, the final score is more to do with how much grip we have left, or how we escape each other's attempts to gain dominance.

I revolve around, searching for an advantage. The fight becomes more determined and more frantic. We're both exhausted and making mistakes. Hands and legs slide against sand-covered flesh. Fingers, wrists, and ankles all ache as they press and pull. Then something in me detects that the end is approaching. Leon's attempt to push my head to the side is weak. I grip his arm and stretch it back out from his body. Then I put pressure on his wrist and hand; it's just enough to let him know he has reached his limit. He raises his other hand and points his index finger into the air. His submission ends the match.

I fall onto my back and gasp for air. The dazzling sun hangs overhead, and I cover my eyes. My heart is beating furiously inside my chest. The hot surface sticks to me as I roll over onto my knees and look across at Leon. As he starts to move, I reach out. We clasp hands before helping to pull each other to our feet. Leon is still grinning, and I return his look this time.

"Wash yourselves," says Demetrius, "I'll give my opinion when you return."

"I didn't think he was going to let us stop," says Leon as we walk through the overgrowing plants that encircle the palaestra.

"I think it's the longest I've ever fought in a single match," I reply. "Do you think Demetrius is pleased?"

"Yes, I think so. He wasn't frowning as much as usual. That's the closest you'll get with him."

A loud cough in the background lets us know that Demetrius can still hear us.

Leon leads me to another part of the palaestra that must have once been a bathhouse. The pool is still there, but it's nothing more than a collection point for a spring that you can open to hold fresh water. It's full already.

"It's fresh from under the hillside," says Leon. "We can drink some further up, but I wouldn't drink this. It's just for washing here."

I pick up a strigil and so does Leon. It feels good to get rid of the oil and dirt. We scrape the exhaustion away and help each other around our backs. The joking continues. Leon makes fun of Demetrius again. He doesn't appear to care if our trainer overhears. I'm sure that Demetrius can, but maybe he just chooses not to listen, or if he is listening, he has chosen not to acknowledge.

With the sand and grime gone, we plunge into the pool. It's cooler, but not cold. I rinse out my eyes and dip my head in the water. I feel alive. The hills that rise above us, the islands that surround us, and the deep blue Aegean Sea, all combine to infect me with a sense of freedom and contentment.

From the anticipation of walking up to the palaestra, my conversation with Demetrius, the contest with Leon, and now the chance to recover in such a beautiful place, I have never felt so vibrant.

"We better go find out what we did wrong," says Leon.

"Or right," I reply.

"Yes." He pauses. "You're new here, Alexander. You'll get used to it."

We climb out of the pool, and I can feel my skin and hair drying almost immediately. Voices call from above us. It sounds like they're making fun or taunting.

"Who's that?" I ask as I shield my eyes to look for the source of the disturbance. I can only see three silhouettes.

"Oh, it's just my sister and her friends. Ignore them, they're just trying to tease us."

"So teasing runs in the family, then?"

Leon slaps me on the back and pushes me back toward the palaestra, but not before he shouts an insult or two himself toward his sister.

I take another look behind me; whoever the figures are, they're already disappearing from view. We return to the walls that surround the old oil room; our clothes are still hanging on a wall where we left them. The sandals are waiting too. I'm dry enough now that the material doesn't stick when I get dressed. I'm sure there might be a bruise or two later, but nothing serious.

Demetrius seems lost in thought when we return, but he acknowledges our presence. He invites us to sit, but he remains standing.

"You both fought well," he begins. "You showed courage, endurance, and maybe too much respect for one another. I could never place the two of you in a contest unless of course the crowd was prepared to stay throughout the night."

"We thought you wanted us to fight on," I reply.

"Until one of you won. Neither of you wished to end the match."

"Then we didn't need to fight for so long?"

"I had seen enough in the first few rounds. After a while, it was only a curious observation to see how you adapted to stress and exhaustion. That *was* interesting... if it makes you feel better." He pauses. "But you might now ask, what was the point? I need to know who I am training. I need to know where you need support and encouragement. Your technique is basic, but as you haven't undergone extensive training, I'm prepared to say that there's promise in the skills you have developed so far.

"Be aware that an untrained mind weakens the body. If you lack discipline, humility, and empathy, then you will fail. Did Gaius not explain these things to you?"

"He did," I reply, "but sometimes I felt as if he held me up as the poor example. The one not to follow."

"And how did that affect you amongst your fellow wrestlers?"

"It made me determined to win my fights, but he didn't caution me if I made a poor decision."

"And so, he kept you as his bad example. Your wins would have proved an added lesson to the students who couldn't match your natural talents. The results of contests are temporary. States of mind through which we accept the results of an opponent's unpredictable actions. Gaius received more value out of you than you did from him."

"And my Uncle Nikos paid him," I complain.

"Yes, Nikos told me. He should learn how to hold on to his wealth." He turns to Leon. "You fought better today. Better than I've seen before."

"Alexander didn't crush me like Dario would have. I felt as if he was being fair. Allowing me a chance to attack." Leon turned his eyes to me. "I learned more from today than any other fight. I know I'm not the best—"

"You're better than you know," I interrupt. "I wasn't letting you choke me for fun."

We both laugh again. Demetrius draws in a deep breath and lets out a sigh that sounds a little frustrated. A withering look restores our calm.

"Humor is good but better in moderation. Within the colonnades, I will expect a serious dedication to achieving great things. I will expect it from both of you."

"So, you are going to train Alexander?" Leon asks.

"It will be good for all of us if I train Alexander." He turns to gaze at me. "It won't be easy, but you will find the palaestra of Delos a different place than you've known before. Do not dwell on the past days. Prepare for, but do not predict the future. The present is the only moment you can control.

"We will begin a tetrad. Four afternoons each week. A day of preparation, a day of trials, a day of combat, and a last day of sparring and exercise."

I nod. "Gaius used that method. I'm familiar with it."

Demetrius gives a small nod of approval but continues anyway. "Then you know each day serves a purpose. The first—preparation. We focus on technique, movement, and discipline. No wasted effort." He lifts a finger. "Then, trials. Harder than a real fight. Endurance, drills, pushing past comfort." Another finger. "Then combat. We fight. We put everything into practice." He lowers his hand. "And on the last day, we refine—sparring, conditioning, sharpening weaknesses."

I know this. I've done this. But something about the way he says it—we fight, we refine—sends a thrill through me. This isn't just training. It's a test. A chance to push harder, to prove I'm more than the fighter I was yesterday.

Four days, one cycle. No shortcuts. No excuses.

I roll my shoulders, feeling the anticipation coil tight in my muscles. Let it come. The sweat, the bruises, the aching limbs. I welcome it.

Because on the other side of it, I won't just be better.

I'll be unstoppable.

"You will continue to experience life in the mornings with your work amongst the harbor and the markets. Do not think I will treat you differently there. I'll expect the same effort and dedication in your labor. The evenings will belong to you, but I recommend you find a place to sit in contemplation. Your mind will need more training than your body."

"I understand, but I was going to ask one thing for the evenings. Can I come here and work on the buildings that surround the palaestra? It will help me practice my carpentry skills and I can help to restore the oil room and the bathhouse."

Demetrius rubs his hand against his chin. I'm sure I can see a hint of a smile.

"Sounds like a trade I cannot refuse. My old friend Nikos has not let me down with his appraisal of your character. I accept your offer. I will send men in the morning to bring supplies for you to work with. Thank you, Alexander."

Demetrius extends his arm, and we clasp hands in agreement, just as the merchants do. I feel excited about my new life stretching out before me. From the gentle shoreline to the summit of Mount Kynthos with its Temple of Zeus, the island of Delos is already becoming part of my soul. There is no turning back now.

CHAPTER XI

"Uncle Nikos, I think Delos is more like Rome than I first thought."

My uncle is concentrating on finding what he needs for his next sea journey. He sends the servants throughout the house to find the things that he's misplaced. I'm surprised he can remember where to steer his ship. He always says that Poseidon will get him to where he's going and that unexpected harbors can sometimes bring a pleasant surprise for profits. So, he doesn't mind getting lost.

He stands up and straightens while he rubs his back to soothe an ache. "I'm getting too stiff. I need to get back on the ocean. I can't cope with ground that doesn't move. Now what were you saying?"

"Am I right to say that the poorer you are the closer you live to the shore?"

"It's not a hard and fast rule but, certainly, the larger houses are higher up. It's considered safer when the storms come inshore. Why?"

"Leon's avoided showing me where he lives. I remember I didn't want to show Lucius and the others from Palatine Hill where I lived in the Subura. I felt ashamed that they all lived in large homes when I had to sleep in a room with many of my neighbors and only curtains to separate us."

"Leon has helped you learn about Delos and working at the harbor?"

"Yes."

"And are you happy to learn from him?"

"Well, yes."

"Then he will be happy to learn from you as well. Explain that you are only living within different circumstances. It doesn't make you better or worse as a person. I can tell you where he lives. Their house is smaller.

It's surrounded by parts of boats, nets, and wicker baskets. The scent of grilled fish hangs in the air. Leon's mother is a wonderful cook, but most skilled with preparing his father's catch of the day.

"They use the fish oil for lights that illuminate the coastline at night. A comforting welcome for those searching for a safe harbor when it's late and darkness falls. Leon has nothing to feel shame about as long as he knows that *you* are not the type of person to make him feel shame. Have you told him much about the Subura?"

"Not about where I lived."

"There you are. He feels bad about living more modestly than you, while you feel bad about where you used to live. Can you make sense of that?"

"No, because it's nonsense," I smile.

"Are you going to work at the palaestra this evening?"

"Yes. Demetrius has arranged for some building materials to be brought over. Leon said he would help me."

"Then when you're ready I'll walk down with you. I wanted to talk to his father about buying some supplies for the ship. We might as well go together." He returns to his search and groans a little more.

Just then, my mother arrives with Selene and a bundle of materials for making clothes.

"Nikos, what are you doing?" she says. "Let Tigranes help you."

"Tigranes is already helping me in another room. Ah, here they are." He holds out two reed styluses for writing on papyrus.

"Is that all you were looking for, brother?"

"All? These are my luckiest writing tools. I always record higher profits with these."

"Your uncle spends too long in the sun, Alexander. He forgets it's the trades that make him money, not the tools he uses to list them."

"It's a system that's worked very well for me so far. What have my lucky reeds paid for today?"

My mother rolls out some of the cloth she's purchased at the market. Enough to make new clothes for all of us.

"Selene tells me you only let her make new clothes when she can no longer patch or repair your old ones. It is time for you to have a choice of what to put on."

"Maybe for a visit to the festivals, I concede, but there's no point in taking new clothes to sea. It's a tough life you know."

"Listen to him, Alexander. I would like to say that it's old age that makes him stubborn, but no, he's always been like this."

"And you have always been—"

"Right, my dear brother?"

"I suppose so," he grumbles, but I can see him laugh to himself. "Now please forgive me, I've promised Alexander to take him to Leon's house. I need to buy some salted fish for myself and my crew."

"But we were going to measure you."

"We're running late. Demetrius is waiting for Alexander to return. We must go. Alexander?"

"Yes, we have to go now," I reply.

Uncle Nikos races toward the front door and out into the courtyard. I grab my bag of tools and follow behind as fast as I can. A pleasant heat remains in the air. The wind has dropped a little, and the sun traces a slow path to the west of us in a pink sky that promises good sailing. It casts shimmering reflections on the water that glitter like the stars in Zeus's heavens.

We set off down the narrow lanes and nod to neighbors. Uncle Nikos is familiar to everyone, but it's only taken a few days for word to get around that I'm his nephew. Now I'm treated like a local, but Uncle Nikos has assured me I'll need to live here for several years to become accepted as an islander.

"How are you getting on at the palaestra? Is Demetrius making you train hard?"

"He's strict, but he knows so much. Sometimes he'll tell us about contests he took part in when he was younger. The stories inspire me. If I can become as good as him, I'll be happy."

Uncle Nikos stops to look over toward his ship, sitting further away at the dock.

"I think Demetrius will want you to be better than him. That's his dream. He may be slower and older than he once was, but there's no reason that he can't achieve his goals through the efforts of another. The goal of raising you to a certain standard of skill is something that falls within his control. Any rewards or fame you gather will be yours, but you will both share in a successful reputation. A winning partnership, if you want to think of it that way."

"I want to do that... for him, for the palaestra, for my mother and you, and..."

"And your father, too. You are a wonderful son, and you always will be to him. Let's walk on."

A row of buildings stands aligned along a path that runs by the sea. They extend out along the bay as it heads south from the harbor. The *Sacred Harbor* as the locals call it, is just as Uncle Nikos described.

Rough-hewn stone walls and earth-covered flat roofs provide space for growing herbs and distinguish them from other houses on the island. Each home has an enclosed courtyard for drying nets and mending lines. Timber piles and other parts for boat repairs lie scattered around the row. A well toward one end is for all of the families.

"This is where Leon and his family live," says my Uncle Nikos. "The third house in the row. Knock on the door and let Leon know you're going along to the palaestra now."

I'm a little nervous about surprising Leon, but a loud cough from Uncle Nikos is already announcing our presence. I strike the door.

I can hear a frustrated voice from inside calling out, *I'm answering*, but it's not Leon's voice. The door swings open.

"Yes?"

Standing facing me is the most beautiful girl I've ever had the pleasure of seeing. My breath leaves me as I stumble to speak.

"I'm Leon, I'm here for Alexander."

"What?"

"Sorry, I mean I'm Alexander. Is Leon here?"

"Hello, Zoe," says my uncle. "I'm here to see your father as well."

"Leon!" she shouts. "Your friend is here."

"Which friend?" is the response.

"I don't know. The new one. I don't think he knows either." She smiles before looking at Uncle Nikos. "I'll get my father for you, Nikos."

She disappears inside and Leon appears in her place.

"Am I late?" Leon asks. "I was going to come and get you at your house."

"No, Uncle Nikos wants to buy salted fish for his sea journey, so he asked me to come with him."

"That's fine. It's not so far to walk now." He calls back inside. "I'm going to the palaestra with Alexander, see you later."

He steps out, and I catch another glimpse of Zoe looking back.

"Are we going?" says Leon.

"Yes," I say, and we start our walk along the sea and through the ruins of the older parts of Delos.

"What do you think Demetrius will want us to work on first?" Leon asks.

I can hear the voices of Uncle Nikos, Zoe, and Leon's father. I turn around to look, distracted by the sound of their conversation. Zoe's name keeps repeating in my head and I feel my heart quicken. I realize that Leon is still waiting for an answer.

"I think the oil room. It needs a new wall to be built and then a roof. It should be cool so that we don't cook while we're preparing to wrestle."

Leon turns and stands beside me. "I don't suppose you'll have seen a Greek fishing village before. It's just a row of houses on Delos, but on other islands, they're much larger. Probably not as large as your old city."

"There were those that fished on the Tiber, further out of the city. They would sail in to sell the catch and leave. There was nothing like here, so pretty."

"Pretty? I never thought of it like that. You do like Delos a lot, don't you?"

We start to walk again and my focus returns.

"Delos is much better than the place I used to live. How many live in your house?"

"My mother and father, my sister, and me."

"In the Subura, where I came from, there might be thirteen or fourteen in the same space."

"How did they all sleep?"

"At different times of the day. Some would take jobs where they worked through the night, like bakers making bread for the next day or guards watching storehouses and ships on the river, and then there are the gangs who roam the streets and ply their trades under cover of darkness. It can be a dangerous place for those who don't know where to avoid. Delos is far different from Rome."

"We have pirates here, but they don't tend to cause trouble. The Roman soldiers guard everything. It's not wise to get on the wrong side of them."

"It's strange, but they forbid Roman legions from entering Rome. There is a guard for the emperor and around his palace. Those that offer protection are the same people who will do you harm. If you don't have wealth to share with them, then it's best to befriend them and hope they'll leave you alone."

"That sounds terrible. Did you make friends with them?"

"I tried to stay out of their way, but in the end, I started wrestling in street matches for them. It was a big mistake."

"What happened?"

"I earned money for my family by pretending to lose fights until enough people had bet against me. When I got the signal from the person who was holding the bets, I would turn the fight around and defeat my opponent. Then I would receive a share of the money. The gang would surround me at the end to make sure I could get away from an angry crowd."

"Wow! That sounds dangerous. Did anyone ever beat you?"

"No, I was undefeated, but they expected me to take damage to make the fight look real. I would have bruises at least at the very end."

"You're brave to have done that. I wouldn't mention it to Demetrius, though."

"I know. It's not what he would call virtuous behavior."

"You were just trying to help feed your family. I didn't know that life in Rome was like that. I think I'll stay here after all."

"My old trainer, Gaius, would speak about not wasting our thoughts on an idea of how other people live better lives. He would remind us that a virtuous person could live a good and simple life, without the need for lavish surroundings. I thought it funny that he said this from within the garden of one of the finest houses in Rome, but deep down inside I could acknowledge the lesson he was teaching.

"A rich patrician in Rome might well see this island and the idea of living a few short steps from the sea as his dream. He might envy you eating the freshest fish, just caught and grilled directly from the sea, and your view of the sunset over the Aegean. You don't get to see a sight like that if you live within Rome."

"I've never thought of it that way before. I was worried that you wouldn't like where I lived. I know I shouldn't have. You're a good friend, Alexander. I'm glad that you came to live on Delos."

We continue walking in silence for a while, both lost in the moment until the palaestra looms into view. Demetrius is sitting and waiting for us. His gaze is fixed on the ocean, but I know he'll be aware of our presence. He turns to face us just as we arrive.

"Are you ready to start work?"

"Yes," I reply, "we were going to start by trying to rebuild the oil room."

"Have you built walls before?" he asks.

"No, but I can take my time and learn."

"I applaud your commitment, but we may have to move faster. I have slaves who have the knowledge. They will work with you. You know them. The same men who help you at the docks."

"I didn't expect to be organizing men for the work."

"There is much they can teach you. A slave is still a man or a woman. They have experiences, skills, and talents of their own.

"One of the greatest philosophers, Epictetus, was born into slavery. He taught about the loss of physical freedom, that it could not enslave the mind. He believed that true freedom lay in the control of your own thoughts, actions, and responses, and virtue remained the path to happiness. In hard conditions, it is still possible to find meaning and purpose.

"I have already spoken to the men who are keen to help. They want to join you in bringing this palaestra back to its former glory. It is a chance for them to still stake their place in history. Such a building can long outlast the builders. Somewhere on the stone, they may carve a name, a date, or the image of a god. They know they are giving a tribute to the deities of Delos with their efforts, and when The Great Delia arrives, they will be content with the part they played."

"The Great Delia?" I ask.

"Every four years on Delos, there's an important festival. We call it The Great Delia. It's a very important religious festival dedicated to Apollo and Artemis. Priests purify the entire island to renew its sacred status. Important officials will travel from around the city-states of Greece to conduct business and political discussions. For a few days, Delos takes its rightful place in the center of our world.

"The town's taverns and squares fill with music, poetry, and entertainment, and in the past, when this palaestra was in a better condition, there were games. Amongst the athletic events, there was an important wrestling contest. The best contenders from across Greece would congregate for the title of champion." He pauses and looks around at the palaestra. "I think it's time to bring these games back. Time is short. We need many hands to do the work, and time to train you and Leon for the contest."

Demetrius allows himself a smile and there's a new excitement in his eyes. Leon and I stand open-mouthed in shock.

"We will get the chance to compete?" I ask.

"I don't want the two of you just to compete, I want you to win."

We raise our hands and cheer at the prospect of taking part. We make enough noise to attract the attention of other islanders walking along the shore."

"Calm down for the moment," says Demetrius, "there's a lot to do, and I have a reputation to protect. I'm not known around here for my frivolity."

"What can we do to get started? We're both here and ready to work."

"I will assemble the men tomorrow to begin the construction. For tonight, look around your feet. Below the grasses and the rubble lies a stadion for running races. Uncover its route and start to bring this place back to life."

"You want us to pull weeds?" asks Leon, disappointed.

"It's no less important than any other task, and the two of you will need to use the path you create for training."

"We'll do it," I confirm, "we'll work hard to get the palaestra ready."

"Good. I know the two of you won't let me down. Now, I have other business to attend to this evening. Spend some time here and get started. I'll still expect you at the harbor just after dawn."

"Yes, Demetrius," we both reply.

Without another word, he rises and returns to the center of town. Leon and I are bursting with excitement, only tempered a little by the task that lies ahead. Parts of the old stadion reveal themselves the closer we look. Some parts are less overgrown than others, so we pick an easier section to begin our work.

"Demetrius has been waiting for you, Alexander."

"He wants both of us to compete."

"That's not what I mean. He's been good to me, and I've worked hard for him. He trusts me and he puts up with me talking back," he smiles, "but you have reawakened something inside him. I can see it. He has noticed something in you that makes him want to win again.

"He was a great wrestler, according to my father. He traveled across the Aegean and the Mediterranean. He was famous and saved enough in prize money to begin his business when he gave up competing. My father said that's when he stopped smiling. He was a Stoic. He accepted his change in circumstances and became a successful merchant instead of a successful wrestler, but something was gone from his life and his nature couldn't hide it. You've brought it back. I promise you."

"Did your father see him wrestle?"

"Yes, he's younger than Demetrius, but I think he was almost thirty years old before Demetrius stopped. That was fifteen years ago. The same year you and I were born."

"How old is your mother?"

"She is thirty-three."

"And Zoe?

"My sister is sixteen, but she makes me feel that she's a lot older and wiser."

"And is she?" I laugh.

"Maybe, but I would never let her know."

We work, laugh, and talk throughout the rest of the evening. Maybe we could have cleared a little more than we did, but in the area where we removed the plants and stones, you could at least run a quick sprint.

We practice running against one another as the sun begins to set into a ball of crimson red. Lights around the harbor and town are already burning brightly, while torches set out for the Roman guards flicker around the buildings.

Somewhere in the distance, faint strains of music drift on the persistent breeze. Twilight stretches across the sky. It's time to go home. I insist that we walk to Leon's house first. I know enough about the paths to my house now. I no longer get lost when finding my way home.

All the way back we talk about the games. I wonder how the contestants will find out that Demetrius is going to stage a competition.

"Word will travel on the ships that sail in and out. Tell your Uncle Nikos when you get home. He'll spread the word in all the ports that he visits, and then I'm sure it will reach the ears of Apion. He travels around the islands and arranges fights between different wrestlers. There is nothing he loves more than supplying the best competitors. He's an old friend of Demetrius who I know will want to play his part.

"If you impress Apion, he'll want to arrange fights for you. Dario, who used to train with us, is overseas with him now. If you want to be a successful wrestler, then you can't do much better than Demetrius as a trainer and Apion as a fight fixer. This could be your chance."

"This could be our chance," I insist. "You said you felt different when we practiced together. You've done so much for me, now I want to do something for you. I want to help you with your wrestling. It would be incredible if we ended up facing one another in the final of the games."

"I don't know about that, but if I can avoid being defeated in the first match, then I'll be happy."

We reach the courtyard at Leon's house. I bid goodnight as he opens the door to walk through into his home. I linger just a little as voices rise from the inside. He's told them about the plan that Demetrius has hatched, I'm sure of it.

I stand for a few moments, looking across at the harbor. The lights are now reflecting in a darkened sea as it laps against the shore. I try to clear my head, but one word keeps repeating. A name that makes me feel like I've never felt before.

I start to walk back through the twisting maze of lanes that lead back to higher ground. The town is far from asleep. The taverns of Delos are as busy as the taverns of Rome, but there's a distinct atmosphere on Apollo's island. There's no sense of threats around the corner. People who have drunk their fill of wine tend to just smile and nod as they stagger past me. The music provides a lively backdrop that only begins to fade near the end of my journey.

I enter the house to find my Uncle Nikos still looking for items he's lost. Tigranes rolls his eyes to suggest it's been like this all day. My mother and Selene are clearing up from a few hours spent cutting and stitching clothes, and Na'amat arrives to ask me if I want to eat.

"Would you like supper, master?"

"Yes, I am hungry, thank you. Please, my name is Alexander."

"Yes, Master Alexander." She is gone before I have the chance to ask again.

"How did your work go?" my mother asks.

"I don't know how much we accomplished, but I have exciting news. Demetrius wants to bring the palaestra back to its former glory, before The Great Delia."

Uncle Nikos drops a small clay pot to the floor, and it smashes into pieces.

"The next Great Delia, in four years?"

"No, he wants it ready for this year's festival. He's going to set his slaves to help us rebuild the oil room, the bathhouse, the stadion, and more. He wants to bring the greatest wrestlers of Greece to compete, and he wants Leon and me to take part."

"That is fantastic news," says my mother. "What do you think, brother?"

"It sounds like the Demetrius we all grew up with has returned to Delos. I would never have thought I would see him like this again. Was he serious? I'm sure he wasn't drunk."

"He was very serious. He warned us about how much we would have to do to get things ready, to train, and still to do our work at the harbor. He wants to bring the games back. Leon said that you might start to spread the news."

"I'll speak to him in the morning before I put to sea. I only want to deliver the news as he sees fit."

Na'amat arrives with octopus, pickled vegetables, some bread, and a goblet of wine. I turn my attention to the food. My mother watches me as I eat. It's one of those looks when I know she has something on her mind.

"Your Uncle Nikos told me you met Leon's sister this evening."

"Yes, she answered the door, that's all."

"What's her name?"

"I don't remember."

My mother knows I'm avoiding the question. The smile that passes between her and Uncle Nikos speaks louder than words.

CHAPTER XII

It doesn't matter how early I want to begin my day, Na'amat is always up earlier to prepare porridge for my morning meal, Tigranes brings a large bowl of water for me to wash the sleep from my eyes, and Selene lays out clean clothes for me to put on.

I still feel guilty about being served in this way, but over the past few weeks, I've begun to get to know them all better. Tigranes is even helping with the restoration of the palaestra. He's very practical and can do a good job of anything I ask him to do.

He was a farmer before slave traders captured him. He told me that farmers didn't just grow food or tend to animals, but they also had to work to build storehouses, or places to keep their herds secure from wild beasts looking for prey. He has a good sense of humor, but it covers a sadness. He lost everything when invaders raided his land. What they couldn't steal, they burned to the ground. In the violent struggle to defend the little that he owned, he was the only member of his family to survive.

The more I learned, the more the words of Demetrius and Gaius were starting to make more sense; Tigranes had taken on a new life. He would never forget his past, but it didn't stop him from doing all he could to find contentment and peace within himself.

Talking to him helped me to acknowledge the grief of losing my father. It was common ground between the two of us to have lost people we loved. His advice on how to cope and turn my focus to the new opportunities that were in front of me has helped me settle on Delos.

There were still nights when I would wake to the sound of my mother crying in her room. The strength that she would put on display each day was a mask to cover her sorrow. At first, I would cry with her, silently in my room, but Tigranes has shown me how to find a resolve within myself. It didn't just help me. I could become stronger when my mother was weaker. I could carry the burden for both her and myself, at least until the passing of time dulled her pain.

Uncle Nikos was still at sea. He had promised to return soon, but "soon" felt endless when days slipped by unnoticed. The Greeks measured time by the moon's cycle, watching for the new moon to signal the start of another month. But I preferred the Roman method—eight days, steady and predictable. Today marked the eighth. As the first light crept over the horizon, I climbed Mount Kynthos to the Temple of Zeus, as I always did, to watch the sun rise over the sea. Maybe this time, I would spot his sails.

It was never a lonely pursuit. Many of the pilgrims who visited Delos wanted to witness Apollo and his chariot climbing into the sky. People would find their space, alone or with friends, to welcome the first glow of light and the departure of the night. We would all sit in quiet contemplation. The breeze stirred into life along with the dawn, as if to carry the whispered prayers of the devoted to their gods of choice.

It took me a few visits before I knew who to offer my own thoughts and prayers to. If I was in Rome, it would have been Minerva, but on Delos, it was a different name for the same goddess. Athena was who I hoped would hear me; she was the Greek goddess of wisdom, crafts, and war. I could ask her to help me make the right decisions, to help me with rebuilding the palaestra, and to help me with my battles in the skamma pit.

This morning was the completion of another seven days. As I left my room, I could see a bowl of warm porridge already waiting for me. I sat down to it and ate. My mind ran with the tasks that were ahead. Demetrius had warned us he expected a busy day at the docks. There had been some poor weather for a few days, and he suspected it would have delayed ships in other ports. Intuition told him that many would arrive at the same time.

Then there was training to follow. The seventh day that marked my visit to the temple was also the fourth day of our tetrad. I would spar with Leon and exercise to build muscle strength. We had cleared the stadion in the first few days after we began rebuilding the palaestra. It offered us the chance to run, build up our stamina and help our breathing. Demetrius told us it was good for the heart and the lungs. He said it would help us sleep, which, he said, would help our bodies repair themselves. Whether it was all the work, training or both, I was becoming more confident about taking part in The Great Delia.

I finish my meal and make my way out of the house. The sky is already starting to reveal thin strips of cloud. I make my way through the twisting lanes to steep steps that climb the side of the hill. It's a much older part of Delos that has survived through maybe hundreds of years. A young crescent moon watches over my ascent. It will soon fade from view when Apollo makes his presence felt.

I reach the summit and look around myself. As is normal, there are small groups of people gathered to take in the spectacle. I have my spot that I head for. Most people avoid it as there's only room for two to sit. When I take my place, the faint lights of Mykonos glow toward my left. The lightening sky now shows the outlines of rocky outcrops in the water straight ahead. To my right, there's a sound that distracts me, or should I say, a voice. I look over to a group of five people gathered nearby.

It's Zoe.

I don't know what to do. I don't want to stare at her, but it might be rude for me not to say hello; yet if I do say something, her friends might not be happy with me interrupting them while they're here to witness the dawn. *Should I just wave over?* The longer I take to decide, the more awkward I feel about talking to her. I fix my gaze out to sea. Maybe I can speak to her once people are ready to leave.

"Leon said you walked up here some mornings."

I spin around, and she's standing there, looking down at me.

"Every seventh day. I'm counting how long my Uncle Nikos has been away."

"You should use the Greek method. Follow the cycle of the moon; it's easier. Do you mind if I sit down?"

"Yes, I mean no, I mean yes, please sit."

I shift along the flat rock I use as a seat, making room for Zoe to sit beside me. She laughs as she does so.

"Do you always say the opposite of what you mean?"

"I'm sorry. It's still early in the morning. I *am* Alexander."

"And I *am* Zoe. Leon's sister, but you know that. Leon talks about you a lot, but I'm sure he doesn't mention me that often."

"Only when you've annoyed him," I smile.

"Oh, well, maybe he does. I annoy him a lot. Do you like it here on Delos now? It must be different from living in Rome."

"It's a lot different, but now I've lived here for a while, it feels more like home. I think I was born in Ostia. My mother and father traveled to Rome soon after that. Were you born on Mykonos, like Leon?"

"Yes, we were both born there. It makes me happy to sit here and look at it across the water. I don't really feel that I've left my birthplace. We have other family who live there, and I can visit when my father decides he'll sail over for celebrations."

She pauses as the first rays of the sun begin to take shape on the horizon. We shield our eyes as we take in the view. Tiny insects begin to hover and buzz in amongst the grasses, then swallows arrive to feed on the wing. It's like a performance for the gathered crowd. The air that moves on the sea breeze carries a scent that I remember from the gardens of wealthy patricians in Rome.

Jasmine.

"It's beautiful," I pause, "the dawn is beautiful."

"Every day is a new beginning," she replies.

The hillside goes quiet as all contemplate their thoughts and send out their hopes for good fortune. They all appear so focused on the dawn, but I can't settle. I want to talk to Zoe. I want to find out more about her, and I feel she's waiting for me to ask something.

"Won't your friends want you to sit with them?" I whisper.

What am I saying?

"Do you want me to leave you on your own? Do you want time for your own thoughts?" she asks.

"No, no. I didn't mean that. I'm happy to share the rock." I smile, and she smiles back.

Thank goodness.

"Leon's made me so welcome on the island. I wanted to meet with the rest of his family, eh, your family, both of your family... oh, you know what I mean."

"I hope you don't trip up in the skamma as easily as you trip up on your words." She covers her mouth to stifle a giggle. "Leon would like you to meet our family, but he's still shy about our house, compared to where you live. If you ask him to invite you, then he won't refuse."

"He doesn't need to feel that way. I've tried to explain. He's been a better friend to me than any in Rome. I want him to know that there's nothing about living a little higher up the hillside that makes us different."

"The life of a fishing family is simple. We all work together to take care of what we have, look after the boat, and prepare the catch for market. Leon does less at the moment. Working for Demetrius, training with you, and now helping to rebuild the palaestra. He doesn't get much sleep. He still tries to help our family in the last hours of the day or the first hours of the morning. He'll be helping to get the boat ready right now. How does that compare with your day?"

I feel a sense of guilt. "I didn't realize all the things he had to do. I suppose I've forgotten what life was like in Rome. There are servants that live with my Uncle Nikos. They don't allow me to do anything in the house. They call me *master*, and I can't persuade them to stop."

"You don't like it?"

"No. I've got to know them all better. Tigranes has been helping at the palaestra. I want to think of him as a friend."

"It sounds like you are friends. Regardless of circumstances that brought you to the same place. It sounds as if you and Leon both suffer from the same complaint. Ask him today, and I'll make sure that my mother plans to cook something special."

"You would do that? That's very kind of you."

"Maybe I'm not as annoying as my brother says."

She stands and smiles before returning to her group of friends. I watch as she goes, and the others train their eyes on me. I turn away and look out to sea, then over to Mykonos, where the town sits bathed in the light of the rising sun.

It's time to go to work. I can see ships starting to approach the island. It's the usual race to be first now the cover of night has lifted. I make my way to the steps that descend the hillside. I take a final look back. Zoe is in conversation with her friends. I want to stay, but I can't. There's a full day ahead, and a nice dinner at the end.

***

As I arrive at the dock, I keep my distance from a ship carrying men and women for the slave market. The crew on these ships are tough and fearsome people. Leon has told me it's better to avoid them. They don't care who they take to the next port in chains. The Roman guard tends to appear in numbers when they're in the town. I think even they feel a little unsafe around them.

It's followed by a second vessel. Demetrius is paying close attention as it approaches, but he still finds time to cast a look that I know means I've arrived later than expected. Leon is already organizing the men who will bring the cargo onto the dock. I go straight to the slaves that draw the cart to market and make sure they're ready to transport the first items when Demetrius settles his trades.

Merchants flock to the side of the harbor to view the goods on offer. Demetrius has a good eye. He picks out supplies he can use for the palaestra's decoration: plaster, pigments, and tiles for crafting mosaics. Delos already has a good supply of marble and granite that we can repurpose with the right tools, but we need more than we have, so iron and wood are also on his list of things to buy.

Hands shake in agreement, and when the goods are in our possession, Demetrius parts with payment. He has been spending a lot to restore the building, but even so, we've never seen him look so eager. Everyone he speaks to at the harbor is told of the revival for this year's Great Delia. The return of wrestling to the festival is an exciting prospect for many.

He'll draw Leon and me into the conversations if we're nearby. He's starting to remind me of my father, boasting of my talents in front of the people he would challenge to fight me. He shows confidence in our chances of success.

That's how he appears in public, but when we train at the palaestra, Demetrius returns to the role of instructor. The training is hard and relentless. The rebuild of the sphairisterion is complete, its floor covered with a fresh layer of sand packed firm by our constant drills. This is where we often begin, hurling and catching leather balls in rapid succession. The coarse leather scrapes against my palms, the weight of each throw solid and demanding.

Demetrius's gaze tracks every movement, his eyes narrowed in that calculating way of his. He's looking for hesitation, clumsiness—any sign of weakness. The games might be meant to sharpen our reflexes, coordination, and endurance, but I know better. They're also meant to test us, to see who crumbles under pressure and who thrives.

By the time we move to the stadion, sweat clings to my skin, my shoulders aching from the constant motion. Here, there's no laughter or playful jostling. Just the steady thud of feet pounding the packed earth, each lap a battle against our own exhaustion. Stamina and strength, Demetrius says, are the true measures of discipline. Sometimes we race along the shore to and from the palaestra. Demetrius knows how long it should take, and if we're too slow, he'll make us run a route over Mount Kynthos.

I feel stronger and my mind is becoming clearer. I have an increasing awareness of how I created my own obstacles in the past, by not believing in myself enough. The dedication to training is making me more positive about myself. The spirit and energy that exists all around me on Delos is transforming me into a better person.

The only break we have is when Demetrius decides it's time to discuss Stoicism. Sometimes, developing our grasp of the philosophy requires just as much discipline as wrestling. Now and then, you reach a point of understanding, something that improves you in the fight, or else improves your attitudes about living a virtuous or healthier life. Demetrius insists that these skills are just as important as any others if we want to be champions.

We wait until the hottest part of the day before finally entering the pit. The rebuilding of the oil room is still underway. The roof is under construction, so there are some shaded areas where we can apply our oil without burning. The weeds are gone from the floor. It's now level and comfortable to step on. Two amphorae of oil sit there for our use. It still isn't quite like Palatine Hill, and it will need to provide more for all the wrestlers who might attend the games, but for now it's all that Leon and I need.

The day is well past the halfway mark. I've climbed Mount Kynthos to take in the rising sun, crossed the island to go to work, toiled at the harbor, run along the shore, taken more exercise, and only now are we getting to fight.

Leon is good. He doesn't give up, and he doesn't back down from a challenge. Maybe he just smiles and laughs a little too much, so I try to teach him how to look stern and intimidating to an opponent. It doesn't work, we just end up laughing together at his poor efforts to put on a fearsome expression. But maybe that unreadable jolly face of his will be his opponent's distraction.

The bathhouse is still an open pool from a redirected spring, but at the end of a long day it's still a relief to plunge into the cool water. It's late afternoon and we can both stop for a short while, but the talk continues about the approaching games.

"Do you think we'll both reach the final?" I ask.

"It would be good," says Leon, "but it sounds like there could be more than a few contestants. We've got no idea what they'll be like until they get here."

"Maybe we'll learn something from my Uncle Nikos when he gets home. He might know some that are going to travel for the contest."

Leon washes his face and seems to wipe an angry look away. "The one I really want to beat is Dario."

"You don't like him?"

"There's not a lot to like about Dario. He likes himself so much, I don't think he needs anyone else's help. We've known each other for years, but that makes no difference when you're wrestling him. I know that you let me escape the odd hold, or you make a misstep to encourage my reactions. Dario just looks for interesting new ways to beat me up. If I can make him submit in the skamma, then that's a victory for me."

"You will be good enough," I reply. "Tell me how he fights, and I'll prepare you as best I can."

"Thank you, friend. It's the only thing that I know I won't like about the games. I thought I might have seen the last of him, but the contest will draw him home to Delos."

"Do you think I can beat him?"

"Maybe. I hope you can." He sighs. "I suppose we better head home for something to eat, before the evening work."

"Uncle Nikos says your father prepares the best fish. I never ate a lot in Rome. It was too expensive for us."

"Too expensive? I didn't think there was a cheaper food. It's all we eat most of the time, but I suppose it's because my father catches it. There's always mackerel and sardines to grill, and mullet or even bream if he's lucky."

"That sounds delicious. I'd love to try it."

Leon looks thoughtful for a moment. "Then join us. My mother has been wanting to meet you and your mother. I'm sure they would be pleased to share what we have today."

"My mother?"

"Yes. Bring her with you. We'll have enough, I promise."

We dress and head back into town until we reach the point where we turn in different directions. I head further up the hill while Leon carries on toward the row of houses that sit closer to the harbor. I'm sure my mother will be happy to go, but sometimes a parent can embarrass you even without intending it. I smile to myself as I ask the gods to make sure she is on her best behavior.

***

I wasn't wrong. My mother jumps at the chance to visit Leon's family. She forces me into new clothes, although I put on clean clothes in the morning. She examines my hair and my nails for dirt, even though I just bathed at the palaestra. This is all before I get to even step outside the house.

Then I'm instructed to take some tomatoes from our kitchen and choose a small amphora of wine to take with us as a gift. I know that Uncle Nikos keeps a tally of his wines. I'll need to tell him when he returns. I go back to the main room as Selene helps with my mother's hair.

"We better leave soon, Mother. They'll be expecting us."

"Alexander, this is Delos. Everything will happen at the right time. The fish will go on the grill when we get there, not before."

"I know, but—"

"I'll just be a few moments, now wait outside in the courtyard."

I go outside and sit below the shade of the trees. It's true that the pace of life is different on the islands, and no one likes to dine in the full heat of day. I have a feeling that Leon and I won't make it to the palaestra tonight, but we'll work harder tomorrow to make up for lost time.

I still haven't quite adjusted to the peace of this place. If I was in Rome, then we would wander the few steps from our room to Caeso's. It was always busy, there were always crowds walking by, and you had to time it perfectly to get a favorite seat. There is none of that here. Even though I have never worked so hard in my life, living on Delos makes me feel free and far away from the endless crush of the city. Each day I spend here makes me realize how lucky I am.

Demetrius told us to always expect the unexpected in our lives. The death of my father on the Danube River led to events that brought me here. I whisper to him. I want to let him know that our lives have carried on. I talk to him about my training and the games, and I invite him to be with me when I fight against the worthiest of contenders.

"Are you ready, Alexander?"

My mother appears in the courtyard. I'm not sure how long she's been there, but I'm sure she's overheard me talking with my father. Her smile is kind. I think she's proud of me.

It doesn't take us long to walk down to the shore. I'm glad because the amphora is weighing me down. My mother asked if we should get Tigranes to carry it, but we agreed that he deserves a night off along with Selene and Na'amat.

When we arrive at Leon's house, the sun is dropping lower. It colors the clouds as well as the sky, which takes on hues of gold, yellow, orange, and pink. Leon's father is standing at the entrance to the courtyard along with his mother. Leon and Zoe are standing behind them. I can see that they've forced Leon into his better set of clothes as well.

"Welcome, Alexander, and welcome, Elena. Welcome to our home. My name is Thalasso, and this is my wife, Kera."

We all greet each other with small hugs and kisses on the cheek.

"And this is my daughter, Zoe. I know you've met Leon already."

Zoe steps forward and hugs my mother before kissing her on the cheek. Then she steps back while offering me a small wave. I admit to myself that I'm a little disappointed.

We go into the courtyard and sit down on different styles of chairs. I'm sure the neighbors have brought furniture over to seat everyone. A fire is already starting to smolder amongst coals. The smoke rises above us, and the breeze pulls it away, leaving only the pleasant scent of the grill. The waves roll in against the shore, only a short distance from us, creating a quiet steady backdrop that is calming and reassuring. We offer the gift of the wine which goes down well. My mother notes I've chosen one of the most expensive wines. She jokes that Uncle Nikos will be mad at me, but he's never mad. We all drink to his health and safe return.

Leon's father takes over the grill and wants to tell us everything about the fish he's cooking, the herbs that are best to serve with them, and how precise you have to be to know the right time to transfer the food to the plate. Even though he talks like an expert, I notice that Kera is keeping a careful eye on what he's doing and providing instructions for him to follow.

We all enjoy the meal. Fish in a marinade, other pieces in sauce, and grilled sardines we eat whole. Then there's bread, lentils, cucumber, and the tomatoes we brought with us. I never realized, but they are difficult to get on Delos and expensive. I think the tomatoes are more appreciated than the wine.

The darkness falls and the stars take up their positions in the sky. Distant music joins the sound of the waves and the odd call of a seabird. The scent of the grilled fish and coals has gone, and instead, it's a jasmine perfume that fills the air.

Our parents sit together in conversation, while Leon, Zoe and I sit in our own spot. The lamps around the harbor and the market square help to create a perfect atmosphere.

"Which god do you believe in, Alexander?" Zoe asks.

"Oh, here we go, Zoe. Let Alexander enjoy the evening. I apologize for my annoying sister."

"Alexander can speak for himself," she replies, while Leon sighs.

"My father worshipped Minerva, or Athena as she is here. I followed him I suppose. There are so many gods here on Delos."

"To me, there's only one god. I know it's not a popular belief, but I believe that it will grow. My friends and I are always happy to spread the word to others."

"Leon told me you are a Christian."

"He's right. I don't know if he approves, but God has blessed him with a pleasant nature. He accepts that I have my faith. I can't complain."

"Hold on, did you just say something nice about me, sister?"

We all laugh, but Zoe won't allow a diversion from her thoughts.

"So, would you like to come to one of our meetings? Would you go with me?"

Inside myself, I'm screaming yes, but I don't want to show that. After all, maybe I'm not accepting for all the right reasons, but the thought of spending more time with Zoe is too much to turn down. I try my best to keep a calm expression.

"When do you meet?"

"Every seventh day, on Hēméra tou Hēliou, the Day of the Sun."

"So, you count each seventh day as well?"

"I don't believe I said that I didn't."

Leon looks confused. He's not aware of our conversation at dawn, and I don't think it's the right moment to mention it. If I do, it will look as if I've set up the entire dinner to make this happen. Then I realize I didn't set it up, Zoe did. I smile as I nod back.

"Yes, I'd like to join you for a meeting. I'd like that very much."

Leon just shakes his head, and the subject changes back to the up-and-coming games. He's happier about that.

CHAPTER XIII

"Master Alexander, let me look at you."

Selene spots me trying to leave the house early, even before breakfast can be served.

"I have to go out, Selene."

"You have plenty of time."

"My mother will fuss if she sees me."

"And she is right to fuss. You are going to meet a nice girl and visit where she worships her god. Your mother only wants you to be your best. She has given me the power over your appearance today." She smiles. "Have something to eat at least, and I will approve your release."

Na'amat walks past us at that moment with a plate of figs, grapes, pomegranate, and some bread and honey.

"No olives. Just as you like it," she says.

"Thank you, Na'amat. I'm really not hungry."

"Your mind tells you that, not your belly," says Selene. "Eat some, and I will let you go."

I sit down and try my best. The fruit is refreshing, and the honey is sweet. I pull at pieces of the bread, enough to make some space on the plate. I push the rest to one side to make it look as if I've eaten more.

"Can I go now?"

Selene passes judgment on my efforts. She sighs before she speaks. "Have a pleasant day."

I'm out the door when the words have barely left her lips. It's early morning, but the heat pours down from the sun. My skin has darkened since arriving on Delos. Working beside the ocean each morning and spending most of my afternoons oiled for training has had its effect on me. I feel healthy, and today I feel good. I thank all the gods I can think of before I reach Zoe's home. I know I'm going to learn about the Christian god, but I still want to make sure all the others have heard me, and so will bring me good fortune.

I don't run. I don't want to appear out of breath or sweating. I can hear my mother's advice even though she's not with me. The island is starting to come to life as I arrive at the shoreline. Leon and his father are already busy mending nets. Zoe had said he was always up early to do his share of work for the family.

"Have you come to help us?" he calls out, as I get closer.

"What are you saying, Leon?" shouts his father. "You know better than to go against the wishes of your sister. I wish to have a peaceful day." We all laugh. "Although you are early, Alexander. We still have to break our fast, but you can join us."

"No, it's alright, I—"

"I insist. Get your sister, my son. Tell her that Alexander is here." Leon puts down the net and disappears into the house. "Sit beside me, Alexander. Do you know much about fishing?"

"No, when I came to Delos, that was the first time I had been on a ship. My father was in the Roman navy, though. I know he loved the sea and his life sailing amongst the islands."

"It's true. The sea is too powerful to resist once you fall in love with it. It is a life you commit to that brings many rewards, and yes, some dangers. It can be calm and placid, other times it rages and battles against you. Once you understand how to live with the sea, then you understand how to live your life. Today you will hear many tales about fishermen.

"In Zoe's faith, they are very important. There are many lessons that she repeats to me after her meetings. I have lived too long under the guidance of Poseidon. I fear he would be angry with me if I turned away, and more than once I've needed his help to reach home. I expect Zoe's god would be the same with her, so I respect her views." He pauses. "Today is important to her. She wants to share that with you because she thinks you are a good person. Poseidon thinks you are a good person, too."

"I am interested in learning about her beliefs. I can see how much it means to her."

"If it doesn't speak to you, then you should be honest. It's not respectful to agree in words when your heart lies somewhere else. This is a small island, where secrets cannot hide for long. Be honest. You'll find that all the gods appreciate that. There we go. That is all I have to say about religion and daughters." He smiles. "Now let's eat."

I still don't feel like having another breakfast, but I am concerned it might insult the family if I refuse. I'm sure all the others have been hiding behind the door of the house, as they appear as one to organize the morning meal.

We're all sitting together in the open air within a few moments. The sun is sparkling on the sea and the heat continues to rise. Neighbors call out greetings for the day and all the family take their turn at responding. I like it here amongst the row of houses. It's almost like a small village of its own, even though the center of the town is just a few brief steps from here.

"Are you looking forward to your day, Alexander?" asks Kera.

"Yes, I don't know what to expect, but I think it will be good." I notice Zoe smiling with a wide grin.

I think I've said the right thing.

The islanders of Delos are not concerned with rushing. Maybe it's good that I've arrived early, as breakfast lasts a long time. The talk is full of comments that make me laugh. They all share jokes at each other's expense, though it's clear to see they are a close family. Eventually, we empty the plates of food and finish our cups of watered-down wine. Only then is our breakfast over.

Then Zoe bows her head and clasps her hands in prayer. "We thank you, Father, for this food you have provided. May it nourish our bodies and strengthen our spirits. As we break bread together, may we remember the love and sacrifice of your Son, Jesus Christ, our Kyrios. Amen."

"Amen," says the rest of the family.

"Are you all Christians?" I ask.

"No," says Thalasso, "but we can still offer our thanks to the god that Zoe follows."

"Or else..." smirks Leon.

"What was that you said?" she replies, clenching a fist at her brother.

"Hey, Alexander. Do you think Zoe would make an excellent boxer?"

"I'll box you, Leon!"

"That's enough, you two," says Kera. "It's time for you and Alexander to be off, Zoe. Are you going as well, Leon?"

"Not a chance," teases Zoe.

"I don't know which god I'll worship today," Leon answers back. "Maybe Dionysus. You get to drink more wine at his temple."

"There will be no more drinking for you today," says Thalasso. "It's nets and baskets for you, and that means silent and sober prayer to Poseidon while you work."

"Whatever gods you all worship," laughs Kera, "get on with it. I have trinkets to make for all of Olympus. The visitors to the shrines always look for something to take home, and I like a nice peace in the air to carry out my work."

Kera leads Zoe back to the house with the plates, while Leon and Thalasso return to their mending. I wait for a few moments on my own and start to think about the day ahead. I saw her friends at dawn on Mount Kynthos, but none of them came over to speak. Leon told me once that they don't tend to mix with people outside of their group. Maybe that's why people in Rome didn't trust them. I was starting to worry they wouldn't like me if they knew I was a Roman.

My worries fade away as Zoe reappears from the inside of the house. "Are you ready?" she asks.

"Yes, let's go. Are you meeting at the amphitheater, the ruin?"

"Soon. We still have time for a walk along the shore. If I'm going to introduce you, I need to know more about you."

We step out of the courtyard and follow the row of houses to a worn path that weaves its way through the grasses. We walk over shingle and step between rocks, to hug the closest route alongside the rolling waves.

"Can you swim?" Zoe asks.

"No, not really. This is the first time in my life I've lived so near the sea."

"That's terrible. I'm sure Leon will teach you if you ask, and I wonder why Demetrius hasn't suggested it. It's good for you."

"Maybe. I think I'm like your brother. We both prefer dry land."

"Don't be like my brother please," she smiles. "One of the miracles written about in our Gospels tells us about how Kyrios walked on water."

"Walked?"

"There are many miracles he performed."

"And people saw this?"

"Yes, it was his followers, his disciples. They were rowing on a rough sea. The wind blew hard and stirred the surrounding water. Out of the darkness, they saw Kyrios walking toward them. I think they thought he was a ghost."

"I'm not surprised," I reply. "So you believe in miracles?"

"Miracles happen all the time. It's God's way of bringing healing and restoration into our lives."

"Restoration? I suppose a miracle has just happened for me. A few months before I came here. I thought my chance to become a successful wrestler was gone. For my mother and me, life was harder. I was beginning to fall into the hands of a local gang. I fought for money, but not honestly. We were cheating the people who bet on the matches.

"Then from nowhere, my Uncle Nikos appeared. He brought us to Delos, to live in his house. He introduced me to Demetrius, who introduced me to Leon, who told me about you."

"Who is now telling you about God and Kyrios. Do you see how miracles work?"

"Yes," I smile.

We stop for a moment and stand face to face. Zoe is so beautiful. The breeze doesn't touch her hair. The scent of Jasmine surrounds her. Her almond-shaped brown eyes meet my gaze, and for a brief moment, the rest of Delos might have disappeared. Only the sound of the waves rolling on the shoreline lets me know there's still a world around us.

"So, what have you been building at the palaestra?"

The sudden question draws me back from my thoughts. "We're restoring it so that it's ready for the festival. Everything needs some work, but there are many hands helping. I think we'll have it ready soon."

"Can you show me?"

I feel awkward. "I'm not sure if Demetrius would be happy. Certain people aren't able to enter the palaestra."

"By certain people, you mean women?"

"Well, eh, yes. It's a tradition."

"A tradition? I don't think the walls will tumble if I walk within them. Me and my friends have been watching you train from higher in the hillsides. You know Demetrius. He'll not have missed that we were there."

"He's never mentioned it. You've watched us often?"

"I've watched you. You are a good wrestler. Demetrius likes you better than Dario, I can see that."

"Dario? Leon has spoken about him. He's fighting across all the islands here."

"He'll be back. He is traveling with Apion the fight fixer and his mother Maria. You should train hard. I think you can beat him. I want you to beat him."

"Leon said that he isn't a good person. I think he likes to throw his weight around in a match."

"In and out of the skamma. He hurt my brother with chokes and holds, but he hurt me as well."

"What do you mean?"

"Dario is a good-looking boy. He is strong and confident. All the young girls of the island fall for his charms. At least until they find out what sort of person he is."

"Did you fall for him?"

Zoe nods and seems to wipe a tear from her eye. It's not the answer I wanted to hear. I feel my heart sink and my shoulders drop.

"Others warned me. 'You think you'll be the one to change him,' they said. To make him a better person. I was sure for a while that he was the one for me, but then I started to hear whispers that I wasn't the only one for him. Lying and cheating, to Dario, is no more complicated than breathing."

"And did you leave him?"

"No. I stayed true. It was only when he left with Apion that he told me our time together was at an end. I cried at first, and even though he had broken my heart, I still rushed to the dock to see the ship leave. I waved him away, telling myself that he would return to me. As the days passed and my hope faded, I became angry."

"I think you should be angry with him."

"It wasn't just him. I was angry with everyone—my family, my neighbors, the whole of Delos. But mostly with myself for having been a fool. It was then that I turned to God. I found the teachings of Kyrios spoke to me. At first, I prayed to God that Dario would return, full of regret and longing for us to be back together. I wasn't thinking. I was being told how God could help me, but I wasn't listening. There was something I thought I wanted, something I thought was best for me.

"It took time for me to realize that the longer I held on to the past then the worse my life would become in the present."

"Demetrius tells us that dwelling on the past is futile," I reply, "and can lead us into suffering. The future is beyond our control, so it's right to concentrate on the present." I pause. "So... are things different now?"

"Yes, I know now. Kyrios has shone a light on my life. Dario cannot take me back to the darkness. Now take me to the palaestra. If Demetrius spots me, I'll just hide like normal."

Zoe returns to smiling as we continue our walk along the shore. A thousand thoughts are cramming into my head as we make our way to the south of the island. I didn't like Dario from what Leon had told me, but now I really hate him. All I want to do is make Zoe happy. I can look after her. I can protect her. I hope she can see that.

The sound of building work lies ahead; hammers on stone, wood being cut, marble and granite being carried and put in place. I've never stood back and looked at it from a distance, but the palaestra is much bigger with the addition of new rooms. The oil room is complete, the bathhouse is just about finished, and an area to hold the spectators under shade is just beginning construction.

"It looks incredible," says Zoe. "None of us thought that Demetrius would ever make this happen. He talked about it for years, but he didn't have the energy within him to make a start."

"So, what do you think changed him?"

"Not what, but *who* changed him. You changed him. He sees something in you that reminds him of himself. What can a wrestler do when he is no longer able to win against younger men? He must accept that he keeps himself alive by training others and passing on his knowledge. He thought, like all of us, that Dario would be the one, but he could see before anyone else that his young apprentice would never be a true champion. I think he's been happy Apion has taken him away."

We walk on and up to the colonnades. There are two skamma pits now: the dry pit we're always used to, and now a wet pit, next to water and shade to keep the mud from drying out.

I spy Tigranes approaching us. "Do not wait here long with Leon's sister," he calls. "Demetrius will be back soon."

"We won't. We have somewhere else to go today. I just wanted to show Zoe all the good work that everyone's doing."

"This showman doesn't take the applause he deserves," he says to Zoe, as he returns to his work.

"I do like the applause, at least in the skamma," I object, "but there are too many working here for me to say it's my work."

"I think I know what he means," says Zoe, looking into the pit. "You show humility and patience. Kyrios tells us those qualities will lead you to peace and fulfillment."

"Maybe after I beat Dario," I grin.

Zoe rolls her eyes. "I think it's time for us to go to our meeting."

***

The theater is huge compared to other buildings on the island. A large platform lies littered with rubble and blocks of granite. It sits at the center of row upon row of tiered, stone seating. There is space for thousands of people to assemble here. I wonder how large Delos must have been all those years ago.

A group of about thirty people gather in the center seats, facing a smaller group of five who stand on the scaena. They've brought containers of papyrus scrolls. One man is preparing to speak. The others bow down to him. He carries a crook that gives a sense of his authority. I can see him looking at me as we take a seat. He doesn't need to have the skills of Demetrius. I'm sure it's easy to pick out my unfamiliar face in the crowd.

The people present are older than us, but a small group that looks the same age sit together. I recognize some faces from passing them in the streets or at the market, but I don't know their names.

"Is this a new member of our group, Zoe?" says one of them.

"I hope so," she replies. "I'd like you all to meet Alexander."

Myrto, Eirene, Aglaonike, Leonidas, and Apollonius, all stand to introduce themselves. The welcome is genuine, and they all express wishes I will discover Kyrios in my heart. As we settle down, whispers flow between them. I think they're protective of Zoe. Leonidas keeps me talking while Myrto and Eirene move to sit between Zoe and myself. I can't protest, but I wish they would let me sit next to her. As everyone turns to look toward the stage, Zoe appears to understand my predicament, directing a last smile before the meeting begins.

"Listen to Paul," is all she says. The others nod in agreement as he begins to speak.

Paul begins by thanking everyone for attending. He comments on his flock growing by one and looks at me while asking what has inspired me to join them. The various faces in the crowd turn to me, and with a little embarrassment all I can think to say is, "Zoe brought me."

In amongst the giggles, Paul keeps a serious look on his face.

"Zoe brought you because Kyrios inspired her to do so. It is God who has shown you the way to his church."

I nod to let him know I understand. He bids me welcome before unrolling parchment that is handed over by another of the followers. Then he begins to tell the story of Moses, a legend about the Ten Commandments and leading the Israelites from slavery.

I notice that among the congregation, there are a few slaves that I recognize from houses near my uncle's. Paul insists that all will find freedom if they follow Kyrios. I wonder if it's that faith which allows them to endure their circumstances. Stoicism tells me that the way to find freedom is from within yourself. Paul speaks of it differently, but I can understand his meaning. As I nod my head with the others, I can feel that Zoe is looking across at me and observing my reactions.

She would be a good wrestler.

Paul continues to speak. He talks about the parable of the sower and the casting of seeds onto different soil. He talks about how God's message is proclaimed far and wide, but only those who can commit to nurturing its meaning will reap the rewards.

I know that he's sincere, but I think about how belief in other gods isn't so different. My father believed that Minerva would reward him. Many of the islanders devote themselves to the Greek gods. Their lives aren't terrible or miserable as a result. Zoe's father relies on Poseidon to fill his nets with fish, a prayer that is granted on most days. I want to ask questions, but this is not the garden of Gaius, I know I'm here to listen, but most of all I'm here for Zoe. I take the moment to snatch a glance, as she sits with her gaze fixed on the stage. I can see how devoted she is.

Paul's talk reaches its conclusion. As he returns the scrolls of parchment to their containers, the other four who are on the stage with him step forward and begin to sing. I don't know the words or the music, but everyone else seems to be familiar with it.

"You'll learn the songs eventually, if you come back," says Leonidas.

I detect a lack of trust from him. I start to wonder if Zoe brought Dario to the group. It annoys me to think that she might have. I do my best to sing the words the crowd repeats most often. I want to look as if I'm trying. I want to be better than Dario...

As the singing stops, Paul walks forward with his crook in hand. He looks toward the top of the hills, where the shrines remain for the *false gods*, as he calls them. He offers a prayer, and all bow their heads and close their eyes to focus on his offering. I take the chance to look over at Zoe, wishing I was sitting beside her, and not separated. A chorus of *Amen* pulls me out of my thoughts.

Once again, the others on the stage line up, this time with bread and wine to share out. Everyone around me stands, and I feel as if at least one God has heard my prayers when Zoe crosses over to join me and lead us down onto the stage.

"Is it feasting now?" I ask.

"We call it Communion. Just follow what I do."

"I'm really not that hungry, honestly."

"Don't worry," she assures me. "You only eat a small piece of bread and drink a small sip of wine, but they have blessed it, so it's good for you."

For a brief moment, she extends her hand to guide me to my position in the line of worshippers. The touch of her fingers sends my heart racing. If this is truly God's work, then I'm happy to give my thanks.

Once we've all eaten the morsels of bread and drunk from the same cup of wine, we return to our seats. Paul offers some last thoughts before concluding with a blessing for all those who have attended.

After the ceremony is over, the small crowd of Zoe's friends are keen to know what I think. They are friendly, but I feel like all my answers are being studied. Even after the meeting is over, they follow on as we walk back toward Zoe's house. I wonder if they will ever leave us alone.

Each of them wants to share some of their knowledge of God. All I can offer in return is what I have learned from studying Stoic philosophy, and about the benefits of living a virtuous life and respecting those around you. It seems to grant me some acceptance, but until I can learn more teachings of Jesus, I think I will have some way to go to earn their trust. At the moment, I wish they would just go home.

Whether it is Zoe's God that hears me, or Minerva, or any of the Greek pantheon, at one point, they decide to leave. I think Zoe is secretly as relieved as I am. As they walk out of sight, she leads me into the courtyard of her house and pulls up two wooden stools for us to sit on. We sit side by side and face the sea.

"I hope it wasn't too boring for you," she says. "It's important to me now to share my faith."

I suddenly realize that Dario didn't go to the meetings with her. I remember that she only found her God after he departed. I feel better being the only person she has wanted to invite to share her beliefs with.

"I want to learn more, but not just the words from the priest. I want to know more about you."

I panic as the words fall into a moment of silence. We look into each other's eyes, with only the backdrop of the waves landing on the rocks a short distance away.

"Are you there, Zoe?" Kera's voice breaks the moment.

"I need to help my mother now, but I don't mind if you call for me again. I know the parable spoke of the different soil. I think Paul was talking to you. He is wise enough to know not everyone will react the same way, but I think he could see, like I do, you are someone to be trusted."

She stands up and begins to make for the door. As she steps away, I want to say so much more, but my mind has gone blank. She's just about to enter the house when she turns and sighs. Quickly stepping back toward me, she reaches to the sides of my face and pulls me into a brief and wonderful kiss.

I'm struck dumb as she turns once more and disappears inside the house. I brush my fingers against my lips. I can't believe what just happened. As I walk back toward home, my head is in a spin, my heart is beating fast, and I have such a wide grin that I'm drawing odd looks from those who pass me in the narrow lanes that weave through the town.

When I reach the house, I have to sit in the courtyard to catch my breath and relive the day in my mind. Selene appears to ask me how it all went. I don't recall saying anything in return, but I think my expression is enough of an answer. She goes back inside and leaves me alone with my thoughts.

CHAPTER XIV

ELENA

"Nikos. It's good to have you home, brother. Alexander will be happy to have his uncle back in the house again. I think between Selene, Na'amat, and myself, we've been making his life a misery."

"Did I just catch sight of Alexander along the shore with Leon's sister?" Nikos replies. "I don't think it's my tales of weights, measures, and bad weather that will interest him right now."

"She's a lovely girl, and I approve. They get little time on their own. Demetrius is making sure the palaestra and the games are at the forefront of everyone's minds."

"I'm sure he is. I'll talk to him later, but I've done my best to spread the word in the ports I visited. It will surprise me if the games don't attract good contestants."

"Alexander will want to know that as well. Oh, and don't expect to see much of Tigranes until the games are here. Alexander has recruited him to watch over the rebuilding. We seldom see him around the house."

"Are you telling me I need to take on more servants? Business is not as good as it once was. I may have to buy less of my favorite wine."

"Oh yes, the wine."

"Elena? Don't tell me—"

"It's alright." I laugh. "Maybe just an amphora or two less since your departure. Alexander wanted to make a good impression with Zoe's family."

"But, with my wine?"

"Don't panic. I'm sure you'll get a good price on salted fish for your next voyage."

"It better be the best price, for it's the best wine," he says while tapping over his heart with his hand. "Is there any other bad news, dear sister?"

"No, there's no bad news. Thank you for bringing us here, Nikos. I feel I have come home. The years in Rome with Marcus, I could never replace, but it was only he and Alexander that made me want to stay. It was survival rather than living the life that I wanted. Now I've returned, there's so much for me to look forward to again. So, thank you, thank you for all you have done."

I stand and embrace my brother for a moment before stepping back and covering my nose.

"I still smell of life at sea?" he smiles.

"You smell of something. I will get Selene to make a bath for you."

"And Na'amat to make me something to eat. Anything but fish."

"There is lamb. It will take time to roast."

"For dinner, yes. Maybe just some mezes for the moment. Flatbread, hummus, dolmades, some saganaki, and some wine," he pauses, "the cheap wine."

"Yes, of course, my brother."

"I will change out of these clothes at least."

He wanders out of the room, and I walk out into the garden. Na'amat is sweeping the courtyard. The sea breeze carries sand and dust from the rest of the town. It's a never-ending task to keep it clear.

"Give me the broom, Na'amat. I'll finish here while you make some mezes for Nikos."

"Yes, mistress. I'll finish clearing the path once I've prepared the meal."

"No, I'll finish it. I'm not too proud to do what I can for my brother's house."

"He may be angry, mistress."

"Angry? We're talking about the same brother, aren't we?"

"I understand, mistress."

She smiles and leaves me alone. I look around myself. There are small areas that still need to be swept, and there are some plants that could do with attention. Nikos loves his roses, but they need some pruning and the heads of dead flowers removed. A small pair of bronze shears lies close by the plants. Na'amat must have been thinking the same thing.

I settle down on the ground beside the flowers. High, hazy clouds are stopping the sun from being so fierce. The shade of the high walls that surround our home is just enough to make the later morning pleasant.

Curious chaffinches and sparrows hop and flutter about nearby. They call out, asking for crumbs to feed their families, while the faint buzz of bees humming in the background can be heard. The hovering insects focus their attention on the same flowers. I avoid interfering with their task.

I take in a gentle breath of rose-scented air and turn to look toward Mount Kynthos. It is easy to see why the gods love this island. It is a true paradise. Apollo blessed it with his birth. Is this the place where the sun first climbed into the sky, drawn by his chariot? I bite my lip hard as I think about the sin I committed against him. I have had to live with that for almost sixteen years.

Yet the gods have not descended to wreak their wrath on me. The island hasn't opened up and swallowed me whole. I know it is only men who assume the power of the heavens to stamp their authority over the people they control. It is their proclamations that divide out those who they judge to be sinners. If Apollo or Zeus want to exact revenge on me, then I won't be difficult to find.

"It's all nonsense," I say to myself.

Marcus and I should have stayed. We shouldn't have run or seen Rome as an escape. Leaving the freedom of Delos behind was the mistake we made. We were young, and Marcus was sure he was doing the right thing to protect me.

I smile at the thought of Alexander with Zoe. There is so much about them that reminds me of Marcus and myself. The young son of Rome and a daughter of the island that sits at the very center of the world. Alexander is respectful like his father. He has dreams like his father.

"I will do my best to help his dreams come true, Marcus. Lend me your strength if ever I need it. Just know that we are happy, and that Delos has welcomed us back."

I start to work with the roses. I listen to the breeze in the faint hope that I might catch a whisper from the one I loved, but it's only the small birds and insects that persist. One chaffinch edges closer to me in short hops. It holds its head to the side. The bright red of its plumage reminds me of the Roman cloaks and tunics.

"Are you Marcus?" I ask. "Have you come to watch over me?"

Na'amat reappears from inside the house. "Would you like to eat, mistress? There is enough food for you and Master Nikos."

"Yes, I will, thank you, Na'amat. I'm afraid I haven't done so much, but I'll help you later and from now on we will work in the garden together."

"I can't ask you, mistress."

"And you're not asking me. I'm offering myself for the duty. I love being out here. No one on Delos should spend their life under the cover of a roof. It is too special a place."

"I know what you mean, mistress. Your brother has been kind enough to allow Tigranes, Selene, and myself to stay. We are all each other's family now, and Delos is our home as well."

"Nikos is always full of good intentions. It's a pity his sister fell from grace."

"Mistress?"

"Nothing." I smile. "I'm just wallowing in self-pity. Your mezes are just what I need to feel better, but can you throw some crumbs out for the birds, especially the chaffinches?"

"Yes, mistress."

I return to the main room of the house where Nikos is already reclining and eating in the Roman style.

"Help yourself, Elena. There is too much food here. I'm hungry, but this will weigh me down for the rest of the day if I eat it all."

"I think she made the food for the both of us."

"Oh, alright, that makes me feel better. Please eat."

"I'll take some of the flatbread and hummus, some stuffed grape leaves, and feta cheese."

"The baba ghanoush is good. Try some."

I make up my selection and sit facing Nikos. He stares at me with a suspicious look on his face.

"What's wrong, Elena? You can't hide your feelings so well."

"I can't settle today. I don't know what it is. Everything has gone so well about returning to the island. I just wonder how long it can last."

"It was so many years ago. You were young and in love. Sacrilege was not part of your plan. Believe me, there are many worse crimes than the one you committed."

"Yes, but my crime was against the gods."

"Then where are the lightning bolts? I know that Alexander suffered on the trip here, but you know as well as I do that the wind hardly blew as we made our way from Ostia." He looks thoughtful as he crams down more food. "You have been hiding away since we arrived. We need to do more to get you back into life. You cannot watch the days pass by even if the view is pleasant. There could even be another love for you. You are still young, sister."

"I will go out more, I promise, but I'm not looking for a replacement for Marcus. In fact, I want him to know that."

"Aphrodite will make those decisions for you and don't think that she reacts well to being ignored. You will only recover from the last few years by living a full life here. Once you are confident that there's no threat to your safety, then you'll be able to enjoy life again, and all it can offer. We shall walk to the market and harbor together after our meal, and once I've washed the salt from my skin."

"I'm not sure."

"Elena, you must. I insist you will be safe."

***

The sound of the market creeps up as I walk with Nikos along the twisting narrow paths, hemmed in by houses, shops, and the many places to eat and drink. Glimpses of the sea appear through regular gaps between walls. The white crests and waves of blue water reflect a beautiful sky above us. The clouds from earlier have melted away, leaving a shimmering haze in their place. The bright light of Apollo shines down upon all his followers, even me.

The faces of his chosen people smile and welcome all to his birthplace. It's important for the islanders to show hospitality to strangers. Those who visit the temples and shrines come in peace. They're not the invaders who once ravaged the shores of these islands. As we walk along, Nikos notices the greetings I receive from new as well as old friends.

"Surely, you must feel better knowing you are part of Delos once more?"

"I do, but guilt still raises its head now and again. Forgive me if I return to old ways from time to time."

"There is nothing that should make you feel guilty. Themis, Justitia, and Ma'at are all far too busy with other concerns. Please relax, Elena. You are home, that's all that matters."

"You're right."

"Of course I am. Now think about how you can best fill the days ahead with joy."

"I may have a marriage to plan."

Nikos roars with laughter. "Poor Alexander!"

"Zoe and I will do the organizing. Alexander has nothing to do with it. He just needs to turn up." I smile.

I am joking, a little, but it provides some fun as we take our time amongst the market stalls. Linen is in plentiful supply, but also cotton from Egypt, and even rarer, silk that's arrived over greater distances. I notice that Nikos is happy to distract me toward other stalls when I let the expensive fabric glide through my fingers.

"Leave the cloth to me. Every pair of hands it passes through adds something to the price. The further east I can sail, then the cheaper it will become."

"And how long would that take?" I ask. "Alexander might be as old as you are now by the time you return."

"But it would be less expensive," he pleads with a wide grin across his face.

We move to a large stall that sells all kinds of pottery: for the house, feasts, and items of every size down to the little figurines and keepsakes that I know Zoe's mother makes at her home.

Four amphorae draw Nikos' interest. They all depict figures of wrestlers in different poses. A matching set, which the stallholder insists on selling together.

Another form of combat then breaks out, as my seafaring merchant of a brother takes on the convincing nature of the market trader. The wit and haggling skills are on full display. I smile as they tell one another how poor they will be if they buy or sell at the wrong price. They are both enjoying the sparring too much, so as I await their agreement, I pick through the tiny figures of the gods who gaze out at the customers. A small clay dolphin takes my attention.

I hold the item up to my eyes. The little clay creature looks as if it's smiling back at me. My choice doesn't escape the observation skills of the market trader, who seizes the opportunity to influence Nikos.

"Ah, the beautiful lady has wonderful taste. This is your sister, Nikos?"

"Yes, Elena," he confirms.

"Elena, you are graceful like the dolphin, and just as wise, I'm sure. Do you know how the dolphins swim? They travel from east to west each day. They follow Apollo as he charges across the sky, and each night they return to the east, so that they may greet him when he returns over the horizon on the following day.

"The dolphin is sacred to Apollo. They are like his children. I know that he is offering his blessing. Can't you hear his words on the breeze, dear, graceful, and beautiful lady? He is telling me that if only your brother can strike a fair price for these wonderful amphorae, then I must give you this dolphin as a gift from the god himself."

I can't help but giggle at the trader's offer. We all knew that Apollo wasn't speaking on the wind. The hot air was only flowing from the seller's charm.

"Very well," sighs Nikos, "as long as you have them delivered to my home today."

"Consider it done, my friend. They will be at your house before Apollo leaves us."

"And the dolphin?" asks Nikos a little sarcastically.

"Oh yes, and the dolphin too, my friend." He waves and smiles as we turn away from his stall.

"Maybe I should do the buying on my own from now on," Nikos grumbles.

"Now, now, you said I should get out more and meet people," I remind him. "Maybe he was right, and Apollo is letting me know I am still one of his children. A beautiful dolphin."

Nikos shakes his head. He is happy for me, if not for the ultimate price of the amphorae. At last, I am starting to settle. Everything about Delos refreshes my soul. As we step onto the area that lies between the market and the harbor, cheers arise from a crowd in front of us. A new ship has just docked. It's attracting a lot of attention.

"What's the commotion?" I ask.

"I have a feeling that I might know. I'm sure I can hear the booming tones of Apion."

"Apion?"

"A showman. Someone that Demetrius needs to make his games a genuine success. Follow me."

It looks like half of the island is rushing toward the dock. I had seen things like this in Rome when the crowds flocked around renowned athletes or gladiators, but I never remembered it ever happening on Delos. I've missed so much in my years away.

We push our way through the crowd. Nikos is always polite yet firm as he removes any who stand in his way. I follow close behind, and we emerge from the busy throng into the center of a circle surrounding Demetrius and the man I presume is Apion, a tall and imposing Nubian, well dressed, and displaying a confidence that naturally comes with success.

"Apion!" calls my brother.

"Nikos! It's good to see you again. My ship has followed you to Delos. We were on Santorini when word reached us of the games."

"So, you'll be staying on Delos until then?"

"I have a wrestler to prepare. Undefeated on our travels so far."

"You have Dario with you?"

"He's somewhere over there."

Apion points to an even more tightly packed crowd. I can barely glimpse the person who is in the middle of the adulation. The name means something to me, though. Alexander has mentioned him more than once and not in a good way. I'm curious to see him, on my son's behalf, to get the measure of him. I know before too long they will face each other in the skamma.

I excuse myself from the praise and backslapping that's being exchanged between my brother, Apion, and Demetrius. I don't think they notice me leaving to be honest. I cross the dock to join with Dario's many fans. Boys who want to be like him, girls who want to be with him, and gamblers who want to profit from him.

A sea of hands extends around and over him. What seems like twenty conversations are happening at the same time. To his credit, he tries to answer everyone with words that tell of his triumphs and trophies. I can see him more clearly, and I admit that my first thought is that he will not be a measure for my son.

Alexander always talks about his ability to read others in the fight. He doesn't realize that he inherited that talent from me. I know within seconds that pride is Dario's weakness. It leads to arrogance and a lack of focus; it exposes vulnerability. My Alexander has stronger principles, even if Dario may match him in physical strength.

I'm only a few feet away and I hear the crowd mention Leon's name and then Alexander's. They're telling Dario about his new competitor on the island, but he only shrugs at the thought of his fellow wrestlers.

"Yes, where is Leon?" Dario asks. "I thought he would have been here at the harbor to greet his sparring partner. I haven't thrown him face-down into the dirt for weeks. He'll be missing the taste of sand."

He bellows a laugh at his own joke. I can see that the talk about him is true.

"There's a new wrestler on Delos, Dario," says one of his adoring fans." He's from Rome."

"They all fall the same way, my friend, regardless of where they were born. Whoever this Alexander is, he will know the might of a contender from Delos."

"That is a title you will have to win, Dario."

Demetrius has walked up behind me. His commanding presence calms the crowd, and they part to allow him through to face Dario.

Dario's bravado fades in front of his old mentor. "I will earn it, Demetrius. I have learned much since I left with Apion. I am better than when I left the palaestra."

"I'm happy for your success, but it also sounds like you may have forgotten some of my teachings already. Those that wish to win should not make assumptions that will leave them open to defeat."

The crowd falls silent. Some of the crowd sneer at Demetrius. Whispers in the crowd side with Dario. They question: *who does Demetrius think he is?* Dario remains respectful, but he knows he has the support of *his* crowd.

"I learn from many. I have chosen the teachings that mean the most to me. I return here with over thirty victories to my name. I will always show you respect, Demetrius. I am someone who began learning in your palaestra, but you must know it is the wisdom born of the contests fought for Apion that makes me a champion."

Demetrius returns a formidable glare. I think even Dario realizes he has said too much.

"Then I urge you to remember more of your beginnings, Dario. Leon has improved, and as for Alexander, you will not find it so easy to defeat him."

"I look forward to it," Dario grins. "Alexander, whoever he is, and wherever he is from."

"I should expect to see you return to training then? If you expect to win in the games."

"Why not? It will help me stay in good shape if nothing else. I will train with your Roman, but he shouldn't expect any favors."

"Nor will he." The objecting and assertive voice of a mother catches all by surprise. I will not have him demean my son before he has even met him.

"This is Elena, Alexander's mother," says Demetrius.

"Elena?" another woman's voice calls from the crowd, and she steps out in front of me.

"Elena, this is Dario's mother, Maria," says Demetrius again, while stepping back as if half-expecting a fight to break out.

"I know perfectly well who she is," Maria continues. "Elena and I go back many years. There is only one year between us. We were neighbors until she left for Ostia, with a child in her belly. And your child, is he the Alexander that they speak of?"

"Yes," I falter. Maria and I did not separate on good terms. It left me wondering how much she would choose to remember from those days that lay behind us. "Alexander is my son."

"I remember worrying about you. Was he born at sea?"

"No, we made land before his birth. The gods were on our side."

"Then Apollo's blessings be on you and your family. How is Marcus?"

"Marcus fell in battle some months ago."

"I am sorry, Elena. He was a good man. Come, walk with me, away from the crowd. Let me offer you some comfort. I also lost my husband to war some years ago."

A sea of eyes surrounded me. The brief conversation has changed the mood of the crowd. Dario smiles with some sympathy. Demetrius flicks his eyes to the side to suggest that following Maria is the best idea, as she extends her hand toward mine.

I silently agree and allow her to lead me to the side of the harbor that overlooks the Roman fort. The noise of the crowd strikes up again as soon as we walk away. I feel this is not going to end well.

We only travel a short distance, but far enough away from the crowd for us not to be overheard. I can feel her sharp fingernails poised over my hand. Like daggers waiting to inflict a wound. So, when she turns to face me, her rage is not a surprise.

"What do you think you are doing, coming back to Delos? How do you think the gods will choose to punish us all?"

"Apollo's light has crossed the sky without fail every day since I came back to my home. You know as well as I do that the law was written in fear. Those in Delphi are obsessed with the thought of a warrior king who can claim Delos as his birthplace. One who might want to reclaim the great store of silver that was once kept here. It has nothing to do with the gods."

"So you say, but then you would. Remember though, it is the people who will pass judgment on you for what you have done."

"There is no need for this, Maria. No one needs to know. No one needs to pass judgment."

"Are you asking that I keep your secret? That I risk my own fate to protect you?"

"We were friends once. Does that mean nothing?"

"Our friendship ended when you stole Marcus from me. I have only hated you since then."

"So, what are you going to do?"

"I'm going to follow your example. You waited on your moment. Now, what can I steal from you? I will let you know when I am ready. Your return to Delos will cost you, of that I am certain."

Maria pushes me out of the way, knocking the clay figurine from my hand. The little dolphin smashes into pieces in front of me. Perhaps the gods are sending me a message after all.

CHAPTER XV

Calm yourself, Alexander.

My head is ordering my heart as I start the oiling of my skin, preparing for the contest. Dario seems to be relaxed as he readies himself for our fight.

Is it only me who feels the tension?

But I have learned that what appears on the outside is not always what is taking place on the inside.

Demetrius has warned us. We are in training, and he intends for both of us to be fit for the games. He carries a rod with him today, and he intends to use it if he feels that we need encouragement over our conduct.

I'm trying to keep my thoughts clear, but it'll surprise me if Dario can't hear them. He hasn't spoken up until now, and I'm sure he's not predicting failure for himself. For my part, I try to steady myself with long, slow breaths, but then he disrupts my concentration.

"Why are you doing that, Alexander?"

"Doing what?"

"The breathing. It makes you sound like an ox that's sick."

"It helps to improve concentration and focus."

"Ah, I see. Concentration takes time. What if your opponent doesn't grant you time? I'll warn you now, I'm quick."

"But am I quicker?" I reply.

Dario stops and makes a point of looking me up and down from head to toe. "No, I don't believe you will be."

He smirks, and silence falls again. There are only the sounds of the strigils and the oil being poured. I feel my anger grow. Zoe has told me many things about Dario and my head is full of revenge for what he has put her through, but I know these emotions interfere with my performance. I cannot allow him that advantage. I cannot disgrace myself by letting my emotions control me. I know I am better than that.

The oil room is the first stage of a contest. It is here that you must first try to judge your opponent. The tone of their muscles and frame. The scars and marks that tell a history of their battles, and the ability to read their state of mind. Are they calm? Nervousness can show itself in many ways, and it's not always bad. As long as the tension keeps me alert, then I am happy with suffering the effects of anticipating the fight.

Apion enters the room and breaks the atmosphere.

"You have done a good job with this place, Alexander. There have been so many changes since I was last here a few months ago. What do you say, Dario?"

"It's alright, I suppose. A lot better than it was, but still nothing like the kind of palaestra I'm used to."

"Have you asked Alexander about the place where he used to train?"

"What?" Dario can't hide his surprise.

"According to Demetrius, young Alexander here once trained on Palatine Hill in a palaestra that could rival Demetrius' own. That right, Alexander?"

"Yes, I trained with Gaius for a time."

"I know Gaius. He is one of the best, Dario. You should know what you're facing. It pays to enquire about your opponent."

"I'll know him soon enough," he replies.

It's normal for the wrestlers to leave the oil room together, but Dario strides out on his own, leaving me to follow behind in his footsteps.

"He's hard to respect, I know, but he is good, and he's been beating the best of all for many miles. He has earned his confidence. You will not beat him today, I think." Apion smiles.

"Well, I will surely try."

"Take some advice. Unless he slips up and leaves an obvious open-ing, then allow him to triumph without having to break your bones. Demetrius doesn't need a win to spot a wrestler who is a winner."

"But Demetrius has a keen and discerning eye. He will know if I give up the fight."

"Think of it as conceding defeat and not giving up. Dario has been in the full throes of the fights I arranged for him; you have been sparring with Leon." He pauses. "Don't get me wrong, I like Leon, we all do, but he won't help you improve."

"And Dario will?"

"Yes, he will. Whether he realizes, that is a different matter."

"Why tell me this?"

"You fought for Gaius, and now you fight for Demetrius. I haven't seen you wrestle, but I trust the judgment of both the men who have. I am not a wrestler. I am a fight promoter. Two contenders from Delos will earn greater recognition."

"I'll do my best as I always do. I can gracefully concede a win by Dario if that is what transpires, but I will not hand it to him on a silver platter." Apion shows a wide smile. "He will earn his win as will I, and we'll both learn something."

He bows and invites me to join Dario in the skamma.

***

Dario is already waiting at the edge of the sand and in conversation with Demetrius. I'm sure he's been talking to him about my training in Rome. He is arrogant, but not stupid. I stride forward with confidence. Leon stands to the side and mouths a message of support. He's eager to see Dario fail, and I don't want to let him down, but I'm confused as I stand opposite my opponent. Is Apion trying to encourage a friendship between us? Zoe will not be happy about that. I want revenge for her, today at least, but again, I must control my emotion and keep a clear head.

There is no time left. Demetrius stands between us and signals the start of the contest. We both drop low into our stances. Our height matches up, and our hands come up against one another. We circle, testing distance and balance. Dario is true to his word. He wastes no time in moving in for a quick attack. He pulls and snaps down on my neck. I pull away, but he continues to repeat his move. It forces me to react with instinct rather than planning. Our grip on one another changes at a fast and furious pace. Our heads clash together and every time we make contact, I detest being so near to him.

My anger is growing. His speed and reactions give me no time to fight back. His hands attack and defend with equal intensity. The fighting is furious. Our grip on one another changes at speed. Slaps sneak their way into the combat. Dario doesn't mind missing a grip on my arm if he can glance his palm off my face.

The pain stings, and the afternoon sun burns above us. I swallow dust and sand that's kicked into the air. Demetrius encourages the ferocity. Leon shouts for me, while Apion calls out to his fighter. The palaestra seems to raise the level of the noise.

We both fight for the advantage and neither of us will back down. I can feel my frustration grow. I can't break through for an attack. I take more risks even though I know I shouldn't. Then Dario senses our match is on his terms. He grimaces as he manipulates me into constant defending. He pulls on my wrist and down on my neck.

He is wearing me down.

He only needs me to delay my reactions by the smallest measure. I feel the grip on my leg and my balance has already gone. He twists me to the side and over my head. I crash down to the side, with no time to protect myself. A crunching agony courses through every part of me, and Dario's knee drives into the side of my body. An added attack when I'm already down.

Demetrius breaks us apart with a word of warning for Dario, but that doesn't alter any of my resentment. Of all the people, I cannot let *him* beat me. As I pick myself up, he takes the moment to taunt me further.

"What did the great Gaius teach you?" he asks. "I'm looking for a proper match, not a brawl that I could have in a tavern. You are slow, Alexander, and that's in your head as well as your body."

"That's enough," orders Demetrius. "Fight again."

I won't get caught the same way twice. I block and focus on ducking out of his grip. He pulls at my wrists, my elbows, and my shoulders as we weave left and right, back and forward. The sand stings below my feet. His breath is like a fire on my jaw as our heads draw together.

He is winning.

I've never felt this way in a fight. I have to win. I'm desperate to repay him for his attacks against Zoe and Leon. All I need is one good opportunity, but he's not prepared to allow me the opening. The pressure keeps up. I cannot plan for an attack, and his instinct is better than mine. His leg sweeps behind me, and the movement of his weight is enough to carry me over. I end up staring at the sky, watching Dario grin back in my face.

"How long would he last on the road, Apion? How long until the games, Demetrius? What can he hope to achieve? Rome will disown him. They won't want him as a contender. The emperor will give you the thumbs down if you fight like that, Alexander."

I pick myself up again. Sweat and oil drip from me. I look at the gaze of the others. Demetrius shows no hint of emotion, Apion smiles, Leon is disappointed, and Dario is sure in his ability to triumph. I don't want to be here. I'm not ready. I won't win. I might as well end this, but I dare not throw the last point to my opponent. Demetrius will not tolerate any sense that I have given up.

How do I beat him?

"Fight," Demetrius commands.

I have to face him with his own game. I go in hard and fast as I try to dictate the pace. I reach for his legs, forcing him to step back from the combat. I steady myself in the center. I force him to move around me to look for an opening. I keep up the attack, but he blocks or outsteps me on every move. Then it ends. He pushes my face to the side and locks his arms around me. He pulls me in and changes his stance. Once again, I'm brought down with a throw. It's over.

"Enough," says Demetrius. "I have seen enough."

"He was better on that last point," says Dario.

His words bruise me further. I know that there's no encouragement from him. He steps out of the pit and without a look back, he strides away to wash himself clean.

"Don't lose heart," is all that Apion says as he follows Dario out of the palaestra.

"You should get yourself cleaned up," says Demetrius.

"I don't want to right now. I've been too near him already today."

"Do not blame him. He did not defeat you today. You are the master of your own failing."

I look to Leon, and he seems to agree without speaking.

"What could I have done? He has been fighting in contests when I've been working at the harbor, or mending walls and fixing paths and tracks. How can I learn to be as good as him without the same experience?"

"These are questions I can answer for you. I invite you again to wash. If we wander out to the hills, the sun will roast the oil on your skin. You will become distracted as you burn. Allow Dario his triumph. There is nothing you can gain for the sake of those you love today."

Demetrius knew the reason for my emotion—for my distraction and my mistakes. He knew I had arrived at the fight with the wrong motivation. My feelings for Zoe, my desire to win only for her, was obvious to him, even if it wasn't apparent to Dario.

"Go. Make yourself clean. Accompany him, Leon. You can both learn something from Dario's triumphant mood in victory."

***

"You will fight better, Alexander," Apion insists as he draws the strigil against Dario's back.

"He'll have to fight better," Dario adds. "There are many who are going to make their way here for the games. You have a lot to do to beat any of them. The wrestlers from Mykonos, Naxos, Palermo, and even across to Armenia, have all been told of the Great Delia games returning. We heard of it on Santorini. Nikos, the merchant, has spread the word far and wide."

"My Uncle Nikos," I reply.

"Nikos is your uncle? Of course he is. You should at least be able to keep us all laughing if he is your uncle."

I don't reply. I don't want to talk to Dario, and I don't want to encourage him to talk back. Instead, I plunge into the pool and cover my head with water. The cool bath makes me aware of every part of me that hurts. I stare into the water as the conversation carries on around me.

"Is that Zoe and her friends further up the hill?" I hear Dario asking.

I look up to see him waving toward her. She turns and walks away without waving back.

"Maybe I shouldn't have split up with your sister before I left, Leon. It was cruel of me. I should make amends while I'm back on Delos. She is good company."

"You have no chance of becoming friends with Zoe again," remarks Leon.

"No? She can't resist me. Who else on this island can compete with me? You will see."

I allow myself a small smile. I step out of the pool, ready to tell him he has lost more than he knows during the time he has been away, but Leon gestures for me to say nothing. I do as he asks, but it seems that everyone bows down to Dario. My frustration increases, and I'm happy when he decides that it's time to leave.

"Thank you for the contest, Alexander. You were a little unpredictable. I like that. Your lack of training is all that counts against you. Time will improve your practice, but you'll do better to accept that you won't beat me. You can help me win the Great Delia as a fellow student of this palaestra. Take your place on my side, and I promise I won't break any of your bones."

My blood is boiling. He can see my rage. I want to attack him then and there, and I know that Leon and Apion can both sense it. Dario can't resist one last comment to push me as far as he can.

"Three more days of the tetrad this week. I hope it won't be as tense as today. Get your Uncle Nikos to tell you some jokes that you can share with us tomorrow. You never know; we might even become friends." He smirks once more and walks away, with Apion following on.

I watch him as he returns to the palaestra and Demetrius. They talk together with Apion, and Dario makes it obvious that he is talking about me. He's mimicking some of my moves, pointing in my direction. I can hardly contain myself. Then a large splash of water hits me on my back and my head. I turn around to see Leon smiling and holding an empty bowl.

"You still need to cool down," he says.

"You're right," I reply. "How can anyone put up with him? Why does Demetrius even want to train him again?"

"Demetrius doesn't judge others. You know what he'll say to you. You must focus on yourself. Don't ruin your own progress by objecting to how others behave. You must rise above it. You must strive to be the better person. That's what's important. Don't concern yourself. You had him worried on the third point."

"Did I?"

Leon nods. "Yes, we could all see it." Apion glanced at me with a look of approval. "We could all see that you were adapting to Dario's style," Leon continued. "You just didn't have enough time today, that's all."

"I wanted to beat him. I wanted that more than anything, for Zoe and you."

"Forget about that for the moment. Work hard. You will beat him. Remember, you are on Delos, not Rome. Nothing moves fast around here, and we're all used to it." He smiles. "Whichever day you beat him, then you can be happy to know that Zoe and I will take great pleasure in your victory."

"I still want that day to come soon."

Leon laughs and performs a perfect impression of Demetrius' voice. "Victory will come when you work hard and dedicate yourself to all that is virtuous. There are no shortcuts on the path, Alexander."

We laugh together. I fetch my tunic and put it on. By the time I am ready to return to the palaestra, I can see that Dario is leaving for the day.

"I suppose I better find out what the real Demetrius has to say."

"His advice won't be as good as mine," Leon assures me.

We walk down to where Demetrius and Apion are still standing. They notice us approaching them and their conversation stops.

"Have you settled yourself?" Demetrius asks.

There is something about the tone of his voice. He expects me to know and be honest about why I lost. I know there's no point in lying.

"I didn't offer Dario respect in the skamma because I don't respect him out of it."

"You lost control of yourself," replies Demetrius, "and long before you walked into the pit."

"You have talent," says Apion, "and your mind is good—"

"When it has focus," agrees Demetrius.

"I'm sorry, Demetrius. I know I shouldn't allow things to control me. Things I can't control myself."

"Then there's nothing lost today. You have learned an important lesson. Which I'll expect you to keep in mind from now on. It is lighter training tomorrow. There will be no combat. I will expect to see you, Dario, and Leon working together to improve your strength, your stamina, and a sense of harmony within our place of learning. Are you prepared to do that?"

"Yes," I reply.

"Then perhaps this is a good time to let Apion speak. He has a proposal for you."

"Which contests did you fight in at Palatine Hill, with Gaius?" Apion asks.

"I only trained with Gaius. I wasn't with him long enough to be part of a contest."

"Then you didn't fight in Rome?"

"Oh, I fought in Rome, on the streets and courtyards of the Subura. I fought for money to live rather than glory or titles."

"I see." Apion looks thoughtful and smiles through fingers he holds over his mouth. "If you fought in the streets, then there were few rules for you to follow."

"Only to stay in the fight until it was time to win."

Apion bellows out a laugh that echoes around the stone columns. "Yes, here is an unpolished diamond, but a diamond no less, Demetrius." He pauses and gives me a discerning look, as though assessing how to take the unpolished stone and make it into something of beauty and worth. "How can we reveal Alexander's true value?"

"Work," says Demetrius. "Alexander, when you take stock of the cargo that arrives by ship each day, you organize your duties. You set yourself tasks that make your goals easier to achieve. You want to finish in time so that you can train at the palaestra. You work with Leon, and between the two of you, with joint effort and discipline, you both appear for wrestling each day. You are successful because you instinctively know how to succeed.

"In the afternoon, you cycle through the moves and the throws. Repeating them each day. Your muscle has memory. Your body learns in the same way as your mind. Your heart and lungs build up in silence. You do not need to question yourself about how you are becoming more accomplished. You can feel it as each hold or throw becomes a natural extension of your core strength.

"Then in the evening, you work for the benefit of all. You develop your knowledge and skills by observing and listening to others. They can tell you why the roof will not cave in around you, or how best to direct the flow of water around this place. Each time you can stand back and see another task completed, you can look at what you have accomplished and know that your actions have had an effect not just in your world, but the world of others. When your virtue can extend to create harmony in the lives of other people, then you are ready to shine, just as a polished stone.

"Do not limit yourself to a single thought, which, in turn will limit what you can achieve. I ask you again, are you prepared?"

I nod and smile, while Apion places his hands on my shoulders as he looks into my eyes.

"Let us see if we can prepare you for life as a wrestler. I can see that Demetrius has faith in you. Give me a few days. I will make a short sea trip and call in a few favors from friends. I will tell them I have a new and exciting find who I need to try out. I will offer a purse or two to those who will agree to a match. I will expect you to win, but I will not give instructions or a signal of when you should move for victory. You will be free to fight to the best of your ability and to build a reputation. You will begin to learn about the excitement of the contest, the drawing of an opponent, the perfecting of your skills in a match. Your timing, your breathing, your movement. All the disciplines that will transform you into a champion for the future.

"And so, it is my turn to ask. Are you prepared to accept the challenge I lay down, Alexander?"

It takes no time to respond. "Yes!" I gasp.

***

I've stopped caring about Dario now. Leon and I walk back along the shoreline toward the town. The sea breeze has blown away the tension and hurt I was feeling. I know my mood has transformed on a promise, but what a promise. Apion wants to start me out on a wrestling career.

I'm always mindful at these times to thank Minerva and my father. I'm sure wherever he is, he will be happy and proud. I keep his memory so close. I don't think he has ever left me.

I question Leon about Apion and the fights he organizes.

"He puts on large contests for enormous crowds. He makes a lot of money, and not just for himself. The wrestlers who sign contracts with him will also do well, and travel far."

"And he's choosing me for this? I can't believe it."

"I don't think I should keep telling you how good you are. I don't want to turn you into another—"

"Dario!"

"Yes, Dario. Wait! Alexander, where are you going?"

Leon's voice trails off behind me as I pick up speed and run toward his house. Dario is standing with Zoe. Trying to touch her hair. I fly back into a rage. Leon's calls for me to slow down have the effect of drawing Zoe and Dario's attention.

"Is he bothering you, Zoe?"

Dario looks at me with surprise. "Bothering? What are you saying?" A look of realization passes across his face. "You think that Zoe is *your* girl?" he laughs.

"Zoe is... is my friend."

"Your friend? Then don't worry, we are all friends together. Zoe and I have been friends long before you blessed Delos with your arrival."

"Alexander," Zoe interrupts, "my mother has invited you in for some dinner with us. Leon, the both of you go inside the house. Dario is just leaving."

"Come on, Alexander," says Leon.

He places his arm around my shoulder and guides me through the courtyard and through the front door of their house. I can hear Dario snigger with contempt as I leave them alone.

"Alexander, are you going to have dinner with us?" Kera smiles. "Thalasso had to take some fish to one of the taverns, so we'll eat a little later. He doesn't return with haste from that place. Sit with us."

It's the first time I've been inside the house. The light flows in from the doorway and two small window spaces that look out over the sea. I can just make out Zoe and Dario still talking to one another.

Why doesn't she just tell him to go away?

"Is your sister alright?" Kera asks Leon.

"Yes, she's fine. Zoe won't fall for his words again."

"I don't like him," I say.

Kera shakes her head. "None of us have ever liked him, Alexander. We had put up with him for Zoe's sake in the past, but she's making better choices these days. Don't worry."

Even with Kera's lack of concern, we all watch to be sure that Zoe is safe. She's telling Dario something that he's not happy to hear. He looks angry as he turns away and walks off toward the harbor. Meanwhile, Zoe steps inside the house with a smile on her face.

"Did you tell him to go away?" asks Kera.

"And stay away," she replies. "I feel better now that I have been able to say it."

I hang my head slightly. "I'm sorry, Zoe. I wanted so much to beat him in the skamma pit today."

Zoe flashes a full smile at me in return. "You have beat him today, just not in the way you expected."

CHAPTER XVI

Another morning of hard work at the harbor has passed. The port is busier than ever as merchants crowd to offer their wares in readiness for the Great Delia. The ships bring in building materials, textiles, spices, and livestock, all to provide for a growing population who will attend and participate in the event. The demand is driving prices higher for the limited supplies. Demetrius has to be more observant than ever and make sure he can secure what he needs. Word about the good business on Delos has reached the surrounding islands.

The military fort is also growing in size. The garrison will double to make sure of Rome's authority over the crowds. Dignitaries will soon arrive from Delphi and other important city-states, and they'll bring their own guards and servants, so space is being cleared where the slave markets will normally take place. It will transform into a small city of tents with its own areas for cooking and washing.

Then there are the old buildings that have been empty for many years. Some islanders intend to offer lodgings to the many visitors who will soon be arriving. New taverns and shops will also open to serve them. Meanwhile, musicians and poets are preparing to provide entertainment, already competing for the best spots to draw an audience and make money.

There is a great, shared excitement on the island. It feels like Delos is the center of the world, just as Uncle Nikos had said.

"Oh, I'm too tired to wrestle today," Leon complains as we make our way along the shore, "and the sea looks so good. Should I go for a swim or a fight? I know what I'd prefer."

"I can't swim, but I'd like to learn," I reply.

"Perfect. I'll tell Demetrius I've been training you when he asks why we're late."

"I don't know. He's expecting us both to work with Dario today."

"Do I look like I care?" Leon smiles. "Swimming is an excellent exercise for your whole body, and it's good fun. We're on Delos. It's the most natural thing to do."

I look down along the coast. The palaestra stands out more than ever against the background of the hills. New blocks of marble and new buildings have increased its size. The sound of hammering echoes out from around its walls. Then I turn and look at the sea. It's calm and lapping against the shingle. A deep blue expanse that salts the air. I feel like it's calling me to escape the heat.

"Oh well, I suppose Dario can run a few extra times around the track until we get there. Can you teach me to swim?"

"I can make a start. Let's go!"

We race to the water's edge and remove our tunics, leaving them lying on a nearby rock. I step into the water. It's warmer than I expected. Leon takes a few more steps and dives forward into water that's deep enough for swimming. I follow him a little more cautiously. I sink myself down in the water to make it look like I'm doing the same, but I'm still steadying myself with my feet on the ground.

"No cheating," Leon laughs, "the sea wants to support you. You can float. You don't need to sink."

He swims back over to me and places a hand behind my back. "Stretch out with your feet and your arms. Pretend you're a starfish stretched out under the sun. I won't let you drop." He supports me as I lie back and allow the water to flow under me. "Now relax. It is a beautiful day. Let Poseidon cradle you like a new baby!"

We both laugh. The water feels wonderful around me. Much better than the baths, and not so crowded. A few others are out enjoying a swim, but it's peaceful and quiet. I can almost feel myself drifting off to sleep when I see Leon standing and waving both his hands at me.

"You're floating," he says.

I suddenly realize he's not holding me up and I panic, quickly splashing and disappearing below the surface. I gulp in some of the sea before finding the ground with my feet and standing straight up, brushing the water from my eyes.

"You are doing well. You've learned to swim underwater already." He laughs. "Now let's try to learn the proper way."

Leon is an excellent teacher. It doesn't take him long to give me the confidence to push off of the ground and kick my legs out behind me, stretching with my arms to pull myself forward.

At first, I'm just splashing for the smallest moments, but then I start to go a little further, then a little further still. My confidence starts to build as Leon encourages me, and before I know it, he's left me to practice on my own. He pushes further out to sea. He's a strong swimmer who has grown up so near to the sea that it's in his nature, just like his father, and my father too.

My opinion about Leon has changed over the time we've been friends. People often talk down to him because he's not been so good at wrestling in the skamma, but he's good at so many other things, and so many people trust him to do a good job; like his father does when he's mending nets, or when Demetrius relies on his initiative at the harbor. I have a lot to thank my good friend for.

I concentrate on trying to improve my efforts. The water is crystal clear all around me. It's just as well, as there are plenty of sea monsters believed to swim around these shores, but thankfully there are none today. It's only Leon that kicks the water up over my head as he swims up to me.

"Hey!" I shout as I splash water back at him and a contest begins to throw as much of the Aegean over one another as we can.

We lose track of time, but Delos has that effect on you. It seems like we've been laughing and talking, splashing and swimming for ages, when I spy a recognizable figure standing in the distance, glowering in our direction.

"That's Demetrius. We better get going," I say.

We rush to collect our clothes and resume our journey to the palaestra. Demetrius turns and walks ahead of us. He knows full well that we've seen him and that we'll follow on to offer our apologies for being late.

Walking quicker than normal, we soon reach the palaestra. It rises in front of us and looks magnificent as we approach it from the shore. It has become a maze of buildings with paths and shaded areas for people to gather, the oil room and bathhouse are complete, and both now sit within a small area that also has a dedicated dressing room and dust room. Most of the work remaining is for a place for the athletes to train and warm up for the contests, plus decorative work to make it more impressive for the spectators.

A little higher up the hill, the favored slab that Demetrius likes to sit on to face the sea is still there. Now it sits beside small benches and fresh-planted shrubs and young trees. It reminds me of Gaius's garden. This is where we will meet to discuss philosophy and develop our minds toward living a more virtuous life. Demetrius insists that it is the most vital part of our training.

I can see Tigranes working at placing a small stone table between the seats. I wave to him, and he returns the wave as Dario appears.

"Remember, he's a slave, Alexander," Dario sneers. "It's not good to be too friendly. You might need to punish him one day."

"Tigranes is no longer a slave. He is a free man who continues living at my uncle's house."

"He still acts like a slave."

"He acts like a friend."

Dario shrugs his shoulders. "You call him what you like, I'll call him what I like." He turns to Leon. "Demetrius wants to speak to you before we wrestle. You've to go see him now, alone," he insists.

I'm still raging at the mere presence of Dario. I feel hot again even after the cooling swim. I decide to join Tigranes to stop myself from getting into a fight. Unfortunately, Dario continues to follow me, even though I'm sure he realizes he's annoying me.

"I'm sorry for you, Alexander."

I keep my head down as I walk up toward Tigranes. I just don't want to even speak to Dario, but it doesn't put him off from wanting to speak to me.

"You probably thought that life was very easy here on Delos. A beautiful island, with many beautiful girls, and you, a handsome young Roman, but then you had to pick Zoe."

I stop in my tracks and turn. "What did you say?"

Dario smiles. He does so because he knows he's got my attention. "We are friends, aren't we?" he replies. "Or at least we are fellow wrestlers under the leadership of Demetrius. That must count for something?"

"We meet to train with one another. Only because Demetrius insists that we will both improve. Friendship is based on shared virtue and values. I don't know you well enough to judge you yet, and neither do you know me. There is such a thing as a terrible friend."

Dario shakes his head. "Don't tell me you actually listen to those stories that Demetrius tells?"

"You think they're unimportant?"

"The only thing they've taught me is how to nod in the right places, to make it look like I'm agreeing, but when he tells me how to stretch someone's foot to near breaking point, or how to apply a choke on an opponent, then I listen."

"You need to listen to all of his training if you want to be a champion."

Dario laughs in my face. "I have toured around every island, breaking and bruising the bones of those who spent too long with their heads in the clouds. Maybe the only thing it helps is their understanding of how I defeated them. You use your head for blocking an attack, that's all. Not too much, mind you. It will waste your good looks."

His sniggering look makes me turn away. Tigranes stands up from his work. He looks just as uncomfortable in Dario's presence as I feel. I get the impression that they already know one another well, from when Tigranes was still a slave.

"The garden is looking beautiful, Tigranes."

"A garden with a view. It's the favorite place for Demetrius. He'll sit here whether bright sunshine or storm. We kept his favorite place to rest. I think he would be angry if we swapped it with a bench."

"He better not think I'll be sitting up here when the wind is raging and the rain is lashing," Dario complains.

Tigranes shrugs and directs a frustrated look in my direction. "I better get on with other work; we're still finishing the spectators' area. You'll have quite a crowd for your contest. Many people will come to see you win."

He directs a defiant look toward Dario as he begins to walk back down to the palaestra.

I sit down on one of the new stone benches. Today is calm and bright, but there's always at least a small breeze that arrives from the sea. The sounds of the harbor and town are distant, but enough to let you know that Delos is alive with people going about their business. I could sit here for hours and enjoy the natural world around me, but Dario continues to cause a threatening air. I can hear him planning his next insult before it emerges from his lips.

He walks around, nudging blocks of stone on a new wall. Eventually, one of the heavy stones gives way and cracks as it lands on the ground.

Dario sniggers. "Did you build this wall? It's not very strong. It could have caused a nasty accident. I'll be warning Demetrius that he has to make sure that everything is safe."

"Leave it alone. You pushed it down."

"Do you plan to stop me, Alexander?"

A silence falls. I want to fight him. If we were in the Subura, he wouldn't win. My father would give me the signal and I would pounce. He would land so hard that he wouldn't want to stand and face me again.

What should I do, Father?

Dario keeps walking around the circle of the garden, looking to make more mischief. When nothing more gives way to his feet, he begins to lean with his weight, cracking a branch from a young sapling.

"Stop it, Dario. Demetrius will not be happy."

"Demetrius won't know. Not unless someone tells him. But you're right, I'm only playing games with you. Demetrius will see that I'm just impressing my authority. He needs a winner for the Great Delia, and you have already lost a fight to me. Stoicism tells us you must practice and prepare for outcomes that you would not want to happen. You see, I pay attention sometimes."

"One win doesn't make you the champion."

"No, but it puts you at a disadvantage. I have already scored the first point. Now you have to fight with that defeat in your mind, and I know your weakness." Dario stands over me, looking down. "Does it annoy you to know that Zoe and I were together? Does it make you fill with rage when you think of how I may have held her? Her kisses are sweet and passionate, but maybe you don't know that yet."

He's not wrong. He can fire me up into anger with simple words. He steps out of range as I stand and try to slap him across his jaw.

"Hey, you two. What's going on?" Apion is striding toward us. "Whatever it is, keep your fighting for the skamma. Demetrius is not too old to take on either of you and win. Now calm down."

"Yes, calm down, Alexander," Dario laughs.

"Get down to the palaestra, Dario," Apion orders. "Your training should have started ages ago."

"It was Alexander and Leon who kept us late."

"Go. Now."

Apion might not have been a fighter himself, but he's threatening in his own way. I'm sure he's used to dealing with all sorts when running his contests. A mere wrestler is below his level of authority.

Dario shrugs once more and glances against one last stone to knock it to the ground.

"Watch what you're doing," says Apion.

"It was an accident," he smirks as he walks away.

Apion sits on the stone bench opposite me and invites me to be seated once again, facing him. I feel ashamed. I need to keep myself under control. Apion studies me, and I notice more about his clothes. Indigo is the dominant color. A dye that comes from a far-off land. You need wealth to afford the robes and tunics that are colored with it.

"You two were fighting over a girl?"

I nod and look away out to sea. I'm still having trouble settling down with the thoughts of Dario and Zoe running through my head.

"Demetrius would be unhappy to see you lose control with such ease. I'm sure he has spent hours telling you that control is all important. You must understand what he means and not just allow his words to land on deaf ears."

"Like seeds falling on the path and being trampled?"

"You could put it that way." Apion pauses. "You must give Dario credit for how he controls his situation. You've met a handful of times, and like it or not, he already has ideas of how to control you as a prospective competitor. Who's the girl?"

"Zoe. Leon's sister."

"Ah yes, I've seen her. She is very beautiful."

"Dario doesn't respect her. He mistreated her when they were together."

"And I can tell you for certain, he will have no more respect knowing she is with you. When he walked off the ship in Delos harbor, he couldn't have guessed that someone had taken his place so perfectly. A new prospect for Demetrius, a new boyfriend for Zoe, and a Roman, not a Greek."

"I was born before my family arrived in Rome."

Apion laughs. "You will need to live here for fifty years before people will stop calling you a Roman."

"I suppose so."

"Dario is a good wrestler. He will have a wonderful career. *If* he follows my advice and guidance. It's only taken him a few short days to work out how to win back some of what he might have lost. Every time you stand to strike him in anger, then he has won. If you blackened his eye today, do you think that Demetrius would have applauded?"

"No." I hang my head.

"No," Apion echoes. "I think you understand the challenges ahead, and that is why I'm here to talk to you. I am entering you into a small contest on Mykonos. Eight wrestlers, including you. You will fight three rounds if you survive to the end, and there will be a purse each for the finalists. You need this experience, before the Great Delia. Demetrius will allow it as long as you agree to take part."

"Of course I'll take part. Why wouldn't I?"

"Demetrius doesn't always trust me as much as he might. I don't favor any one wrestler over another. I will take you to the contest with a good heart for your victory, but my head will tell me where to place my wager on the winner. If you get badly beaten up or suffer a break, then your chance to compete in the Great Delia may be over. It is your decision to make."

"Will Dario be at the contest?"

"No. He will remain here. He's had many fights over the past few months. It is recovery that he requires right now. Dario just needs a few warm baths and some time throwing Leon about the skamma pit to keep his fitness level where it should be."

"I hate that he doesn't give Leon a chance."

"And that is up to Leon to control," Apion sighs. "Listen to me. I can see what others have seen. You are an outstanding athlete. You are strong and agile, with the stamina to survive a hard fight, but it is your own mind that fights against you sometimes. You must focus on being the best version of yourself and not be driven by anger, jealousy, or frustration. If you can combat those enemies, then you'll find your entire life will improve. I promise you. Set that example for others to follow and then, in turn, they will make their own improvements."

"I understand. I'll calm down. I want to be the best person I can be. In and out of the skamma."

"Good. There is an enormous world out beyond these islands. Sights and sounds you could never imagine. Your experience of Rome will have prepared you for some of what lies ahead. Before long, you will fight in the shadow of the remains of the Colossus on Rhodes, or against the backdrop of the Great Pyramid of Giza. Then you might even return to Rome to earn the favor of Emperor Marcus Aurelius. Are you ready for the life that Apion can show you and which you alone must seize?"

A wide smile stretches across his face. His belief in me settles my mind. "My father always said there's a day that childhood quietly leaves. You cross over into a world where you have to embrace responsibility with a sense of duty and purpose. He said challenges were only opportunities to grow and develop who we are."

"Your father was wise, and he knew the day was nearing for you when he gave you this advice. I think you are ready to take on the world. Should we tell Demetrius?"

I nod and smile, and we both rise and walk the short slope down to the palaestra.

I stop for a moment and Apion stops alongside me. "There is just one thing," I say to him.

"Oh? And what is that?"

"I don't seem to get along with the sea very well from aboard a ship. Can we go early so I can recover from the tempest that will be inside my stomach?"

Apion laughs and slaps me on the back.

Demetrius is busy examining some of the completed work, while Dario and Leon are working out in the exercise area. They are playing a ball game and there seems to be good spirits between them. Maybe Apion is right about me not picking fights on behalf of others. In fact, I'm sure he is right.

Demetrius looks over as we draw nearer. "It is too late for any sparring today. Did you enjoy your swim, Alexander?"

"Yes, Demetrius." I shuffle on my feet.

"Good. It's excellent exercise. Keep it up now you know how but find time that is not normally spent here."

"He spends all his waking time at the palaestra," says Apion. "He's even rebuilt half of it for you."

"He's played his part. I'll grant him that."

It looks like Demetrius might smile, but you can see him cautioning himself against expressing humor. "Has Apion told you about the contest on Mykonos?"

"Yes, I want to do it. I'm ready."

"Let me tell you something about Apion, then. He organizes entertainment and sport. This time it's a wrestling contest, tomorrow he might look for gladiators to face a pride of lions in an amphitheater. Be sure you know what you are getting into before he leads you there."

"I won't feed him to the lions. Well, maybe when he's too old," Apion laughs.

"If I'm too old, then you will be older," I smile.

"That is a fair and wise assessment, you have my word, there will be no lions involved."

"When do we go?"

"Three days. Time to get some last-minute training. We'll stay on the island for one night either side of the contest. You'll be back on Delos in good time."

"Without injury, I hope," Demetrius adds. "Dario! Leon!"

Both come running into the palaestra on the command from Demetrius. It's never a good idea to dawdle when he's calling for your presence. They're both still catching their breath from their game when they arrive.

"We'll change our training for the next few days. Alexander is going to compete in a contest on Mykonos. We must do all we can to make sure that he represents Delos to the best of his ability. Tell me, Apion, has Dario fought some of the other contestants before?"

"Yes, two or three. He fared well against them."

"Then, Dario, you will help your fellow student with any knowledge you have. Tell him what to watch out for, which attacks or defense they favor. I'll expect you to recount your fights with them, and how you won your points. You will act out the role of the opponent. You will offer how he can beat you and let him practice the moves that he needs to improve."

"But..." Dario protests, while Demetrius returns an icy stare.

"Leon, you'll work on improving his fitness. At the harbor, on the track, or in the sea. Push him hard. Make sure he won't fail from lack of effort."

"You can rely on me, Demetrius," Leon grins. "We'll start with a run up and down Mount Kynthos at dawn."

"Dawn?" I ask.

"You can always start earlier if you want," Leon replies.

"No, it's alright."

Apion booms with laughter. "Good. Let's work together. It is good for the body, the mind, and the soul."

"And your purse," Demetrius reminds him. "My first contest was on Mykonos. I'm sorry I won't be able to see you compete, but there's much still to do for the Great Delia. I'm sure you will return triumphant, and your fellow students will be eager to hear your tales of victory."

Demetrius is careful with his words. We all know his meaning. None of us are more important than the other. I lock eyes and clasp a hand with Dario; we both understand that for the next few days at least, it is time to call a truce.

CHAPTER XVII

ELENA

My son is facing his first real contest.

I can't help but think of Marcus looking down on us. He would be proud and I'm sure he would speak about nothing else. I would have ended up telling him off for giving Alexander too big a head.

But I am just as pleased.

The garden of my brother's home is a mass of color. Hibiscus, poppies, and his favored roses are all reaching out for their share of the sunlight amongst the oleander, lavender, and rosemary. The olive tree is in full bloom, providing shade and leafy branches for the small birds to rest on.

The chaffinches are here as usual—including the one that's my favorite—braver than the rest, or less timid, at least. He thinks about hopping onto my hand for some crumbs, but he's not quite ready. He calls to the other birds whenever there's food to be shared. He looks after his family. I'm sure it's Marcus keeping an eye on Alexander and me. A private thought that I quietly hold on to, but it brings me comfort on certain days to think the gods granted him a way to be with me on Delos.

I take in the scented air as I walk toward the entrance of the courtyard. A view of the sea lies straight ahead. The waves are calm. It will be an easy crossing to Mykonos later today, and I hope old friends will welcome us when they find out we're there.

I turn around to see Nikos climbing the path toward me. He waves and greets me with his well-known smile. It's still early, but he's already been down to the harbor to check that his ship will be ready for sailing.

"It's another fine morning," he calls as he approaches.

"I'm glad," I reply. "We want to get Alexander across the water without too many problems."

"It will be a pleasant voyage, I assure you. He won't need to test his sea legs today."

"Does Demetrius still have him working?"

"Yes, until the last moment. He's spared training today, but that's all. There is still much to be done in time for the festival. But don't worry about that, for I bring interesting news. A rumor is circulating about a certain Gaius from Rome attending our games."

"Gaius?"

"Yes." Nikos nods. "Demetrius sent a private message without even telling *me*, his oldest friend. He plans to send the winner of the Great Delia games to fight against a contender from Alexander's old palaestra."

"Does Alexander know?"

"I'm surprised you didn't hear him calling out from the harbor. The response from Gaius just arrived by ship this morning."

"Maybe Gaius is regretting his decision to reject Alexander."

"Maybe. I think it's more likely unfinished business between Demetrius and Gaius. They still want to compete against one another, the old fools! But it's an excellent incentive for Alexander, to put in the work and earn the chance to prove his worth."

"Thank you, Nikos."

"What did I do?" he laughs.

"You brought us here, to a new life and new opportunities. I'll always be in your debt for that."

"There is no debt to be paid. I'm enjoying life with you and Alexander in my house. I'm even starting to take an interest in wrestling, but don't tell Demetrius. He thinks I've been interested from all the years of listening to his tales." He fakes a yawn. "That reminds me, I should have a short sleep before we sail, so I'm ready to steer the ship."

He grins and strides into the house, scattering the chaffinches into the tree. I look up to find my favorite small companion looking back down at me.

"Are you happy now, Marcus?" I smile.

I take one last look at the sea and then my eye catches Dario's mother, Maria. She's climbing the path to our house. I step back out of sight in the hope she hasn't seen me, but it doesn't take long for her to be peering into the courtyard.

"Elena, may I come into your house? I owe you an apology."

"Oh, Maria. I didn't see you there." I think she knows I'm lying. "Please come in, you are welcome here."

She steps forward and kisses me on each cheek while holding me by my shoulders.

"I am sorry, Elena. It was a shock to see you when I arrived back on Delos. I never thought I would see you again, and then there was all the excitement of Dario coming home to his followers."

I'm caught off balance by Maria's change of mood. I thought she hated me, but I can't turn down an offer to make peace. I return the gesture of greeting.

"Thank you for coming to see me. Would you like something to eat or drink? We can sit here in the garden in the shade of the trees."

"Would you mind if we go inside your house?" she replies. "Much of what I have to say needs to be spoken in private, and the sea breeze on Delos often carries our words along to the flapping ears of neighbors."

"Of course."

I smile because it's true. Delos is a place where everyone knows everyone. It's hard to keep secrets from those who live on the other side of the small walls.

Maria follows me into the main room of my brother's house. I can see her eyes spinning around and taking in the comfort that I've become used to in recent weeks. Nikos is one of the wealthiest islanders. I don't know what Maria's house looks like, but I'm sure that Nikos lives a far more comfortable life.

"Your brother has expensive taste. You must feel very lucky to be living in this place."

"I do. It's very different to the life I lived in Rome. I appreciate my change in circumstances."

"But Rome must have been exciting. Delos is such a quiet place in comparison."

"It was at first, but we had to find somewhere to live, and our accommodation was small and poor. We had each other, but life was hard from the very beginning. We had a baby to take care of. Marcus was quick to find work, but it meant that I spent a lot of time alone. Many Romans can speak Greek, so language wasn't a problem, but people in the city look after themselves first. It's hard to find people to befriend and rely on."

Maria gives a sympathetic nod. "I'm sorry that you had to flee. You left in the night as if you were racing to escape the sunrise itself. I want you to know that I understand, Elena. I would also have run from the wrath of Apollo for committing such a sin. Even if it was unintentional."

"I carried Alexander inside me for only eight months. We had planned to leave the island in time, but the Fates had other plans. Clotho, the spinner, is the one that casts the first thread of life, and only she can choose the moment of birth. The other gods are not her masters."

"Poor Elena. The choices of the gods provide both a blessing and a curse on the mortals who live under their rule. I know you are a good person. You have a kind heart. I know that you do not wish misfortune on others. Please hear my plea, for I have not shared your secret all these years, and in some manner, I have taken on responsibility for the sin."

"You were not involved, Maria. We only passed each other in the street when Marcus and I were making for the harbor. That is not a sacrilege."

"But I didn't just pass you and Marcus. You were carrying a bundle in your arms, a precious cargo for your journey—your newborn child. I witnessed the event and yet I said nothing. I chose to remain silent. Would Apollo choose to punish me for aiding your escape?"

The room falls silent. I can't work out why Maria even wants to discuss my breach of a law that wasn't set by Apollo, but by people who rule, alleging their authority through him.

"I'm sorry you had to witness the events of that night, Maria. We had been friends for so many years. I wouldn't want to involve you."

"We *had* been friends. I was with Marcus before you. I was once the focus of his affection, and you knew that. I had no reason to protect you at that time, but if I revealed your crime, then I might also have suffered from accusations of helping you. My first silence was for my own self-preservation."

"I thought the trouble had already passed between us. You had taken a husband by then, and Dario was already a small child. You had a life on Delos with a family to support you. What I would have given for that? I felt so alone with the choice I had to make. Maybe Apollo saw my exile as a fitting punishment for my crime and left me alone?"

"And maybe that's true, but yet you choose to return. Have you any idea the trouble that could cause, if your secret were to be revealed? All the misfortunes to befall every soul on Delos would point to the time you set foot back on the island."

"But it is a secret," I protest. "Those that sailed away with us are long gone. A Roman patrol ship with its crew, you and my brother are the only ones who know."

"Yes." Maria lets her response hang in the air. "So please let that show you that even after our falling out, I remembered an earlier time in our lives. Those were happy days. Know that while I asked forgiveness for myself, I also lit a candle and prayed for a good life for you, Marcus, and your child."

"I thank you, Maria. I appreciate what you have done for me. If there's a way that I can repay you for your kindness, then I will."

"I cannot accept anything from you. I only need to know that my life will not suffer as a result of keeping the secret. I am proud of Dario, just as you are proud of Alexander. He is doing well. It has made me happy to see him find success in the skamma. He has worked and trained hard for his achievements. The prizes he shares with me have led to a better life for both of us. In recent days, I've become used to feeling that the gods had forgiven me for not confessing what I knew. We are fools if we think that they need to be spoken to, like the priests, to know what is in our hearts."

"I'm sure Dario will continue to be a wonderful son for you. Alexander has told me how fine a wrestler he is. He has been helping my son at the palaestra to prepare for a contest on Mykonos."

"I know. Dario has also been speaking about Alexander. I know that he can appear full of confidence, and some might even say arrogant, but he looks after me all the same. He is concerned about providing a good life for both of us. Like Alexander, he lost his father to war.

"First, Demetrius taught him, then Apion took him under his wing, just like they are doing now with Alexander. It is making Dario fearful for his future. He did not expect to meet a formidable competitor on his own island."

"But Alexander hasn't beaten him," I assure her. "He says that Dario is a tough opponent. He says he is fast and strong."

"Dario knows that it is only a matter of time. *That* is the secret that he holds. He knows that one day Alexander will surpass him. It is a knowledge that can only come from the close quarters of a fight. Dario will never reveal it to anyone other than me. He is worried about his success falling under the shadow of your son's. And now I wonder if this is my punishment. To be shown a glimpse of what might have been, only for it to be snatched away by the baby that murmured in your arms as you sought to outrun the dawn."

"Maria, there's an opportunity for both to succeed. They do not place each other in the shade by striving to be the best they can be. I ask you to not look for the wrath of the gods where it doesn't exist. If my life had gone ahead as planned, then Alexander and Dario would have grown as friends. They would have trained with Demetrius together from being young boys. They would have helped each other to success."

"Do you really think that Alexander wishes success for my son? That thought brings me comfort."

"I'm sure he does. Alexander would not wish to harm Dario's ambitions. The fight only lasts in the skamma until they score the winning point. Alexander will not see Dario's success as a challenge to his own."

"Thank you, Elena, your words make me feel better. I'm glad to have had this conversation with you. I better not take up any more of your time. You'll have a fine evening on Mykonos ahead of you."

"Yes." I sigh with a little relief. "Everyone says it's the last preparation Alexander will need before taking part in the Great Delia. My brother says that the champion of our games will earn a fight in Rome, before Emperor Marcus Aurelius."

"Then it's good to know that you and Alexander understand the need to repay the debt between us. It will be a fine gesture to *allow* Dario to win the contest and let *him* fight in Rome."

"What? That's not what I meant."

"I realize it is only if they face each other in the final round of the contest. I'm sure the appreciation you will offer and the help that Alexander can give, will help lay that sin of many years ago to rest. Dario should be the contender from Delos. It is his rightful place. A different outcome might mean I'd have to release myself of the burden I've carried for many years. Believe me, I wouldn't be happy with myself, but I have to look after the interests of my son. I've already done what I can for yours. I bid you a safe and pleasant journey to Mykonos."

In an instant, Maria turns and leaves without looking back. She doesn't allow a response. I'm angry with myself. *What did I say?* I'm stepping angrily around the room, my fists clenched, when Selene appears.

"Is everything alright mistress?"

"No, Selene. I've made a terrible mistake. I've had a conversation that I shouldn't have allowed."

"I was worried, mistress, when I saw you bringing Maria into the house. She has a reputation for mischief-making. Can I pour you some wine or run water for a bath? Your brother is snoring loud enough to shake the island. I think you have some time to prepare for your journey."

"Yes, Selene, thank you. I need to calm myself and clear my thoughts. There is something that has hung over me since I returned here. Maria knows she has the power over my situation. She has the key to unlock Pandora's box."

"Mistress?"

"Forgive me, Selene. Maria can ruin the lives of all in this household and our entire existence on Delos. I can't let that happen, but for now, I don't know how to escape her trap."

"Ask the gods for help, mistress. There are so many shrines and temples here. At least one of them may help you."

"Unfortunately, I think the gods may be the last ones to help me."

***

Nikos didn't need to know where the sun was to know the time of day. He was able to wake and be ready to leave at just the right moment. As he comes back into the room, it must've been clear that I'm upset.

"What's wrong, Elena? You look annoyed about something."

"I think I'm just nervous for Alexander. This is his first proper contest, after all."

"He will be fine," he says. "Selene told me we had a visitor when I slept?"

"Yes, Maria." My voice wavers. "She came to wish good luck to Alexander."

"Maria? She must be mellowing with the years., but we'll take her effort to support us as a good sign." He looks around the room. "Did she steal anything? I'll have Selene check for the most expensive items. Now it's time to go."

We step out into the courtyard where Tigranes is waiting with a bundle of my belongings wrapped up for the journey. The talk between the three of us distracts me a little, but the chatter returns to the Great Delia. How the palaestra is nearing completion, and rumors of the wrestlers who will be accepting the invitation to take part. It sounds like there will be many with an excellent reputation. Perhaps the chances of Alexander and Dario meeting are slim enough.

My worries don't leave me. What if Dario loses early and Alexander goes on to win? Will Maria remain silent, or will she still seek to hurt us?

We arrive at the harbor and my brother holds me back, allowing Tigranes to carry on toward the ship.

"I don't know what she said to you, Elena, but do not worry about Maria."

"She still remembers that night, Nikos."

"And she has said nothing in all the years between then and now. It would be a risk for her to reveal what she knows now. Whatever she wants from you, we can come to an arrangement. People always have a price. If I've not learned that in all my years, then I've learned nothing. Now settle yourself. We have a pleasant sailing ahead and will be on Mykonos in good time to share food and wine with old friends and family—and speaking of family—the young ones have spotted us."

Alexander and Zoe race over with bright smiles and an infectious joy that dissolves my anxiety. I'm happy to see my son so excited.

"It's almost time to leave," says Alexander. "I thought you might be too late."

"Late for my own ship?" Nikos grins. "It doesn't move unless I'm on board."

"Yes, Uncle, and then it moves too much and makes me sick."

"Not today, I promise you," Nikos replies. "The sea is like glass; you will stand as a young warrior on the prow as we glide into port. Like a hero, returning from an epic quest."

Alexander puffs out his chest in response and Zoe pretends to gaze with adoration upon him. They make a beautiful couple. I'm so happy they've found one another.

"Well, I suppose I better get myself on the water," says Nikos. As he starts to board, he nods to me. "We should let the lovers say their goodbyes for the moment. We'll bring him back in good shape. Don't worry, Zoe."

I follow Nikos to the deck. There is something magical about sailing, even over a short distance like today. I feel as if I'm suddenly in a different place, even though we are still in the dock. The crew have already prepared a place for me to sit, and they fuss around me as an honored guest. This is not the hard sea voyages they are used to making. It's a simple task to complete with some time to spend on Mykonos before we return. So, all are in good spirits. All, except for me.

Secrets are a weakness we place upon ourselves. Hiding the truth can cause pain within our hearts and allow others to take advantage of our situation. Maria can control me without lifting a finger because the secret we share gives her strength. I have to have the courage for myself, but what would it do to the people I love? Would the island turn against us? I can't answer these questions now.

There is maybe one chance of escape. Alexander can't meet Dario in any of the matches at the Great Delia. I don't know enough about arranging the fights, but I'm traveling to Mykonos with someone who does. Perhaps Apion can help me? Yet I can't tell him why.

He is next to embark and offers a polite bow and a smile as he takes his place beside me.

"I'm looking forward to this. Alexander will do well. I'm sure of it."

"He's excited. Do you know who he will face first?"

"No, they choose an opponent at random. They draw a token inscribed with the other wrestler's mark. That is always the way with these contests."

"So, you can't arrange a fight in advance?"

"I won't pretend that it doesn't happen. Sometimes they will fix a certain match. Especially if there's a demand from those who will place high wagers, but not for something like this. It's better for Alexander to not know what's ahead and for him to be able to judge an opponent in the skamma and not out of it. Why do you ask?"

"Oh, nothing. I'm just learning about how the contests take place."

"You'll enjoy it." Apion smiles. "I will wager before long, you'll be calling out for Alexander to *kill him*, or *break his arm*."

"I would never do that." I blush.

"Forgive me, I've seen it so many times. Often the crowd is more aggressive than the contenders. So, where is our champion?"

Apion rises to his feet and bellows from the deck. "Alexander, it is time to leave!"

"Make ready to sail!" calls Nikos.

Alexander grabs Zoe for one last hug, before racing over to leap onto the deck. A friendly crowd waves us off and raises a cheer as the ship pulls away into the sea.

"You smell of Jasmine," I say as Alexander draws closer.

"I'm sorry." He smiles with a little embarrassment. "I wish Zoe could have come with us."

"I think it is better to not have the distraction," says Apion. "I need you to concentrate on returning to her as a champion."

"I will," he says.

He rushes to the side of the ship for one last wave, but I watch his shoulders and his mood sink as Dario appears beside Zoe at the dockside. He makes a show of placing an arm around Zoe as he waves back at Alexander.

Dario's just as bad as his mother.

Alexander watches Zoe pull herself free, but he can see that Dario is being persistent as the harbor begins to fall further behind us. I can see Alexander clench his fists. Fortunately, Apion sees it as well and brings him back from the edge before he jumps into the ocean and tries to swim for shore.

"Just wait until I get back," says Alexander in disgust as Apion returns with him to sit beside me.

"You can trust Zoe. Dario is nothing to her," I reassure him.

"Don't let him under your skin," offers Apion. "If you do, he will always beat you."

I take Apion's advice in, along with Alexander. I'm letting Maria get under my skin and I know it. Marcus would always say that threats only harm us if our minds allow it. There are maybe things we cannot change, but we can face adversity with courage and wisdom.

"Can I have some time with my son?" I say to Apion as Alexander slumps down beside me.

"Of course, dear lady."

Apion pats Alexander on the shoulder before joining Nikos and leaving us alone.

"Why did he have to do that, Mother? I thought there was a sense of peace between Dario and me."

"I think you know that Dario only seeks to annoy you. He doesn't believe he will beat you in the end."

"I don't believe that."

"His mother said as much to me this morning. She expressed his fears on his behalf."

"So why does he try to intimidate me?"

"Control. You are always telling me how Demetrius teaches you about it."

"Yes, but—"

"Am I wrong?"

"No, I suppose not. I know what you mean."

"Trust Zoe and try to keep your mind clear. I think you take that part of your nature from me. I felt the same way earlier today. Dario's mother caused just as much of a rage inside me this morning, but it's wasteful to dwell on what might be or what might have been. None of it should be important when we step forward in life's next adventure, or in your case, into the skamma on Mykonos."

"You know that Dario and Zoe were together once?"

"Yes, and I know that she is much happier with you. And, of course, Maria was your father's first love. So, you see, your father and I, you and Zoe. We've both caused trouble for this one family without even trying. What you see as your own good fortune can draw out envy and jealousy from others. Even if you live the best and most noble life you can, it can still affect those who do not feel they've received their share of the same opportunities. You will survive these conflicts as long as you keep your composure and your humility, and don't forget courage and wisdom. Do these things and you will stay in control of anything you face in life."

"I understand. I can feel Father standing by my shoulder. I can hear his words as well." He pauses. "How did you and Father meet? There's so much about your life on Delos I don't know. You've never really spoken about it."

I take a look around, and as Nikos had promised, the sea is like glass. The gulls travel alongside, believing that all ships carry a morsel or two for feeding. Alexander sits waiting for my response.

"Yes, we have some time to pass. So, I should tell you the story that will live with me always."

CHAPTER XVIII

ELENA

"I will never forget that day, for many reasons. It started off the same way as any other. I turned up to work at a kapeleion that used to sit near the harbor, where they served the best Thasian wine. It was the first thing I looked for when we arrived back on Delos, but I saw that it is long gone. The owners were old, even back all those years ago. They've passed now, and so has their business.

"But back then it was very busy. It was the first place that many would head for when they left the ships with their hard-earned pay. The Roman fort was also nearby, and many of the garrison would come in to drink and even eat every now and again. It was a strange mixture of people who had reasons to mistrust one another, but the atmosphere was always good. People tended to mind their own business, and just indulge in tall tales and coarse humor.

"I never had an unpleasant experience working among them. The owners commanded respect, and customers had to show good manners if they didn't want their visit to be brief. The young girls who worked there, like me, were safe from harm. Trouble would happen in other places, but not in the kapeleion.

"Regular customers would have a favorite table. It wasn't hard to see that deals and trades were being made in the darker corners that sat furthest away from the Romans. There were a small group of local islanders who frequented these seats, one of whom was Jason, the son of Demetrius."

"Demetrius has a—"

I held up a finger to stop his question. There would be time for that later.

"Jason wasn't like his father. For a start, he never took an interest in wrestling. He had learned something from his father's attempts to train him, but he didn't have the discipline to practice. Demetrius, I'll say, handled very stoically his son's failure to follow in his footsteps. He didn't allow time to dwell on disappointment, and instead, he created opportunities for Jason to learn the skills of the merchant. How to negotiate the best price and the best quality in trades, how to know what buyers wanted and just the right time to sell, and how to build a network of contacts for information and knowledge.

"In this area, Jason did very well. He enjoyed the life and the thrill of barter and making profits. He was a charming person to speak with, always smiling. I think he must have got that trait from his mother.

"For a while, it looked like Demetrius would be able to stop working and dedicate his time to restoring the palaestra. Everything appeared to be working out for his family.

"But Jason wasn't reliable. I could see it most days when he arrived at his table. He would have coins to risk on dice games, which he loved to play. Living your life on the chance roll of the dice is not a good way to give yourself a firm foundation to build on. Sometimes he won, but often he lost. Those days wiped out his profits as well as his charming nature.

"It's a story as old as time itself, but his losses continued even when his purse was empty. He started gambling with favors and promises to pay. The people who allowed such terms began to gather like moths around the flame. All the workers could see that the company he was keeping was not the sort that Demetrius would approve of. Not that Jason's father ever frequented our premises, but you know Demetrius, he would have known what was going on.

"And that is where your father enters the story. He was just another customer at first. He stood out because he was always polite, and he never drank as much as some of the others. He was very handsome—I can't deny thinking that. Me and all the other girls thought so, but it was Maria who he fell for first. For many months, he was still just another customer. He was part of a regular crowd, and we would only speak in passing when he was ordering food or wine.

"Some days he would be out at sea on patrol, others he would oversee activity at the harbor. It was his job to check that Rome received its share of the profits from the goods that were landed and sold. That's how Rome makes money from its empire. The garrison fort overlooks the harbor to remind us of all of Roman authority and our required tributes to the city.

"Demetrius and your father struck up a wonderful friendship from the start. Marcus wasn't a wrestler, but he loved the sport. He would look around the palaestra some days. Walk around the ruins and imagine what it must have looked like in past times. He would often meet with Demetrius there, just to listen to his tales and discuss philosophy. In those days, we lived under the rule of Caesar Antoninus Pius. His time in power was just and fair, and although he never promoted Stoicism like Marcus Aurelius does now, I think most people would say the old ruler adhered to the same principles.

"What I'm really saying is that your father had a lot of respect for Demetrius and valued him as a genuine friend. He knew that Demetrius loved his son and had placed a lot of faith in him. So, it troubled Marcus when he could see across the kapeleion and view the company that Jason was starting to keep.

"There were times he spoke to Jason, taking him aside to give him words of wisdom. I think it worked, to begin with, but as Jason's debts rose, his willingness to listen fell. If Marcus tried to approach him while in the company of his new friends, Jason would often hurl insults. Some Romans would have thrown him in prison for that alone, but Jason could rely on the fact that your father was a good man who wouldn't do such a thing. Jason took advantage of this to appear tough in front of the crowds. Your father would just shake his head and return to his table. He could tolerate the insults. What he couldn't tolerate was the name Jason was bringing on Demetrius.

"Weeks passed, Maria was still with Marcus, Jason was getting worse, but life on the island kept going at its slow pace without too much disruption. It was a beautiful morning, and I had started work early to help open up the kapeleion. We knew several ships would arrive that morning and we would be busy by the middle of the day. I was sweeping dust away from the entrance when Marcus surprised me. *Come this way,* was all he said. He took the broom from my hand and led me around the corner of the building into a small lane out of sight from everyone on the main street. It scared me. I thought I had done something wrong, but Marcus was quick to calm me down.

"'Elena, I need your help,' he said. 'It's important. I want to save someone from a terrible fate, and I want to help a worthy friend, but I need you to aid me.'

"I asked him what I could do to help him and he told me Jason was in trouble. It didn't surprise me. He held out some coins that he said were fake, with nothing more than a thin silver covering, something criminals used in trades and which were spreading across the islands.

"I asked him if he thought Jason was behind it. He said others were responsible for making the coins, but he was sure they had persuaded Jason to help with the distribution. He said he just needed more information, and that is why he needed my help. He wanted me to pay a little more attention to Jason's table when I was nearby. Listen in a little more than usual to the discussion. He said anything I could report to him would be helpful.

"I didn't want to get anyone in trouble, especially the son of Demetrius. He made it clear that it was Demetrius he was trying to protect. Jason had already squandered his father's kindness and efforts to give him a good start in life. Demetrius knew he was becoming too fond of gambling, and he was well aware of the presence of fake coins. However, he still cared for his son and chose not to suspect his involvement."

This crime can carry a punishment of death, I told Alexander. Marcus wanted to end it, without involving Demetrius' son.

"I told him I would ask the other girls to help and I would do what I could. He told me it must only be me and that I should not discuss this with anyone. The more people who knew, then the more risk of Jason and his less reputable friends finding out. So our meetings were always in secret.

"I was still uncertain. Your father was serious about his request, and I felt I could trust him. I suppose I knew even then that he had a kind soul, but it was the fact that he had chosen me and not one of the others. I asked him why he picked me.

"'I have a high opinion of you,' he said. 'I've watched how you are with the people you serve. They trust you too. Everyone falls for your smile and the sparkle in your eyes. You always have pleasant words for everyone. You are the best choice by far to help me, to help Demetrius. Believe me when I say you will be safe. Don't act differently. I only want you to keep your eyes and ears open a little more than usual. Now please, go back to your normal day. I will wait here a short while, so no one sees us together.'

"He handed the broom back to me and ushered me to go. I went straight back to sweeping. The owners didn't appear to have noticed that I had disappeared, or if they did, then they didn't say.

"My head was spinning. The secret task was one thing, but it was also a delight to know that Marcus had noticed my smile and my eyes. What would Maria have to say about that?

"The days passed into weeks. Marcus would wait for my arrival, ahead of the other workers. I repeatedly brushed the dust over to the little lane and would slip around the corner when I thought no one was looking. To begin with, I couldn't offer him much that was helpful, but I was learning more about the traders who sat with Jason, and how to pay attention to the little signs.

"I noticed two men in particular who appeared to have plenty of coin to spend. They would often play dice against Jason, and for large amounts, which they always seemed to lose. I'd seen that before with others and it often caused frayed tempers and maybe even a fight, but these two seemed to be so happy to lose to Jason. It was as if they wanted to give him their money, and what better way to do it? If Jason was receiving payment for a trade or providing a service, then he would have to account for it. Demetrius would have a record of prices and terms of agreement, but nothing like that was needed for a lucky win in a game of dice. It was just a chance event where the odds seemed to always be stacked in Jason's favor.

"At first, I thought that Jason was just cheating. It's well known in dice games, but then he would lose again to a different group of people before he had time to put his winnings to good use.

"The rich men who he always won against began to appear more often. It didn't take me long to learn their names in passing. The small conversations that happen with the customers can fill out a picture of their lives. Once I knew their names, I learned they were from Syros and the name of their ship. They traded marble and pottery, and people thought them to be respectable, and wealthy from conducting an honest business.

"In my mind, it just made the situation more suspicious. One morning I decided to share my thoughts with Marcus. As normal, I went outside to sweep the dust away from the door. I looked around into the little lane and he was standing waiting, but there was a distinct look in his eyes as I drew close. Before I began to speak, he placed a finger to his lips to keep me silenced.

"'Elena, I've made an error in asking you to help me,'" he said. 'Please accept my apologies. The last thing I want to do is place *you* in any danger. I should have thought out my plan more clearly before I asked you. It was wrong of me.'

"It was the way he spoke to me that made my heart jump. I wasn't expecting to feel that way, but I carried on, regardless of what he said.

"I told him about the two merchants from Syros who were passing money to Jason for winning at a game, and that it might have been how he received payment. They were doing it right under the noses of the Roman garrison. He even cheered and created a noise when he won, but I thought it was all a show to mislead all around him. The two merchants only played against Jason. If anyone else asked for a game, they politely and firmly refused.'

"Marcus went thoughtful and silent. He still seemed uncomfortable. He said that was the information he'd been waiting for. There had been a rumor that Syros was at the center of the problem, and he planned to investigate my suspicions, but he told me again he did not want me to do any more with this. He told me to go back to my normal day's work, without acting as a spy for him.'

"I told him I enjoyed being a spy. But he was adamant. Marcus couldn't shout, but his whisper was a command. It upset me. Just when I felt I had done something good, he was acting with anger.

"'Look, I'm sorry, Elena, things have changed. I didn't know you a few weeks ago. You were the popular serving girl who could charm all her customers. With a cool head, I could see the advantage of gaining your help.'

"He paused for what seemed an eternity. Then he shocked me with his confession.

"'Now it's only my heart that I hear. It beats faster whenever I am near you. I spend my days worrying that I've led you into danger, and I curse myself for that.'

"I told him I was not in danger. Though it made me happy to know that he cared, and I told him so.

"'I don't just care about you. I love you.' I will never forget those words.

"A stunned silence surrounded us, neither of us could speak. I could only feel my own heart beating. I took a sharp intake of breath as he took my hands in his.

"'Elena. I hope you feel as I do,' he said. 'At first, I walked away, noting only what you could tell me, but as time has passed, I've got to know you. The longer we spend meeting, the more difficult it becomes to walk away. I'll understand if you want nothing to do with me, if I have hurt or angered you, but I think about you night and day, and I only feel happy when I'm near you. I'm sorry if I've said too much.'

"Inside I was happy, but your father had chosen Maria over me, I wouldn't let him off that easily! I told him he couldn't have feelings for both Maria *and* me and he would need to prove that he could respect me as a strong woman, or else he might give me up for the next pretty girl who fluttered her eyelashes. I insisted that he should trust me to finish the job of trapping the fraudsters. I knew where and when it could be done.

"Then I took my time, of course. Your father looked at me with the slight sulk I became used to over the years, and I told him that once I knew from Maria's own words that their partnership was over, I would wait a little while longer, and then decide if we should be together.

"He looked a little disappointed but happy at the same time. So, I finished telling him what I knew. The merchants had said they would go, but be back in two days, but what's more, they were talking about a delivery. I was sure this meant that they were bringing in some of the fake silver for Jason to disperse on his own voyages.

"Marcus seemed impressed with what I'd been able to discover. He thanked me once again and left. We had spent longer than usual together and the owners of the kapeleion spotted us leaving the small lane. They gave me a suspicious look, but I said nothing and just smiled sweetly in return. I'm sure they thought I was up to something, but nothing related to Jason and the traders.

"And so, the next morning came. I was up very early before the sun rose. I knew that Marcus and the men from his garrison would be lying in wait for the merchants to land. There would be trouble, but I had set everything up, so of course I wanted to see what happened and if the traders would get caught committing their crime.

"As I left my house, I could see the ship approaching the harbor out of the half-darkness. Few landed at that time of day. It was obvious something was going on. I hurried through the streets to be nearer the dock.

"I was just passing through the market when I had to jump out of sight. From out of another side street, Jason appeared a few feet in front of me. He was walking with speed, looking around himself, but thankfully he didn't spot me.

"I kept following from a safe distance. I could see the ship docking. Ropes were being cast to tie up against the side, and as usual, some of the slaves were gathering to help unload the cargo. Jason went straight over to them, issuing instructions in the same way that Demetrius does when merchants arrive. For a moment, I stopped and told myself that Jason was just helping his father, by attending to a ship that had arrived early, but deep inside I knew that wasn't true.

"I hid myself behind a large stack of boxes and crates to get a good view of the scene. The ship had come to rest. The two traders appeared from on board and leaped over to greet Jason. It looked like a normal landing, except that the sun was still to rise and only torchlight could let the slaves see what they were doing.

"The first few items to come off the ship looked normal, but then there were smaller boxes that one slave should have been able to lift if you were judging it by size, but instead they were heavy and needed two to carry.

"Jason was paying special interest and following to make sure where it was being placed on a waiting cart. He wasn't interested in anything else. He ordered his slaves to work at a fast pace. Everything was happening quickly.

"And then I froze. A hand clamped down on my shoulder and spun me around. I gasped and called out in surprise. It was Marcus. He placed his hand over my mouth, but it was too late, I had alerted those at the ship, and before I knew it, marines from the Roman garrison were rushing out of the darkness and onto the harbor.

"'Go, Elena,' was all Marcus said to me before he raced away with sword drawn. Jason, the traders, and their crew tried to fight back, but they were no match for trained Roman soldiers and were all soon captured. The shouts and the calls from the Roman ambush were already drawing others out from their houses to see what was going on. Delos has suffered invasion so many times that I'm sure they were worried it was happening again.

"The gathering crowd made it safe for me to retreat from the scene, but as I walked away, I saw the lone figure of Demetrius, doing what he normally does, observing the chaos of the busy dockside, picking out the calls and the conversations. He doesn't show emotion much, you know that, but on that morning, I felt a great sadness from him. His shoulders looked like they were straining under a heavy weight. He cast a look over toward me for a brief moment, and I felt he knew of my involvement. He could read the emotion on my face because I was not as skilled at hiding it from sight.

"The Romans were quick to uncover the boxes of fake silver coins, and without further hesitation, they set about placing Jason and the traders in manacles and chains. I could hear his protests, but that did little to dissuade his captors. Before long, he was being led past us and into the garrison's fort, where a prison cell would be waiting.

"Marcus walked over to Demetrius. He opened his hand to show some of the fake silver coins.

"'I'll do what I can, Demetrius,' he said, 'the garrison legate will want to question them. I'm sure they will keep the prisoners until they have more information. We won't have long, but just know that I will do everything within my power to help Jason survive. You have my word.'

"Demetrius nodded solemnly in return. For the only time I can ever remember, he turned away from the dock and from the town as if it was the very last place he wanted to be. He was a lonely figure, walking against the tide of people still rushing to find out what had happened. Jason's name was already passing around the lips of many. On Delos, you can never get far enough away from bad news, no matter how much you try, but I think he knew that the palaestra was the place where he would have time to contemplate his thoughts without disturbance.

"Then Marcus turned away to the fort without saying another word. I realize now that he didn't want to be seen talking to me, in case the local people became angry with me for helping the Romans. I was disappointed at first, but the more I thought about it, the more I considered just how good a man your father was. He was always thinking of how he could help, whether it was Demetrius, Jason, or me.

"The sun was rising into the sky on another day. The fuss was dying down, and the morning light was returning the day to normal. I went back to my job, where most of the talk was about the capture of Jason, but no one accused me of being involved. I was just the person who smiled and talked as I served the food and drink in the kapeleion. I thought that everything was over, but there was still to be one last twist in the tale, and one last request from your father.

"A few more mornings passed, and I was back to sweeping up at the start of my day. I was starting to miss the meetings with Marcus, so I would still look around into the lane, just in case he was waiting, and on one particular morning, he was.

"'Elena, are you alright?' he asked. I told him no one suspected my involvement. Most of the customers said that Jason was just too loud in front of the Romans. That he only had himself to blame. They thought he was stupid rather than bad.

"'That may yet save him,' he said. 'I'm sorry to say but the legate wishes to make an example of him. He is planning a public execution as a deterrent to others. He will make an example of Jason.'

"He told me the other traders had already bought their freedom. Only Jason stood to be punished. And that even though Demetrius was wealthy, he was from Delos. The legate felt he had to demonstrate authority. Jason was to face execution in three days' time.

"I told him the islanders would be angry to see that only he was facing punishment.

"'And that is what I am hoping,' he said. 'Elena, can you do what you can to spread the word? Make sure that there's a large audience to witness the event. The will of the public may be the only thing that can save him. I will do what I can, but I'll need the people on my side. Please do what you can. It will be the last thing I ask. I am in your debt, and Demetrius is also in your debt. Demetrius does not know your hand in this, only that you have helped him.'

"So, he left into the crowds and disappeared from view. The next part was simple. Spreading the word on Delos was never difficult and it was easy to encourage the people to be outraged. People knew that Jason had committed a crime, but no one wanted his death.

"Before I knew it, the day was upon us. The legate gathered the garrison in the main square and the people crowded around them. The normal business of the day had stopped, and everyone crowded into every space to see what was going to happen. I think the size of the audience took the legate by surprise. He seemed nervous as the guard led Jason out in front of his executioner. He was to be strangled rather than crucified. That was the one concession that the legate would make for Demetrius and his status on the island.

"As the moment neared, the crowd became more unsettled. The calls to spare Jason's life grew, and the garrison soldiers began to look nervous. It looked like a riot might start, many of the Romans were reaching for the hilt of their swords, and the fervor was increasing among the islanders. Then I could see Marcus speaking with the legate. They exchanged words for a moment before the legate seemed to agree to whatever Marcus was suggesting. Then your father stepped out alone to quell the crowd and resolve the situation.

"'People of Delos,' he began, 'we only seek to see justice done. A serious crime committed by Jason of Delos reflects on the reputation of the entire island, and that of the good people who live with respect for the law. This crime undermines the functioning of the empire, and so it counts as treason against the emperor. There is only one fitting punishment, and that is death.'

"The crowd's anger increased. Their calls became louder. Jason looked around himself with a look of disbelief. I'm sure he wasn't even sure why so many had gathered to defend him. The executioner looked impatient to carry on with his work, but your father raised his hand again to call for silence."

I recited Marcus's speech to Alexander exactly as it was said on that day: "'Emperor Marcus Aurelius is fair and just. Were he among us I'm sure he would seek a way for this issue to have a balanced resolution that allows all to honor the last judgment in this matter. Each human life has its worth, even that of a criminal. Each time a life stops, the loss extends to family, friends, and even larger communities. So how do we resolve this issue for the benefit of all? The punishment must fit the crime, and this is not a crime without victims. It is a theft of trust as well as value. It disrupts the balance and harmony that a community needs to act as one. So let me be clear that Jason must face consequences for his actions. The question is what will satisfy the law, the emperor, and you the people?'

"Murmurs passed around all that were there, and then Demetrius stepped out of the crowd. He faced Marcus and the legate. He looked on with grim acceptance over the fate of his son. This time, it was he who raised his hands to silence the crowd. His deep voice resonated around the square.

"'There is perhaps a way to avoid a punitive decision. For is justice not the way toward restoring balance and order among us? My son allowed his fate to fall into the hands of others. Lack of virtue and proper consideration for the results of his actions on others is the main reason he stands under your judgment now. Such a young man still has time to change, to redeem himself, and make amends for the harm he has caused. I ask you to spare his life today and let him serve a sentence that will offer him the opportunity to grow and learn from his mistakes.'

"The legate summoned Marcus over. The conversation was carried out in whispers. We were all straining to hear what was being said. They nodded to one another, and Marcus saluted his commanding officer before returning to face Demetrius and the crowd.

"Your father believed Demetrius' words were wise. He said the legate would make an offer to find a way through the situation that is acceptable to all, especially the emperor. He proposed a choice for Jason. His choice was to have his life end with no more delay, or make a formal oath and request to serve Rome directly as payback for his crimes. He could decide to join and serve in the legions, to show his appreciation for leniency by Rome, to show loyalty to the emperor on the field of battle up until such a time as he earned forgiveness for his actions.

"Demetrius walked over to face his son. None of us knew how this was going to end. The entire square of people fell silent. Then Jason seemed to stand taller. No words passed between them, but it was as if an understanding between them formed a new peace, between son and father.

"Jason then announced before all that he would accept the mercy offered to him today, and that he would spend his life in service of the emperor.

"A cheer went up from the crowd. Justice was enacted without loss of face for the authorities. I knew, and I think Demetrius knew, that it was the virtuous intentions of your father that had saved Jason's life. A bond formed between Demetrius and Marcus that remains unbroken, even today, though your father is no longer with us. Demetrius will always defend you in the same way that your father defended Jason.

"And as for me. I kept your father waiting a few weeks longer. I didn't want to be seen to be rushing into his arms, but he waited and was patient with me. I think he knew I had fallen for him long before I did, but that is the story of how we became a couple, a man and a wife, then a mother and a father. I miss him so, and sometimes I still look around into that lane hoping he will still be there, but I know in my heart, he will never leave us."

CHAPTER XIX

My mother's story makes me realize more than ever that Delos is my true home. As our ship arrives on the island of Mykonos, Apion puts a hand on my shoulder. He has a reputation, even if I don't. His arm placed around me is already sending a message to the gathering crowd. I am a contender, and in my mind, at least, I am *the* contender from Delos. I'm here to win for myself, as well as the people who know and believe in me.

With great excitement, I launch myself from the ship onto dry land. It's my first time on the island I've only ever gazed at from the top of Mount Kynthos.

"Welcome to the land of Hercules and the giants," says Apion. "Tomorrow you should think about him when you're summoning your strength. Some of the wrestlers you might face are taller than you and some heavier, but you will beat them. I do not doubt it."

"I can't wait for the contest; I just wish Zoe was here with me."

"She'll be waiting for you when you get back, but you must let me tell her some stories about your victories. I have a talent for that," he smiles.

"I think the truth is fine."

"Sometimes." Apion grins as he walks toward a crowd of friends.

"It's so good to be back here," adds my mother. "There are people here I haven't seen since I was the same age as you. I hope they remember me if they see me."

"I'll point them out," says Uncle Nikos, "at least the ones that are worth meeting up with again. Some will welcome you with all they can offer, but others keep an eye on the costs of reuniting. I won't let us get caught up with those who just enjoy spending *my* money."

The port at Mykonos is just as busy as Delos can be, but the houses stretch around a long curving bay. I can see that more people live here compared to Delos, and some of the buildings are so near to the sea, it looks as if the houses might fall below the waves. It doesn't take me long to feel settled in this new place. The winding streets are just like those I've come from, but they stretch further around the island. Tables of fresh fruit scent the air, and places to eat and drink all point out toward the sea. The seats face west to catch the sunset. For those who worship the Greek gods, temples to Apollo and Poseidon lurk around corners and at the ends of small lanes.

It's late afternoon and still warm. I feel ready to find somewhere to rest when Uncle Nikos leads us to a small green door that almost glows against the white walls that surround it. Vines drop from a small balcony in an upper room My uncle knocks to announce our presence and almost immediately it opens to reveal an older man and his wife.

"Nikos!" they both exclaim. "And Elena!" they cry again.

They rush past my uncle to embrace my mother, and she bursts into tears at seeing them.

"Agathon and Thestylis! I can't believe I'm standing outside your house again. Alexander, this is my cousin and her husband."

"My cousin as well," announces Nikos, trying not to be forgotten.

"This is Alexander?" asks Thestylis. "Your son?"

My mother nods her head with the most beaming smile I've seen for a long while, and before I know it, Thestylis has me in a hug, almost squeezing the air out of me.

"Be careful," laughs Agathon, "he has a contest arranged for tomorrow; don't injure him."

"I could never injure such a beautiful boy!" she replies. "It's you, old man, that I save my wrath for."

Everyone laughs together. Agathon takes my hands in his, stretching out my arms.

"He's strong too. I hear you are training with Demetrius."

"Yes, I have been."

I don't know what else to say. They know a lot about me already, but I don't know who they are. I think Agathon senses that I'm surprised.

"Don't worry. Your uncle has kept us informed of all that's been happening. Welcome to your actual home. You must visit us often from now on, or Thestylis may be angry."

"And that wouldn't do as I would nag your Uncle Agathon."

We all laugh again, but I don't think my aunt is lying.

"Come in, come in," says Agathon, inviting us into their home.

We walk into a small room with a kitchen at its side, then through to the main living area with a higher roof where sunlight streams in from the courtyard. Then there's a garden area, where a table sits surrounded by some chairs, flowers cling to the walls, and a set of wooden steps lead up to rooms on a higher floor. Neighbors wave down to us from another balcony, and my aunt immediately starts telling them about the famous wrestler who's staying with them. Then she introduces my mother.

They gasp and race to come down into the courtyard and greet us all. Before I know it, the little garden is filling up with new friends. Plates of fruit, fish, and feta soon appear along with wine. Everyone wants to know all about me, and when they find out I'm here for the contest, they all assure me they'll be there to cheer me on.

Some of them know the wrestlers I might face and start to give advice about what to watch out for. They tell me that one of them prefers to tempt you to overreach, another favors a certain choke hold, and one of them will nip you with a bite if he can get away with it. But everyone says I will beat them.

Apion arrives in amongst the small crowd and makes his way into the center of the garden. The excitement grows even more. Everyone knows him, and with the rich-colored robe he wears, he stands out from others.

The talk becomes more serious now he's here, and to my disappointment, Dario's name is being mentioned more often. People ask him why Dario isn't here. He answers that he's resting his other champion before the Great Delia, but then he says something that shocks me.

"Dario is a great champion, but Alexander will be greater. I will tell you to place your wagers on him every time. He will soon grapple with the best Rome can offer. Be proud to be sharing a cup of wine with him. For this will be the first place where he becomes known to the world of wrestling, and those who value their reputations will need to face him in the skamma. Alexander is the finest wrestler I have ever seen." He pats me again on the shoulder and whispers, "Trust me. I will do the talking and bring an audience like you could never imagine."

***

I wake up early. Fortunately, I ate enough the night before to stop the wine from hurting my head this morning.

"Are you alright, Alexander?" asks my mother from the corner of the room where we've slept.

"Yes, I'm ready. I feel good. Where's everyone else?"

"Apion is staying with others, but he said we should make sure you've eaten before he arrives today, not too much, just enough. Nikos and Agathon are already down at the harbor. Your uncle needs to see what's being bought and sold. He never stops working even if he's meant to, and I think I hear Thestylis preparing a meal. Don't let her force you to eat too much," my mother smiles. "Now go and wash yourself. There is water in the courtyard. Be clean and ready for the day ahead."

"Did you hear what Apion said about me last night?"

"Not when he said it, but plenty of people came and repeated it to me."

"He thinks I'm better than Dario. Someone even asked if we faced one another who would win, and he said it would be me. He was sure of it."

"Just be humble. You know what Demetrius would tell you. Focus on what you need to do to win today, don't get caught up in the fame and fortune of the future. It will distract you from the task ahead, and then you might never get what you desire. Only consider Dario if you find yourself drawn against him."

My mother is wise, but I would have been just as happy to hear her agree with Apion. She can read my thoughts and smiles at me as I go down the steps outside our room, to the courtyard where a large bowl of fresh clean water is waiting for me.

"Good morning, Alexander," Thestylis calls from inside in the kitchen. "Come through and eat before the others. You get to have your first choice before anyone else today, or they will face my wrath."

"I will," I shout back, as I splash the water about myself. It's cold, but it's already refreshing me in the morning heat. It's going to be hot in the skamma today. I can feel it already.

The others return to the house, and we all join each other in the garden. My new uncle and aunt, my mother, and Uncle Nikos will all be there. Some of the neighbors from last night reappear to let me know they are coming to shout for me.

I'm so excited about the next few hours. This is going to be a proper contest for the first time. It's not street fighting or training fights in Rome, this is the real thing with a prize at stake for the best wrestler of the day.

The talk between everyone makes the morning pass, and before I know it, Apion is standing at the entrance to the house.

"It is time to go, Alexander."

My family gathers around me, silent but expectant. I step outside, where a wooden cart waits, sturdy enough to carry us all. Two donkeys stand harnessed, their ears flicking as they shift their weight, the leather straps creaking with each movement.

"We don't have far to go," says Apion. "The palaestra is in the agora, but we shouldn't just walk there. We have to create an impression when we arrive."

It takes a few moments for the donkeys to be persuaded into moving, but once we're underway, I feel as if I'm at the center of a parade. The cart doesn't move fast, so all the others following me to the contest are able to walk along behind us. Some of them are already cheering my name. My mother and Uncle Nikos look proud as the cart drives through the busy street. Apion keeps me talking to stop me from being nervous, even as he calls out to the crowds to come and witness the event. The more who turn up to watch, the more money Apion will make. It's easy for me to understand that.

The road becomes more congested as the palaestra looms into view. The cart pulls up to a halt just outside and I can see an entrance that's only for the competitors. It's small, but it's still like entering the arena as a gladiator. Only Apion can accompany me from here on, so I stand for a moment to receive everyone's good wishes. Uncle Nikos and Agathon will be able to watch from within the palaestra, but my mother and aunt have to stand further away, on a hill that overlooks the place where I'll fight.

"You won't see us, but we'll see you," says my mother.

"And you'll have no trouble hearing us," my aunt insists.

Apion ushers me forward into a covered area. A small corridor opens out into a room that's only lit from windows positioned high on the walls. The sun strays in but can only cast its light over a small area. My fellow contestants take their first look at me in the half-darkness. They whisper words to their own trainers. Some smirk in my direction as if I don't deserve to be amongst them, but I know that is just part of the game. The contest is always easier if you can unsettle your opponent in those first few moments. This might be my first event, but my fights in the Subura have taught me how to convey my strength in return. None of them will beat me this early in the day.

A large table sits in the room with two amphorae. Three contest judges sit beside it. The head judge in the center issues instructions to the other two to collect our tokens. I panic slightly. I've haven't seen a token since I was at the palaestra in Rome.

"Don't worry. I have one prepared for you," says Apion.

He hands me a small piece of wood with a lyre-shaped mark on one side, and a single letter A on the other.

"The letter is for Alexander. The lyre is for Apollo. The combination will mark you out from the others. This is your token for the fights you will enter. When the judge comes round, place it in the amphora, and wait on the invitation to choose your competitor from the other jar."

I can hear the noise of the growing crowd outside, but the mood inside the room is tense and quiet. The judges collect our tokens, placing half into each amphora. The head judge stands to his feet and explains the rules of the contest. There aren't many; no gouging of eyes, no biting.

I look around for the wrestler who has a reputation for using his teeth, but no one reacts. After a pause, the judge places his hand in the first jar and draws out the first token.

"Pallas from Naxos," calls the judge.

A small reaction passes around the room from the other wrestlers, and Pallas smiles.

"If you weren't here, my money would be on him," Apion whispers. "Ask the gods that he doesn't pick you for his first match. I'd like you to get the chance to warm up first."

I gulp as Pallas walks toward the other amphora. He spins the tokens around inside and makes his choice, handing it over for his first opponent to be declared.

"Pallas will face Acis, from Mykonos."

The two men smile at one another. I can tell they've fought each other before.

"Good," says Apion, "Acis is a local hero. He will have the crowd with him so he might win that bout."

They then select a second pair to fight. Four wrestlers have been chosen and four are still to be revealed. I don't have long to wait, as it's now my turn for my name to be drawn. The judge invites me to step forward and choose my opponent. I know it will be one of the two wrestlers facing me on the other side of the room, both look strong, so there's no point in trying to choose one over the other.

I plunge my hand into the jar and spin the last two tokens with my fingers. I can feel one that seems to stick to my grip.

Help me choose, Father.

I pull out the token and hand it to the judge.

"Alexander will face Asterion, from Crete."

We smile and bow toward one another. I can see that we are almost the same height and build. It will be a good match.

Now the draw is complete, my excitement starts to build. The contest will begin soon, and the judge tells us to enter into the spirit of the contest with respect for all involved. He asks Pallas and Acis to prepare for the first round, and then for the rest of us to prepare in turn. He points out slaves who are there to aid us in the oil room, and others who will fetch and carry anything we need, fresh water, or fruit if we need it.

Pallas and Acis take their leave, accompanied by their trainers, while Apion walks me to the side.

"Stay on your feet for this first one," he advises. "He's better when he has you on the ground. He hates being lifted. It makes him angry to think that he looks weak. All I can say is try to throw him as high as you can."

***

"Alexander of Delos."

The herald's voice cuts through the air, sharp and final. A shiver runs through me. This is it—my first time stepping into the palaestra.

I push forward, the sun striking my face like a slap. Blinking hard, I let my eyes adjust to the blinding light. The skamma lies ahead, its sand already marked with the scars of past matches. The crowd stirs, voices swelling as I approach. A rush of energy floods my chest, setting my pulse hammering. They're cheering for me.

Asterion's name is called next. A smattering of voices rise for him—a smaller group, tight-knit, likely those who traveled with him. But the rest... the rest call for me. The realization sends a thrill through me. Even in the Subura, when I fought, the crowd was never on my side. But here, for the first time, their voices lift me. The judge steps between us, holding his rod as a barrier. His gaze flicks between us, steady and unshaken. "A fair fight," he instructs, voice firm.

I nod, shoulders rising with my breath. There's no time to assess, no time to measure Asterion's weaknesses. All I can do is trust in my training. Trust that I'm ready.

The rod lifts.

A roar erupts from the crowd.

Asterion drops into his stance, muscles taut, his body coiled like a spring. I match him, knees bent, weight balanced. The heat of the sand rises through my feet, but I keep my focus locked on him. The noise of the crowd urges me forward, pulsing in my ears. I want the first point. I need the first point.

Asterion lunges, and I meet him head-on.

Hands clash, forearms smack against each other in rapid succession. Our heads knock together with a dull crack as we fight for control, neither giving an inch. We circle, shifting, testing, looking for an opening. My breath comes hard and fast, my skin slick with sweat, but I drown out everything—the roar of the crowd, the heat licking at my skin, the sting of Asterion's blows. Focus.

Asterion grabs for my neck, again and again, trying to snap me down. Just like Dario back home. But I've learned. This time, when he drives me downward, I don't wait. I explode to the side, twisting away before his grip can tighten.

His stance wavers.

Now.

I launch into him with everything I have. The impact is brutal. A burst of breath escapes him as my force drives him back—out of the pit.

The crowd erupts. The first point is mine.

But there's no time to celebrate. The judge waves us back to the center. My chest heaves, but I catch a glimpse of Apion's approving nod before Asterion barrels toward me again.

He hasn't learned. He thinks I got lucky.

I see it in the way he sets his jaw, the way his shoulders coil, tense with frustration. He's convinced he can drag me to the ground, force me into his game.

I won't let him.

The moment he lunges again, I'm ready. Waiting. I shift—one quick, precise step to the side—breaking his contact. His footing falters, and that's all I need.

With a roar, I slam into him again. The force sends us both skidding, but when the dust settles, Asterion is on the ground.

Second point.

The crowd surges, voices rolling over me in waves. "Alexander! Alexander!"

I catch a flash of Nikos and Agathon's faces in the sea of people. But I'm searching for someone else. Father. I know I won't see him, but still, I picture him there, standing among the crowd, giving me the signal to finish this.

Asterion sees the shift. He knows he has to risk something now. His stance tightens. Then—

He lunges.

I dip low, letting his chest meet mine, and in an instant, my arm hooks under his. Momentum takes over.

Asterion's feet leave the ground.

For a heartbeat, he hangs there, weightless. And I know—I know—he's mine.

The world spins as we crash down, sand exploding around us. My vision blurs with the impact, sky and soil flipping before settling back into place.

I press down. He doesn't move.

The judge's voice barely reaches me over the roar of the crowd. "Victory!"

Mine.

***

"Who do I face next?"

"A man from Kithnos," Apion replies. "He's got the strength of a bull, but also the brains."

He smiles as he taps his head. "Just don't let him gore you into submission. Use his weight against him and you'll win."

"Is he the one that bites?"

"If you let him close enough. Keep moving, stay clear of those teeth, and he won't get the chance."

I just have time to clean myself from the first fight and have more oil applied for the next. The slaves who work at the palaestra know what they're doing. They have well-practiced skills to prepare the wrestlers with speed.

I can hear the result of the fight before me. Pallas has won his next round and in no time at all.

"Nobody said this would be easy," says Apion as he reads my thoughts.

My own match is soon underway. No one wants time for the audience to pause. It's important for the excitement to continue rising toward the climax of the contest. Before I know it, I am looking into the eyes of the bull from Kithnos.

Apion wasn't wrong. He charges from side to side. He doesn't care if he misses his target, he just carries through with the mass of his body. The sweat and the oil make it hard to grip and hold him. I have to focus on avoiding him. I notice that each charge saps his strength. I don't need to defeat him right away. In a few moments, he will defeat himself.

One last time he charges. I crouch in toward him and, as we come together, I stand and push up with every part of my body. He ends up in the air, flying out of the skamma and onto his back. He lands hard, gasping for breath. His trainer can't move as he holds his index finger in the air. The second match is mine with one throw.

As I step away from the skamma, my pulse still pounding, my skin slick with sweat, I catch Pallas watching from the sidelines. Arms crossed, head slightly tilted—assessing. There's a glint in his eye, not just approval, but calculation. He's pleased. Not because I won. Because now, he knows I'm worth his effort.

I roll my shoulders, exhaling slowly. A much harder fight lies ahead. Victory is close, but so is defeat.

Apion strides up, his face unreadable. I brace for his usual sharp critique, but this time, he offers nothing—just a smirk and a solid clap on my back.

"Luck, Alexander. And don't worry—I didn't bet against you."

I huff a laugh. The moment is over too soon. The final match awaits.

Pallas stands ready, his stance casual but deliberate. As I step forward, he smiles and extends a hand—a show of camaraderie, but also something more. True contenders want opponents who will push them to their limits.

I take his hand, and his grip tightens. Not crushing, but enough to send a message.

Strength. Control. A test.

I hold firm, refusing to yield. Our grips lock, a silent exchange of will and power. Then, after a beat, Pallas gives a slight nod—acceptance. Respect. We are both here to win, but we will enjoy ourselves on the journey to victory.

For the last time today, the rod lifts between us.

The crowd hushes. The moment stretches, balanced on the edge of something unstoppable. Then—it drops. Pallas moves first. I'm ready. I remember what Demetrius has taught me—what he has drilled into me: the need for quick decisions, the ability to stay in control, and the instinct to expect the unexpected. He trained me to brush off the sting of an open hand, to push through the burning strain in my muscles, even when they're ready to give out.

I fall first in this match. Pallas takes the point. Then I hear my father's voice in my mind.

It is not the first score that counts. It is only the point that brings triumph that matters.

I know I have to accept that the best win comes from a hard-fought contest. I will learn from the falls as much as I learn from the throws.

Our contest grinds on. Advantages are rare, but over time they reveal themselves. I score twice against Pallas before he once again scores against me. The people around us have seen a good final round. It has been fair and well fought. Neither of us will hold our heads in shame, but one of us must win.

We scramble for the move that each of us needs to claim the prize. It is training, reactions, and instincts that need to come together in perfect timing, and perhaps even some luck, as Apion said.

We scramble, muscles straining, breath ragged. This is it—the moment that will decide the match. Training, instinct, and raw force collide as we fight for the final advantage.

Pallas grips my shoulders, trying to snap me down. He's strong, his hands like iron clamps, but I've felt this before. I've trained for this. I shift my stance, lowering my center of gravity, refusing to be dragged under.

Then, I see it—the slightest gap in his balance.

I drive forward, slipping beneath his arms, my head pressing hard against his ribs. My hands lock around his waist. He stiffens, but it's too late.

I pivot sharply, hooking my right leg behind his, and twist my hips with everything I have. Pallas lurches, his footing breaking, his body tilting at an angle he can't recover from. With a final surge of power, I drive him backward. His feet leave the ground for a heartbeat before crashing onto the sand, his shoulders slamming down.

The judge steps in, rod in hand, scanning Pallas where he lies. Then, his voice rings out:

"Alexander is victorious!"

The roar of the crowd washes over me. I can pick out all the voices of the people I've known for less than a day, the laughter and joy from

Nikos and Agathon, and somewhere in the distance I'm sure I can hear my Aunt Thestylis.

I push myself upright, breathless, victorious.

Pallas blinks up at the sky, stunned. I extend my hand, and he takes it without hesitation. As I pull him to his feet, we share a champion's embrace—a brief but unspoken moment of respect. He may not be satisfied with the result, but I know he's satisfied with the fight.

"I hope we meet again, Alexander."

I turn toward Apion, who is grinning from ear to ear.

"Start getting used to this," he says, clapping a hand on my shoulder. "I'm rarely wrong about my choices."

CHAPTER XX

A gentle breeze returns us home. As my uncle's ship steers a route, cutting through a clear and beautiful sea of blue, I keep a hopeful eye on Mount Kynthos. I'm sure that Zoe will be there with her friends, watching for our passage back.

There's a cheerful mood on board. Food and wine, treats that were packed off with us are being distributed; stuffed flatbreads with cheese, honey, or nuts and fruits, cakes flavored with seeds, and one of my favorites, sesamou, a bar of rolled sesame seeds and honey. My mother is keeping guard over a very special cake, melitoutta, made with more honey, cinnamon, and nutmeg.

"Can't I just have one piece?" I ask.

"No, that is for us to share when we get home, with Zoe, Selene, Na'amat, and Tigranes. Do you want Zoe to think that you ate her share?"

"No, I suppose not."

"We'll all have a nice dinner tonight. The cutting of the melitoutta will help to mark an important occasion." My mother pauses in thought. "Are you excited to tell Zoe your news?"

"Yes, I can't wait."

"I could see how you were attracting attention after your win. The ladies of Mykonos were keen to be near you last night."

"I'm not like Dario. Zoe is special to me. Like you and father."

"Well, maybe I should keep the cake a little longer. We'll need something for the wedding feast."

I know my mother's teasing me, but I also know how I feel about Zoe. The thought of being with her makes me happy. As Delos looms larger in my view, I thank the gods again for bringing me to this island, and to her.

"Aunt Thestylis will make more cakes by then." I smile, and my mother shakes her head and laughs back at my suggestion.

Uncle Nikos is behind me, standing by the steering oar. He's busy giving instructions to the man who controls it. I don't know how many times he's sailed in and out of the Sacred Harbor, but he doesn't need maps this near home. Experience tells him where to set our course, ensuring the ship will glide perfectly into the dock.

Apion is standing at the prow. He beckons me forward. The sea is calm, and I can step across the deck with ease. Maybe I'm finally learning how to hold my balance as the ship moves up and down over the water. He points at the small piece of sesamou that I'm still chewing on.

"That is your last for now. You are still in training for the Great Delia."

"I'm just celebrating."

"A celebration doesn't last for days unless it's an important celebration."

"Like winning the Great Delia?"

"Hm, I'm not sure. Maybe winning in Rome, under the gaze of the emperor."

"Do you think I can?"

"If Gaius had trained you in earnest, then maybe you would have already achieved that."

"Gaius only wanted money that my family didn't have."

"We all want money. It buys nice things and allows us to live in splendid houses, but Gaius has allowed it to lead his decisions. I'm sure he's already regretting the decision to send you away from his palaestra."

"I'm not so sure. He only accepted me because of a friendship he had with a commanding officer. One that my father served when he was a marine. When my father died in battle, there was no need for Gaius to support me any further."

"So indeed, your family bore a significant cost in return for your few weeks of training. Much more than the coin offered by your fellow students. Gaius should have recognized his debt to your family. He should have committed himself even more to building your success. He saw what I can see, what Demetrius can see. He has made a mistake, and he knows that he will regret it."

"It is good of you to say that."

"Alexander, do not misunderstand me. I am the showman. My own reputation and the business I run give me no skills in telling you how to wrestle, but I have witnessed more fights than many. I know the world you want to enter and those you will have to face. There are great champions across Greece, the Roman Empire, the Parthian Empire, Egypt, Cyrenaica, and Carthage. Where would you like to start? Do you think that the great Gaius of Rome is coming to the games at Delos for nothing when all he values is money?"

"He wants to see me win?"

"No, he wants to see you lose. So that he can hold his head high among others he demands the respect of and tell himself he made the right decision in letting you go. He certainly doesn't want your name to return to Rome, and I'm sure it torments him that Demetrius is now your mentor. Gaius cannot afford to keep his status on Palatine Hill if his judgment and reputation suffer a loss. So, for the moment, no more sesamou to swell your belly. Train hard, work hard, and win the contest, then you will discover a good life for yourself, your family, and that girl over there on the dock."

I spin around to see Zoe a short distance away and I wave my arms to her. "I won!"

Zoe returns my wave, claps her hands, and cheers. The noise attracts others, and soon the other traders and men who work at the docks are lifting arms in response to news of my victory. Apion places his arm around my shoulder. He takes his share of the applause just as he takes his share of the prize, but I don't mind.

Apion and Demetrius believe in me. The few days journeying to Mykonos and back have shown me more about myself than I have ever known. The story of my parents' meeting, new family in the place that is now my home, the contest with all its ceremonies and traditions, and the good fortune granted to me by the gods. I have never felt better.

I leap from the side of the ship and onto the dock, rushing to take Zoe in my arms. Her eyes are bright, and her smile is beautiful. The scent of jasmine fills the surrounding air. I've missed her so much, even though we've only been separated for a few days.

"You should have been there. I dedicated my win to you."

"I'm so proud of you, Alexander. I promise I'll join you on your next trip. Everyone is sure you will win the chance to go to Rome. Well, almost everyone."

She nods toward Dario who is standing half concealed amongst the people at the docks.

"Did he cause you any trouble while I was away?"

"No, he was just trying to annoy you when you left on the ship. As soon as you disappeared from view, so did he. He knows I've picked my champion." She smiles. "So, you can let me breathe."

"Oh, yes, sorry." I let her go. "I can't wait to show you Rome."

A slap knocks across my back. It's not an attack, but enough to make me flinch. There are parts of my body still bruising from the contests.

"So how did you do?" says Dario. "You've taken a few hits, I see. Did you win or did you just not lose? Who did you fight?"

I have to keep calm. Each time Dario annoys me, he has scored a point. I place my arm around Zoe's waist; I know that will annoy him.

"I fought Asterion from Crete, the Bull from Kithnos, and Pallas from Naxos in the final. They are strong wrestlers. The wins weren't easy.."

"You did better than I thought you would. Pallas is a good wrestler, but I don't know of Asterion. Sometimes Apion will pay for farmers to make up the numbers. They can get lucky in a fight, but they have no training; you shouldn't count such men as anything but a warm-up exercise, and as for the Bull, you only need to step out of his way. He knocks himself out in the end. Still, a good start in your career, but you'll need to do better for the coming contest. I feel I'm getting back to full strength now. I will be ready for the games. Zoe even said to me last night that I was looking better than ever."

"Last night?"

"He's lying," Zoe protests. "I never saw him last night or any night. He's just trying to make you mad."

"Lying?" says Dario. "Maybe we drank too much wine together, and you've forgotten."

"Don't listen to him, Alexander."

I've had enough of this.

I step forward, pushing Dario away with both hands. He stumbles, but more in surprise than anything else.

He responds immediately; we are in a fight, the kind with no rules. I've just enough time to push Zoe behind me before he sends an open palm crunching into my jaw. Dario relies on his speed, with the first punch followed by another, and another.

Zoe's screams alert everyone beside us, but the crowd enjoys a fight. They circle around us, just like the people in the Subura, baying for more.

I use my feet to create distance between us. I'm used to fighting like this. I can take the knocks and stand back up. I aim kicks at Dario that he has to defend. Leaning back, I direct my full strength into his hip. He snarls in pain, but then he takes hold of my leg, pulling me over and slamming me face down into the hard wooden planks that cover the dock.

The fall knocks the air from my lungs as Dario rains punches down on my back. I push with my arms, lifting him with my full body and casting him to the side. The fight resumes, this time we stand facing each other, circling and adjusting our height. Dario goes for his favorite move, snapping down again and again on my neck, trying to break me with constant attacks. This time I know better—I know how I can defeat him, just like Asterion from Crete. Dario loses control as I dodge to avoid him and charge into his side. The crowd around us parts and allows him to crash into a pile of crates on the dockside.

"Stop, Alexander," Zoe shouts as she tries to pull me away from the fight. Dario is picking himself up, but there's no reason to end the fight if he wants it to continue.

"He needs to be taught a lesson," I insist.

No sooner are the words out of my mouth than Dario has rushed over. Throwing his full weight against me, it's now my turn to fall. We end up in a tangle, each of us looking for a choke or a hold that will bring victory. I get a lock on his foot and start to build the pressure. He is going to submit or risk his foot being broken. I grit my teeth and apply my strength.

"STOP!"

The crowd backs away and the face of Demetrius glowers from above us. Apion and some of the other onlookers separate us. There are angry faces everywhere; Apion, Uncle Nikos, and Zoe. Meanwhile, Dario's mother has emerged from the crowd and is screaming at my mother and shouting at the nearby Romans to arrest me. She's accusing me of attempted murder.

I think the Romans have been betting on the fight; they don't want to get involved, and even if they did, this is the Sacred Harbor, and in this part of Delos it is Demetrius who decides what will happen. He signals for two crates to be brought forward, and then for Dario and me to be seated on one each. I notice blood running from Dario's ear, while blood also drips from my nose.

"The fire of youth burns bright for a reason," Demetrius begins, "but this is wasteful. It does not serve you, either of you. Who is the victor out of this? Who earns the prize? Is this all for the sake of pride?

"Pride leads only to harmful behavior, a false sense of your own importance, to arrogance, envy, and resentment. You both want to win, that much is clear, but you will win nothing if you can't avoid the pitfalls of pride.

"Or perhaps you seek to defend an honor. For a family member, or a lover. Has your brawl settled this matter? Or has it only made more reasons to continue with the violence? Alexander, look at Zoe, and then your family. Do you see delight in their faces, or shame and disappointment? Point out the honor you have defended.

"And Dario, what does your honor earn from today? Everything you have worked for? It might have been for nothing. Honor is a quality that's not restricted to wrestlers, but some athletes feel public approval can burnish it. The winner takes it all. Nothing could be further from the truth. It's about acting with integrity at all times, even when no one is watching. Judge yourself on how well you have demonstrated the correct behavior. Can others find inspiration from your name?

"Well?"

Dario and I hang our heads. I'm sure he feels the same as me. Demetrius leaves us with a lesson, that pride often comes before a fall from a position of honor.

We sit silent, ready to accept any punishment that might affect our chances of competing in the Great Delia.

"I expect both of you at the palaestra tomorrow. Ready to train. If you want the good people of Delos to be shouting your name, then you must work to earn that support. Time is running short. In days, the first competitors will arrive. Men experienced enough to smell your fear and strike at your weakest points. End this feud here. I will not tolerate it again."

When Demetrius walks away, the people return to what they've been doing before the fight started.

"I'll take your mother home," says Zoe, as she gives me a hug. "She doesn't like you and Dario fighting, and she seems to worry about Maria."

"Yes, take her away. I need to speak with Apion. I'll see you later."

Maria is dragging Dario over to a group of Roman soldiers. She's still complaining and trying to get me arrested. The Roman guard isn't interested, and when one of them looks at me, he angles his head to suggest I take my leave.

"Do as the soldier says," Apion comments from behind me. "Don't let the Romans feel pressured into leading you into a cell."

"Maybe I deserve it," I reply.

"Maybe you think you do, but it will cost me to get you released, and that's not part of my plan. Now go, disappear for a while, and try to grow a little wiser along the way."

I step from the harbor to the shoreline, and before I know it, I'm already walking past Zoe's house. A familiar voice cuts through my thoughts, easing some of my anger.

"Time for a swim?"

"Leon, am I glad to see you!" I scowl at him. "Where were you? No time to welcome home the Champion?"

"It's good to see you too, my friend. Sorry, I wasn't there. I was doing some extra training. I want to be ready. Congratulations on the win—it seems you just can't stop fighting." He grins.

I shake my head and smile back. "No, it seems that way."

"How mad is Demetrius?"

"I don't know. I think he stopped us just to avoid any actual injuries before the Great Delia, but he chose to deliver wisdom rather than punishment. He can see through us all. It's not enough for him to observe just what his eyes can focus on; he looks through you and seems to know why you're making certain decisions." *What will I have to do to match his skills?* "He must have been impossible to beat in the skamma. How can you win over someone that can not only predict your next move but has already worked out all the reasons for you making it? I think now I'm understanding how Stoicism and wrestling work together."

"Then tell Demetrius that when you see him. He'll forgive your mistakes all the sooner for that."

"You're sure?"

"I've been training with him a long time. He taught me how to read people as some of my first lessons, and now I read him. I think it really annoys him. Come on, let's get into the sea; it's calm and welcoming today. It will help you relax."

We rush to the brink and throw ourselves into the water. It's a little cooler than the warm air. It feels good, except where the salt exposes two cuts I've taken in the brawl, but I know it will help them heal. I lie back and float for a while, feeling the bright sun on my face, allowing the gentle waves to roll underneath me. I look at seabirds overhead, gliding smoothly and without concern. Only small bleached clouds interrupt the cerulean sky as they puff slowly across the heavens. The scene is tranquil and relaxing, but I can trust Leon to not let that last long, and soon enough, a mass of seawater crashes on my face, proving my point.

"Wake up, Alexander. Don't go to sleep out here. The Sirens will sing into your dreams, and you'll sink forever.

"Why you...!" I spin around in the sea and a water battle starts between us. In a few moments, neither of us can see from the drops running over our eyes, but we keep going, splashing, sometimes falling in the water, and laughing hard like children do before they are ruined by the world. Eventually, we both submit and make our way back to the rocks where we've left our tunics by the shore. Uncle Nikos is standing there, waiting for us to return to land.

"Do you feel better now?" he asks as we draw nearer.

"Yes, Uncle Nikos. My friend came to the rescue. He has a wise old head on a young body."

"I agree. It's easy to see that Leon might be the only wise head on this island. He even has the wisdom to hide it under his humor. Though I admit sometimes he does that so well, he can't even find it himself."

"I think your uncle was saying nice things about me. Was he?" Leon asks.

"Yes, I think so." I nod. "I'm sorry, Uncle Nikos."

"I know. Just don't repeat the mistake. Demetrius will run out of patience in the end."

"I won't. Do you think my mother will be alright?"

"Yes. Both she and Zoe are on your side. It's Maria and Dario who dare not darken our doorway for the next few hours. In the meantime, Maria is dragging Dario around the market square, trying to appeal to those who view her son as being the innocent party. They linger where cake or wine is on offer as a comfort. I would wager that was her plan all the time. She seems to enjoy herself a little too much."

"And Apion?" I ask.

"Already in the tabernae, stirring up excitement for when the two of you will meet in the skamma at the Great Delia. He'll make sure that he profits before either of you kills the other."

"We won't kill one another."

"Maybe. I promise I'll only gamble on a winner, not a death, if that makes you feel better. The only question is where do I place my bet?"

He pauses, but the silence goes on far too long for me. "Uncle Nikos!"

"Of course!" he bellows. "Of course, I expect you to win, but get back to training as soon as you can. It is time for all of us to be serious. The Great Delia will be here before the week is out. You must use every moment to prepare. Run, lift your weights, spar, and learn. Dario is fast. If you allow him through, then you know he can score against you. He is a formidable opponent. You must grant him that respect. He can beat you... if you let him."

"I'm never going to do that. I swear on—"

"I do not need you to swear on anyone or anything, Alexander. Show you have the discipline you need to be a champion. That has more meaning than a promise to a god who might decide to make you honor it. That's never a good idea when dealing with Olympus. What do you say, Leon the Wise?"

"Just rip his arm off, Alexander, or a leg. I don't care."

The noise of us all laughing attracts Leon's father over from his house.

"Well done, Alexander. They tell me you won the prize on Mykonos. Congratulations! Please come and share in some wine. I want us to celebrate together."

"He knocked Dario over at the dock as well," says Leon.

"Then that is even more reason for wine. Come, my friends. Come on, Nikos; can I tempt you as well? I picked up something that comes from Trinacria. I think you might appreciate it, with some nice grilled fish, olives, and bread."

"Thalasso, you make a fine offer that I can't refuse."

"No olives for me," is all I say as we walk toward the house.

"And no wine for you either," Uncle Nikos reminds me. He makes his apology for not accepting the offer but laughs and says he will take my share.

***

The afternoon leads into an evening full of laughter and good spirits. I only drink a few sips, while Uncle Nikos only eats a little fish and indulges heavily in the wine. Thankfully, I am there to support him back up the hillside to our house. As soon as we arrive, it is clear to my mother just how much he must have had to drink.

"Nikos, what have you been doing?"

"Sharing the afternoon with good friends, my dear sister. We Greeks debate matters of the world while we enjoy its many gifts. That is the mark of a civilized society."

"How much of the gifts did he drink, Alexander?"

"An amphora."

"To himself?"

"Maybe a bit more." I smile. "He insisted on drinking my share to save me the trouble of a headache tomorrow."

"It is not the quantity of wine, Elena, it is the quality of conversation. Thalasso and I are both men of the sea. We have many stories to share. It takes time."

"The stories were good. Uncle Nikos was so funny."

"Thank you, my boy. You see, Elena, I am a wonderful influence on your son, but I confess I am tired now. I will take myself to bed."

We all giggle as he staggers out of the main room and after only a few moments we hear the crash of him falling over a piece of furniture. Everybody bursts out laughing.

"I'll get him," Tigranes shouts.

My mother shakes her head and wipes a happy tear from her eye. "What am I going to do with your uncle?"

"A good sleep and breakfast will help him recover," I insist.

"Zoe and I were waiting for you to come home to share the cake, but I can see you have both been celebrating already."

"It was your father, Zoe. He was happy to celebrate my win. We didn't think we could refuse."

"And is he the same as your uncle?" she asks.

"Maybe not as bad."

"Well, we left you some cake. There are two slices left. Take it out to the courtyard with Zoe and enjoy what's left of the evening."

"Should I walk you home, Zoe?"

"No, it is too late. Zoe will stay here; there's room beside me in my bed. Which is where I'm going right now, to sleep and forget about Maria."

"Maria is not worth worrying over. Once I beat Dario at the games, then we'll hear no more from her."

"Goodnight, Alexander. You two go out to the garden."

I'm happy to do as I'm told, and so is Zoe. We sit together on one of the stone benches. A sky full of stars covers us from a cobalt sky and I feel I am in the throne room of the gods. Waves lap in the distance, the seabirds call and moths dance around the garden's low light from the lamps. It's a perfect night. We sit in silence at first, gazing into each other's eyes. Zoe is so beautiful. I can't believe how my life is changing, how lucky I am.

"Maybe you should try the cake." She smiles.

"Oh, oh yes. Is it nice?"

"It's delicious. Your aunt on Mykonos is an excellent baker."

"Yes, I know. My aunt kept talking about taking out her wrath on people, but she was very nice to me."

"Do you think she would like me?"

"She would love you, Zoe. I can't wait for you to meet her."

"I can't wait either. I want to follow you across this world."

"Really?"

"Yes, really. I'm sorry I wasn't with you."

A silence falls again. We place down the half-eaten cake and take each other's hands. We lean toward one another, awkwardly at first, but then our lips touch, and we kiss. A brief moment when the rest of the world seems to stop. I know in that instant that we feel the same way about one another.

We both sit back and quietly giggle.

"Zoe, if we're going to travel the world together, there are arrangements that have to be made."

"Arrangements?" She laughs some more. "There's time for arrangements. You just need to win the Great Delia first."

"I will win it. If there was any doubt before, then don't doubt me now. I will win it. I'll win it for you."

"Just for me?"

"Maybe for just one more kiss." I smile.

Zoe pecks me quickly on the lips and then stands. "I think I better join your mother now. But awaken early; there is somewhere on Delos that I don't think you've seen yet, and I want to be the one to take you there. Goodnight, Alexander."

"Goodnight, Zoe."

She turns and disappears inside the house. I brush two fingers across my lips and draw in the last of the jasmine fragrance. All my dreams are coming true at once.

CHAPTER XXI

I'm the last to awaken this morning. Although I'm still tired after the contest on Mykonos, I'm sure I'll be ready to return to the palaestra in the afternoon. Either Selene or Na'amat brought a bowl of fresh water into the room while I was asleep, with a clean tunic laid out for me.

I can hear a lot of conversation coming from the main room; Uncle Nikos joking, my mother groaning at his comments, Zoe joining and encouraging the fun. Tigranes is leaving for the palaestra to work on the last few parts of the building to be finished. Selene and Na'amat are talking about what needs to be done for the day, to help feed and look after us.

I wash and get dressed. I leave my room and walk into the bright sunlit entrance hall. The doors of the house are lying open; it's as if the garden is reaching inside the building. The heat releases the fragrant scent of the flowers and fruits; the birds are singing and chattering with one another, and the fresh air of the island makes me take a few deep breaths and appreciate the new day.

"Is that you, Alexander?" my mother calls.

"Yes." I walk into the main room where everyone is finishing their first meal of the day.

"I'll get you something to eat, Master Alexander," says Na'amat. "Cheese, figs, bread, a little fish?"

"And some honey?" I reply.

"Not too much," says Zoe. "He has a contest to win."

"Yes, Mistress Zoe." Na'amat nods and smiles.

I frown, but Zoe knows that I'm not serious. "I know I need to be fit, but honey isn't bad."

"I know that. We all want you to be your best. I can't wait for you to face Dario and show him who the best wrestler on Delos really is."

"Zoe, please don't mention that boy's name in our house!" my mother snaps. "I was having a lovely morning until you brought him up."

My mother's reaction causes a sudden silence to descend upon the room. It isn't like her to speak like that, especially toward Zoe.

"I'm sorry, Elena, I didn't mean to upset you," Zoe replies.

"It's alright, Zoe. I know you're excited about the games and Alexander doing well, but I would like to go one day without hearing mention of Dario or his mother. They ruin everything, or at least cause us trouble every time we have something to celebrate. I would prefer if someone else beat him on the way to the final, that's all."

"We won't mention them again, Mother, don't worry." I nod to Zoe, and she nods back in agreement.

"Take some air in the garden, Elena," says Uncle Nikos. "The chaffinch is waiting on his breakfast."

"Yes, that's a good idea, brother. I don't know why I feel this way today. There is so much talk about the Great Delia. It's crowding all of my thoughts."

"Then I'm sure the scent of roses and lavender will help to soothe you."

"Yes, please excuse me."

My mother leaves the room. I look over to Uncle Nikos, while Zoe appears sad for upsetting my mother.

"Elena still returns to her grief from time to time. When you share so much of your life with someone, their passing can take time to live through as well. Small actions or a few words can trigger a memory that turns into grief or sorrow. Your mother is cheerful; she just needs the comfort of knowing she is not alone. She needs to know that Marcus is never far away, even though she cannot see him."

"I'm sorry, Uncle Nikos," Zoe responds.

Uncle Nikos smiles. "You have nothing to be sorry for. I would be happy to see Alexander win against Dario, but I think your mother is right. If someone else knocks him out, then I think there will be fewer repercussions after the contest is over." He pauses. "I'll sit with her for a moment."

Uncle Nikos leaves just as Na'amat enters with my meal. I'm not so hungry, but I know I have to eat something, or I'll have less strength when I need it in the afternoon.

Zoe whispers a few quiet words in prayer, then turns to look at me. "Jesus tells us that those who are weary or burdened can go to him for rest. Do you think that your mother would come to one of our meetings?"

"Maybe, but she never speaks about religion. In Rome, there were so many gods to worship that it was easy to not worship any at all. I don't remember her praying or making an offering to a god in all that time. She would not have accepted Jesus while in the city. People frown on the new beliefs. Those who follow Jesus do not believe that Caesar is divine. That can create problems in Rome."

Zoe nods in acceptance. "I hope there's a path for her to find him one day. Kyrios welcomes all that believe in him and live by his words... but today, I will allow *you* to go back to the origins of Delos and the myths of Apollo."

***

Once Zoe told me where we were going, we organize ourselves for a walk to the north of the island, and because we are visiting a sacred site, we gather some more figs and other small fruits to take as our tribute.

My mother and Uncle Nikos are still in the garden as we leave the house. "We're going out now. Zoe is taking me to the Sacred Lake."

"Where?" Once again, my mother bites on her lip.

"The Sacred Lake," I confirm, "the birthplace of Apollo. I can't believe that I've never been. It's the reason that most people come here."

"Is that not against your religion, Zoe?" my mother asks. "You must not treat the gods of this island with disrespect."

"They are only going for a walk on a beautiful morning, dear sister." Uncle Nikos turns to us. "Go now, enjoy your walk. Your mother needs a rest, and I'll get Selene to make her a bath."

"We don't need to go," I say.

"Just go, the two of you, now."

Uncle Nikos looks very serious about us leaving. We walk out of the garden and into the street that heads for the main town. Neighbors greet us and we return their wishes for a good day, but it's only once we reach the crowds of the market square that we talk to one another about my mother being upset.

"She must be worried about you," says Zoe. "Was she like this on Mykonos? Maybe she just gets nervous when you're going to fight."

"I don't think it's that. Maybe it's just what Uncle Nikos was saying. She misses my father every day."

"I know. It must be terrible for her. Do you think it upsets her to see us in love? Maybe it makes her memories come back."

"No, she told me a story on the way to Mykonos, about how she and my father met. I'm sure she'll tell you one day. Her memories of him bring her comfort, and in the story, she was as courageous as him. I know she loves you. She keeps telling me she is organizing our wedding."

"Really? She will need to sort that out with my mother." Zoe smiles.

"Maybe I'll just go to the palaestra when you are all doing that. There will be less fighting there."

"They have plenty of time to make agreements. If we are to be together, I hope you will find room in your life for Kyrios. That is a decision you have to make with sincerity."

The conversation drops again. We arrive at the Temple of Apollo, where the lake sits before the main buildings of the shrine. We find ourselves in a perfect place, even though the markets are still nearby. Small groups of pilgrims, or couples just like Zoe and me, all find a small place around the shore of the lake, to sit and make their peace with the god of the sun.

"Let's sit here," says Zoe as she picks her spot.

It's far enough away from others to make us feel alone. The sun sparkles and shimmers over the lake. Just sitting by it, I can feel the power of the gods. I'm looking out over the birthplace of Apollo, while in the same moment, I'm thinking of how I can turn to following Kyrios.

"It's lovely here this morning," says Zoe. "So quiet, and only us. No fighting or squabbles, no worries. Have no fear about our future. I can hear your mind working on your dilemma. Be still for the moment. Breathe in the peace."

She rests her head on my shoulder. I place my arm around her and she settles her head on my chest. Her hair brushes against me and the familiar jasmine scent fills the air. I want Zoe in my life every day. I can't imagine life without her.

"I want to accept your faith, Zoe. I have to believe it will bring us together."

"Even though you know it will not be a simple path?"

"Something brought me here. Something saved me from falling into the hands of the street gangs. Each fight in the Subura could have been my last, yet here I am in this paradise, at the center of the world. Living in a magnificent house, with a wonderful family, and you. Do I thank Minerva for my father? Apollo for the power of the island? Or Kyrios because he has brought the most special person into my life?"

I pause and look across at the temple and the pilgrims who have traveled many miles to be here for just a few days.

"It is time to make an offering."

Zoe sits up and watches me as I place the small fruits on the top of a rock. I know the birds will find them when we're gone, but for the moment, I must dedicate them to an invisible power.

"I offer this tribute in thanks for the good fortune I have found since leaving Rome. I wish to ask for happiness and health for all of my family, and for Zoe. I ask that we can grow in our relationship. Kyrios, please accept this offering as I submit myself to your love. I will follow your guidance. I will seek truth in your teachings. I accept I am turning from the false gods. Minerva gave my father hope, and I live on this island dedicated to Apollo. Those who love me will understand my reasons for devoting myself to following your light."

"Those are beautiful words." Zoe embraces me. "I believe you. I believe you meant them."

As I hold on to her, I'm still looking at the temple, and now a worry passes through me. Have I just angered those gods that I should have appeased? Was I right to make such a proclamation here? I hide my feelings with a smiling face as Zoe pulls away to gaze into my eyes.

"I've never been so happy, Alexander. To hear you speak these words means so much. I have taught myself not to trust the people who only say what they want you to hear. Those people only want something for themselves. They don't care. They only love themselves, not others."

"You know that's not me. I won't let you down. I promise."

"Don't fear your choices," she continues, as she leads me to the lakeside. "Blessed are the pure in heart, for they will see God."

"I've made my choice without fear. This is how we can go forward in life. I want us to see this world together. I want us to share the triumphs and the rewards. I want us to have a beautiful place to live that is ours. For that, I will work, and train, and fight. I'll never give less than I can against any opponent."

"I know you will win. I believe in you, but I'll still be a little happier if you defeat Dario."

A last hug and we walk off back through the rest of the island. It feels like nothing can stop me, but something still doesn't sit right with me about turning from Apollo on the grounds of his temple. I'll speak to Demetrius about it. He will reassure me.

***

I leave Zoe at her house, where Leon is waiting to join me for the rest of the journey.

"Where were you this morning," he asks. "The dock is busy with people and goods arriving for the games."

"Did Demetrius notice?"

"Demetrius notices everything, but he doesn't always say something at the time. Train hard today and I'm sure he'll allow the one morning missed."

"I'll work late tonight on the palaestra. There's not much to do, but enough to make sure it looks the best we can make it."

"You and Tigranes and the others have made such a difference with your work. Restoring the palaestra has restored Demetrius as well. He even looks younger. In fact, tell him that and he'll definitely let you off of missing work."

We're still laughing and joking as we arrive at the palaestra. The new white marble stands out against the green hills that rise above and the deep blue sea that lies below. It glows with a vibrant energy. New wrestlers who have arrived early for the games are already training in the exercise areas we've built.

Demetrius sits in a group with other trainers and mentors who have traveled with the contestants. A panel of judges is being chosen to oversee the event. Stone benches are being finished off. Enough for the largest crowd I'll ever have wrestled in front of.

Apion greets us and steers us toward a man seated by the skamma pits. Today, the rules only allow a small amount of time for sparring. So, Leon and I ask to be paired. We can help one another learn from mistakes and each other's ideas. We understand and trust one another to only help and not hinder our chances of success.

Dario is already training. He's working out with others that he knows from previous fights. There is a camaraderie between them. They respect him and as much as it pains me, I must respect him too, if I'm to defeat him.

As the afternoon moves on, excitement grows. We run, lift weights, play ball games, run through warm-up exercises, and work on the moves we want to perfect. I'm aware we're being watched by many who might have to take us on, so when we finish our time in the skamma, we clean ourselves as fast as we can so that we can take our turn to watch those who are still going through their own practice.

"This feels like the real thing now," I say to Leon. "The games are only days away. I can't wait for them to start. It will be fantastic to step out in front of the crowds."

"I've got to admit I'm nervous," Leon replies. "This is my first real contest. If I can win my first round, then I'll be happy."

"You can get further than that. You've come along so much in the last few weeks."

"That's because I have you to train with and not Dario just beating me up. I haven't spoken to him since you came back from Mykonos."

"Me neither, but it's best that way."

I look across to the other side of the palaestra. Dario is in with a group that's standing around Demetrius. We catch each other glancing for a brief moment, but he looks away. He focuses on the sparring, which is still taking place. His mood seems different today. Demetrius has probably already spoken to him. I'm sure I will get my talk later.

As the training sessions come to a close and most of the wrestlers and trainers pack up and leave for the day, only a few stay behind to discuss the games and the refurbished palaestra. They offer congratulations to Demetrius before they leave. Soon, only Demetrius, Leon, and I remain.

"The two of you worked well together today. I'm pleased, you gave a splendid display of fitness and strength. No one will think of either of you as an easy win."

"Thank you, Demetrius," we both reply.

"Rest and return tomorrow for more of the same. I will see both of you at the dock in the morning. There are still supplies arriving, along with pilgrims and ships of dignitaries. Our work increases at the time we could do with it being easier, but everything we do prepares us in some way for the contest. It sharpens our minds and stretches our muscles just a little more."

He allows a silence to fall and concentrates his gaze on me. That's my warning to not try to take a day off from work again. Demetrius doesn't scold you; he just expects you to show integrity and virtue. That is something I can only do for myself. If I don't, then I know that my chances of achieving my goals will suffer. Demetrius is offering me the respect that I will make the right choices without being told what to do. I let him know that I understand with a nod of the head, no words need to be spoken. Leon and I turn to leave, but Demetrius has one last request.

"I've just remembered, Alexander. Before you go, I want you to examine the benches that overlook the palaestra, can you take a look at them before you go?"

Leon and I stop and exchange a brief look between us. Maybe I'm still to be punished for my fight the other day.

Leon mouths the words, "Tell him he looks younger," before smiling and walking on without me.

I turn back to face Demetrius. His expression shows little reaction, but somehow, I think he could read Leon's lips.

"Follow me," he says.

In silence, we climb the slope. The sun is beginning its descent, but much of the daylight has still to pass. The sea breeze always blows on Delos. It picks up as we rise out of the protection of the palaestra buildings, but it's still warm, and as we turn to sit and face the sea, it keeps our faces free of blowing hair. A perfect scene extends out below for us to gaze on. I look at the benches and the work looks well finished.

"Don't worry, they are better than I remember, good enough for us to have a last talk about what lies ahead. I can tell you are ready to rise to the occasion."

"I can't wait. This has been my dream for so long."

"It has been my dream, too. To see the palaestra returned to its former glory. I can tell you one person who would have been so pleased to see this, your father. When he was on the island, he would walk along and visit from the fort. He would gaze at the ruins of what was once a magnificent building and try to recapture the days gone by in his mind. We were good friends you know."

"Yes, I know. My mother told me the story of how my father tried to save your son."

"He saved him, at least for his fate to catch up with him on another day. Your father took a significant risk in forming a plan to help him avoid the executioner. If they were to discover his plotting at the time, then he would have faced punishment, too. He did a lot for my family. I missed him when he left for Rome with your mother. He kept the palaestra alive in his own way. Reminding me of former glories and encouraging me to relive my own career.

"But time fills the gaps in our lives with other tasks. Your Uncle Nikos and I worked as partners and built a business. He wanted any excuse to sail. I was content to trade from the dock. It has worked well, and we have grown wealthy, but it never satisfied me, until one day when he returned with a very special cargo—" Demetrius smiles. "You."

"Me?"

"It was like Marcus returning, but with the gift of youth, while I had aged. You arrived on Delos just like he had, and I could see from our first meeting that you shared his energy and willingness to do your best for the people of this island.

"Not all the Romans are so concerned. They are happy to serve their time far away from the wars to the north. They do what their commanders ask of them and nothing more. They dream of going home, wherever that is. They have a life, a wife or a family where they came from. Delos is not the place for them, but your father was different. I knew it would only be a matter of time until he partnered with a local girl."

"My mother said that he first went with Dario's mother."

"Unfortunate, but true. He was stoic about the situation. First, he acknowledged that their partnership lacked the right foundations. He learned lessons for himself to improve his character, and then he released all that was past, before realizing what, or *who*, was the perfect person for him."

"I've found my perfect partner, but I worry I've made a promise that I will have trouble keeping. Can I tell you?"

"You can always talk to me. I've lived my own life. I won't say that I got everything right, but if you have concerns, then I'm always here to give advice where I can."

"I went to the Sacred Lake this morning with Zoe. I made an offering to Kyrios and not Apollo. It made Zoe happy, but I've worried all day about whether I did the right thing. I worry that I wasn't as sincere as I appeared. I was thinking all the time that Apollo might strike me with a lightning bolt."

"Lightning bolts kill few. Apollo has a terrible aim it seems, but treachery can smolder if it's allowed to live. You work hard and train for your contests. You devote time to becoming a better wrestler, but that is so much simpler than becoming a better person. Trust that you can reveal your concerns to those who care. You know I'll suggest that if you are for one another, then a rash promise is easy to forgive. If, instead, you find that you cannot face the truth, if you cannot acknowledge a mistake, then *you* will suffer. The lightning bolt might strike, but not through Apollo's efforts."

"I understand what you're saying, but Zoe devotes herself to her church."

"Kyrios does not expect his followers to be perfect. All he asks is for them to have faith that he will guide them in the right direction. He preached about forgiveness, and he endured suffering for them.

"I say again, your fear will build in your mind as time moves on. Do you believe that she doesn't have the power for forgiveness? Truth brings balance and order into life. Repay all those who have faith in you by being the best person you can be. Will you confess your sin?"

"Yes, I will." I pause. "Maybe after the Great Delia?"

Demetrius nods his head. "I can't tell you when or how. I know you will be miserable if she is angry with you before the contest, so I will remain silent, but just know this, we all believe in you. Your family, Zoe, and I. We all believe you can win. All of us, plus one more person, Gaius. He arrives just before the games begin, but in good time to see you fight. If I ask anything of you, then let Gaius see the person you have become since arriving on Delos, not the person he thinks he remembers."

"I will. I promise."

"Then you will fight before the emperor in Rome. I'm sure of it."

CHAPTER XXII

"Master Alexander. Master Alexander."

My eyes open to see Selene in a panic. "Have I overslept? The games are today, don't tell me I've slept too long?"

"No. Master Alexander, it is still late, but your mother wants to speak to you... she's very upset."

"My mother? What's wrong?"

"She needs to tell you herself. Please go to her now."

Selene leaves me to get out of bed. I shake the tiredness from myself. My heart is racing about what might be wrong, on this night of all nights. I must have only been asleep for a short while.

I splash my face with cold water and dress as quickly as I can. I can hear my mother sobbing even before I walk into her bedroom. Selene is sitting, comforting her, but she rises as soon as I arrive.

"I'll leave you alone. Please hear what your mother has to say."

"What's upset you?" I sit down where Selene has been and hug my mother to let her know that I'm here for her.

"I'm sorry, my son. I'm sorry for ruining the life you might have had. Just know that your father and I always wanted the best for you. You are the most important person in my life. I will give you everything within my power to help you find happiness."

"I know you love me, Mother, I've never questioned it. My family is so important to me. What's wrong?"

My mother stops her tears; she seems to gasp for air at first, but then her breathing slows. She takes my hands in hers and looks at me with a deep sadness in her eyes.

"Alexander, I have lived through a lie for your entire life. I thought I had escaped its curse, but Apollo has only waited for the right time for his revenge."

"Apollo? A curse? What do you mean?"

"I committed a sin against him, the greatest sin of all. No child can be born on the island of Apollo, it is sacrilege. The punishment can be severe, exile at best, or even death if the priests demand it."

"I don't understand. Who's the child you speak of?"

"You are the child, Alexander."

"I thought I was born near Ostia before we reached Rome."

"That was what we had to say to protect ourselves. You were born early, a month early, and you were born here on the island. Delos is your birthplace. It is a secret your father and I have had to keep for your entire life."

"But if no one else knows, then we're safe, aren't we?"

"Some others know. Your Uncle Nikos, because you were born in this house. The servants who aided me that night are long gone, and so are the Romans who allowed us to sail off before the sun rose in the east. Your father arranged a sailing, and his commanding officer agreed. Even the Romans knew that the child of one of their men being born on the island could cause a lot of trouble up to the highest levels of the legions. It was that serious." She pauses. "Then there was one other person who witnessed our escape—Dario's mother, Maria."

"Maria knows I was born here? Is that why she's causing trouble for you?"

My mother nods her head and begins to sob once more.

"She visited me weeks ago. She complained that she felt her life was going to suffer now that I had returned to the island with you. She told me that Dario was earning a good living to support them, and now you were threatening to take it away, stealing his chance of success."

"I'll make sure I'll steal it now that I know this. Maria cannot threaten you and get away with it."

"No, Alexander, no. I'm sorry to burden you with this tonight. I hoped that something would remove the threat, but I dare not ask Apollo for his help. Maybe you can, maybe you can be at Mount Kynthos for the dawn. Make an offering and ask that you do not meet Dario in the draw. Ask that another contender has the strength to defeat him. For it can't be you.

"Maria made it clear to me—if you defeat her son at the games, she is prepared to reveal my crime. If that happens, then our lives could be in ruin. If you face Dario in the games, then the only way you can save all of us is by losing to him."

Silence fills the room. I can't believe what I'm hearing. It's too much to take in all at once. My head is spinning with a thousand thoughts of what can be done. The sun will soon rise and then the games will be underway. There's no time to talk or find another solution. I suddenly feel cold, although sweat is dripping from my brow. I need something to give me hope.

"Surely, the priests will not punish us? It was so long ago. Have they punished anyone else?"

"Many years ago, yes. That's why there have been no births here for a long time. Maria knows that the Great Delia brings the highest priests of the Greek cities to Delos. They're here from Delphi, Thebes, Sparta, Argos, and many other places. I can't imagine what they will do when they are all assembled to judge us. It causes my heart great pain to ask you, but if you have to face Dario, you must let him win."

"Then I'll lose my chance to fight in Rome. I've made promises to Zoe and Demetrius. What will they say if I throw the fight?"

"You will live to fight another day, and your day will come. I promise you. You are still young. If they send us into exile, then there will be no Zoe, no Demetrius to train you, and they will never allow us to return to Delos. If they choose death..."

"Maria could hold this over our heads forever. How do we know that she won't tell the priests later?"

"There is still a risk for her. Things may not go well for her fate if they discover that she has known all these years and not told anyone. The small offering she is making depends on Dario's continuing success as a wrestler. If nothing happens at the games to harm his chances, she will remain silent."

"Can we trust her?"

"I think so. Each success for Dario will leave her with more to lose. It will reach a point where it will be too much. Then we will be safe."

"And how long will I have to live in Dario's shadow? I thought the gods had brought me the good fortune to achieve my dreams and have a perfect life. I realize what you mean when you say Apollo decides the perfect moment to enact his revenge."

"That's why I thought you might ask him for his help?"

"I can't. When Zoe and I visited the Sacred Lake, I denounced my following of the old gods and made a proclamation of my faith in Kyrios. I chose to do this as I looked over Apollo's birthplace. Now, this is my punishment. He is withdrawing all the gifts that Delos brought me. It would have been better if we remained in the Subura. At least I might have earned good money from the street fights. The friends we had there were good to us. Why did you decide to bring us here? Why show me this life for it just to be taken away?"

"I am so sorry, my son. You must believe me when I say this. I want you to have a good life, and you can, as long as the secret is safe. Do you wish you never met Zoe?"

I sigh to myself and look to my mother. I can feel her pain, but my own heart is heavy as well. "I will do what you ask. Please try to rest until dawn. Apollo will make his judgment. If I end up drawn against Dario, then I know the sacrifice he demands, and I will accept it."

"No one else can know, Alexander. Not even Zoe. Sharing the secret will endanger anyone who knows. Do you understand that?"

"Yes, I understand, but it just adds to the burden of thinking about it. You have my word. I will not put us in danger, but I will do everything that I can to get as near to the final as I can, and you must be happy even if I lose. Promise me that."

"Thank you, Alexander. I couldn't wish for a better son."

"Sleep and rest. Know we will be safe."

My mother settles down and closes her eyes. I look at her for a moment as a peaceful stillness takes over within her. I don't return to my room but go out to sit in the courtyard. I sit on the bench looking out to sea. In the far distance, lightning flashes with a low rumble of thunder. Apollo is busy punishing someone else.

"Is your mother alright, Master Alexander?" Selene speaks from the entrance.

"Do you know the secret, Selene?"

"Yes, your mother told me. She was so upset, she needed to tell someone."

"So, you're cursed too?"

"The gods cursed everything I came from when they witnessed my family murdered and my abduction into slavery. Many like me didn't even survive the sea crossing. Was I blessed by a god, or was it only luck that led me to this house and the benevolence of your uncle? Wherever life leads us, we must still search for all that is good. That comes from within, not from the summit of Olympus. Goodnight, Master Alexander."

Selene is right. I sit outside for a while longer, considering all the teachings I have received about Stoicism. This was my test. To realize what was within my power to control, and to accept what was beyond my reach.

Many questions run through my mind. Some I remembered from my father, some from the garden of Gaius, and others from the teachings of Demetrius. I wish that I could speak to him now, but what more could he say? I've listened, and now I must act. I will hold my head high in the skamma and at the very least I will make my mark. If Dario wins, then it will be on the very last point at a time of my choosing.

***

All of Delos is rising with the sun. The broken sleep makes me slow to start, but Selene and Na'amat have made a special meal that they say will help my strength and my stamina. After eating and washing myself, I feel better about facing the day.

Everyone is excited. My mother is more like her old self, better than she's been for a long while. When Zoe arrives at our door, my mother fusses over her and makes sure she feels welcome. Uncle Nikos is still telling his terrible jokes, but the laughter is infectious.

Of course, everyone keeps insisting that I'm going to win. The others don't notice sympathetic glances from my mother and Selene, but I know what I have to do. I have a plan—there will be thirty-two contestants. The battles will be fought over five rounds, *if* I make it to the final. Dario and I might not face one another, but that's not within my control. I accept the praise in friendly spirit, but I will give each match a clear focus. Looking to the future only encourages fear.

"Time for us to leave," Uncle Nikos announces.

As we walk together toward the palaestra, there's great anticipation in the air for the events of the day ahead. The Great Delia has already been underway for the pilgrims and the priests. Many rituals have been taking place, and the sea breeze carries the smell of incense to every corner of the island.

Symbols and ornaments of the gods are present around every home, from small figurines to larger statues. There can be no doubt in anyone's mind—Delos is the island of Apollo.

The crowd is growing larger as we approach the palaestra. I can hear many voices commenting on the building. For the pilgrims, the day's events will be a highlight of their visit. A glorious tradition of wrestling has returned to play its part in the celebration. For local residents, the restoration of the palaestra is a potent testament of the importance of Delos as the center of the world.

As the path narrows toward the entrance, we meet Leon and his parents.

"Are you ready?" asks Leon.

"There's no more time left. We have to be ready," I reply.

Within a few more steps, we have to part from our families. Leon and I must enter the area for competitors to take part in the draw and learn the order of contests in the first round. The task of security belongs to the same men who work at the docks for Demetrius. They know Leon and me well; we have no trouble passing inside.

Here, our families must part as well. Only men may view the contest from within the confines of the palaestra, and among them, only a chosen few from the higher echelons of society accompanied by their supporters and bodyguards, may enter.

The rest of the public gathers on the hillside slopes above. They cannot see everything, but word will soon spread of who is winning and who is losing. Vendors weave through the crowd, selling food and drink, while wagers are placed on those deemed most likely to emerge as champion. The ever-present Roman guard watches from a distance, ready to intervene should a fight break out beyond the skamma.

We soon leave the sun behind as we enter the dim half-light of the judges' room. This is where the draw will take place for the first round. It's not like Mykonos where there were only a few taking part. This time there are the thirty-two contestants, their trainers and patrons, officials, and guards. Over a hundred people have crammed into the room, surrounded by the echoing noise of all the voices in conversation. It is still early morning, but it's already hot in here.

The tokens are being collected into two amphorae. I have mine from Mykonos, and Leon produces his own. The symbol on one side looks worn by the passing of time.

"It was my grandfather's, and my great-grandfather's before him... I painted the first letter of my own name without removing theirs. It makes it stand out with the letters of my ancestors, not just my own."

"That's a precious object. It will make your heart strong in the contest to know they're with you."

"Just as long as they make my arms and legs strong as well. Then I'll be happier."

We head for the judges' table and confirm our entry from a list they already have. They make us place our tokens in different jars. That means we might face one another in one of the rounds.

"Go easy on me." Leon smiles as we shake hands.

Apion appears out of the crowd as we stand to await the draw.

"This will be a fine contest for both of you today. Enjoy the event. It will take the full day to complete, so pace yourselves. Between rounds, eat food for energy, and drink to replace the fluid you will lose under the heat of the sun."

"So, who have you bet on?" I ask half in fun, but Apion changes the subject.

"Look over to the back wall. Can you make out the figure standing next to Demetrius?"

"Gaius!"

"He arrived on the last ship to dock yesterday. He stayed in the house of Demetrius, and as far as I can see, they have been in talks all morning. Something great is being planned for the winner of this event. Forgive me if I leave you now, but I believe they will need my expertise. We could have a lot of fun and really make a name for ourselves in Rome. Don't you think, Alexander?"

I nod in agreement as Apion leaves to introduce himself to my old trainer.

"How does it make you feel to see him again?" Leon asks.

"I feel angry. I know he wants me to lose. All I can hope is that he places bets along the way, and I cause him to lose money as a result."

Our eyes meet for a moment. He stares at me while still reacting to the surrounding conversations. I sense a fear from him. Today is about reputation, his against mine. For a moment, I almost forget my promise to my mother. I want to show Gaius how wrong he was to cast me aside. That's until Dario enters the frame of my view. He stands with his back to me, as Apion introduces him to Gaius. The fight fixer has an interest in both of us. He has told me I can win; has he told Dario the same?

The chief judge stands to announce the start of the draw. The games are about to begin.

***

"Fight!"

I adopt my stance against a man from Athens. He's much older than me and very experienced. My round is one of the last for the opening matches. Dario and Leon have both won their first contests. Now I have to win my own.

The crowd is excited and the air charged with energy. Lining the palaestra are leaders and influencers of the city-states. Wealth and influence surround me. Any one of these men could ask me to fight in their palaces or their own games. The winner of today will be able to demand large payments from any one of them. Larger if Apion has his way.

I distract myself, looking for the money in the crowd. Just like in the old days when my father would sit amongst them, encouraging them to bet against me.

My back hits the ground of the skamma with a thump. Again, just like I did in those old days, I have taken the first fall to heighten the interest.

As I stand back up, I catch a look of concern from Demetrius and a sly smile from Gaius. I think only Apion can read my mind; he realizes that I am working up the crowd's enthusiasm and expectations. They cheer with greater volume as I turn the fight around and secure my place against the next competitor. I am giving them the show they want.

The fights follow a cycle—the winners assembling to draw another opponent, preparing in the oil room, taking part in the fight, and then cleaning the oil and the dirt to begin all over again.

Leon loses his fight in the second round of the contest. Dario goes through with the fastest victory of the day. I haven't seen his matches, but the word spreads that he is a favorite for the title. The third round has reduced us to eight. The crowds in the judges' room have already thinned as most of the contestants are now gone. Leon, always the loyal friend, stays beside me to offer support.

The next draw places me against a recent foe, Pallas from Naxos, who I won against on Mykonos. He smiles as he acknowledges our contest. He will want to even the score, and if his reputation is true, then he'll not leave me the same opportunities.

Our fight is hard and tiring. He is a worthy competitor who has learned from me as I have from him. This time it is not a show as he takes the first two points. I have to battle to recover once again. The crowd is growing used to my comebacks. They want me to snatch victory from defeat, but in this round, it saps my strength. I win with a high throw and the audience jumps to their feet on the point of my win. Apion is leading the cheers, while Gaius is growing in frustration and losing coins from his purse. I offer him a smile.

"You're doing well. We are only one fight away from one another." Dario joins me for the penultimate draw. "I look forward to crushing you in front of your new followers."

"You might draw me this time. The final might not be between us."

"Whenever we face, it doesn't matter. Apollo will favor the pure who are without sin."

"Then he'll favor Alexander, not you," says Leon.

"I don't think so, eh, Alexander?"

Demetrius can see there's trouble brewing. He walks over to address us together.

"I am expecting a good fight if you two are drawn together. Dario, do not underestimate Alexander, he may surprise you today."

He pauses and looks me in the eyes.

"Alexander, learn not to fall into traps. I'm sure Dario will not allow you the same opportunity to turn the tide of your fight with him."

We turn to face the judges. I wait, holding my breath. Although the others don't know, there's only one route to my victory—Dario must fight this round against a different opponent where I need him to lose. Any other result will mean I have to give up the last battle, to save my family and everything I hold dear.

The chief judge picks the tokens from a single amphora and declares the next two fights.

"Alexander of Delos will fight Nikolas of Artaxata, Heracles of Thebes will fight Dario of Delos."

The gods are teasing me or offering me a chance. I can't tell, but my fight is first. I'll make sure I'm in the final.

***

Whether Nikolas has made it through the early rounds with luck rather than skill, the pressures of the whole day have taken a toll. He's tired when I face him, his energy and stamina sapped from the struggles of his day, the heat of the sun, or perhaps even a late night of wine in the evening before. Whatever it is, I beat him without a struggle, and now I have the honor of the fastest win.

I rush to clean myself and return to the audience to watch Dario. My only chance of winning is if Heracles can do the job for me.

As I stand silent amongst a raging crowd, I ask all the gods I know to help the man from Thebes. Any that will hear me, be it Apollo, Minerva or even Zoe's God. I ask that they grant Heracles the power to defeat Dario. The fight is one of the most brutal of the day. Dario relies on his speed as much as ever, but Heracles has greater strength. The fight becomes frantic as it comes down to a last score.

There is no obvious winner between these two, and in the end, the gods choose to aid Dario in his quest. A final choke on his opponent causes the defeated man to raise his index finger in the air. His submission also signals my defeat. I drop my head as the people around me roar for the final contenders. A climax where I already know the result.

Time passes too quickly. Demetrius and Apion offer last words of advice to both of us. There are plenty around to prepare us and make sure we arrive in the skamma together.

"Make me look good," Dario whispers amidst the loud calls from the audience. I spot Demetrius among others on the benches. He looks disappointed... as if he's aware of what I'm about to do. Demetrius observes everything and it seems he can look into my soul. I'm sure he knows that my fight is gone. Gaius sits beside him. He's calling a win for Dario. I see him parting with more coin. I'm sure he's trying to earn back what he lost. He will recover his money.

I fight as hard as I can. This time I score first. I catch a look of doubt on Dario's face. He scores the next two points through his own talent. It's then his arrogance comes to the fore again. He teases me into an error. He talks into my ear when we press our heads together.

"I stand for Apollo. I am his champion. I have not desecrated his birthplace. I am his chosen one, Alexander. I am not a common street fighter, who cheats the poor for the little coin they have. My father died facing his enemies, not stabbed in the back like yours; and my mother did not bring shame to this place. It is time to fall from grace, Alexander. It is time for my victory."

I let him claim what he knows is his already. I drop my guard and look over Dario's shoulder. I'm looking for my father. I want him to tell me what to do. The pause is long enough for Dario to use up his last burst of speed. I'm suddenly separated from the ground. The world revolves around me and, as I crash down in the pit, my collarbone and left arm tear apart. The pain of dislocation causes me to scream with all the power in my lungs, but it goes unnoticed among the triumphant cheers for Dario.

The last image I have is of Dario's arm being raised in the air by the chief judge, then Leon and Tigranes are around me. They are quick to manipulate my arm back into place. The second jolt of pain causes me to black out.

***

It's late when I come around in my uncle's house.

"He's awake," I hear Zoe's voice say.

I'm propped up on cushions in a room full of people. My mother's face is ashen, but happy to see me awake. Zoe sits closest. Uncle Nikos sits beside Demetrius. His face shows little emotion, yet he dominates the room with his presence. I feel that the others are waiting for him to speak.

"I'm sorry, Demetrius," is all I can think to say.

"What are you sorry for, Alexander?"

I look at my mother. Her face tells me that the secret is still a secret.

"For losing. I wanted to win so much. I wanted to repay your faith in me."

"My faith in you has little to do with winning a wrestling contest. I didn't read the signs with my own son until it was too late, but that experience taught me how to read the signs in others. You didn't win today because you decided to lose. You spent the day convincing the audience that you were powerful yet fallible. You could take the throws and come back to win. You told your story well, and most left without suspecting a thing. What inspired you to make that choice? Think before you answer. For only a virtue I have missed may offer you redemption from this break of trust and faith."

The pain was still coursing through me. Uncle Nikos handed me a cup of wine.

"Take a drink and a breath, Alexander. Speak when you are ready."

"You think I tried to lose?"

Demetirus sat somber with a look of defeat. His silence was difficult to bear and finally he answered.

"Not just me. Gaius knows you were too good for Dario. He saw something in your performance today that will help him justify casting you out of his palaestra. He says you will only fight for the ill-gotten gains of a criminal venture. He considers you a trickster who engages in fraud. He wonders about who was issuing your instructions. He even hinted I might be the unknown beneficiary of your schemes.

"After everything I have done, his comment exposed a weakness in myself. It brought my son's memory back to haunt me. I never saw Jason again after he joined the legion. He didn't die at the hands of the executioner, but I didn't see him age even one more year. His life was over within months. I tortured myself for years that I had let the problems of his character fester and grow, and it was only the words of Seneca and Epictetus that have helped me find peace. I promise you I cannot put myself through it again. Tell me what thoughts drove you to this."

Everyone in the room is awaiting my reply. My mother can't look at me. Zoe holds my hand, but I can feel her fingernails press into my palm. She wants Demetrius to be wrong with all her heart. I think Uncle Nikos knows what's going on, but he'll never offer his thoughts outside of those who share the secret. I decide to face the anger of Apollo once more.

"It was someone I knew from the Subura, He contacted me a few days ago. Word had traveled back to Rome that I was on Delos, and news of a great wrestling contest had reached those from my past. The man I knew led a gang that organized fights. I had fought for him before. He sailed in on a galley and didn't take long to find me. He offered a large share from a wealthy audience. He insisted that this was an opportunity that neither of us could miss."

A gasp goes around the room. Demetrius stands to leave.

"I cannot save you from this, just like I couldn't save Jason. You have caused many powerful people to lose small fortunes on you today. You have deceived them, just as Jason deceived others with his fake silver. How do you think they would treat you if they were to discover this?" He pauses and looks pained. "I owe your life as a debt for my son's. I will say nothing; this will pay what I owe in full. Others will offer you work; someone might even offer you training when you recover. I hope this sum of money was worth it."

Demetrius steps out of our house without a second glance.

"He'll soften in time," Uncle Nikos assures me. "Maybe in ten or twenty years."

"What have you done?" Tears begin to roll down Zoe's cheeks. "How long could you do this for and not tell me? Was that your plan to make a career for yourself? To lie and to cheat and take people for fools? And I would be the biggest fool, believing every word you say to me, believing you with all my heart."

"Zoe, I'll make up for this, you'll see. This will never happen again, I promise."

"You know who used to promise me that? Dario. I fell for his pleading again and again. I thought you were different. I believed you were different, but you are worse than him. Dario doesn't have the intelligence to plan something like this. How can I trust you again? I can't stay here a moment longer. I can't even breathe the same air. Like Demetrius said, I hope you find what you want in life, but it's clear that it isn't me!"

"Zoe!" I call, as she runs for the door.

I try to get up to follow her, but the pain pins me down.

"Zoe!" I call again, but she's gone.

My mother, Uncle Nikos, and I sit in silence for what feels like ages. We know the truth. Guilt hangs over everyone. There is no point in saying words that might cause further hurt. I can only pray we have appeased Apollo and his chariot will soar over brighter days ahead. That is the only remaining hope that I have.

CHAPTER XXIII

LEON

"Leon, it's time to go for your training."

My mother is standing on the shingle, calling me back from the sea. I take a last plunge into the water to clear my head as I head for shore. I stretch my arms out against the water; they're bruised and tender from the beatings I've been taking again from Dario. My wrestling is improving, and he doesn't win so easily, but he still triumphs as my body suffers the consequences. I admit I am struggling to stay focused, and I think more each day about giving up. I was never good at hiding my feelings. My mother can see it on my face as I step back onto dry land.

"Have you still not seen Alexander?" she asks.

"No." I shake my head. "I didn't think someone could disappear on an island this small, but he's managed it. I ask Tigranes if I see him at the dock. He says Alexander's shoulder is recovering, but that he rarely leaves the house. His mother is the same."

"You should visit him. You are his friend. You can help him, I'm sure of it."

"I worry he'll think I've betrayed him. He'll know I've been helping Dario to train for the fight in Rome. Zoe could convince him more than me."

"I know, son. I've tried to speak to her, but you know your sister, she feels let down. She punishes herself for placing her trust in another boy, and she still compares Alexander and Dario. She should trust her mother, at least. I know the differences between them." She looks over toward the fishing boats. "Your father is angry with his daughter, but that is normal. He wonders where the money is that Alexander got. Who were the criminals? And where are they now?"

"He knew the local gangs when he was in the Subura. That much is true." I look at my mother. "You don't believe this either?"

"I only know what I know, because of the tale your sister came home with. Why would Alexander lie? What or who was he trying to protect? You must find out, Leon."

"Me?"

"Out of everyone, you have never lost faith in him. You were close enough to have learned something before the Great Delia, but that never happened, did it?"

I shake my head.

"I worry about you as well. I didn't think I would see days go by where you didn't smile or laugh, but that happens more often now."

"Life is not so good at the moment, that's true. I help my father with the nets, then I go to work at the docks, and that's not the same with my friend missing. Then I train with Dario most afternoons. My life has gone back to the way it was before, and I don't want that."

"Then you must take the action you can. Think about it... someone knows the truth."

"Dario?"

"Yes. Dario."

"He insists he won the fight without Alexander's help. He's annoyed that Demetrius still won't give him full credit for the victory. That's why he still fights so hard against me. He still has a point to prove and knows Demetrius still lacks confidence that he's good enough for Rome."

"So, he won nothing in the end."

"Other than the applause on the day, no. He will claim his prize, his right to compete before the emperor, but I wonder if he truly believes he can win."

"Then get to the truth. Maybe even Dario will thank you for it."

We both look at one another with disbelief and a smile.

"I'll try my best."

"That's all I can ask... It's all any of us can ask."

My mother is right, but how do I persuade Dario to tell me anything?

The sight of the palaestra doesn't bring me joy at the moment. Everywhere I look I can see the places where Alexander has worked. This is as much his place as anyone's. It makes me angry to think that he's the one person who can't come here. At the same time, Dario is benefiting from everything that Alexander helped to build. Why can't Demetrius see this is wrong?

It won't do me any good to hold on to my bad feelings. I have to work out how I can get the truth from Dario. I can only do that if I have focus and control. I put on a brave smile and walk toward the skamma where Dario is practicing moves on his own, under the watchful eye of Demetrius.

"I'm here. Sorry I'm late. It's taking a little longer to finish my work at the dock right now."

Demetrius ignores the meaning behind my words. He still hasn't found a suitable replacement for Alexander, which makes my job harder to do.

"I appreciate your efforts," he replies, "they don't go unnoticed. We all have much to thank you for. Isn't that right, Dario?"

"Eh, yes. Thank you, Leon."

Dario can hardly utter the words, but I can see he will do anything to stay near Demetrius. There is something about him that has changed. I can sense it. The old Dario would still be full of swagger over his win at the Great Delia, but now he seems more withdrawn.

If Alexander is innocent, then Dario must be suffering from guilt, and Demetrius has given us many examples of how guilt can weaken us when we dwell on something from our memory. We cannot control it, so guilt serves no purpose. If I'm right, then Dario is weakening himself by holding on to something that is devouring his concentration. An idea flashes across my mind.

Maybe this is the weak point I must attack.

I put on my most enthusiastic look for the benefit of Demetrius. "So, what are we doing for training today?"

"Just exercise, some running, some weights. I have to meet with some new traders this afternoon. They are offering business with the Egyptians, and I want to make sure that I'm involved."

"I'm happy to work in the skamma as well, to give Dario the extra time that he needs."

"Do you think I *need* the time, Leon?" Dario's voice is full of scorn.

"You are the champion of the Great Delia, but do you think that the champion of Rome is not preparing? Or do you think he's lying back on a couch, eating grapes served by a slave?"

Demetrius nods his head. "Leon is right. No matter how good you think you are, Dario, we should concentrate on how good your opponent is. Whoever he is."

"Alexander once told me that Gaius' champion is called Lucius," I tell him, "the son of a very important senator. They say he's been wrestling ever since he could walk. Alexander has trained with him. I'm sure he would be able to help you with his knowledge."

"Did Alexander beat him?" Dario asks.

"I don't think so."

"Then his advice will count for nothing. We do not need him, do we, Demetrius?"

Demetrius sits in silence and gazes back at me. I know he can understand the wisdom of what I say. It's easy to see that Dario is unhappy with the lack of a response.

"Demetrius?" Dario repeats his question. His voice shakes. *He is nervous.*

Demetrius nods his head toward Dario. "You are right. He cannot return yet. His deceit was a crime for which he has exiled himself. No one has seen him. We cannot know the nature of his heart, and whether he is repentant for his misdeeds."

"What will it take, then?" I reply. "I could try to talk to him. I could maybe convince him to explain what happened. That's if he doesn't think that I've turned my back on him."

"We do not need him," Dario objects. "Leon, you cause trouble with words and thoughts that will only make this situation worse. Demetrius is right. It is actions, not words. Alexander has been causing trouble ever since he arrived here. He is not one of us. He is Roman. Who is to say that he is not sending word to Gaius about how his champion should fight me? Perhaps his gambling friends are already arranging the odds."

I can see that Dario is covering up something. *My mother is right.* Meanwhile, Demetrius darts his eyes between both of us. I know he can see what I can see. Nothing escapes his gaze.

"Can I trust both of you to wrestle in my absence? You are training, not fighting. I don't expect to hear of injuries on my return."

We both nod in agreement, but I conceal a thought.

There may not be injuries, but there may still be pain.

Once Demetrius has left for the day, we begin by warming up with a run, a ball game, and some stretching followed by weights. I push Dario to lift more. I encourage him to go further and faster than ever before. As he forces himself to beat his own records, he fails to notice I'm lifting nothing at all.

I praise him. After all, he is doing well. I am not lying, but I know that Dario's body is under stress. He is doing too much. In his mind, he is becoming stronger, but he is tiring his muscles just before a match. With an exhausted body, the first advantage he will lose is speed. His favored method of attack.

"Maybe we should go to the skamma," I suggest.

"Not yet," he replies. "This is good for me."

I let him continue. The veins are standing out on his arms; the sweat is lashing from his brow, and his eyes bulge as he takes on even more weight. I shout more encouragement, cheering him on. It's only when Dario decides he has done too much that he declares a stop.

"I feel good," he insists as he gasps for breath.

"Maybe we shouldn't fight now," I reply.

"Are you scared? You've seen me lift more weight than ever. I've never felt more ready to fight."

"If you're sure?"

"Yes, let's prepare."

We walk to the oil room. The sun heats every part of the surrounding air. I can see that Dario has lost a lot of fluid, but energy courses through him right now. It persuades him he's unbeatable.

As we begin to cover ourselves in oil, I can see he is slowing down. His muscles are rushing to repair themselves. I know his reactions will suffer. Before we are anywhere near the skamma, I'm securing an advantage. Now it is time to press the attack on his mind.

"Demetrius might invite Alexander to return."

"What? No! Alexander threw the most important fight for some coin. Why would Demetrius forgive him?"

"Forgiveness is an important quality that Demetrius encourages us to consider. Why would he not forgive Alexander himself?"

"You know that Alexander must explain his reasons before Demetrius would even consider it. If Alexander knows what's good for him, he will leave Delos on a ship under darkness and never return. He's lying about the gang and the gambling."

"He's lying? How do you know?"

"Because I was better than him on the day. It was my skill, not his cheating. He just didn't want to admit it to Demetrius."

"Dario, I have stayed loyal to Demetrius and the palaestra. I have played my part in helping you prepare for Rome as much as I can, but many at the final of the Great Delia felt that Alexander threw the fight. That means they think he let you win. Demetrius thinks he let you win. Your victory is hollow unless you can prove he didn't cheat, don't you see?"

For a moment, I'm unsure if Dario agrees. Or if he is going to lash out. His face shows a mix of anger and frustration. He knows I'm making sense.

"You know I'm right," I continue. "How can you be sure that he didn't cheat? How can you prove to Demetrius that you were the winner on the day?"

"I don't know. I don't know!"

"Be calm," I insist. "We would be better off thinking about this than wasting more energy in the skamma."

"Demetrius will know when I beat Lucius in Rome. Then my success will prove it."

"You still need Alexander. I'm not good enough to match you. My body is just a map of points where you have bruised me. You need the best opponent to prepare for Rome. You need Alexander to give you the best chance of winning the fight."

"No! He can't return. His family deserves nothing but shame for their actions. He is as bad as his mother."

"Elena? What does she have to do with it?"

"Sin runs through the whole family. It has done so for years. They must leave Delos and never return. Now enough of this. I'm more than ready to fight, and erase Alexander from my thoughts. If you are here to help me, then finish your preparation and meet me at the pit."

He strides out of the oil room, leaving me alone. He is tired, and now he is angry. I've scored two points before our contest begins.

I have to slow down my own thoughts. I know I'm closer to the truth. What is the sin of the family? Why is he talking about Elena? Alexander did tell me that his father knew Maria before Elena. There is bad blood between the families. Something that hangs over all of them. I wish I could ask Alexander now, but for the moment, it is Dario I have to keep working on for a confession.

I finish oiling myself and leave the room, into the sun. It's a short walk to the skamma pit. I take a long, slow breath to steady myself. I will seek one more advantage before we even begin with our stance.

"Let's get started," calls Dario. His patience is fraying.

I can see he is suffering under the heat, so I offer a change to the plan.

"It's hot. Why don't we fight in the wet skamma? The mud will help us stay cool."

Dario looks around at the other pit, kept wet and under shade. It's a harder challenge, but since I've suggested it, Dario will not want to back away.

"Yes, why not? It might be raining in Rome on that day. We should do some practice in it."

"Alexander told me that Gaius trains his students in a wet skamma."

"Fine, but please stop mentioning that name. I don't want to hurt you, Leon, so please allow me to quell my rage."

We walk over to the shaded area of the palaestra, and as we do, we see Zoe and two of her friends further up the hillside, perching on the slopes above us.

"You see. Your sister will come back to me in the end. She knows who the best choice is."

"My sister devotes herself to Kyrios more than ever. I think even you will have to concede that you cannot win that contest."

Dario smirks. "I know which gods say what happens on Delos, and it's not Kyrios. Apollo will hear my prayers and answer hers."

We walk onto the darker, less steady soil that surrounds the wet skamma pit. I watch my step as I find a place to start. I rub the soles of my feet into the ground, to dig into a more solid stance. With no hesitation, we both step forward and start the fight. A fight I'm determined to win.

I can feel Dario use all his strength, but the soft ground stretches his legs as he tries to push against me. I can see his face strain with determination. Those torn muscles are beginning to hurt him. He breaks and then attacks again before I can defend, but his efforts to push me out of the pit cause him to slip and stumble.

He falls to his knees in front of me, giving me the opportunity to spin around his back and position my foot against his leg. I lock a grip around his shoulder, and I push it toward his head. He scrambles for a move to throw me, but the ground is working against him; his weakened muscles are working against him, and so is his vanity. He knows that Zoe is watching, and that increases his desperation. I have him where I want him.

"How can you hope to win in Rome, Dario, if I'm beating, you now?"

I apply all the force I can. The mud helps me pull him over onto his back. The first score is mine. He pushes me away and we return to our feet.

"You didn't beat Alexander, did you?"

"I did, and I'll show you how. You were lucky on the first point."

Alexander has taught me well since he came to Delos. He has taught me how to read my opponent. How to watch their balance, how to use their own weight against them, and when to pick just the right moment to attack.

Our hands battle for grip on one another. The mud and the oil mix on our skin. It's becoming harder for either of us to gain the advantage. I just need to make sure I can stay out of his reach and grasp. There are no judges to force us together. I just need to avoid his attempts to snap down on my neck or reach for my legs. Just long enough to see him lose control.

The shifting ground and the intensity of the fighting result in us falling together. We struggle and stretch for a hold that will lead to a score. Our fingers strain and our skin burns as we wrestle for superiority. Dario recovers his position and returns to his knees. He pushes free, but the effort leaves him open. I bring an arm across his face and slam him onto his back. His frustration is easy to recognize as he calls out an agonized scream. He didn't expect this; especially not from me.

"Get off," he yells as he gets back on his feet. This time he pauses for breath. I can see that he is feeling worse because of how much he trained.

"Do you want it to stop?"

"Stop for you? Leon?"

"You cannot win. Even if you beat me in the skamma. You are in more pain than you know. You have been part of the deception all this time. You fixed the fight, and the longer you run away from your part, the worse it will be for you."

"I beat him. I am the champion of the Great Delia. You all saw me win."

"We saw Alexander lose."

"You don't know what you're saying. You'll all thank me one day when Alexander and his cursed mother leave this place."

"Why is she cursed?"

Dario doesn't offer an answer. Instead, he lashes out with his hands and gives up on the rules of wrestling. If that is how he wants to fight, then I'll match him. Maybe I've not been the best at wrestling over the years, but I've lived a life where I've worked hard. Life at the docks is not easy, and trouble breaks out. Now we are in a street fight, just like Alexander in the Subura. It's as if I can hear him shouting from the side. Telling me how to take the kicks and the punches, before fighting back with my own.

Dario becomes like a cornered animal. Every time he connects, it carries all the energy he can summon, but then each attack also saps his strength. He begins to stagger and step back on himself. Blood starts to run from a cut on his brow, seeping into his eye. He tries to wipe it clean, and I seize my chance to swipe a kick behind his leg. He collapses on his back. He's down on the ground, but he's not yet beaten.

I grab his leg and spin him. With his face pressing into the ground, I drop to my knee and lock my arm around his ankle. I press his foot to the side and lift him up. He will submit. The fight is over, but I still need him to admit the truth. I use all the pressure I can bring.

"Why did Alexander hand you the contest?"

"You know why!" screams Dario. "I submit."

"I don't see your hand raised." I press again. "Why did Alexander give you the win?"

"Sacrilege!" Dario screams. "Let me go!"

"I still don't see your hand raised. What sacrilege?"

"Alexander is the sacrilege. He was born here on the island. I'm raising my hand. I concede."

I press on his foot one last time before letting him go. If for no other reason, I want to guarantee our match is over. We both sit facing each other across the skamma, covered in dirt, sweat, and blood. We both gasp for air and stare at one another.

"How do you know he was born here?"

"My mother knew. She saw his parents escaping with him when he was a baby."

"So, you decided to threaten them with what?"

"What do you think? They could have lost everything if my mother told the priests of Apollo. He had no choice. He still has no choice. I'll deny anything I've told you."

"You screamed out your last words of the fight. We had witnesses, remember?"

I look up to the slope where Zoe and her friends are already leaving.

"You were always proud to tell us about ignoring the words of wisdom that Demetrius offers all of us. You've refused to recognize it as part of your training, but if you only had paid attention. If you had listened and understood the lessons, then you would have been able to hold your head high. You won the Great Delia without virtue. Who was the real deceiver?"

"You can't threaten me. I can still make trouble for everyone."

"Including your own mother? She is involved. Do you want her to suffer? You will find the people of Delos will turn their backs on you for good if you decide to take that action."

"Once I win in Rome, I'll be happy to leave this place. What is there for me here? Apion will find me fights. I'll grow rich. I won't need anyone from Delos to support me."

"You won't win in Rome. You know that. You've lost to me today."

"You tricked me. If it was a fair fight, you never would have beaten me."

"So, now you want a fair fight? How does it feel to be cheated? Will you tell Demetrius how I gained the advantage? I'm sure he'll want to know."

I stand up and turn to leave. "I'm going to wash myself and head for home. Don't come near me again. I'd consider what you do next carefully, Dario. Reputations can be raised or ruined with each ship that sails in and out of our Sacred Harbor. You cannot escape fate, but you can still make the right decisions to shape its course."

I turn my back and walk away. My heart is beating fast. I'm shaking and not sure if Dario will attack me once again, but nothing happens. I clean myself and dress. I look over at the palaestra where Dario is still sitting. His head is in his hands. I'm sure he knows I am walking away, but he doesn't make eye contact.

I step onto the path and look over to the shore. Demetrius is there, and he stands looking back at me for a moment before he turns to face the sea.

He never went to meet with Egyptians. He's been here all this time.

My body is aching as I carry on toward home. I've just had the fight of my life, one that I won. My mother stands waiting outside the courtyard of our house. She smiles at my disheveled appearance. We don't need to speak, not just yet, but the truth will come out over dinner and wine. Like one of my father's great tales of the sea. This will be a day to remember.

CHAPTER XXIV

I admit I have been hiding from Apollo, ever since he handed down his punishment to me and my mother. We both made offerings every day to appease him, but we were frightened to go outside when his chariot was high in the sky.

My mother confined herself to the house, not even venturing out to the garden to sit among her beloved chaffinches. I had done the same at first, but then I asked Selene to fashion me a cloak with a cowl so that I could hide myself from view. Even then, I only ventured out in the dark of night, under the light of the silver moon that was Artemis, or Diana as I knew her from my time in Rome.

It still took me some time to go near the palaestra. The white marble stood out even during the darkest hours. A star-filled sky gave just enough illumination for me to stretch and work on my injury. I used the lightest weights and was careful to replace them in the exact position I found them. I didn't want anyone to know I had been there.

I wandered around the colonnades, the running track, and the preparation rooms. Then I would climb to the small bench where I used to sit with Demetrius. I tried to hear his words just as if he were speaking to me, but the only sounds were from the wind, the sea, and the calls of gulls. It felt lonely and cold at times. I would pull my cloak around me and venture down to the shore. The fishing boats and merchant ships sat idle, perhaps just the noise of crew returning from a taberna.

I'd wander near Zoe's house, hoping to glimpse her from afar, but she never ventured out at night. Every now and again I would hear her family talking, but I could never go nearer to make out their words.

My heart was heavy, and my mind recalled that day repeatedly. I didn't blame anyone, not even Dario. At first, I accepted that it was only

Apollo's will. He would have found another way to exact his revenge if Dario and his mother hadn't caused our problems.

Then my thoughts began to change. Men had decided that it was a sin to be born on Delos, not Apollo himself. It was the priests who handed out punishments on Apollo's behalf. Did Apollo even know about the crime?

As I worked on regaining my fitness, a strong resentment grew within me. Delos is my homeland. It is the place of my birth. Why should I feel guilty about belonging to such a beautiful place? I love the island and its people. Over centuries, warring nations, pirates, and invaders have committed terrible acts against a people who only wanted to live in peace. They would take over and impose their rules and laws, only to suit them and not the gods.

Our suffering was an effect of laws enacted by the present rulers. It was they who were offended, and they were the reason we were hiding away, out of fear of what they would do.

Each night that passed I would stay out longer. My day was lit by the moon and stars, my night was when the sun was high in the sky. I would end my walk on the top of Mount Kynthos, asking Artemis for the strength to wait there for the first light of dawn.

It took a long time to find the courage, and I began to understand how all of us were living under the same darkness, even Dario and his mother. I found it in myself to look at events from more than one direction, to realize that we were all victims of this curse. So many people are affected by the laws of men they would never meet.

There was only one way to be certain we were not being punished by the gods. I needed to face the first light of a new dawn. I needed to climb to the Temple of Zeus and be there to face Apollo and his spears of lightning. If he decided to strike me down, then that would be the end of all my shame, but I knew he was also a god of healing, so maybe there was still a chance. If I stood before his judgment, then maybe I could find a way out of this turmoil.

So, here I am, ready to accept my fate. I pull my cloak around myself and sit on the hill's summit, facing east. Faint lights still glow on Mykonos. I smile to myself as I make a promise: if I was to survive the dawn then I would visit my aunt and uncle. They would show me kindness no matter what I had done.

Other shapes start to surround me. The usual pilgrims who congregate for the dawn. They are true believers, but they're ordinary people. Would they seek to punish me for being born here?

I sit and wait.

The sky is retreating from the black of night. The breeze begins to blow a little harder. Then the first rays of dawn appear in front of me. The horizon illuminates with soft pinks and shades of orange. I clasp my hands together as the sun climbs into view—a shimmering red that chases the stars from the sky.

Words of prayer surround me. All asking for a share of fortunate blessings. Meanwhile, I stay silent. Apollo will know I am here. I keep my thoughts to myself, but just like the others, I'm here to ask for his favor.

The chariot has taken to the sky. It seems to race upward as it emerges out of the sea. A full circle of fire shines across the island and drapes it in golden light. Long shadows from the ruins of the temple stretch out. The sky transforms into a bright crisp blue, bringing change to the color of the sea. The day is here, and I've survived. I don't know what lies in front of me, but I bow my head in thanks.

I close my eyes, but I can already feel the heat of the new morning. I can hear the sounds of birds calling across the waves... I can smell the scent of jasmine and the soft touch of Zoe's arms around me. I sit back, startled.

"I'm sorry, Alexander. I was wrong to doubt you."

"Zoe, how did you know I was here?"

"You still count the days like a Roman. I knew you would be here."

I stand and return her embrace. "Thank you. Thank you for coming to find me."

"It's not me you should thank. I'm afraid to say it's to my brother that we all owe a debt."

She smiles and steps back as Leon steps forward. He also hugs me like an old friend.

"What are you wearing?" he smiles. "Have you become a priest?"

"No, it's what I've been using to hide from the priests."

"Then take it off; you won't need it anymore."

"Why, what's happened?"

"I had a fight with Dario, and do you know, I actually won!"

Leon and Zoe both giggle. How I've missed both of them! I feel that Apollo has shown me his forgiveness, and he's sent two of the most important people in my life to tell me.

"I'm glad you beat him, but what else has changed?"

"I *persuaded* Dario to tell the truth."

"Dario told Leon how they threatened you before the fight," Zoe adds. "We know that you were born here, Alexander. We can only imagine how they used that against you."

"But I don't want you to know, Zoe. It's dangerous. That's why I wanted to protect you all, that's why I told the lie about the gang from Rome. I didn't want you caught up in our problems."

"It's all changed now. Maria and Dario only had power over you as long as they kept us apart. We are together again, and others know."

"Others?"

"My mother wouldn't even let me in the house last night before I told her everything that had happened, then of course, Zoe and my father." Leon smiles. "And something tells me that Demetrius knows. He was nearby when I forced Dario to tell me the truth."

"You beat him?" I laugh.

"Yes, I beat him. Did you think that I couldn't?"

"I was always sure you could. I'm sorry I missed it."

"You've missed far too much. It's time to take your rightful place back in the palaestra."

"Demetrius said that?"

"Well, maybe, not exactly, yet. That might still need a little conversation. Don't fear him. Demetrius only tries to do what he thinks is right. He knows that none of us are perfect, but as long as we strive to do the right thing, I don't think he'll be angry You were only trying to protect the people you loved."

"Maybe not the right way," Zoe teases.

"But there's no crime that you committed. Maybe Apollo wants an official contender from Delos." Leon looks to the sky. "Look, no lightning, I'm still here."

"That's a pity," jokes Zoe. "Just close your eyes, my brother."

Zoe pulls me forward and kisses me on the lips.

"Oh, stop it you two," Leon complains. "Let's go to your house and see your mother. We have to let her know the news."

***

We run down the stone steps that stretch along the side of Mount Kynthos, and into the narrow lanes that weave between the houses. Neighbors give friendly greetings as we pass by them. I think they're surprised to see me. I'm sure some thought I had left the island. All their faces are smiling, happy, and welcoming. I pause just outside my own house.

What have I been frightened of?

"Let me go in first," I say to Zoe and Leon. "Wait here in the garden for a moment."

I enter the house and pass Na'amat, leaving the main room. She notices Zoe and Leon and gasps covering her mouth. I place my finger to my lips to signal that she shouldn't say anything. She nods and smiles back.

My mother looks up from the table. Her expression is tired and weary, but she realizes that I've waited until daylight to return.

"Are you alright, Alexander? I was worried when you didn't come back."

"I had to test if Apollo was still angry with us. I waited to watch for him arriving, I climbed Mount Kynthos and sat where his light would shine on me."

"I'm happy that you are venturing out, but the gods don't always act when we expect them. I have been thinking more and more about us returning to Rome. To take us back home, where we will be safe."

"No, we are home. We will be safe. We've shut ourselves away for too long when all we ever needed to do was trust those who love and support us. We cut ourselves off from the very people who could take our fears away and left ourselves to grow weak under the threats of Maria and Dario. We will not live that way for another single day. Will you step out into the garden with me? It's a warm and beautiful morning, here in the center of the world."

"I don't know, Alexander. I'm still not ready."

"Just out to the garden. We'll take some bread for the birds. Father wouldn't want this life for us."

"Yes, you're right."

I offer my hand for my mother to stand and take her arm to lead her out into the courtyard. She bursts into tears of happiness as she sees the smiling faces of Zoe and Leon, waiting to greet her. Hugs and kisses are exchanged. I can see the stress and strain disappearing like a mist that melts away in the warmth of a new day.

Selene and Na'amat also appear to celebrate the reunion. We all find a place to settle in the garden, and even the chaffinches descend among us, curious about the goings-on.

"Tell my mother, Leon. Tell her of your victory in battle."

"Battle?" my mother asks.

"With Dario," Leon replies.

"Oh, are you alright?"

"Maybe you should ask him." Leon smiles.

"I don't understand. You fought Dario and won?"

"Why is everyone so surprised?" Leon pretends to be annoyed but joins in the laughter. "I knew that he was hiding something. He changed after the Great Delia. At first, I just thought he was unhappy because Demetrius refused to accept that he had done enough for the win against Alexander. I knew that frustrated him, but as time went on, he just wasn't Dario anymore, if you know what I mean. He worked at his training, but his heart wasn't in it. If I could see it, then I'm sure Demetrius could. He would go straight home after training and speak to no one. I had to find out what was going on."

"So, you decided to fight him to find out?" says my mother. "That was taking a risk."

"I think it was my mother's idea if I'm honest, and I didn't want to go home and tell her I'd changed my mind. But there was another twist. Demetrius had a meeting with someone. He left us alone. Although I'm starting to wonder if my mother had organized that as well." He smiles.

"Not completely alone," says Zoe.

"My sister was above the palaestra looking down. She sat with her friends to watch me taking a beating."

"That's not fair. I was cheering for you, and although I hate to admit it, you fought well. I am proud of you, brother."

"Thank you, dear sister." He laughs. "For all the joking, the important thing was that he confessed what had happened. He told me that Alexander was born on Delos and that his mother had seen you escape, Elena. She knew about the birth, and she used it against you to force Alexander to give up the fight. So, we know the truth, and ever since, I *haven't* seen the sky turn into a storm."

A silence passes for a moment, and my mother's favorite chaffinch hops toward her. She smiles as she looks at Leon.

"Alexander's father always used to say that there were four virtues above all others. Wisdom, justice, temperance, and bravery. You have shown yourself to have all of these. My family has much to thank you for, Leon. You have saved us all from years of regret and wrong decisions. I was about to leave Delos for good and hoping that Alexander would come with me. I couldn't force him, but I knew he would be a dutiful son. That was all he was doing when he tried to protect us with stories of gangs and gamblers. The fear that had grown inside of me might even have pushed us back to that very place. Back to the Subura and a harsh existence in Rome..." She pauses for thought. "But I still worry, will Maria continue her threat? Has anyone seen them since you fought her son?"

"We're going to walk to the palaestra now," I interrupt. "Demetrius needs to be told the truth from all of us. Once we are honest, and the truth is out, then I'm sure he will help us."

"Yes, you're right. Demetrius will help. I'm sure of it."

We nod in agreement and let the rest of the morning pass. There's a lot more laughter as Leon describes the details of his fight, complete with a play where I have to act out the role of Dario. I pretend to scream out in pain as Leon places his foot on top of me, raising his arms like a champion. Selene and Na'amat join us for the end of the entertainment and bring us all food and something to drink. They also hug Zoe and Leon. It's like we are a long-lost family, all reunited.

The sun reaches higher in the sky. All of us know that Demetrius will be heading from the docks to the palaestra.

"We better go," I say. "It's time to face whatever comes next."

***

I'm nervous as Leon and I near the palaestra. I think we both are. I hold a strong feeling within myself, a sense that this time I have gone too far. I lied and let Demetrius down, and now maybe I'm about to do it again, by telling the truth. I have to hope that Demetrius would take my admission in the way I intended. That he would see that I'm trying to change myself for the better. That I'm trying to take control.

As we walk into the complex, we immediately see that Demetrius and Dario are sitting in the garden area. Demetrius is on his favorite place, while Dario faces him from one of the stone benches. I know they have seen us approaching, but both keep their gaze fixed on one another and their conversation shifts to silence. Dario hangs his head. I'm sure it is in shame, but I haven't come here to add to his torment. I hope he will see that in the end.

"Demetrius."

"Alexander, you join us from out of the shadows. How is your arm?"

"It's better. I've been working to improve it."

"I know. I'm often around this place at night as well."

"Then you saw me?"

"Yes, but it was not the time for us to meet and talk. I left you to your exercise." He turns to Leon. "And I see at least one of us still stands without injury. Dario's foot seems to have suffered some damage. Perhaps you will need to go to Rome and fight Gaius' champion, for I'm running out of contenders."

"I'm sorry, Demetrius," says Leon. "I didn't mean to injure Dario."

"It will heal. The body is more than capable of repairing itself, it's our thoughts and emotions that can take longer to mend. All of us have lost control in the rush to score a victory, even me. I have to consider my part in this, what I didn't see, or what I refused to look at because of inconvenient truths. I wanted a win that would equal my past glory, and what I was prepared to trade was the fate of you all. For that, I am sorry."

"Demetrius, I came back to offer my apologies. I lied to cover another lie."

"You rushed into another lie because of my anger. I confronted you and left you no choice. Like you, I have spent many nights considering my error. We all make mistakes, and I have studied long enough to know the first step to dealing with them is to recognize them. Accept them for what they are, an opportunity to change.

"It is the correct course of action to reflect on the mistake and then consider how to avoid it happening again. After that, we must learn from it, before letting it go. Then we can grow from the experience."

"I want to grow. I want us to move forward together. We all respect you, Demetrius, and what you've done for us. I'm sure I speak for everyone."

Demetrius sighs. "I appreciate your words, but fate is not in my hands for the moment. This palaestra might have been better left a ruin rather than be allowed to destroy the fortunes of such young lives as yours and Dario's. You and Dario should be friends. You should be there to help, not hinder. Each should push the other to greater success. Instead, an unresolved rivalry weakens the pair of you and for all my years and experience, that is something beyond my control."

Demetrius stands. "Follow me, Leon, you have done all you can. Alexander and Dario can only find a way forward between them. The fate of this place hangs in the balance of the decisions they will make."

I watch the pair of them step back down the slope and disappear from view. Dario is sitting looking at me, but there's no anger or malice in his expression. I sit opposite him and start to speak, but he stops me, raising his index finger as if submitting in a fight.

"Before you say anything, I want you to know that I've told Demetrius everything. I've cleared you from any part in this and let him know that we pressured you at the last moment. I've told him I cannot fight in Rome, as it was never my fight in the first place. If I had won in the skamma, I would not have changed as a person. My own arrogance would have caught me in the end. Someone would defeat me and bring me down. In fact, someone did, and little did I expect it would be Leon."

He smiles ironically. "This is not a new feeling. I've lived with it since the Great Delia. I cheated and then I hurt you further on purpose. I gave in to rage and anger, and that was when I lost all control. I was condemned from that point to just carry on and wait for the day you would return. I had enough faith in you that you would find a way back. Believe me when I say that I feel better about bringing this situation to an end. Gaius will expect someone in Rome, but it can't be me. I've already said this to Demetrius, so you can't talk me out of it."

Dario's words surprise me, but only because I expected him to be the same person as before. There is a change in him today, and I must meet him in the same place. It's time to end our war.

"Thank you for what you've done. That's taken more courage than a wrestling contest. I'm like you. I don't want this to carry on. I arrived on Delos not knowing I was going to find such a capable enemy. From the start, we circled each other in and *out* of the skamma. We both had good reasons to compete, and both of us could still find reasons to fight even now, but that's only if we keep looking at the past.

"Even enemies should be able to change and move on. I understand why your mother feared that the gods were turning against her. Why it seemed that every part of your success was being taken by someone who Apollo should have dealt with years ago. It's important for you to know that I felt Apollo was punishing me when I gave up the fight. Was he angry at all of us? Maybe he just wanted Leon all along, and that's why the sun god broke both our bodies."

"Maybe," says Dario as we laugh together.

"You have done something good, Dario. You've used your control to heal much of what was wrong. I thank you again. My mother will thank you too." I sit back and breathe a little easier. "How is your mother?"

"Relieved, like me. It might take her some time to face your mother, but she is sorry. They have a lot of history between them, much more than us. The healing might take longer."

"If we can make peace, I'm sure they will follow. Can we agree to work toward the contest together? We can help each other recover and then decide who is the fittest of us to take on the fight."

"No," Dario replies. "I've made my decision. The fight is yours, and you have my support. As long as you agree, I'll be here to help you train.

There will be other fights for me. You know Apion won't let me stay away from a contest for too long. His purse wouldn't agree."

We shake hands in agreement.

"You need to work on your speed," Dario grins. "You're too slow."

We walk down to the palaestra carefully. Dario is still limping and now that we're officially on the same side, I feel sorry for his pain. Leon looks hopeful as we return, and Demetrius is as hard to read as ever, waiting for our response.

"Well?" he asks.

"We've talked and both of us are clear in our understanding of what was wrong and how we want to make change for the better. We want to work together to prepare for the fight in Rome. That is if you think we can all work as one."

"And who will wrestle Gaius' champion?" Demetrius asks.

"I've offered my support to Alexander," says Dario. "This was always his fight, and I want to make sure he has the best chance of winning."

Demetrius nods in agreement. "I will also offer my help. What do you say, Leon?"

"I'll help too. Don't worry, I'll get them both up to my standard."

From the first light of dawn that day, until the sunset in the evening, Apollo showed us his healing powers. The clouds that we had all lived under were now gone from our lives.

As Artemis returns with her moonlight, my mother and I join Zoe, Leon, and their parents for more food beside the sea. The aromas from the meal swirl around us and another amphora of my uncle's wine helps ease our spirits.

"Will Uncle Nikos be back tomorrow?" I ask.

"He'll be back sooner if he smells his best wine being opened," my mother laughs.

The nightmare is over. I can look forward to each day again, and now I can clear my head and prepare to return to Rome.

CHAPTER XXV

I want to say that life returned to normal after the decision that I would fight in Rome, but that's not true. Every day has new meaning and importance. I've returned to spending my mornings working at the dock, but the afternoon training at the palaestra is much more intense. We are all working together for the next fight.

Dario and Leon are with me constantly as we run, stretch, lift weights, and wrestle. I know I'm going to fight Lucius, so we concentrate on practicing how to defend against his style of fighting, then we spend time on new ideas for attacks and holds, to perfect each move.

Apion is looking after my general fitness. He makes sure I'm eating the right food, getting the correct amount of sleep, and working out with just the right effort for muscles, lungs, and heart. He doesn't just oversee me at the palaestra; he oversees my home life and makes sure that Selene and Na'amat prepare everything I need. Uncle Nikos says that Apion is in our house so much he'll need to charge him for lodgings.

Even Leon's parents are playing their part, bringing me fish fresh from the sea along with healthy herbs and vegetables from their garden.

Meanwhile, Demetrius watches over all of us. We all rely on him to guide us in working together. Sometimes he watches from afar, sitting in the palaestra garden, where we gather after training to listen to his wise words. He'll tell me how to improve my wrestling, but he'll also prompt me to think about how I live my life and how I can establish patterns that will help me grow stronger as a person.

He doesn't just want me to be a good wrestler; he wants me to become a better son, neighbor, and citizen. He often mentions the words of the Stoic philosopher Epictetus. He asks me to commit the words to memory and then act on them. He assures me that this is the way to becoming a true champion. He wants me to inspire others and set a good example.

I have to admit I am starting to see a change within myself. I can discipline myself to work and train better. I have the courage to confront new challenges as I no longer create reasons to worry. Regular practice is helping me make the right decisions in the skamma and the right choices for my life.

As the evening light descends, Zoe guides me with the words of Kyrios. She is patient and happy to school me in her religion at a slower pace. I still look to Apollo each morning and evening to thank him for his healing, but as I listen to Zoe's thoughts and beliefs, it has made me understand the importance of ritual and faith in her life.

Tonight, the stars spread out across the sky, and the harbor lights cast reflections upon a calm sea. We walk together along the shoreline, happy and content.

Zoe stops and looks out across the waves. "I'm sorry for the time lost between us. I should have trusted you more and sought to understand your actions. I sat my brother down and thanked him. It was he who remained a loyal friend when the rest of us deserted you. It wasn't any of the gods who saved us all. It was just a person who we all underestimated."

"Leon has grown up faster than the rest of us. He just chooses not to let us know," I smile, "but I still think the gods play their part."

"Maybe, though I still only believe in one God."

I shake my head a little. I know Zoe is agreeing with me in her own way. We continue our slow walk back to her house. No matter how long we take, the time to say goodnight always arrives too soon. As we part, I linger for a moment longer, deep in thought.

For the first time, I think about how this is my birthplace. I am the only one I know who can make that claim. Delos has a spirit and a history that goes far back in time. I feel as if it flows through me. It's the blood coursing through my veins, the air that I breathe. I feel it's great power around me and within me. I owe everything to this place and its people, and now I am ready to show my gratitude. It will be the greatest honor I can ever achieve, to wrestle under the name of this sacred island and make it known throughout the world.

***

Pain sears through my back as I crash to the ground in the skamma. Leon looks down at me from above with a wide grin as Dario laughs and pats him on the back.

"How did you do that?" I ask as I pick myself up off the sand.

"I've been working on some new moves. I'll teach you."

"The new Leon is dangerous," Dario adds. "You can't take half-chances with him. He reads us better than anyone these days."

"Thank Alexander," Leon answers. "He taught me how to observe my opponent. Sometimes the fight can be over before it's even started. Isn't that right?"

"Yes, I know I've said that, but when did you learn those tricks?"

Leon smiles back at Dario. "Maybe someone else has taught me how to bring a surprise or two to the fight. I guess by learning from you *and* Dario, I've become the most dangerous threat on the island."

"Am I going to have three wrestlers from Delos now?" Apion quips. "That would be something people would pay to see."

"I don't think I'm quite ready," Leon replies.

"Yes, but I organize fights for the future. I have to plan for your happiness, but also for mine, my friend." He grins.

"For the moment, we will just focus on the next fight." Demetrius reminds us all not to think too far ahead. "Stop for today, clean up, and spend some time in the bath, Alexander, then we will talk some more. Dario and Leon, you two can go. Thank you for your help today."

We all return to the oil room and use the strigils to remove the worst of the dirt from our skin. Leon and Dario have discovered they make better friends than enemies, and good humor has now replaced the old tensions that used to exist between us. The noise we make as we laugh and joke might have annoyed Demetrius in the past, but he knows it's increasing the bond between us.

Demetrius remains a serious figure, commanding attention whenever he speaks, but I can tell he's savoring this moment in his life. The palaestra is in pristine condition, and his wrestlers stand united, supporting one another. Even Dario has begun joining our philosophical discussions.

This must make him feel as if control is returning—as if the balance he's worked so hard to build is being restored. Every step we take forward as a group, driven by his virtue and integrity, allows him to grow, pushing him toward new goals.

I understand now—when we work together and share in success, we don't just help ourselves. We lift each other.

I step into the bath. The days are becoming cooler on Delos at the moment, but they're never cold and the water is still refreshing under the sun's glare. The others leave me to relax and recover. I soak in the water and fall into a daydream where I see Rome on a festival day, with its streets lined with people who gather for feasting and entertainment. In my head, I'm watching parades of dancers, musicians, acrobats, and animals. Then I remember our visit to the Circus Maximus and my last full day in the city. The excitement of the chariot races taking place before the emperor is something I will never forget.

I will have my moment before Roman crowds.

I step out of the water, dry myself, and get dressed. The day isn't over for me yet, and Apion will want me to eat. A plate of bread, fruit, and nuts is always waiting. He insists I eat it within a short time after training. He says he cannot tell me how to fight in the skamma, but he will send me into battle in the best way he can. I trust him and follow his instructions just as much as the others, especially if it prepares me to meet Lucius.

As I walk back to the palaestra, I see that Uncle Nikos has joined Demetrius and Apion. They are in the grip of a discussion about Gaius, but of course, Demetrius notices that I've returned and silences the others.

"I have good news," he says.

"You were talking about Gaius?"

"Yes, we didn't want to speak about this too soon, but we had to inform Gaius that you were taking the place of Dario... and he wasn't happy about it."

"What did he say?"

"I'll spare you much of that. He was going to cancel the contest at first, but I've known him for a long while. My words still carry weight."

"Eat, Alexander." Apion pushes the plate of food over to me. "Gaius will not risk his reputation for himself or his champion if he thinks that there's even a chance you might seek to help increase the fortunes of Rome's underworld. He will have no part of it if he suspects their involvement. It has taken some time to convince him otherwise."

"As Apion says, it has taken time," continues Uncle Nikos. "We had to admit that your start in wrestling was not the best. Only by giving ground to his suspicions could we hope to persuade him you were not the perpetrator of crimes, only the victim."

"So, he accepts that?"

"We still had to explain your loss to Dario," Demetrius sighs. "We could all see that you allowed Dario the win. You fooled much of the crowd, but not those that know you and believe in you."

I bow my head in shame. "But you all know why I had to take that action."

"It was still the wrong action to take," Demetrius replies. "We know the danger you were trying to avoid, but Gaius asked us how we could make sure that there would be no more reasons for you to alter the course of a fight. Could I answer with honesty? It took me time to find the correct response to his question. I had to convince myself before I could convince Gaius."

"I'm sorry, Demetrius. I promise I have learned from my mistakes. You have all helped me realize that I should have been honest from the start. I know it is not always the easiest path. I know sometimes it can have difficult consequences, but these past few weeks have shown me the truth can release us from fear."

"We have seen your transformation," says Uncle Nikos. "But Gaius only remembers the Great Delia. I also wrote to him. I told him that my nephew was once a boy who was prepared to do all he could for his family, even if it was sometimes less than honest. I reminded him—not all live the privileged life he and many of his students enjoy on Palatine Hill."

"Gaius wasn't always wealthy," says Demetrius. "When I was fighting him in the early days, we were both poor, but the memory fades for him. Perhaps by choice. He has become too accustomed to his life amongst the rich and powerful."

"You were able to convince him, though?"

"No," Demetrius says. "In the end, an unexpected voice spoke for you—Lucius."

"Lucius!"

"When Lucius learned the contest would be between you two, he used all his influence to vouch for your integrity. He argued with Gaius, insisting you were the proper test for any champion. It seems even your opponents believe in you."

"Then I owe my gratitude to Lucius."

"You do." Demetrius gazes at me. "When your uncle wrote to Gaius that his nephew was a boy, he also went on to say that you had since become a man. That is an important step. You can no longer rely on others to make decisions for you. You must demonstrate in every fiber of your being that you have taken control of your way forward in life. When all of us work with you now, it is as peers with mutual respect for one another. That respect is born out of shared values and principles—integrity and honesty."

He looks to Apion, then Uncle Nikos. "Gaius has agreed to the contest. There is no more to be hidden between us. When you step into the skamma in Rome, all our reputations will stand aligned behind you, Alexander of Delos."

I sit in silence for a few moments. This is an important time to choose my words carefully.

"My father told me this day would come. He said there would be no fanfare, no great parade. He said I would only wake with a greater sense of my place in the world. He said the challenges I would face would then be my own, and I would find solutions through inner strength, fortitude, and dignity. He told me to listen to good advice, but the course I would set in life would be my own decision." I look around at the faces of the men around me. "Thank you for your belief in me, thank you for your patience, and thank you for the knowledge you have shared. Today I understand what my father meant. I believe he will stand beside all of you in Rome. I will fight for this victory with everything I have."

"I think this is a moment to celebrate." Uncle Nikos smiles. "Perhaps, Demetrius and Apion, you could join us for dinner and wine at my house tonight? I guarantee I will serve the best for your esteemed company."

"Well, that's a reason to celebrate in itself," says Demetrius.

"That sounds very good," says Apion. "Am I to allow Alexander to miss a day of eating and drinking the right things?"

Demetrius frowns.

Uncle Nikos laughs.

"Once you've drunk my best wine, I think we'll all miss a day."

***

My mother doesn't react well at first when we arrive home with the news.

"You could have given me more warning, brother."

"It was just in the moment, Elena. I thought it would be good to bring everyone together before we travel to Rome."

"So that's Demetrius, Apion, Leon, Dario, Zoe, and the three of us?"

"Well, yes, Tigranes, Selene, and Na'amat as well. Oh, and I invited Leon and Zoe's parents, then some of our neighbors, so they don't complain about the noise. Maybe about twenty people."

"Twenty! Do we have enough food to feed them?"

"Yes, yes. I'll organize it. I'm a merchant, after all. I'll get everything we need for a good price and arrange for it to be sent over."

"We need to prepare the house. Twenty will be too many for this one room."

"Half of them will end up in the garden. Don't worry, Elena."

"Zoe and Leon are going to come and help us," I confirm. "We'll get everything organized in time."

"Alright, it will be nice to have everyone around for the evening. If you told me before, we could have invited Agathon and Thestylis over from Mykonos."

"Ah, didn't I say? I sent my crew and ship over to get them. They should be back before sunset."

"Nikos!"

I don't think my mother is unhappy; she loves being in a house where she can entertain friends and family. Back in the Subura, our home was too small, our meals and our celebrations were always in the taberna, so she never got the chance. Tonight is going to be special.

Zoe and Leon soon arrive. My mother has a list of duties to be carried out; cleaning is at the top, but also helping Selene and Na'amat with food preparation. We search for extra lamps to light the house and the garden. My uncle's idea of inviting close neighbors seems to have turned out well because they arrive with extra cups and plates, places to sit, and tables to hold wine and food. Many also bring extra food, and their own favorite dishes to share.

Uncle Nikos returns with a group of men carrying even more, and a musician with a lyre who he spotted in the market square. He's paid him to provide music for the guests.

Before we know it, the evening is underway. There's more food than I've ever seen in one place. There's lamb, goose, octopus, squid, and oysters, plates of vegetables, cheeses, bread, lentils, chickpeas, and my not-so-favorite olives, but I leave them alone.

Everyone is in good spirits and all the talk is about our trip to Rome. My mother makes sure she speaks to everyone to make them feel welcome. It's a great relief to her after all the weeks of isolation. Meanwhile, Uncle Nikos is always at the center of the laughter, which is not surprising, but Demetrius is standing beside him enjoying the jokes, and that is a rare sight.

"My boy, my wonderful nephew!"

Aunt Thestylis arrives, and she's going to make sure everybody knows it. She wraps her arms around me with such a powerful hug that any wrestler would be proud of it.

"And is this Zoe? Oh, such a beautiful girl for such a beautiful boy. When is the wedding? I will make a special cake for you, and you'll name your first daughter after your favorite aunt, yes?"

We all laugh together, but I know Aunt Thestylis is being serious behind her smile. Uncle Agathon just rolls his eyes and offers me some more wine.

Selene appears out of the crush of people to find me and my mother. "Mistress Elena, there's someone at the entrance."

"Tell them just to come in," replies my mother.

"No, mistress, I think you should see them first."

I follow my mother out to the entrance, and I catch the eye of Uncle Nikos before I leave.

He's up to something.

It doesn't take long to see why. Dario is standing out on the street along with Maria. Both of them look nervous.

"Maria?" The tension is apparent in my mother's voice.

"Elena, I should have come to see you before now. I am sorry for how I have behaved and the trouble I caused for you and Alexander."

Maria hands over a small arrangement of cut flowers as a gift.

"These are from my garden. I know it isn't much, but please accept them as a gesture of peace between us. Your brother invited us along this evening, but if you want us to leave, I will understand."

"No, Maria, I do not want you to leave. I want nothing more than for us to be friends and put the bad days behind us. Alexander has been telling me how much Dario is helping him. I appreciate it, Dario. Of course, you are both welcome to our house; please come in and enjoy the company."

My mother ushers them into the garden. She takes Maria by the hand and leads her through the other guests. Dario and I just smile at one another.

"I suppose we are able to be friends now," Dario laughs.

"Maybe strange friends that spend each afternoon fighting each other," I reply. "But I'm also grateful for your help. Please come in and have some food; the lamb is excellent, and so is the octopus."

Not everything will heal in one night. There's still some hesitation to overcome on both sides, but the atmosphere is helping to repair the damage. My mother and Maria are soon reminiscing about their teenage years and growing up on Delos. It sounds like they were good friends, to begin with, so I think there's hope for the future.

I do my best to talk to everyone. Many say it was a shame about my injury at the Great Delia, but they offer comfort that I won't be that old in four years' time when it returns. They don't suspect any wrongdoing on the day, and so to let go of the past, I don't correct them. I accept their sympathy and share their optimism for better days ahead.

Demetrius waits until I'm on my own before he approaches.

"Thank you and your mother for the hospitality this evening."

"Are you going?"

"There are still ships arriving in the morning. I have to keep a clear head, unlike your uncle. He reaches a level of frivolity that I could never match I'm afraid."

"Don't worry, I'll be there with Leon."

"No, I've told him, and I'll tell you to have a day of rest tomorrow. I greatly value the work you both do, but I'll manage for a day."

"Thank you. Thank you for everything, Demetrius. I can't wait to fight in Rome."

"You will do well. And thank you for giving me something back that I thought lost. It is difficult when age dictates your limits. I don't feel old, and I'm sure I could still beat many that are half my age, but unexpected events can lead us away from the path. I worried for a while that it had happened to you. I at least had completed my days of contests when life presented me with problems to overcome. I was able to retreat into memories to preserve my sense of worth, but they are only pictures from past days. They can't save you from a sense of failure.

"I tormented myself for years after my son's exile. I read the teaching of Epictetus many times. His words spoke to me about how I could make the changes I needed to improve my life. It was then that I returned to the ruins of the palaestra, and I invited Dario and Leon to join me. That was the beginning. By passing on my knowledge to others, I was able to reclaim some of what I had lost. I was able to take control. Perhaps one of the great mysteries is that once you take control, fortune begins to turn in your favor.

"And so, you arrived with your mother on Delos. I could see you were sick from the journey; you were a little frightened and unsettled, but I could also see you had character and strength that would help you succeed. I felt I owed your father so much that I didn't hesitate to support you, but I have to give you the respect you deserve. It is your control and your integrity that has brought you to this point. It is your attitude and commitment that has drawn so many to join you in your cause.

"You are the finest wrestler, and if I allow myself a little vanity, you have many dedicated, able, great men working around you. Be confident, friend."

Demetrius takes my hand and shakes it. It's as if I can feel him passing on an energy of all his years of experience, and with that, he turns and disappears into the night.

"Are you alright, Alexander?" Zoe asks from behind me.

"Yes, I'm better than alright. I am so ready for this contest."

"Come on you two, grab a lamp each," shouts Uncle Nikos as he leads everyone else from the house.

"A lamp? What's happening?"

"We are going down to the shore."

"Now?" Zoe giggles.

"I can't think of a better time. Come along, follow us."

We pick up two lamps from the garden and join the end of a line of bobbing lights as it weaves its way down through the narrow lanes of Delos. The tabernae are long closed and many people are asleep, but it doesn't stop the chatter, the laughing, and some singing as we make our way to the side of the sea. I keep hearing the word. Kalamatianos.

"What are they talking about, Zoe?"

"The Kalamatianos? It's a dance."

"I don't know how to dance."

"Are you Greek?"

"Yes, I am."

"Then it's in your blood. You don't have to learn it."

We all join hands in a circle, but Aunt Thestylis takes her position in the center and guides everyone around her. We step back and forward, to the left and the right. I get the steps wrong at first, to everyone's amusement, but Zoe is right; it's in my blood, and I soon know what to do. Every few steps we separate into pairs, and I spin around with Zoe on the shore, and then the circle joins again. Uncle Nikos leads the singing and as everyone joins in, they can probably hear us on the other islands, but no one cares. We are all celebrating together, and I've never felt such a sense of belonging in all my life.

CHAPTER XXVI

The days following the celebration have passed, and now the time is upon us. I'm glad to know the sea is calm for the start of our sailing. Uncle Nikos welcomes us all back on board his ship; Demetrius, Apion, my mother, Zoe, Leon, and Dario are all with me. Bags and boxes follow us on, carrying our clothes and other supplies.

Our course is set straight across the Aegean, as direct as we can make it. But Uncle Nikos warns that the Etesian winds might have other plans, tugging at our sails and slowing us down. If they're kind, we'll reach Italy in ten days. If they're not—well, fifteen if we're lucky.

Tonight, we'll make our first stop on the island of Milos, following the well-worn paths of merchant ships. The waters here are familiar, safe. But beyond Milos, the open sea waits. We'll skirt past Kythera, hugging the coast of the Peloponnesian peninsula, where the cliffs rise like the backs of sleeping giants. Then comes the crossing—the Ionian Sea. Deep, endless blue. If the weather turns, there's no shelter, just us and the waves.

Once we reach Sicily, we'll stop in Palermo to take on fresh water and food. From there, the Italian coast will guide us like a stretched-out arm. We'll pass Naples, where the southerly currents will finally work in our favor, pushing us toward Ostia. And then—Rome.

When we dock, the scent of seaweed and salt will give way to the heavy, spiced air of the empire's heart. Ox carts will rattle over the worn stones of the Via Ostiensis, carrying us straight into the heart of it all—past towering columns, shouting merchants, the ever-present hum of a city that never truly sleeps. Capitoline Hill will be waiting. And with it, whatever fate has planned for us.

The games will begin a few days later. A procession on the first day will end with chariot races, then overnight, the Circus Maximus will transform to host boxing and wrestling events. Lucius and I will fight our contest as a special event to open the games of the second day. The timing will guarantee that along with thousands of spectators, Emperor Marcus Aurelius will be there to watch the fight.

Almost two cycles of the moon will pass before we return. Well-wishers watch us leave and cheer for us as the ship departs the dock. Many have come to the harbor early just to watch us go. They shout out for us to return with the emperor's laurel crown, the prize that I'll be wrestling for.

I will miss you, Delos.

We all wave back and make promises of victory. Apion places a hand on my shoulder. Demetrius might have trained me, but it's the fight-fixer who considers me as one of *his* wrestlers.

"You will bring back the crown this time," he says.

"I can't wait. I know Lucius. I know Roman style and rules. It's not so aggressive unless you're fighting in the street."

"Those days are over, Alexander. Do you know how large an audience there will be in the Circus Maximus?"

"Thousands."

"Try tens of thousands and you will be closer. Did you not hear the roars when you lived in Rome?"

"Yes, though I was only there once. Uncle Nikos took me there before we came to Delos."

"And what do you remember?"

"The thunder of the chariots, the noise of the spectators. The whole place moved and rumbled as the horses raced around the track."

"Do you remember the emperor sitting high above you?"

"Yes, he was far from us though, and the Praetorian Guard were out in force. Someone from the Subura would never get near him."

"And that is what we are going to change. Beat Lucius and you will line up with other winners from the day. The emperor himself will present you with your trophy."

I'm speechless. We're only a short way from home and already my mouth is going dry at the thought of what lies ahead. Apion bellows out a laugh.

"Get used to this. You will meet many emperors, pharaohs, kings, and queens. You will face their champions, and you will receive good grace in coin and treasures in return for the entertainment you provide. The bigger your name becomes, the higher the price will be. Trust me, the riches will follow."

I smile and nod, but his words do not excite me like they once would. The promise of riches and fame feel hollow. I remember early lessons from Gaius and countless conversations with Demetrius, Uncle Nikos and Leon. I've come to know that riches are not always wealth, and wealth is not always riches. True wealth lies in strength of character, in mastering myself rather than the world's fickle applause. Fame and fortune are shadows, beyond my control. What I can truly command is my own effort, my own virtue.

I step toward the prow. The waves grow restless, lifting and dropping the ship with a steady rhythm now that we're beyond the calm of coastal waters. Zoe joins me and grips my arm, her fingers tightening slightly as the sea sways beneath us.

"Why was Apion laughing?"

"All the money he's sure I'm going to make for him." I smile. "He was telling me how the winner will meet Marcus Aurelius to receive the prize."

"I know you can do this. Is Lucius a fair wrestler?"

"He is. He was kind to me when I first went to Palatine Hill. We were becoming friends until I made trouble for myself. The last time I saw him, he turned away from me, but I think that was under the orders of Gaius. Demetrius says it was Lucius who pressured Gaius into allowing the match to take place."

"But Gaius must have wanted the fight to happen as well."

"Maybe in the end, but Lucius's father pays a lot of money for his son's training. I'm sure Gaius wouldn't want to displease the family, and he won't believe I can win. He never has. So, what does he have to lose?"

"I think it's more likely that he'll realize what he's lost when you beat his champion. Then he'll know the mistakes he made."

"I give thanks for his mistakes. It brought me to Delos and to you. I think about everything that's happened since I first sailed on this ship. The changes that have taken place. When we reach Rome, I want to take you to where I used to live. We can eat in our local taberna, and I'll introduce you to Caeso. He'll want to meet everyone and hear all my stories."

"Do you miss Rome?"

"I'm not going to lie. It is a different place. You'll see when you get there. People, languages, and cultures from across the world, yet everyone will tell you they're Roman. It doesn't have the peace of Delos, and your head will spin in every direction to capture the sights and the sounds; but don't worry, just hold on to my arm. I will always keep you safe."

"Always?"

We pass an arm around each other's waist and look ahead on our journey as the sun rises further behind us. I ask Poseidon to look after us and guide us to the greatest city that has ever existed.

***

The capital of the Roman Empire does not disappoint my family and friends. Our lodgings look down across the city and are in a perfect place to assemble for the start of the emperor's procession.

Drums and trumpets have sounded from first light. A small army of officials is present to sort out the order of the parade. The chief magistrate is to lead, followed by nobles on horseback, then the chariots that will compete in the day's races. The boxers and wrestlers will follow on from there; then musicians, dancers, and actors are charged with making the crowds laugh as they walk.

We stand together as a small group on the edge of organized chaos. I'm to be in the parade, taking my place amongst the other wrestlers. Everyone else has to make their way to the Circus Maximus so that they're in the crowd when the procession arrives.

"Where do I go?"

"I'll take you to your place," says Apion. "I recognize a lot of the other competitors, but I don't know Lucius."

"Just get me close enough and I'll find him."

Everyone else wishes me well. There's so much excitement in the air. Hugs, handshakes, and kisses send me on my way as I follow Apion into the middle of a large group of athletes. The mood is friendly, and although no one recognizes me, many are keen to shake Apion's hand and find out who he is representing. I feel proud when he introduces me. Many of the other competitors nod with respect. They tell me if I am Apion's choice, then I must be good.

I remember watching these parades when I was younger, but to be part of one? It's too good to be true. I can't hide my excitement. Yet the same tug at my heart always gets me. *What would my father say about all this?* I look for his face in the crowd. I know I won't find it, but I'm still sure he's out there. As I look around, I meet the gaze of Gaius. I can see him sending Lucius forward to stand beside me.

"Alexander!" Lucius greets me like his oldest friend.

"It's good to see you, Lucius."

I feel awkward at first. *How do I start to ask how he is?* The last time we met one another he wouldn't even look my way, but Apion steps in to cover any embarrassment.

"So, you are Lucius?" he asks.

"Yes. I am Alexander's opponent tomorrow."

"Alexander speaks highly of you. I'm looking forward to seeing the pair of you fight."

"We didn't know where you had gone after leaving Palatine Hill," Lucius continues. "It was a shock when we found out you had gone to Greece and began training under Demetrius."

"You know Demetrius?" I ask.

"Gaius knows Demetrius. They fought against each other many times, and I've been told they each won the same number of matches. I think that's a reason this fight is happening. It's settling an old score between them. Whoever wins between us, claims the title for their trainer. So, there's a lot at stake when we meet in the skamma pit tomorrow."

"That's the reason? Demetrius never mentioned this. We're fighting for them?"

"You're fighting for more than them," Apion interrupts. "They can take their personal victory, but there will be others out there that want to see this clash of champions. This moment will go down in history as Greece battles Rome once again. At least that's what I'll be telling them when I announce your entrance for the contest."

The trumpets sound from near the start of the parade, and a fanfare heralds the beginning of our march through the city. Drums set a rhythm for our walk, and calls from the organizers go up and down the line to tell us we're underway.

"I better join your family," says Apion. "Remember, Alexander. Offer a bright smile and wave to the crowds, be friendly. Many of the same people will see your contest tomorrow. You want them to be cheering for you when they attend."

He pats me on the shoulder and offers a final handshake to Lucius before heading back into the crush of onlookers.

A loud cheer rises from all the people in the procession, and the musicians who are further behind start to play. The crowd responds, and the noise is incredible.

I look at Lucius; both of us are proud to be in the parade.

"Did you think we would compete against one another at the Circus Maximus, Alexander?"

"Not when I left. I wondered if I would ever wrestle again."

"We were sorry to lose you, but none of us could go against Gaius."

"He was angry with me. I understand why. Not then, but I do now."

"Even though he tells us not to think about the past, he regrets it. I know him well enough to say that."

"He'll still want you to beat me."

"Yes. He wants me to win. Don't worry, the battle is tomorrow, today we can just be friends."

We walk past the Temple of Jupiter, and I think of Minerva sitting there on her throne. Apollo? Kyrios? They all play their part, but I have to acknowledge her as well. She was the first to answer my prayers. I bow toward the temple and offer quiet words of thanks.

Our march winds past the Temple of Saturn and through the Forum along the Via Sacra. We move around the Colosseum's towering arches, the crowds growing thicker as we head toward the Circus Maximus, stretching beyond Palatine Hill.

The clatter of chariot wheels and the steady beat of marching feet mix with the shouts and cheers of the crowd. The air feels heavy with the scents of sweat, spices, and crushed flowers. Even surrounded by the grandest buildings I've ever seen, the noise of the people drowns everything else.

I search the crowd, hoping to spot a familiar face, but there are too many. Their voices crash over me like waves, rising to a roar as we near the entrance of the Circus Maximus. The feeling of thousands of eyes watching me is overwhelming, but I force myself to stand taller, trying to focus on what's ahead.

Still, I can't help but feel a thrill. From the rough streets of the Subura to marching in a procession meant for champions—it feels like I've already won something. But I know the real challenge is still waiting.

Then the cheering soars to a higher level as we walk onto the track. Thousands upon thousands stand to their feet and welcome us all. The horses who pull the chariots know where they are. They begin to react to the crowd like the champions they truly are. The charioteers are all famous in Rome, and most of the crowd are carrying or wearing something in the colors of the stable they support.

We come to a rest and high above us I can see the emperor, Marcus Aurelius, among his guard, his generals, and his senators. He waves to all of us who will take part in his games.

"Can you see your family, Alexander?"

"No." I strain to see someone I recognize. "There are too many people. Can you see yours?"

"It's easier for me. My father is a senator. He's sitting just below the emperor."

Lucius waves up toward his father, who makes a great show of waving back. I can see him point to us, for the benefit of important men who surround him.

I search again for my own family, and just for a moment, I think I see my own father's face in the crowd. I rub my eyes and the vision is gone, but somehow, I know he is here to see me and will be near when I return to fight.

***

The day is here, and the moment I awaken, my heart is racing. I push myself upright, the rough fabric of my blanket slipping to the floor. My chest tightens with the rush of nerves, but I plant my feet firmly on the ground, letting the cool air wash over me.

I draw in a slow, deep breath, then another, my shoulders rising and falling in steady rhythm. My hands unclench, fingers stretching wide before curling into loose fists. With each breath, the trembling in my chest eases, my pulse slowing to something I can control. As I join the others, I am ready for what this day will bring.

"A last meal," says Apion as he places a plate of selected food before me.

"For those about to die?" I joke.

"No, my friend, for those who need energy to win." He smiles.

"At least you're in good humor," says Uncle Nikos. "That's very important."

"Maybe before he enters the skamma, not during," Demetrius remarks.

"Let my son relax for a little while," insists my mother.

They all mean well. I know they're all as excited as I am. I take my plate and sit beside Zoe, Leon, and Dario. They do their best to keep me calm. Zoe places her hand on my back, as we sit together, Dario distracts me with last advice on some of my moves, and Leon is just Leon. He can't even pretend to be serious for too long.

"It's time to go," says Apion.

Ox carts take us down to the arena. The officials show us the skamma pit which now sits in the center of the racetrack, directly in front of where the emperor will watch the sport. The morning seems to hasten toward the time of my contest. Demetrius and Apion remain with me this time, and the rest take their places in the rows of seats.

Next, the officials summon us into a tent to witness the draw of competitors for the main tournament. I see Lucius enter his token. He'll be fighting in more matches after our contest. They draw him against a man from Praeneste, and as he returns from his selection, he walks over toward us, with Gaius at his shoulder. I shrink away, but I can feel Apion's hand pressing against me. It is time to face old fears.

"Alexander." Gaius nods. "And Demetrius. It's a good day for a contest, and to settle old scores."

"Just like old times," Demetrius says, with a glint in his eye.

"You're fighting again after our fight?" I ask Lucius.

"Yes. I've time to recover in between the matches."

"That's lucky. What if you had drawn an earlier contest?"

"That wouldn't happen. When your father helps to rule Rome, the timing of a wrestling match is not a big problem to solve. He just asks the judges for their *understanding*."

As soon as the draw is over, an official instructs Lucius and me to go to the oil room and prepare. It's another tented area on the grounds. As we walk toward it, I catch a glimpse of the full stadium. It's impossible to avoid a rush of excitement.

Demetrius, Gaius, and Apion stand outside the entrance as Lucius and I go inside, where others gather, ready to apply the oil. All I need to do is stand still.

Is this what it's like to live the life of a champion?

Time rushes on, and soon we are out in front of the crowd, ready and prepared for our contest. The chief judge gives a signal to Apion, whose role is to announce the contest before it begins. He steps forward, and I draw a slow, deep breath as the vast audience falls into a hushed silence.

"Imperator Caesar Marcus Aurelius Antoninus Augustus, it is my privilege to address you, your esteemed family, and all our honored guests—Viri Illustrissimi, the most esteemed senators, and Viri Fortissimi, the greatest of generals." Apion performs a deep bow toward the most important people of the city. "And to all the good citizens of Rome, I welcome you to a battle of warriors, worthy of your attention and support."

The crowd cheers. "We all live and thrive under the merciful rule of our emperor, but there have been great battles over the years that have put the men of Rome against men of Greece. Heraclea, Asculum, Cynoscephalae, and Magnesia—all names that echo through history.

Courage and skill in conflict will always decide the victor of such clashes, and today I bring you such a contest.

"For Rome, I present to you, Lucius Cornelius Imperiosus!"

Lucius steps forward into the skamma to a huge deafening cheer. He raises his hands as if already in triumph.

"And facing Rome's champion today, a Greek who grew up among many of you in the Subura. I give you, Alexander, the contender from Delos."

Apion plays his part well. By mentioning the Subura, he changes the reason for the contest. To those in the crowd, this is no longer about Rome against Greece, this is about the ordinary citizen against the elite. His ploy works, and I step into a wall of noise as the plebeians of the city band together to support me.

The judge steps in between us and Apion withdraws to the side. Lucius and I shake hands, and the judge reminds us of the rules of the fight. As he speaks, it's difficult to hear him, but we both know what we're here to do. Suddenly, he raises a rod in the air. The crowd erupts into a wall of noise, and we find ourselves in the fight of our lives.

We both look for an early opportunity. The pressure from the crowd is immense—they want an early score. We circle, adjusting our stances, waiting for the right moment. The judge shouts at us for remaining apart, and then a few moments later, he breaks the fight to give me a warning for not attacking enough.

I don't understand why he's picked me out, both of us have been taking the same approach. It unsettles both me and the audience, who are jeering against the pause in the fighting. I have no time to think as he calls us together again.

I rush into an attack before I am ready, and Lucius is too good to not take advantage. From a misjudged grasp for both legs, he drives his hips into me, slaps down an arm and before I know it, he's behind me, pulling me over by falling back with his weight. He pins my head and shoulders to the ground between his legs. First point to Rome.

I won't make the same mistake again, but Lucius grows in confidence. I need to show more skill if I'm to win this match. I summon everything I've learned over the past few months—the work I've done with Demetrius, Leon, and Dario—but every time I think I have the advantage, the judge intervenes. He won't let me finish moves. I start to worry that I've forgotten the Roman rules, but I know them well enough.

The intensity of the event and the speed we're expected to perform at gives me no time to react or question the judge's decisions. Lucius takes me down once more. He scores the second point and now the cheers from my supporters become more subdued.

I cast a quick glance toward Demetrius before we restart. *He doesn't look happy*. Have I let him down? Am I failing on the biggest stage?

I lock eyes with Lucius again. We drop to matching heights. I remind myself that I know him. I can read his moves. Flashes of the old street fights return to me. It is time to strike back. This is where my father would have sent me his signal to defeat my opponent.

I race in like Dario. Using speed for advantage, I take Lucius by surprise and send him to the ground. He sprawls out, and I move behind, locking my arms around him and pressing down on his head. I roll myself to the side and begin to push him over onto his back. I press forward and I'm just short of pinning him down when the referee breaks the fight without granting me the score.

The jeers from the audience grow louder. I don't know what I've done wrong. Doubts start to rush in, and I begin to hesitate. Again, the judge gives me another warning about not committing to the fight. To be fair, Lucius seems as confused as I am about the calls that are being made.

I won't give up. I change my tactics and start to win by pushing Lucius out of the skamma pit. It works, I score twice and with great speed. The match can go either way, raising the fervor of the audience.

My competitor is not without his own ability. He starts to avoid my further attempts; he defends and deflects with great skill. He catches me off balance and spins me onto the floor of the skamma. I avoid being pinned down, but the judge grants Lucius the point. He has awarded him the contest. It's over, and without warning, I'm left to pick myself up from the ground. The judge raises the arm of Lucius into the air.

Most of the crowd cheers his win, but there are still jeers as well. The judgment doesn't meet with everyone's approval. We're brought together for one final handshake and then I'm hastily ushered from the skamma, pushed toward the oil room, and then the bathhouse. I'm separated from Lucius by the officials. Men swarm around to clean me and then send me on my way. It's all over so fast. Everything I've worked for is over. The sudden ending and my removal from the arena stun me into silence.

***

It's well into the evening before I start to think about what I've lost. We all sit in a large taberna near our lodgings on the hill. The festival moves from the arena to all the places in the city that serve food and wine. Many who were at the Circus Maximus are there to finish their day, and more than a few recognize me. Some come forward to say sorry for my loss, but others say Rome's elite would never let someone from the Subura win. They are angry on my behalf.

Uncle Nikos, my mother, and Zoe do their best to make me feel better about my efforts, but Dario and Leon have drawn themselves away into a corner of the room. They look angry. Meanwhile, Demetrius and Apion are nowhere to be seen.

"I thought we were all going to celebrate together," I say to my mother.

"Dario and Leon are upset for you. They don't want to spoil your meal by arguing about the judge."

"You *were* fighting two people in the skamma," says Uncle Nikos.

"Nikos." My mother wants to avoid upsetting me further, that much is obvious.

"I'm sorry. We agreed," he replies.

"I'm fine," I say. "It's been an exciting time. I'll do better if I get back. I'll try to work on the Roman rules for my wrestling, so I don't make mistakes."

"You didn't—"

"Nikos," my mother repeats, and he falls silent.

The night carries on, but the mood is low. I end up talking about places in the city I want to visit before we leave. We still have one more day, and I want to show Zoe some of the sights. I don't know how she feels, but she's happy to encourage the discussion.

We're almost approaching the end of the night when Demetrius and Apion return. They call Dario and Leon over to join us.

Demetrius begins by saying something unexpected. "I'm sorry, Alexander, and so are Gaius and Lucius."

"What do you mean? They're sorry for winning?"

"They're sorry for how they won. It seems that the judge was *influenced* by a certain senator, anxious that his son wouldn't lose in front of the emperor."

"After you left the arena, I remained behind," says Apion. "When the emperor was handing out the prizes to the winning athletes, not all the crowd cheered for Lucius. Gaius was angry. I could see it on his face even from a distance, but it wasn't the crowd that was enraging him."

"We all watched the fight," continues Demetrius. "It was easy to see that the judging wasn't fair. Apion and I looked for Gaius this evening. We found him at his home."

"What was he like when you saw him? What did he say?"

"He was pleasant. He confirmed our suspicions. It was obvious to Gaius and Lucius what had really happened. Lucius confronted his father, who did nothing to deny his actions. In fact, he assured Lucius that if his position and wealth could continue to buy him victories, then his son should appreciate it. That was the end of the matter, as far as his father was concerned."

"So that's the end of it? What was all the work and training for? Someone who I've never met can just take my dreams and throw them away?"

"I said it was the end of the matter for one person, but not for Lucius and Gaius. They want to arrange one more contest while you're in Rome. There won't be such large crowds or fanfare, but the fight will be fair. It will take place at the palaestra. You only need to agree. Apion will return to Gaius tonight and make the arrangements."

I think about my choices—what I should do. What my father would do. What Demetrius would do. I remember something Epictetus taught: disappointment is fleeting, but how we respond to it is what endures.

Emotions rise and fall. Action is what remains. And right now, I still have control. I can still win.

Not long ago, I lived for the applause. I chased fame, convinced adulation meant success. But that kind of fire burns fast, flares and disappears. What lasts is something deeper—discipline, self-mastery, virtue. That is a legacy worth chasing.

There's nothing left to think about. I know what I have to do.

"Apion, tell Gaius I agree to the contest."

CHAPTER XXVII

The sun is still to rise on this last day in Rome. I've woken up from a dream, or a memory, it's hard to know which. It's left me with a lasting picture of my father. I saw us working together on a piece of furniture. He was teaching me how to carve the wood with intricate patterns and symbols. He was smiling and encouraging me as I tried to copy his work.

I hear his voice: "You have great skill."

"I've learned from you," I reply.

"No." He looks straight into my eyes. "All that you can achieve has always been within you. You only needed to discover that it was there. I'm proud of you, son."

The vision ends there, and I sit up in the darkness.

I'm sharing a room at the lodgings with Uncle Nikos, my mother, and Zoe. They are all still sleeping, or at least I think they are. Zoe yawns and rubs her eyes as she sits up.

"Are you alright?" she says.

"Yes, I just had a dream."

"I know, you were saying something in your sleep. I couldn't make out what it was."

"I was dreaming about my father, then I woke up with a thought in my mind. I need to go out right now. There's somewhere I have to go."

"It's not even dawn."

"It will be when I reach there, just as it is when I climb Mount Kynthos."

"Where are we going?"

"We? You might not want to go, Zoe."

"If you don't tell me where, then how can I know?"

"I need to go to the Temple of Jupiter, to visit the shrine of Minerva. I want to make an offering, before going to Palatine Hill. I don't want to offend you."

"I'm here to support you. I've traveled across oceans to stay with you, and I hope Kyrios will forgive me; I screamed as loud as any for you to beat Lucius to a pulp." She rises to her feet. "I'll take offense if you don't take me."

"It won't take us long," I reply, "we'll be back before Apion has prepared my morning plate of food. I'll be pleased to eat a little more cake and honeyed fruits when we get home."

"I'm sure your Aunt Thestylis will be happy to feed you up. You'll need to learn to sail your uncle's ship so we can visit Mykonos."

"As long as it's a calm sea," I laugh. "Let's go quietly, and not wake the others."

We step out of the room and down a staircase that leads out onto the street. The city's Praetorian Guard is still present. A final religious ceremony will take place later today, so they're needed until the festival ends.

They only glance at us as we enter the temple grounds, perhaps trying to save their energy for when the crowds take to the streets again. Just like Delos, the welcoming of the sun draws other pilgrims. We are not alone as Apollo steers his chariot into the sky. He illuminates the houses of the other gods, as well as the city that encircles it.

The white-robed priests begin to appear. They extinguish torches and light incense. They gather in front of the three shrines and open the enormous doors to where Jupiter, Juno, and Minerva sit on their thrones. Worshippers step forward in turn—each will offer their respects in their own way.

"This is for my father," I say to Zoe. "I've always felt that he has never left me. I thought I saw him in the crowd yesterday."

"His love for you will always live. It doesn't need to be seen to be felt in your heart."

"I think he's waiting. He's staying near me. I think, maybe, he desires to see me achieve success. He believed in me for as long as I can remember, and then, just at the point my life was about to change..." I stare down at the ground and then look to the golden sky above us. "You would have liked him, Zoe."

"I know. And I know you are as proud of him as he is of you. He loved your mother with all his heart, and together, they risked everything for their son. You are special, Alexander. You were the reason they set out in search of a new destiny.

"Born on Delos, raised in Rome—both places live within you. From Greece, you carry wisdom, the hunger to seek truth, to question, to understand. From Rome, you carry resilience, the unshakable will to endure, to rise no matter how many times you fall. You see the world not just as it is, but as it could be. You fight for what is right, even when it costs you. That's why I love you—not just for your strength, but for your heart. Never lose that. Never lose yourself. I don't want you to change. I only want to stand beside you, and carve our own path—together. I love you, Alexander."

Zoe's words fill me with joy, and I can only give one response in return. "I love you."

"Then let's go to the shrine," she smiles. "I'm happy to get your father's blessing along with Minerva's."

We climb the steps and approach the priest who sits beside the offerings. He's the same man I'd seen before. I think he recognizes me as I draw closer. I place a denarius in the bowl beside him. He casts an eye on it before looking up at me.

"Minerva will look with kindness on you today."

"Can you tell me?" I ask. "I had a dream that I was carving wood with my father. When I woke, I just wanted to be here. I had to come."

"The goddess sent you a message, but she does not speak in Latin or Greek. You must search for the true meaning of your vision, but I would say she is smiling upon your fate, wherever it may take you."

"Thank you."

The priest smiles and nods. We walk to the shrine, and I give thanks for everything I've received in the past few months. As I turn and walk away, I recall some of the words of Epictetus. He talks of gratitude being a choice. We choose to focus on the best aspects of our life even when we are in difficult circumstances. By practicing gratitude, we become more virtuous, leading to greater happiness and contentment.

Now it is time to complete what I set out to do.

***

My mother and Uncle Nikos are relieved when we return to the lodgings.

"We thought we had lost you," says my mother. "Apion was going to start a search."

"I was at the Temple of Jupiter. Zoe was with me."

"Yes, well, I knew there was one sensible person with you. That's why I didn't panic as much as I might have."

"It sounds like Gaius is organizing an audience," says Uncle Nikos. "I think it will be a good day. Lucius's father has to attend an event at the Forum, so we should be free of any interference. Not that Gaius will allow any cheating. This fight will be fair. If it is any other way, then he'll not get what *he* wants."

"And what's that?"

"Be under no illusion, he wants you to lose, but he needs Lucius to win on his own merit. Any other way is meaningless to Gaius."

"And if I win?"

"When you win," says Demetrius as he enters the room. "He will accept your victory. He has lost himself a little to the luxurious life that surrounds him, but he's a man of honor. He will offer you the laurel crown on your victory. That is what we came for, isn't it?"

Dario and Leon arrive with Apion. They're more excited than they were at the Circus Maximus.

"The carts are ready to take us to Palatine Hill," Leon announces, gripping the reins.

"Speed, Alexander. Work fast," Dario reminds me.

"We have to get to the palaestra first," Apion adds. "Let's get underway."

We split between two carts, each hitched to a pair of sturdy mules. They aren't the fastest, but they're surefooted, weaving through the uneven streets with ease. The climb from Capitoline Hill to Palatine Hill is easier this way—better to save our strength for the fight ahead.

The city hums around us. Vendors call out their wares, the scent of roasted meat and fresh bread thick in the air. Wheels clatter over stone. We pass beneath the towering insulae, their balconies overflowing with laundry and watchful eyes. Mosaics glint in the sunlight, and marble statues gaze down at us as we ride past, silent and eternal.

The Roman Forum sprawls ahead, its columns and temples catching the afternoon light. As we move past it, the Circus Maximus stretches into view beyond the Palatine's southern slopes, its massive track open to the sky. We veer toward the Aventine Hill and the Tiber, where boats crowd the river, traders shouting over the din of the docks.

As we near the palaestra, the towering walls of the Imperial Palace rise above us, commanding the view. It sprawls across Palatine Hill, surrounded by the villas of Rome's wealthiest, its gardens, orchards, and vineyards spilling down the slopes.

The wheels roll to a stop when we arrive outside a place I know well. The house of Gaius looks busy this morning, and to our surprise, two sentries from the Praetorian Guard are on duty at the entrance to the atrium. Gaius stands between them, ready to greet us. Demetrius is the first to leap from the cart and shake his hand.

"Thank you for this, Gaius," he says with respect. "Today we discover our champion."

I now see what Lucius was mentioning in the parade. I'll not just be fighting for Demetrius today; a victory will grow my reputation as well as his. The guards part to allow us all to enter.

Many of the patrons of Gaius smile at us as we walk through the house. They offer their best wishes for a good contest. I remember some, but not all. They must be very important as other members of the guard stand amongst them, which adds an extra air of importance to the occasion.

Gaius takes us to the entrance of the palaestra. This is a place where women cannot enter. I'm surprised when he ushers my mother and Zoe through and offers them one of the best places to sit, next to a grand-looking chair that faces the skamma.

"Alexander," announces Gaius. "There are some people here to see you."

He claps his hand to a servant who nods in response. The man disappears for a moment, then returns with students from my old training class. It's a reunion I never thought I would see, and they treat me as if I hadn't left.

Lucius arrives last. "Let's help Alexander prepare. It is good to have him with us again."

"Can Leon and Dario join us?" I ask. "They're with me from Delos. Can they help us prepare?"

"Of course," replies Lucius. "We are all brothers in the palaestra." He smiles.

Demetrius, Nikos, and Apion follow Gaius back inside the house. The atmosphere is rising with the heat of the day. I don't want to tire myself out. In fact, Leon *and* Dario are quite insistent that I don't.

The shaded area around the palaestra hums with the low murmur of arriving guests, their sandals scuffing against the stone as they find their places. The judge strides onto the skamma, his eyes sweeping over the sand, checking for any uneven patches or obstructions. Satisfied, he turns to Lucius and me, motioning us forward with a sharp nod.

"I want a fight, not a dance," he says, his voice steady but firm. "Three points wins. Keep it clean. If you stall, you'll feel the rod. Understood?" He doesn't wait for an answer. "Now, get ready."

Lucius and I exchange a glance before heading into the oil room. The heavy scent of sweat and crushed olives clings to the air, a familiar mix that settles deep in my lungs. A single slave, bare-chested and silent, stands ready. He moves efficiently, running the strigil down my arms and across my back, scraping away the dust before pouring oil into his palm. His fingers press into my shoulders, working the oil into my skin with practiced ease. He doesn't speak, but he doesn't need to. His touch is neither gentle nor rough—just another step in the ritual before the fight.

Through the thin walls, the noise from the palaestra grows, rolling over us in waves. I close my eyes for a moment, letting it sink in. The crowd isn't just watching; they're waiting, expectant. Out there, in the skamma, we won't just be two men grappling in the sand. We'll be something more—if only for a few moments.

Lucius claps his hands and rubs them together; the sound is sharp in the quiet room. "Ready?"

I roll my shoulders and exhale. "Always."

We head out to join the others and I notice Leon looks uneasy.

"What's wrong?" I ask.

"Something is up, I'm not sure. The place is filling with the guard."

"What?"

We rush to see what's going on, but Gaius is standing in our way.

"Are you both ready for the contest?" he asks, and we nod in agreement. "Then follow me."

We follow him into the strong sunlight. It's not the Circus Maximus, but the palaestra is full with spectators. Gaius leads us to stand at one side of the skamma pit, facing my mother, Zoe, and the empty chair. I think Lucius and I realize at the same time just what this means.

A commanding officer of the guard steps forward. "All stand for Imperator Caesar Marcus Aurelius Antoninus Augustus!"

My heart is almost beating out of my chest. Marcus Aurelius acknowledges many of the guests as he enters the palaestra. He stops briefly and says a few words to my mother. She can't hide the delight on her face. Then he turns and sits to face us. He gestures toward us with his hand. Lucius and I exchange nervous glances before we bow to him.

I'm stunned at what's happening. Emperor Marcus Aurelius has come to watch us fight. A ripple of excitement goes around the crowd as they can see how shocked we both are and now Gaius steps forward to present us.

"This is a contest that began long before either of these contenders were born, and although it may be hard to believe, long before even I or Demetrius were born. We learn from those equipped to pass on their knowledge. The rules of combat are simple, but the development of self, the gaining of wisdom and virtue, this is the challenge in life. It is not enough to copy the experience of another.

"The champion will question everything taught them. They will use reason and good sense to form their own conclusions. They will acknowledge their mistakes as opportunities to grow and learn, and ultimately, they will realize the responsibility for progress and understanding lies within themselves. They will build on the generations who have traveled the road before.

"Lucius of Rome and Alexander of Delos have one mystery left to uncover between them. Who will best demonstrate the sum of their skill and knowledge in the skamma? Who will capture victory from a worthy foe? This is the contest they've been working for. The prize for the one who stands victorious will be a laurel crown, offered by our distinguished guest. Ave, Caesar, Imperator!"

The crowd repeats the tribute to the emperor, and the judge steps forward into the center of the skamma. He arranges for Lucius and me to face one another. He nods his head at each one of us, steps back, and raises the rod to the sky.

The air vibrates with noise—shouts and jeers, thrown across the palaestra like weapons. Sweat slicks my skin, mixing with the dust of the skamma. The sun bakes everything in gold, the heat presses down. Across from me, Lucius crouches low, broad shoulders rolling with each breath. His fingers flex, itching to strike.

He moves first. Fast. A quick drop, arms shooting for my legs. A desperate attack. But I see it coming before he even shifts his weight.

I step out, pivot sharp, and let him dive past me. He sprawls, the impact knocking the air from his lungs. Before he can recover, I am on him.

A hard knee drives into his ribs, locking him down for half a second. Just enough. My arms cinch around his waist, grip like iron. I push up, legs firing, back arching—Lucius' feet leave the earth. For a heartbeat, we hover.

Then I throw.

He flips overhead, weightless and then gravity reclaims him. The crash is brutal—his back slams into the sand outside the skamma.

Dust erupts around him, swallowing the moment.

A pause. A breath.

Then the eruption. The crowd thunders—some in triumph, others cursing.

Lucius groans, rolls to his side, disoriented.

There is no time to breathe. The judge barely signals before we crash together again. Our hands lock, fingers crushing against one another in a desperate battle for control. Muscles burn, shoulders tight, every sinew stretched to its limit. Lucius is different now—stronger, more calculated. He will not make the same mistake. I see it in his eyes.

We push, twist, shift. Momentum swings between us like a pendulum. Sand grinds beneath my feet as I fight for leverage, my head pressing against his. Control, control—who will break first?

Lucius moves. A sudden jerk—his fingers clamp behind my neck, yanking me forward with brute strength. I feel it too late.

His arms lock tight around my torso. A steel grip. A trap.

A shift in weight—his hip turns into me. His leg slides across mine. And then—he pulls.

My body tilts forward, my feet lose the earth. Gravity betrays me. The world flips.

Impact. My back slams into the skamma, sand exploding around me. Pain blooms across my shoulders, a sharp crunch felt in my spine. The sky tilts, my vision blurs, but I force air back into my lungs. No time to think. No time to hesitate. Lucius steps back, breath heaving, his chest rising and falling in victory. This is his point.

Within moments, we are doing battle again. The noise from the palaestra must be echoing across the city down below us. I see flashes of faces, as we circle one another once again. I catch sight of Zoe. Her hands are over her mouth in prayer.

I feel grateful to have her in my life. I hope her prayers are heard.

Lucius lunges, hands snapping for my head. A brutal, punishing grip—just as Dario always preferred. I allow myself a wry smile, hidden beneath the tangle of limbs and struggle. This one's for you, my friend.

I don't resist—I flow.

As Lucius wrenches me downward, I drop to the side, twisting with the momentum instead of fighting against it. His grip slips, just for a moment—but that's all I need.

My shoulder presses hard into his hips, my hands driving against his waist. I feel his balance falter, weight shifting at the wrong angle. He tries to recover, to plant his feet—but the ground betrays him.

I push.

Every muscle in my legs fires as I drive forward. His heels skid, his body lurches. One step. Another. The edge is near. The moment hangs between us.

Lucius snarls, twisting, trying to drag me down with him. But my positioning is better—tighter, a bit stronger. I drop my center of gravity, brace my feet, and with a final surge of power, I force him back.

Out.

Lucius stumbles, his footing lost. His body spills past the boundary of the skamma, and the judge awards me the point.

My breath heaves, sweat streaking down my back. I know the crowd is making noise, but I don't hear them. None of it matters.

I step back, flex my fingers, roll my shoulders.

One more point. One more fall.

Beneath my breath, I whisper, "Thank you, Dario."

Lucius is far from finished. I can't wait for a mistake—he won't make one. If I want to win, I have to take the risk.

I strike first, snapping my hand around his neck, feeling the heat of his skin, the tension in his muscles. But he reacts instantly. His fingers clamp onto my elbow like iron, locking my arm in place.

Trap.

Before I can pull free, he rolls his head to the other side, shifting his weight. The moment I feel the shift, I know—he has me.

A single-leg attack. Clean. Efficient. Unstoppable.

I barely hit the sand before I hear the point called for Lucius.

The judge steps forward but does not reset us immediately. He knows the moment must breathe. Not for our sake, but for the spectacle. This is the final point, the last fall. The anticipation must rise.

The calls of the crowd swell, a feverish chorus of voices. Some chant my name; others roar for Lucius. Energy hums in the air. The gods are pleased with this contest.

I push up from the ground, chest rising and falling with each breath. My fingers dig into the sand, grounding me, reminding me.

One last exchange.

My body screams with exhaustion. Every muscle aches, every joint burns, but I know Lucius feels the same. I see it in his eyes—a grim, unbreakable determination. Neither of us will yield. Not now. We slam forward, head to head, chest to chest, our breath ragged, our legs trembling under the relentless shifting and grinding in the skamma sand. Every shift, every adjustment, is a battle. The world beyond us—the sand, the crowd, the sun, even the judge waiting with measured patience—fades into a blur.

Lucius moves.

A sudden twist. A grip tightening around my torso. A pivot.

Before I can react, he is behind me, his arms locking around my waist like iron bands. He wants the lift. The final, undeniable fall.

I fight. My muscles strain, every ounce of my weight drops low. My feet dig into the sand, resisting. He heaves, but I refuse to be lifted. My breath is fire in my chest. My legs shake under the effort. I will not fall.

Then—everything slows.

The roar of the crowd stretches into silence. The shapes of onlookers melt into shadows. And in the center, I see one face.

My father.

He is standing there—just as he used to, watching me fight, watching me learn. His expression is unreadable, his presence as steady as it always was.

And then, the signal.

A barely perceptible nod. A command I know in my bones. Now.

A final breath. A surge of will.

I drop—sinking lower, twisting fast, left arm locking around Lucius' waist, right hand gripping his leg. His knee jams against my hip, his balance shatters.

I arch. I twist. I throw.

For an instant, Lucius is weightless. His body lifts from the ground, momentum pulling him free. The fight is over before he even lands.

He crashes outside the pit.

A split-second of stunned silence. Then—the eruption.

Noise explodes around me. Hands pull me upright. The judge announces my victory. It feels like I am dreaming. The crowd is deafening. I turn, blinking, breath still heaving, taking in the faces of the palaestra. They return to focus, their expressions sharp, vivid. I look for my father's face. It is gone.

I know he was here.

I know he saw me win.

Lucius stands, shaking sand from his hair, then extends his hand. No words at first—just the unspoken language of competitors who have pushed each other to the edge.

When he finally speaks, his voice is low, steady. "You got me."

I clasp his hand, squeezing tight, a small smile tugging at the corner of my lips. "Was there ever a doubt, my friend?"

He grabs my neck and pulls me close. We just stand there and breath. There is a silent agreement that this won't be the last time we meet in the pit.

Lucius exhales sharply, smirking through the ache. "Think the old men are satisfied?"

I roll my shoulders. "Not a chance."

The commanding officer of the guard snaps a command, his voice sharp and unwavering. Two lines of soldiers form a barrier between me and the most powerful man in the empire.

"Step forward, Alexander, and kneel before your Caesar."

The world narrows to the sound of my own footsteps. Each one measured. Deliberate. As I lower myself to one knee, the hush of anticipation presses in.

"You fought well."

Marcus Aurelius stands before me, his expression unreadable—measuring, considering. Gaius steps forward, passing the laurel crown into the emperor's waiting hands.

A pause.

The emperor lifts the wreath slowly, making a great ceremony of the moment. The golden leaves catch the sunlight. My breath tightens in my chest. His hands lower, placing the crown upon my head.

"Rise, young man." His voice is steady, carrying the weight of a ruler hardened by battle and tempered by reason. "Enjoy this moment, but remember—virtue, control, and focus are what brought you here. Hold fast to them, and you will find victory beyond the sand."

"All stand for Imperator Caesar Marcus Aurelius Antoninus Augustus!" the head of the guard calls.

The soldiers move in unison, their armor clinking as they form a protective wall around the emperor. As he turns, those present erupt with a final cheer, voices rising in waves that roll across the palaestra.

Most of the spectators follow him in his departure, but those who have always stood by me—my people—remain.

They gather around, hands clasping my shoulders, voices calling my name.

"I had complete faith in you." Demetrius smiles, and he's *really* smiling. I can't help but return a grin.

"I'm glad you can believe it. I still don't know what just happened."

"You won, that's what happened," says Leon.

"I knew you had it in you, I have a keen eye for champions," says Apion. "Clean up and dress. We have a last night in Rome, and we have a lot to celebrate."

"Where will we go, Alexander?" says Uncle Nikos. "Demetrius has assured me he will cover the expense."

Everyone laughs as Demetrius grumbles to himself.

"There's only one place I want to go."

***

"Caeso!"

"Alexander? I don't believe it! Where is my wife? Look, it's Alexander and Elena. You came back to see Caeso, and maybe my wife?"

"We've come here to eat. I've brought some friends."

"How many friends?"

"There are eight of us."

"Hold on, I will sort it."

Caeso rushes past us. Our old table is still where it used to be. He scatters the other customers that have been sitting there and then pulls another table to join two together.

"Sorry, sorry," he says as he moves his customers and their meals to other places. "My friends have arrived. I say friends, they're family, please understand."

I don't think they understand, but Caeso doesn't take no for an answer.

"Come this way," he says to all of us. "Sit, sit. What can I get you?"

"Just what you used to make me. That's what I've missed."

"I will bring you what you ask, though some of your friends look as if they could afford a little more?"

"I think so." I laugh.

As the evening goes on, a crowd forms on the street around Caeso's. The word soon travels to old neighbors and friends. Everyone wants to hear of my adventures in Greece, and my mother sheds many tears, but they're tears of happiness. Leon and Dario find they are popular with the Roman girls, and Apion is ever the showman, entertaining the other customers with tales of his travels. Nikos and Demetrius spend the entire night laughing. I've never seen Demetrius enjoy himself so much. He has ordered enough food and drink to feed half of the street, so Caeso becomes his new best friend.

There is no sign of the evening reaching its end. I'm sure there will be a few headaches in the morning.

"Will you walk with me, Zoe?" I ask. "The place I used to live in is just along the street."

"Yes, I want some time with you. I haven't been able to get near to you today because of an emperor, soldiers, and the wealthiest men in Rome. I was beginning to think you had forgotten me."

"They kept me from you as well," I protest.

We sneak away for a few moments. The wine and the celebrations keep everyone distracted. It's only a few steps along the street and we're outside the building I used to call home.

"It looks dark inside," says Zoe.

"It is. You feel your way at night and try to avoid those sleeping on the stairs."

"I don't know how you could cope with that. Rome is so famous, but I miss walking down to the sea at night. The sound of the waves rolling over the stones of the shore."

"The lights of the harbor reflecting in the water," I reply.

"The smell of the grills cooking fresh fish, the music that flows into the air. I miss it. I can't wait to go back. How about you?"

"Anywhere we can be together. I'm sure that's what my father said to my mother." I pause. "I saw him today, at the end of the match. He gave me his signal to win."

"I knew something had happened. I could see it in your eyes."

"You don't think I'm mad?"

"Well, maybe." She smiles as she holds on to me. "But not for seeing a vision of your father. Do you think he would want you to bring me to Rome?"

I shake my head. "No. He fell in love with a girl from Delos, re-member? And he fell in love with Delos as well, even though it was the darkest secret. He knew it was my birthplace, my true home. I feel he'll be content to know I'm there with you.

"There's something about the island that sits at the center of the world. Whatever lies ahead in life, it will always call me back."

We turn and walk back toward Caeso's. I contemplate if I'll see my father again; I'll always look for him near the end of a fight. I'm sure I'll know if he's somewhere in the crowd, cheering me on to victory and telling me when to make the winning throw.

The celebration fades with the stars, and as Apollo rides once more across the sky, Rome wakes to its own stories. Soon, I will sail for Delos, where the dust of the skamma pit calls me back, where old laurels wither and new trials await, sharpening their teeth. The gods have given me victories, but they do not grant rest—not yet. And truth be told, I would not want it any other way.